TEL AMAL DISTRICT, HAIFA, 10:00 P.M.

The house was dark and silent as a tomb. From what was known about Yakof Gromit, his import/export business had merely been a front for his other illegal activities, not the least of which was arms smuggling. Anything of importance would be upstairs in the man's living quarters.

Pulling on a pair of thin leather gloves, the Mossad agent went up the stairs, moving on the balls of his feet so as to make as little noise as possible. At the top, he stopped to listen. Nothing. A dim light filtered from the outside through the heavy curtains over the windows in the main room. He took a small penlight out of his pocket and switched it on.

Careful not to disturb anything, he stepped across the stained Oriental rug to the ornate wooden cabinet standing along the far wall. Holding the light in his mouth, he had the lock picked in seconds. The cabinet was empty. Bending a little closer, he could see where the dust had been disturbed and a book taken. Looked like the work of Palmyra's KGB henchman.

A sudden slight noise came from behind him. He spun on his heel as he reached for his gun, but the silenced shot beat him to it. The impact shoved him back against the cabinet. He raised his head as a face swam into view.

"You," he gasped. "How . . . did you know I—"

"You leave an easy trail, my friend. I am sorry this had to happen."

The agent mouthed the word "why," unable to say it.

"It is a matter of . . . loyalty," the killer said, aiming the barrel of his silenced pistol just inches from the man's forehead. "First loyalty."

FIRST LOYALTY

GARY KRISS

LYNX BOOKS
New York

FIRST LOYALTY

ISBN: 1-55802-087-X

First Printing/September 1988

This is a work of fiction. Names, characters, places, and incidents are either the product of the author's imagination or are used fictitiously. Any resemblance to actual events, locales, or persons, living or dead, is entirely coincidental.

This book is published by Lynx Books, a division of Lynx Communications, Inc., 41 Madison Avenue, New York, New York, 10010. The name "Lynx" together with the logotype consisting of a stylized head of a lynx is a trademark of Lynx Communications, Inc.

Printed in the United States of America

0 9 8 7 6 5 4 3 2 1

MOSSAD is an acronym for the Institution for Intelligence and Special Assignments—the Israeli Secret Intelligence Service.

FIRST LOYALTY

Prologue

"ANOTHER FIVE MINUTES, MAJOR."

"Any sign of him?"

Roskov had been waiting in the darkness of a side street half a block from the fringes of the growing crowd that had spread out along the Wailing Wall between the gates of the Chain and the Dung since eight. The night had turned very cool but windless, and the sounds of the chanting mob echoed and reechoed off the ancient walls. He hunched up the collar of his long dark civilian coat and pulled the flat-brimmed Hasidic hat a little lower over his eyes.

He could hear the building urgency in the huge crowd that would soon turn to anger. "Trust in God . . . Trust in God . . ." they had been chanting for hours. Men, women, and even children had streamed in from the Jewish sector of the city, and even from Tel Aviv and Haifa and Afula and Be'er Sheva and a dozen other cities. Religious fanatics. The Haredim, who wanted a simpler age; who wanted to return to the old ways of coexis-

tence with the Arabs and the rest of the world.
Fools, he thought. Utter and complete fools.

"Not yet, sir, but he will be here," Roskov's aide,
KGB Captain Petor Bogachev, said softly at his
elbow. "But the cover tonight is perfect."

"Unless he couldn't get through," Roskov said.
He was worried. So much could go wrong. "The
city has been sealed."

"He's here all right," Bogachev said. "There are
a couple of civilian police units on El Wad Street,
and a couple of army squads from the Ein Karem
Barracks over on the Street of the Columns, but
on one else. They don't want trouble. Not now."

Bogachev's walkie-talkie crackled and he
stepped farther back into the shadows as he raised
it to his lips. "*Da,*" he said softly. He looked up at
Roskov and nodded.

"Well?" Roskov asked impatiently.

"He is approaching on foot."

Roskov studied the crowd again. Speaker's plat-
forms had been constructed in front of the Wailing Wall, and soon the rally would begin. He shook
his head. In three years he had nearly burned out.
But now he was close. Very close. Breed the enemy within, he'd been ordered. It is the least suspected danger, and therefore the most devastating.

*Israel must fall if our goals in the region are to
come to pass . . . You are the one, Ivan . . . only you.*

How am I to do it alone, he'd asked the director
at their last meeting in Moscow at the Lubyanka.
I am just one man.

You will find a way. You know the Jews. You
know what they fear most, you know where their
loyalties lie, you know how to manipulate them.
We'll be watching, Ivan Ivanovich. Closely.

Roskov nodded, turning back to his aide. "Everything is set?"

"Yes, sir. We will be waiting for you in the Moslem Quarter. Near the church of St. Veronica."

"You understand the fallbacks in case there is trouble?"

"Perfectly. The accelerants have been set. Within ten minutes there would be a dozen fires within a ten-block radius. Molotov cocktails," Bogachev murmured, chuckling at his own little joke.

Mistrust. Lies, deceit, uncertainty. You are the expert, Ivan, because you have no conscience, you understand the goal. The only goal.

"In that case we will meet at the safe house by the Jaffa Gate," Roskov said, thinking ahead to a dozen different probabilities. He carried his own secret, and it had been an increasing burden all these years. Especially now.

"Yes, sir. Later we will be able to slip across the border into Jordan."

"No," Roskov snapped, the single word sharp and clear even over the rumble of the crowd. Bogachev stiffened. "This is merely the beginning, Petor. We still have work to do before we can leave."

"It would ruin everything if you were . . . to be taken, Major."

"Better to turn back than lose your way, is that what you are trying to say?" Roskov asked, quoting an old Russian proverb. "Fear has big eyes."

"No, sir. Sorry," Bogachev said. He'd seen the look in Roskov's eyes. Dangerous. Unpredictable. It's what made the major so good.

Roskov reached out and patted his aide's arm. "It is time now," he said. "I will not be taken, but before this night is over we'll be one step closer to going home. Heroes."

Bogachev's eyes narrowed, but he said nothing.

Roskov stepped out into the street and hurried

toward the crowd. "Trust in God," he shouted in perfect Hebrew. "Trust in God," he chanted with the crowd, and melted into the sea of bodies, just another face in the mass.

Roskov had been born in a little town outside of Kiev in the summer of 1941 with the Nazis barely five miles away. He remembered none of the war, of course, but his mother used to tell the stories over and over again; how they had fled on foot to the east, always to the east, the sounds of the cannonade behind them, the high explosives lighting up the night sky like not-so-distant thunderstorms. She'd told him about the starvation and hardships throughout the fall that had become nearly impossible to bear when winter set in. Even rats, which for a time had become a food staple, were in short supply. There'd been rumors of cannibalism, and fear was their only constant. His mother had died a few years after the war, and his education had been taken over by the state. But he had never forgotten the stories.

To live, she'd told him often. It is the only thing of any importance.

The mob had grown in size and intensity. There were at least ten thousand people crammed into the square and along the street that paralleled the Wailing Wall. Everyone was shouting "Trust in God!" over and over again, now at a fever pitch. An old man with a long white beard had been helped up onto the platform and was shouting down to the people, his words drowned out in the roar. A half-dozen other bearded old men were exhorting the crowd to calm down, but it would be ten minutes or more before any order would be imposed. The timing was perfect, Roskov thought.

He had worked his way past the speaker's platform, south along the Wall toward the Islamic Museum, beyond which stood Robinson's Arch, where he was supposed to make his contact. The mob was pushing inward toward the Street of the Chain, and it took him a lot longer to make the last hundred yards or so. No one paid him the slightest attention, even though he was pushing in the opposite direction to everyone else. He was dressed as a Haredim. He blended with the mob. It was his specialty: being seen, yet not being seen.

Twenty yards farther and Roskov was shoved up against the rough stone wall of the museum by the passing marchers who were surging forward in an effort to get closer to the speaker's platform. He had to push aside several women, knocking one of them to the pavement. He hastily apologized and helped her to her feet, pushing her forward so that he could get away from the wall; several eyes momentarily turned his way, but then they were swept past in the tide and he was free again.

"Trust in God!" he shouted, the crowd finally beginning to thin, and he spotted his contact standing beneath the arch. He stopped in his tracks, letting the marchers surge around him as if he were a boulder in the middle of a swiftly moving stream. The man was dressed in a long dark coat and a Hasidic hat just like most of the men in the mob. He looked no different than any other Haredim. The cover was perfect, Bogachev had promised, and he'd been correct. They would attract no notice here. Not tonight. Not like this.

"Trust in God," Roskov said, moving forward. His contact looked up, his eyes narrowing. "And Palmyra," Roskov said, reaching him. It was his code name, and ironically the name of a city in Syria.

"I didn't think you were coming," the contact said, relief evident in his voice and manner.

"Did you have any trouble? Were you followed?" Roskov asked.

"No, I got here clean. No one suspects . . ."

"What have you brought for me, my friend?" Roskov asked, cutting him off. "We don't have much time."

The man looked off toward the center of the mob, and as Roskov stepped a little closer he quickly pulled an envelope out of his coat pocket and thrust it forward. Roskov slipped it into the uniform blouse he was wearing beneath his long coat.

"This is a good thing you are doing," Roskov said.

"It's for Israel," the man said. "My first loyalty . . . is to Israel, you understand this?"

"Perfectly, my friend," Roskov said smoothly. There was no trace of a foreign accent in his Hebrew. He could have been a *sabra*. "Is there anything you wish to tell me about this?" he asked, patting his breast pocket.

"It is very dangerous . . . that information."

"The truth is never dangerous," Roskov replied. "You needn't worry, you shall realize your desires. All of them."

"Then it has already been approved?" the contact asked, the first hint of relief in his voice. "The operation has been accepted?"

"Completely. It's necessary. They all see it."

"Yes," the contact said.

"Now you must go," Roskov said, glancing over his shoulder toward the fringes of the mob still pressing inward toward the speaker's platform. "You will call at the usual time."

"Yes," the contact said stiffly.

"There will be more work for you to do."

"Yes," the contact said. He nodded. "Yes, I will call you."

"Trust in God," Roskov said.

"Trust in God," the contact said, and he turned and hurried across the street away from the Wall into the Jewish Quarter.

When he was gone, Roskov hurried around the corner and then through the Double Gate into the Aska Mosque. In the darkness of the big building he shed his long coat and hat, discarding them as he ran out the rear exit, past the Dome of the Rock, the sounds of the mob just on the other side of the Wall. He was now dressed in the uniform of an Israeli Civil Police officer. At the north end of the inner walled holy site, called Haram Esh Sharif, he dug the Uzi light machine gun out of the trash receptacle where it had been hidden for him, unfolded the stock, levered a round into the firing chamber, switched off the safety, and stepped out of the gate just a block away from the Church of St. Veronica where Bogachev was waiting for him.

There were no police or army units in sight, but the fringe of the mob, mostly women and children this far out, were barely thirty yards away.

"Traitors," he shouted in Hebrew at the top of his lungs, and opened fire as the first of the crowd began to turn around to see who was behind them.

A woman and small child were shoved back into the crowd, blood flew everywhere, then two other women went down and others began to scream as the crowd scattered. Roskov continuing firing, spraying back and forth as people trampled each other in an effort to escape.

When the Uzi was finally empty, Roskov laid it

down on the pavement, turned and calmly walked away, the sound of approaching sirens already audible from the distance even over the roar and screams of the dead and dying.

"Trust in God," he mumbled as he disappeared into the night.

1

MASAYÀF, SYRIA, 3:07 A.M.

THE AIR WAS HIGH AND COOL IN THE SYR-
ian coastal mountains. Avram Zemil held up his
hand for the others to stop, his every sense straining to hear or see something ahead of them.

He was a large, well-built man, even handsome
in a rugged sort of way, and at thirty-six he was
old enough to be considered "well seasoned" but
young enough to still believe that what he was doing did make a difference. He was dressed in Israeli Army fatigues, an Uzi machine gun over his
shoulder, a fifteen-round, nine-millimeter Sig-
Sauer automatic pistol in the holster strapped to
his chest, and three fragmentation grenades attached to the web belt at his waist. He could hear
and see nothing ahead in the darkness. But the
PLO encampment was close; he could almost smell
it.

They'd choppered in at maximum speed two
hours ago, running without lights just off the deck
well below Syrian radar, and had been put down
two miles southeast of the small city of Masayàf.
Avram glanced over his shoulder, but he could

see nothing of the glow of the city now lost in
the mountains they had hurriedly traversed. The
much larger city of Hamāh lay ten miles to the
northeast and Hims lay twenty-five miles south,
and between them was a no-man's-land of foot-
hills that gradually gave way to desert.

"What is it, Avram?" Anne Tsgonnis asked
softly. There were four of them on the team. She
was the only woman and as capable as any of the
men. She was a *sabra* and had been in the Mossad
from the day she had finished her military service
five years ago.

They had stopped just below the crest of a slight
rise, the track here narrow, rocky, and ill-defined.
No one had come this way for a very long time. In
the planning stages, which had lasted nearly three
months, they'd gone over every square inch of this
territory in the relief recon photographs, so they
knew exactly what to expect. Now Avram sensed
that they were close, but that something was
wrong.

"Wait," he said tersely. He turned, and keeping
low hurried up to the crest of the hill, getting
down on his stomach and crawling the last ten
feet.

Just at the top he took out his night spotting
scope and peered down into the valley spread out
below him. Scanning slowly left to right, the desert was lit for him in an eerie infrared glow. Just
to the northeast he picked up a track in the sand,
lost it as it dipped into a depression, and then
picked it up again as it curved back toward the
east. Wide, well traveled. There was no mistaking
what it was. They'd all studied the photographs.
The road had been cut from the airfield at Hamāh
straight through the desert. It was the PLO's first
and biggest mistake other than the capture of the

three Mossad intelligence agents who had been held hostage now for one hundred and twenty-two days. The road had been a signpost to the PLO base. No one constructed roads in the desert that went nowhere. Every track had its purpose and its destination.

Directly below, but still three or four miles away, Avram was just able to pick out the low Bedouin-style tents and buildings that were so familiar to him from the photographs. Nothing to mark this encampment as being any different from a dozen or a hundred others across the Syrian desert, except the well-traveled dirt track from the Hamāh airfield. And yet something was wrong. Drastically wrong. He could feel it thick in the night air. But what?

He could make out the distant sounds of a jet aircraft high overhead. Probably out of Damascus. They often sent out night flights to Europe. Life went on despite the conflict.

Then he realized what was odd.

The encampment on the desert below was not dark. He could see a few lights scattered here and there, he could see the glow of electric lights illuminating the interiors of the tents, and he thought he could hear the clatter of a gasoline-driven electric generator, the noise coming every now and then on a chance breeze. But there was no movement in the camp. No guards smoking cigarettes, whose glow would have been clearly visible even at this distance in the night spotting scope; no one moving from tent to tent, no Jeeps patrolling the perimeter. They'd seen that activity around the clock in the reconnaissance photographs. They'd even watched night training maneuvers to the east of the encampment. But there was none of that tonight.

Tel Aviv seemed so very far and unreal to him at this moment, and yet he could not keep out the thoughts. His parents were long dead, there were no sisters or brothers, aunts or uncles or cousins. No wife. Only Miriam. Yet he felt the tug of his safe, secure existence, as much as any Israeli Jew could be safe and secure in the Middle East. The Mossad wanted him at a desk. They wanted him to coordinate operations. Perhap one of the outstations. But he was a field man. He lived for missions like this.

"Once it gets into your blood," Arik Ben-Or, an old friend, had told him years ago, "it will never leave you. You've got the look." And he had. It had to do with loyalty, he'd tried to explain, but it hadn't been necessary; the old man had understood without words. Ben-Or had literally walked all the way from Yerevan, the capital of Armenia, as a young man; eight hundred miles through Turkey and completely across hostile Syria to Tel Aviv, where he started a kibbutz. In the middle of World War II. He was an extraordinary man who now ran the Mossad with an understanding, if iron, hand. He had practically written the book on loyalty and dedication.

Avram took one last long sweep across the camp, then worked his way back below the crest and hurried down to the others waiting for him. All good people, he thought. The best. He had hand-picked them himself. Anne from Haifa Station, Larry Saltzman and Steve Rosenberg out of Tel Aviv, and Golam Lapides, their medic on loan from the Army.

"It's too quiet," Avram said, hunching down.

"They're sleeping. . ." Anne started to say, but Avram cut her off.

"No guards, no movement, no patrols. Nothing."

"Have they left?" Saltzman asked.

"I don't think so. There are lights showing, and I heard the generator. They're down there all right. But something is going on."

"Could they have been warned?" Anne asked.

"No," Avram said, shaking his head. "This entire operation has been too tight. There aren't two dozen people in Israel who know about it. Every one of them beyond question."

"Maybe they spotted us coming in," Rosenberg suggested.

"It's possible, Steve. But they'd have had the Syrian Air Force down here on our ass if that were the case." Avram glanced again over his shoulder toward the crest of the hill.

"Do we abort?" Lapides, their medic, asked softly.

"Not a chance in hell," Avram replied. He looked at his watch. The air strike on the camp was scheduled for 0430 sharp, which gave them slightly less than ninety minutes to effect the rescue operation and get clear. The choppers would be coming in to pick them up in the confusion. The timing was tight, but it would work. He looked up. He would *make* it work.

Tel Aviv, *Three Months Earlier*

Avram Zemil parked his white Peugeot sedan on Lilienblum Street just around the corner from the Central Post Office and worked his way on foot back toward the Land Registration Office on Yafo. It was midwinter but the day was pleasantly warm, a gentle breeze coming off the Mediterranean, the sun high in an absolutely cloudless sky. Traffic was heavy downtown. He had driven over from Jerusalem this morning after Ben-Or's call, disturbed by the peremptory tone in the old man's voice on the phone. They'd been friends for a lot of years. Ben-Or had known Avram's parents, and had been like a Dutch uncle to him. When Ben-Or got that way, something was up. Something not very pleasant.

The location of the Mossad's headquarters in Tel Aviv was a closely guarded national secret. In fact, operations were spread throughout the city in half-a-dozen spots. Israel had learned well the lessons of decentralization. Administrative Functions were located in what was called the Land Registration Office: Annex, through a small courtyard behind the main building. Avram took pains with his tradecraft this noon, doubling back, crossing streets, turning corners suddenly so that if he were being trailed, front or back, he would know. When he decided that he was clean, he circled the block and ducked into the Annex courtyard.

The old woman behind the reception desk in the small anteroom recognized him and buzzed the inner door, allowing him to go straight in past the civilian guard. He took the elevator to the third floor. There was a muted hum throughout the building, of clattering typewriters and computer printers, telephones ringing, people talking. With a worldwide staff of less than two thousand people, everyone in the Mossad wore two and three hats. If you weren't directly involved in a field assignment, you were working somebody's desk somewhere. There never seemed to be enough time. But no one complained. The survival of Israel was at stake. Every day, twenty-four hours a day.

Ben-Or, his mane of white hair in disarray, was in the corridor talking with Alex Paderewski, his chief of staff, when the elevator doors opened.

"Good morning, sir," Avram said, stepping out.

"Afternoon," Ben-Or grumbled, his voice deep, his Armenian accent still strong. "I'll get him started," he said to his COS. "I want you out at Lod the moment the recon flight comes in. Call me from the lab if anything has changed."

"Let's hope it hasn't, Arik," Paderewski said. He nodded his greeting to Avram and hurried down the corridor to his office.

Avram followed Ben-Or into the screened briefing room where all their top-secret conferences were usually held. The windowless room was at the center of the building and electronically swept every minute. It was the most secure spot in all of Israel. The long mahogany table was filled with large reconnaissance photographs, maps, and what appeared to be assessment reports, all of them marked with twin diagonal orange stripes and stamped TOP SECRET, NATIONAL DEFENSE. The door locked automatically when Ben-Or threw the light switch.

"We have trouble, Avram," Ben-Or said without preamble.

Avram dragged his gaze away from the photographs. "I gathered as much, sir."

Ben-Or managed a faint smile. "It's that obvious?"

"Yes, sir. What is it?"

"Ephraim Storch, Frank Pfeiffer, and Chaim Mallekin. Those names mean anything to you?"

"Pfeiffer is one of us," Avram said. He thought

he might have met him a couple of years ago in Haifa. He hadn't heard the other two names.

"They all are. They were running our Damascus network, and doing a damned fine job of it."

"But?"

"They've been blown, and arrested."

"Syrian Intelligence?"

"I wish it were that simple, Avram," Ben-Or said heavily. "No, the PLO got to them."

"When?"

"Thirty-two days ago."

"I hadn't heard anything," Avram said. He was getting a very bad feeling about this. Whenever the Arabs, especially the PLO, grabbed an Israeli, especially a Mossad operative, they crowed about it in the world press the instant it happened.

"We've kept it quiet. But we think we've got them spotted in a PLO training base about thirty-five miles inland from the Syrian coastal town of Tartūs. We've been flying over the place for the past six weeks, and it's been on our A Strike List. Photo Analysis spotted what looked to them like a prisoner transfer last month, but we had no one listed as missing then, so the information was mostly ignored."

"It's our people?" Avram asked. "Are we certain?"

"Reasonably," Ben-Or said. "At least Mallekin is there. He was spotted in this morning's overflight. He was standing in the doorway of the main camp building. He couldn't have heard our aircraft, but something made him turn his face toward the door at the right moment."

"Nothing from the PLO?"

"Not a word."

"Unusual."

"To say the least, Avram. I want them out of

there. In secret. Just the way the PLO grabbed them." Ben-Or looked at the photos for a long moment. "Something is going on. I don't know what, and I don't know why. But this isn't like them." He looked up. "We have enough trouble as it is."

He didn't have to say anything else. The Mossad was still feeling the repercussions from the maverick spying operation against the United States. The debate continued to rage in the Knesset about reassessing, reevaluating the continued role the Mossad should play in Israel's future. Even the moderates, if they had their way, would cut back the organization. By the time they realized their mistake it would be too late—for all of them.

This was to be a test case, then. Another Entebbe, another Eichmann snatch. The Mossad needed it. Israel needed it. They could not fail.

ON THE SYRIAN DESERT, 4:13 A.M.

The PLO encampment lay barely a hundred yards across the desert floor from where Avram and the others crouched in the darkness. They had circled around to the east. From where they waited they could see the main building, which was actually nothing more than a large shack with a canvas roof and tent flaps for windows and doors over a rough wooden frame. To the left was the generator shed, the noise of the machinery loud now on the still night air. To the right were half-a-dozen tents in which the soldiers billeted. Three wood-frame buildings housed the camp office, the armory, and the communications center.

"You take the generator building, Anne," Avram said softly. "Set your timer for 4:25 exactly, which will give us five minutes in the confusion to snatch our people and get clear before the air strike."

"I don't like this," she said. They were all spooked by the silence, and by the absence of guards. Except for the lights and the few Jeeps and trucks parked within the camp, the place could have been deserted.

"Neither do I," Avram said, not taking his eyes off the main building, where they suspected their people were being held. They had rehearsed this scenario for weeks, going over the steps time after time at the exact duplicate of this camp that they'd set up for training outside of Be'er Sheva. In their training scenarios, however, there'd always been guards. A lot of guards around the perimeter whom they'd find and eliminate one at a time. Silently.

Avram touched the haft of his stiletto in its sheath strapped to his right calf. Kill silently. They'd practiced until they could take this camp apart in their sleep. But where were the guards?

Anne disappeared into the darkness.

"Same thing with the armory, Steve," Avram whispered to Rosenberg. "Larry, you take the comms tent."

Both men slipped away into the darkness, leaving Avram and Lapides alone in a slight depression in the desert floor. Because of the tent lights they would be invisible to anyone watching from the camp. Still, Avram felt vulnerable. Something was wrong, he could feel it with every sense. He looked at his watch again. In seventeen minutes three Phantom jets from the air base at Zippori would be coming in on a surgical strike mission. Their actual flight time would be less than eight minutes. At the same moment that happened, two Huey choppers would set down on the desert behind the camp to pick up the team and the hostages, and then make for their transport craft standing by five miles out in the Med.

Avram turned to Lapides. The man was sweating. "Are you all right?"

"I just want to get the hell out of here."

"Just a few more minutes. We'll go in just before the charges are set to blow, neutralize the building, and as soon as everything starts popping we'll get out." They sat very close, their voices low so that the sounds would not carry above the noise of the generator.

"Any chance this is a trap?"

Avram shrugged, grim-lipped. He looked again toward the camp. "Anything is possible. But a trap can spring both ways."

"Let's abort. Three hostages are better than seven."

It wasn't that Lapides was a coward. Avram knew better than that. Sometimes the best strategy was a retreat. But not this time. Not yet. "We won't leave them. We've come too far."

"Maybe they're not even here."

"In that case we'll blow this place off the map. That'll get their attention."

Lapides sighed deeply. He knew how to fight, of course. But he was a medic and officially listed as a noncombatant. He knew his way around scalpels and needles better than he did guns and grenades. "I'm scared, and I don't mind admitting it."

"So am I," Avram said, managing a slight, feral grin. The feeling was always there for every Jew. Israel was surrounded by hostile states. The Grim Reaper was always near, ready to pounce the moment any of them made the slightest mistake. It was there for all of them.

Even his father. General Meir Zemil, Israel's

ablest tank strategist. He'd died in the Six-Day War, leading a charge in the Golan Heights when his tank received a direct hit from an antitank missile. From that day forward Avram had begun to seriously consider his own mortality. And it was on that day too that he vowed to take the fight to the enemy.

Anne materialized out of the darkness as silently as she had left. "There's no one in the camp," she said urgently, hunching down next to Avram.

"Did you set the charges?"

"Yes," she said, nodding. "But there's no one there, I'm telling you! Not a single living soul. I looked in one of the barracks. It's empty!"

"Damn," Avram swore. He tried to think it out. They could not simply turn around and leave. There was no way of calling off the air strike. If their people were in the main building, they would be killed. Trap or no trap, they would have to make sure before they ran.

Avram pulled out his stiletto. Before they left they would have to make sure. "Wait here for Larry and Steve," he said. "If anything goes wrong, get the hell out."

"Where are you going?"

"To see if our people are here," Avram said. "Just keep your heads down."

Avram climbed up over the top, hesitated a moment, and then, keeping low, hurried directly toward the rear of the main building. Seventy-five yards out he heard a movement to his left and he flattened himself against the ground, the knife in his right hand. He saw a movement, then lost it, then saw it again, a figure moving fast from behind the communications tent. It was Saltzman. A second later Rosenburg came around from behind the armory in a dead run.

Jumping up, Avram charged the main building. When he reached the back wall he tore open one of the window flaps and looked inside. A single light dangled from the ceiling of the completely empty building. Nothing had been left behind. Not so much as a single scrap of paper.

Strong lights suddenly came on all over the camp, illuminating the entire area as if it were bright daylight. Avram dropped down beside the building, pulling his Uzi around, snapping the bolt back and switching off the safety.

"ISRAELI DOGS . . . STAY WHERE YOU ARE . . . THROW DOWN YOUR WEAPONS. . . ." an amplified voice boomed across the desert close to the west.

Anne was the first out of the depression, the others right behind her. She fired off a quick burst in the direction of the voice and started toward Avram's position, moving fast and low, zigzagging as she ran.

Machine-gun fire came from behind and to the left. Rosenburg went down, but then rolled right and was on his feet immediately.

Avram laid down a long burst of covering fire, left to right, as they ran. Someone had sold them out. The single thought crystallized in his brain. But who? And why?

A wave of bullets slammed into the building above his head, wood splinters raining down on him. A second hit his left arm just below the shoulder, shoving him backward off balance. Anne was returning fire, and Saltzman swiveled on his left heel, threw something, and a second later was racing to the right, bullets kicking up the sand inches behind him.

Avram relied on his instincts and reflexes. His brain was consumed with the thought of a traitor. It was his only thought as he followed Anne to safety around the corner of the building.

An explosion shattered the darkness beyond the perimeter of the camp and someone cried out. For a moment Avram thought one of the charges they'd set off had gone off prematurely, but then he realized it was a grenade Saltzman had thrown.

Saltzman and Lapides, dragging Steve Rosenberg between them, flopped down in a heap beside them moments later.

The firing stopped as abruptly as it had begun. As Avram's head began to clear, the same voice as before came out of the darkness.

"THERE IS NOWHERE FOR YOU TO GO ... YOU ARE COMPLETELY SURROUNDED HERE ... THROW DOWN YOUR WEAPONS AND LIVE. ..."

Lapides was working on Rosenberg, who had taken a round in his side. He didn't look good, though he was still conscious.

"Are you all right?" Anne said to Avram.

Avram's head was rapidly clearing. He tried to move his left arm, but couldn't. "I'll live," he said tersely. "How're we doing on time?"

Anne checked her watch. "Three minutes before the charges blow. Eight minutes before the strike."

"ISRAELI DOGS ... WE GIVE YOU THIRTY SECONDS TO THROW DOWN YOUR ARMS AND COME OUT INTO THE OPEN. ..."

Time. They needed just a little time. Avram turned to Rosenberg. "How are you doing, Steve? Can you run if need be?"

"Not far, but I think I can make it to the checkpoint if we can get out of here," Rosenberg said through clenched teeth.

Saltzman was crouched down between them.

"Larry?" Avram asked softly.

Saltzman nodded. "I won't be taken hostage. Not by those bastards."

"I'll try to buy us some time," Avram said. "As soon as the charges go off we'll head directly for the generator shed."

"There's a lot of fuel over there."

"Right, they're not going to want to come very close. And if we're lucky, there'll be enough ammunition going off in the armory to keep them confused."

"You're a tough bastard, aren't you?" she said, a faint smile on her lips.

"Don't think I ever had a choice," he said. He got to his feet, swaying as a momentary wave of dizziness ran through him. When it passed he edged to the corner of the building.

"We want a guarantee," he shouted out toward the darkness.

There was a moment of silence.

"WE GUARANTEE THAT YOU WILL DIE IF YOU DO NOT THROW DOWN YOUR WEAPONS AND COME OUT INTO THE OPEN."

"We have wounded, dammit!" Avram shouted. "We need medical assistance!"

"YOUR WOUNDED WILL BE ATTENDED TO," the voice boomed across the desert.

"Time," Avram asked over his shoulder.

"Minute and a half," Anne said behind him.

"SHOW YOURSELVES NOW, OR WE WILL OPEN FIRE ... THIS IS YOUR LAST WARNING. . . ."

"Soon as the charges blow, we go," Avram said. He raised the nearly empty Uzi high over his head with his right hand, and before Anne could reach out to stop him he stepped around the corner of the building out into the brightly illuminated open area. "Don't fire! Don't fire!" he shouted.

"THROW DOWN YOUR WEAPON."

"We need guarantees. Two of my people are badly injured. As you can see, I have been wounded as well. Send us a medic."

"THROW DOWN YOUR WEAPON OR YOU WILL DIE WHERE YOU STAND, ZIONIST!"

It was impossible to tell whether the amplified voice was being broadcast from a remote speaker or a bullhorn, but it was coming from the west, not too far from the armory tent.

Avram, moving very slowly as if he were more seriously wounded than he was, threw his Uzi out ahead of him, the weapon rattling as it hit he sand.

"TELL THE OTHERS TO SHOW THEM-SELVES!"

"They are wounded, as I have said," Avram shouted.

"LET THEM CRAWL LIKE THE DOGS THEY ARE."

"They cannot. We need a medic. . . ."

The communications shed behind him exploded first, the concussion knocking him to his knees. A second later the generator shed blew, flames and burning fuel spewing high into the night sky. All the camp lights suddenly went out, and a split second later the armory tent blew with a tremendous, earth-shattering explosion, rockets shooting out in every direction, small arms ammunition popping furiously.

Lapides, helping Rosenberg, came around from the main building, Anne and Saltzman right behind him as Avram picked himself up off the ground and drew the SigSauer from his chest holster. His left arm hung useless at his side. He was lightheaded from the shock and loss of blood but there was no pain. Yet.

They raced across the camp, illuminated now only by the flames from the generator shed and the exploding rockets. Off to their right someone was screaming. And at least half-a-dozen pinpoints of automatic weapons fire were coming from the desert to the west, but directed toward the main building they had just left. The heat near the destroyed generator shed was so intense that Avram could feel the hair on his head singeing.

A second explosion came from the vicinity of the armory, and Avram looked back in time to see one of the Jeeps that had been parked nearby flipping up, end over end. Soon they were on the other side of the flames, struggling across the desert to the east, while overhead they could hear the scream of the approaching Phantom jets and the much lower-pitched whine of the Hueys' engines coming in low and fast from the sea.

2

■

JERUSALEM, *Three weeks later*

"THERE IS A TRAITOR WITHIN ISRAEL,"
Prime Minister Ezra Harel said tiredly. "There can
be no other explanation." He'd been looking out
the window from his second-floor office toward the
Israel Museum to the south. He turned now to his
adviser, David Sokoloff, one of the very few men
in all of Israel whose judgment he trusted without
reservation. Until five years ago when he emigrated to Israel, Sokoloff had been adviser to President Reagan. America's loss was Israel's gain.

"As much as I hate to agree with you, Mr. Prime
Minister, I must," Sokoloff said. Unlike Harel, Sokoloff was tall, very thin, and almost ascetic in his
looks, with a narrow face and a prominent,
sharply defined nose. His intelligence was beyond
reproach.

A third man was present in the room, but for
the past ten minutes he had held his silence,
merely watching and listening to the other two.

"The question is, David, what are we going to
do about it?" the PM said. His face was heavily
lined, large bags beneath his moist eyes, his face

weather-beaten from years on the desert. He'd been a member of the Haganah fighting the British before and after the war, had been a field commander in the Israeli Army, and over the past fifteen years had actively pursued his hobby as an amateur archaeologist.

"I don't think there's any question that something must be done. But before we run off half-cocked we'd better damned well verify our suspicions. There is a lot at stake here."

Harel waved off the objection. Israel was in big trouble from within as well as from without. The Knesset was meeting at this very moment to continue their debate about how Israel was to be governed. Three months ago he had barely survived a vote of confidence. If another were to be taken today, he was certain he would lose and his party would be out of power. The moderates would have their way; or worse yet, the religious zealots such as those of Jerusalem's Mea She'arim District, the Haredim and the Hasidics, would dismantle the government and the military, leaving Israel wide open for a total destruction that would make the Holocaust seem like a simple Sabbath celebration.

"Operation Brother was a complete debacle," Harel said. "They were waiting for our people. They knew we were coming. They knew the schedule, the routes, everything." He glanced down at *The New York Times* on his desk. "And now this," he said with barely controlled anger. The photograph on the front page showed Ephraim Storch, Frank Pfeiffer, and Chaim Mallekin hanging from the gibbet under the headline: ISRAELI SPIES EXECUTED IN DAMASCUS.

"They were waiting for the excuse," Sokoloff

said softly. "It's why the Syrians didn't announce their capture until after our raid."

"Our *failure*," Harel corrected his adviser. "And yet you continue to advise against a retaliatory strike."

"Not now, Mr. Prime Minister. It's not the right time."

"The Knesset is screaming for bloody murder. If I do nothing, I'm out. But if I order a strike on Damascus, it could mean a new war. Israel is not ready for another war. I would be driven out and the government would fail. The opposition has no capable leadership. Not yet."

"They were spies," Sokoloff said.

"Yes," Harel replied, sighing deeply. "Yes, they were that, David. Nor have we denied it. But until now we've exchanged those we've caught. Am I to order the executions of the dozen or so Syrians or the fifty PLOs we're holding?"

Sokoloff shook his head. "Not that either. We're going to have to find the traitor first. Without that, anything we might do would be doomed to fail even before it began."

What Sokoloff was saying finally began to penetrate Harel's worried state, and he looked at his adviser now with renewed interest. "What are you saying to me, David? Exactly."

"The traitor within Israel is very highly placed among us."

Harel's eyes narrowed but he held his peace, allowing Sokoloff to continue.

"He or she is either a member of your cabinet or someone within the Mossad."

All the air seemed to go out of Harel. He glanced at the third man, then slammed his fist on the desk top, the noise like a pistol shot in the room. "Better we three be the suspects," he roared.

Sokoloff nodded calmly. "We're included. But who else knew about the operation? And, who has the most to gain by Israel's fall?"

Harel followed that thought in his mind. Who had the most to gain? He could think of a dozen, perhaps more. But even more important than that, who had known the exact details of the operation? A dozen men? Two dozen? He'd been assured that the planning had been compartmentalized. The Air Force knew it would have to make a strike from Zippori, but the actual target wasn't given to the pilots until they were actually in the air. A duplicate of the PLO camp they were to hit had been laid out at their training base outside of Be'er Shiva, but the camp could have been any of a dozen similar places within Syria. Even Photo Analysis had been kept in the dark. They had known they were looking at PLO bases. But the one outside of Hamāh was only one of a dozen or more being considered for air strikes. Who knew enough to put it all together? The list, he thought, was still large. Too large. Maybe two dozen people, maybe a few more. And such a list might not even include their spy, who might have found out the details without giving himself away. Or *herself*, as Sokoloff had pointed out. Israel had had her women leaders. Why not women traitors?

"We're at war here, Mr. Prime Minister," Sokoloff said, reading something of Harel's thoughts from the expression on his face.

"You're right again," Harel said. "But we don't even know who our enemy is."

Sokoloff shrugged. "And, we can't simply assume that Operation Brother was his only project. There could be others."

"The Russians?" Harel asked.

"Perhaps. The Americans, too. That entire operation over there was stupid to begin with, but it should never have been exposed."

"We can't blame everything on the traitor," Harel said. "Once we start that there'd never be an end to it." He picked up a file folder from his desk. "This, for instance," he said. "The massacre of seven civilians and the wounding of nine others here in Jerusalem."

"The Haredim thing?" Sokoloff asked.

"Reliable witnesses are sure the killer was a Civil Police officer. He left his weapon. The serial numbers match one of the precinct armory lists." Harel looked up. "We might just as well blame that on our traitor."

"Then let's find him," Sokoloff said. "Before it is too late."

"I'm open to suggestions."

"One man. Someone totally beyond corruption, whose first loyalty is beyond question to Israel, and only to Israel."

"What do we tell him?"

"Everything," Sokoloff said evenly. "But once he starts he is to be left completely on his own. We must not interfere with him. None of us. We mustn't even approach him, or send any word to him, because if we do, the traitor might find out and we will have lost again."

The third man now sat forward. "I can give you three names, any one of whom could do the job."

Harel and Sokoloff turned to him.

"Captain Isser Bauer, Army G-2. I know him personally. He lost his parents and his sisters in a PLO raid of their kibbutz. He's a bit overzealous perhaps, but he is intelligent, and his loyalty is beyond question."

"I'm not familiar with the name," Sokoloff said.

"I am," the third man replied tersely. "The second is Felix Louk, a civilian."

"The Knesset," Harel said. "Intelligence Oversight Committee."

The third man nodded. "His story is very similar to Captain Bauer's. Only he watched his father's brains being beaten out of his head, and he was forced to witness the rape and murder of his mother and two sisters. That was less than three years ago in Beirut. They shouldn't have been there in the first place, but Felix's father was on government business . . . our government's business, as you may recall . . . and he took his family with him."

Harel nodded. He remembered well. And he agreed that Felix Louk's loyalty was beyond question.

"There is one other name?" Sokoloff said.

"Yes," the third man said, turning to him. "Avram Zemil. You know his background. His loyalty is beyond question. He is intelligent and very capable."

"Yes, Meir's son," Harel said, nodding. "He'll want to make up for what happened during the raid. But is he fit? Has he recovered from his wounds?"

"Yes," the third man said.

Harel thought about it for a long moment. It *would* be fitting to send him after the traitor. Who better to find the spy for them?

"Avram Zemil," Harel said. "Get him here. In secret. This afternoon."

The Armenian Quarter of Jerusalem,
noon

It had been twenty-one days since they had been
plucked from the Syrian desert and returned to
Israel, and still Avram could not forget what had
happened. Nor would he ever forget the bitter
sense of betrayal he'd felt when he'd looked inside
the main building of the PLO camp and had seen
... what? Nothing. An empty room, a bare light
bulb dangling from the ceiling. The PLO had
known someone was coming. They had been set
up.

The midday sun was warm on his back as he
walked slowly down a narrow lane below David
Street in the Armenian Quarter, barely aware that
he was rhythmically squeezing a tennis ball in his
left hand, building up the strength in his muscles.
It was too soon, the doctors told him, there would
be pain. But he didn't care.

He'd been given sick leave. But after only a few
days the urge to act, to do something, had become
so overwhelming that at times he thought he
would lose his mind. Finally he'd been given a direct order: Stay away from headquarters until you
are completely healed.

*The room was empty. The single light bulb dan-
gled from the ceiling. Now the lights were coming
on all over the camp.*

He stopped suddenly and looked up, pedestrian
traffic giving him a wide berth as if he were a
crazy man. Directly across the street was Police
Headquarters. For a long second or two he stared
at the building wondering what he was doing here,
wondering why he had come this way, until he
remembered Ben-Or's telephone call an hour ago.

He had isolated himself these past three weeks. If the Mossad considered him unfit for duty, even desk work, he didn't want to be with anyone. Not even Miriam. But he had needed time to heal, mentally as well as physically. Ben-Or's call had come like a lifeline tossed to a drowning man. Or at least that's what he had thought at first. Now he wasn't so sure. Replaying the brief conversation in his mind, he wasn't sure at all.

"I want to see you today," Ben-Or had said.

"I can be in Tel Aviv by one," Avram had said, jumping at the opportunity.

"How are you feeling?"

"A lot better. I can—"

"I'm coming to Jerusalem. We'll have lunch together," Ben-Or had said, mentioning a small restaurant in the Armenian section of Walled City. "Do you know it?"

"Yes," Avram had mumbled. It was Ben-Or's tone. The old man wasn't calling him back to work. This was something else.

"This is important, Avram. Very important."

The restaurant was just around the corner. Avram had the urge to turn around and walk away. He didn't know if he wanted to hear what Ben-Or was coming here to tell him. You're finished, Avram. The Mossad cannot afford you any longer. Too many mistakes. Too many failures. Too many good men are dead because of you.

He was sweating, and all of a sudden he could feel the pain in his arm and shoulder. He nearly dropped the tennis ball before he shook himself out of his daze. He had done what he thought was right, he told himself. For better or for worse it had been his decision. If he had to do it all over again, he'd make the same decision. They had to make sure their people were safe. They could not simply have turned their backs and run away into the night.

Avram looked at his watch; it was just noon. Ben-Or would be at the cafe by now, waiting for him. He wasn't going to keep that old man waiting. They went back together too many years for that. Besides, he had never run away from a problem in his life. His father had taught him that.

He pocketed his tennis ball, crossed the street, and walked around the corner.

Ben-Or was waiting at a back table in the small Turkish restaurant, sipping coffee from an ornate handleless cup. He beckoned when he saw Avram, who moved forward slowly, trying to read the old man's face. But he could not. Ben-Or, when he wanted to, could present a completely neutral front. It as one of the many talents that made him such a great spy master.

Ben-Or rose, and they shook hands. "You look like *dreck*," the older man said. "How are you feeling?"

Avram raised his left arm above his shoulder and moved it around, though it caused him pain, and he forced a smile. "Not a hundred percent yet, but close."

Ben-Or smiled indulgently. "You were always a terrible liar," he said.

They sat down. The waiter came and they ordered a light lunch of *kadin Budu*—meatballs and rice—yogurt, and a small pot of expensive Turkish coffee. When they were alone, Avram leaned forward a little.

"Let's get it over with," he said. "Do whatever it is you must do. I'll understand."

Ben-Or's left eyebrow rose, the slightest hint of amusement in his expression, although now

Avram could definitely see that the old man was troubled. "Just why do you think I called you?"

Avram braced himself. "To relieve me of duty."

"On what ground?"

Avram glanced toward the other diners. "Because of . . . Hamāh."

"What about it?"

"I failed. I should have pulled back when I realized that something had gone wrong. I shouldn't have gone ahead. Anne tried to tell me, but I wouldn't listen."

Ben-Or studied him for a long moment. "Yes, she told me. Steve Rosenberg is fine, by the way. He sends his greetings. He's grateful, you know."

"For what?" Avram asked, genuinely startled.

"For saving his life. Without you they would all have died out there in the desert."

Avram looked down at the tablecloth. "I don't see it that way, sir. Not at all."

Again Ben-Or was silent for a few seconds.

"What do you think happened, Avram? Were you spotted coming up from the coast?"

Avram resisted the urge to blurt out his real suspicions. There was no proof. And it was possible, he thought, that they had been spotted after all. He shook his head. "I don't know."

"But you can guess."

Avram shrugged. "It won't bring back our people."

"No," Ben-Or said heavily. "But you'd better do some hard thinking and come up with the answers. You're going to need them."

Of course, Avram thought. There would be a board of inquiry. His debriefing had lasted barely half a day. They would want more facts. They would want to know not only everything that had happened that night on the desert, but every detail of his life during the entire three months of training.

"When do you want me in Tel Aviv?" Avram asked.

"Tel Aviv?"

"Or Haifa. Wherever," Avram said. In the early stages, before they had moved their training schedule out to the mock PLO village near Be'er Sheva, operations planning had been conducted out of their Haifa station.

"What are you talking about?"

"My interrogation. It's what you called me here for. To order me. . ."

Ben-Or was shaking his head. "I wish it were that simple, Avram."

"What, then?"

"Prime Minister Harel called this morning. He want to see you in his office this afternoon."

Avram's heart sank. It was worse than he thought.

"I thought I'd come down to tell you in person, and to make sure you had at least some of the answers for him."

"He's upset," Avram said, realizing it was a stupid comment even as he said it.

"We all are."

"Yes," Avram said, looking away. "Will you be there as well?"

"No," Ben-Or said heavily. "He asked to see you alone."

THE PRIME MINISTER'S OFFICE, 2:18 P.M.

Prime Minister Harel, coatless and tieless, his shirt collar open, his sleeves rolled up, sat behind his desk, his nostrils flared as if he had just smelled a terrible odor. He and Avram were alone.

"Did Arik tell you why I wanted to see you?"

"No, sir," Avram said. "But I think I can guess. The failed mission. Operation Brother."

"Just so," Harel said. "How do you feel about it?"

"You'll have my resignation if . . ."

"I'll decide who resigns around here. I asked you how you felt about the failure."

"Terrible."

Harel nodded. "Fair enough. But beyond that, I want to know what happened. What *you* think happened."

The lunch lay heavy in Avram's stomach and his arm was aching. He decided that he would rather be almost anywhere else than right here. But the time for mincing words was over. Ben-Or had told him to think hard, and to come up with some of the answers. He had.

"We were betrayed, sir."

"Strong words."

"Yes, sir. But the rest was my fault."

"Yes?"

"From three miles out we watched the PLO encampment, and I could see that something was wrong. There were lights, but there were no guards, no movement, no traffic. Nothing."

"Yet you went ahead with the operation, despite what you could see would probably be an impossible situation."

"Yes, sir."

"Why?"

There was no way to minimize his error, Avram thought. Not now. It was far too late for that. "Because I wanted to make absolutely certain that our three agents weren't still there."

"Even though you knew, or at least suspected that you were walking into a trap?" Harel asked harshly.

"Yes, sir."

"And what did you find? What happened next?"

"I filed a report—"

"I'm asking you, now."

Avram hesitated a moment. The memories were there for him, bright and clear. He'd done the right thing. He went over it step by step.

"In fact, Avram, you risked your own life in a delaying tactic that resulted in the destruction of the PLO base and the saving of four lives, including your own," Harel said.

"But not the three agents we'd been sent to rescue." Avram could see in his mind's eye the photograph of the three men hanging from the gibbet, thousands of people looking at them.

Harel sat back. "You did not fail," he said firmly.

"But—"

"No. Hear me out. It was I. My cabinet. Arik Ben-Or."

Again Avram tried to protest, but again Harel held him off.

"You were correct. You *were* betrayed. Your mission was doomed to fail even before you were landed on Syrian soil. It's a miracle that there were not seven bodies hanging on display in Damascus."

For the first time since that night on the desert,

Avram could feel the old fury rising up inside of him. His muscles tightened, the action almost reflexive. Someone had sold them out. He could feel that he was sweating again, the pain in his arm all but forgotten.

"I believe your loyalty to Israel is absolute," Harel said after a beat.

"Yes, sir," Avram said.

There are two men in all of Israel who are beyond reproach, his father had told him just days before he was killed. Two men with whom he would trust his own life without hesitation: Ezra Harel and Arik Ben-Or.

"I'm going to ask you to do something," the prime minister continued. "Something that you may find personally repugnant. But it is something that must be done if Israel is to survive."

"Whatever I can do, sir," Avram said.

"There is a traitor to Israel in our midst."

"Yes, sir," Avram said. "A spy who—"

"No," Harel corrected him. "Not a spy, but a traitor. Someone in the government, or in the Mossad. Someone at very high levels."

The air seemed to leave the room. Avram found it difficult to breathe.

"I want you to find him for me," Harel was saying.

"Have you any idea who—"

"No."

"Arik Ben-Or is here in Jerusalem. He should be the one to conduct this investigation."

"No," Harel said. "Nor will you tell him what I've asked you to do. This is strictly between you and me. And after you walk out of this office this afternoon you will be completely on your own. This conversation between us never occurred."

Avram was speechless.

"Do you understand what I am telling you?"

"No, sir. Not completely."

"You are to trust no one."

"But surely Ben-Or—"

"No one," the prime minister said, his eyes boring into Avram's head. "Not a living soul must know what you are doing or why. You report only to me—personally."

Avram didn't know what to say. His thoughts were racing on a dozen contradictory paths.

"Yes, sir," Avram said softly.

"Then God go with you," the prime minister said, relief evident in his eyes.

Ivan Roskov, parked in a Mercedes sedan on Hanasi Boulevard, watched as Avram Zemil climbed into his white Peugeot and drove off. He'd been spotted by happenstance in the Armenian Quarter and had been correctly identified as the mission commander for Operation Brother. He'd met with Arik Ben-Or in a small, out-of-the-way Turkish cafe, and afterward had come directly here. To see whom? Roskov wondered. The prime minister? One of his aides? Someone in the Knesset? He would find out.

"Follow him," he said softly to his driver.

3

∎

HAIFA, *Two days later*

THE DAY WAS BEAUTIFUL, IF WARM, AND
traffic along Uno Avenue below Mount Carmel was
dense and frantic. Strollers in the Bahai Shrine
and Gardens took their time at midday. Haifa was
an ancient city that had been rudely hauled into
the twentieth century first by the British in the
thirties, then by the Israelis after the war. It was
a city of heavy industry, and because of its deep-
water port at Kishon, was headquarters for Israel's merchant marine and navy.

Avram Zemil had parked his Peugeot on Prophets Street around the corner from City Hall in the
lower city and had gone on foot toward the Zion
Hotel. There were a lot of tourists. Not so many
as in the holy city of Jerusalem, of course, but
plenty just the same. Westerners, especially
Americans, couldn't seem to get enough of Israel
despite all her recent troubles. Americans loved
the underdog and would continue to visit there
until they perceived Israel as the bully.

He worked his way through the government
complex of Post Office, Town Hall, and Court

House to a small one-story building of white stone just behind the Zion Hotel. A plaque in front announced that the building housed the VULCAN FOUNDARY COMPUTER CENTER. In reality it housed the Mossad's Haifa Station. Inside, he walked down a short marble corridor that opened into a narrow reception room. The building smelled of electronic equipment. A young man in shirtsleeves seated behind a desk looked up and smiled pleasantly.

"Good day, sir," he said. "You have an appointment?" The fiction was maintained with the actual Vulcan Foundary in Haifa's industrial section. The few non-Mossad people who stumbled in here were directed across town.

"I'm Avram Zemil; I believe you were expecting me?" Avram said. For two days he had lived practically in limbo waiting for the doctors to finish with him, and for Ben-Or to assign him here as assistant station chief. They'd not spoken of the meeting with the prime minister. Avram accepted this position as the promotion Ben-Or had been after him to take for a while.

"Yes, sir," the young man said, jumping up and coming around the desk. He was obviously in awe. Avram's reputation had preceded him. They shook hands. "Yoram has been waiting for you all morning. We expected you much earlier."

"Do you need some identification?" Avram asked, digging for his wallet.

"No, sir," the young man said. "That won't be necessary. If you'll just wait here, I'll tell him you've arrived."

"Sure," Avram said. The young man opened a steel door at the end of the corridor and went inside. The door closed with an authoritative snap. Mossad stations were built like bunkers that could be defended if Israel were ever to be overrun. The entire country was a fortress, defensible block by block, building by building, and in some cases even room by room.

There was nothing in the reception room to indicate that this was anything other than the computer center for Haifa's major foundary. A coffee table in front of a grouping of leather couch and chairs held a few business magazines and the company's latest annual report. Avram picked up one of the magazines and thumbed through it. Leaving the prime minister's office forty-eight hours ago, he'd been torn. He was consumed with guilt that he was being set to spy on the very people to whom he owed his first loyalty. Not being able to tell Ben-Or had been the unkindest blow of all.

The steel door opened and Yoram Geller, chief of Haifa Station, came out. He was a short, slightly built man with intensely dark eyes and thick black hair. His face was set in a permanent scowl. Avram knew him slightly and did not like him, though he really couldn't say why. But Geller had the reputation of being a tough, extremely capable administrator and operational strategist whose loyalty to Israel was beyond question.

"You're late."

"I wasn't released from medical leave until late yesterday afternoon."

"We expected you first thing this morning. I was getting ready to send someone looking for you."

"I had a few things to do," Avram said, holding his temper. He remembered now why he didn't like Geller: The man was totally unreasonable. Ever since his wife had been killed by a PLO bomb, he'd become overzealous.

"Have you got an apartment here in Haifa yet?"

"No, sir."

"We'll set you up at one of our safe houses. It'll save us all some time. You have a lot of work to do before you'll be useful to me."

Geller held open the steel door and gestured inside. Avram followed him down a long narrow corridor off which several offices opened. If anything, this place seemed even busier than headquarters in Tel Aviv. A lot of the major operations carried out by the Mossad went through the planning stages here. Whoever Israel's traitor was would have had contact through this station. Everyone who'd had access to Operation Brother would be listed here in the operational records.

"I'm sorry I was late," Avram said. He didn't want to start off on a sour note. If things began to get tight, he figured he was going to need Geller's good will. "I should have called."

"Yes, you should have," the station chief said.

They entered his cramped, overstuffed office, which looked over the much larger Operations and Situation Room, deserted now because at the moment there were no field operations in progress. "Have a seat," Geller said. "There are a couple of things you and I have to get straight between us before you start."

When they were both seated, Geller stared at Avram for a long time.

"I'm sorry about what happened with Operation Brother," he began. "From what I understand you were spotted coming in from the coast. Rotten luck. But it wasn't your fault."

"Thank you—" Avram started to say, but Geller cut him off.

"However, when you realized that the operation had gone sour, you had no business continuing.

You could have gotten yourself and your team killed or captured."

Again Avram had to hold his temper, the accusation even more difficult to bear because Avram still felt Geller was correct.

"But that is behind us now," Geller was continuing. "It will not be mentioned in this station again. Not by me, not by anyone else. Nor will we engage in petty recriminations. What's past is past. Is that clear?"

Avram nodded, not trusting himself to speak.

"As assistant chief of station you will be required to know everything that is going on here. I'm giving you a couple of days to familiarize yourself with operational and personnel records, but the rest you're going to have to pick up on the run. There is a lot of work to be done and not nearly the staff to do it. No dilettantes here. Arik Ben-Or may run the Mossad, but Haifa Station is mine."

Avram had wondered how long it would take Geller to mention his relationship with Ben-Or. Ben-Or had never in his life played personal favorites. Not with anyone, and especially not when it concerned Mossad operations.

"I understand," Avram said.

"Yes, I hope you do, because here we run things my way. When I give an order I expect it to be carried out instantly and without question."

"You'll have no argument from me."

"No," Geller said matter-of-factly. "I won't." He opened a desk drawer and took out a small electronic instrument encased in black plastic, a belt clip on the back. He handed it across to Avram. "Keep this with you at all times. The signal to you will be virtually untraceable. A scattered downlink from our communications satellite. When it goes off you are to report here at once, in person, no phone calls. It'll mean trouble."

Avram clipped it on his belt. He felt tethered. But it was a part of the game. It was the way Geller ran things. And for better or worse, at the moment he belonged to Geller—or at least on the surface he did.

"Anything else?"

Again Geller stared at him for a long moment, as if he were trying to make a decision, or find the answer to a puzzling question by reading the expression on Avram's face, or in his eyes. Finally he shook his head.

"You'll want to get settled in. Housekeeping will get you set up in our safe house. You may use it until you have the time to find a place of your own."

"I'll be in first thing in the morning," Avram said, and he started to get up when his eyes strayed to a framed photograph on Geller's desk. It was of a pretty young woman in a white sundress, standing on a quay, the sea behind her. It was summer and she was smiling.

"My wife," Geller said shortly.

"Yes," Avram said, rising. He thought he should say something else, but he couldn't think of a thing. She'd been killed five years ago. It was a long time.

Geller got to his feet and they shook hands. "I expect we will work well together once the ground rules have been worked out."

"I expect so," Avram said.

"We're all working for the same thing here," Geller said as Avram reached the door. "The future of Israel."

Avram turned back. Where to begin, he wondered. With Geller? Anything was possible. Absolutely anything.

MIRIAM'S APARTMENT, 7:08 P.M.

Avram had used his key to let himself into Miriam Loeb's apartment overlooking the sea very near the casino in the Bat Gallim District of the city. He stood just within the entry hall listening to music softly playing on the stereo in the living room, and feeling the gentle breeze flowing through the apartment from the open balcony doors.

It felt odd, in a way, coming here like this. He'd not been back since the failed operation on the desert. Shame, in a small measure, he supposed. Miriam was chief of the Haifa news desk for Israeli Television One, and Arik Ben-Or's niece. She'd never taken failure lightly. But he'd not come partly because he hadn't wanted her to see him wounded, less than whole.

They'd been together now for nearly seven years. At times their relationship was comfortable, like an old, well-established marriage, while at other times he thought they hardly knew each other. She was a strong-willed, independent woman, five years his junior. She'd married young, to an air force pilot who'd been shot down over Lebanon three days after their honeymoon. His body had never been found in the disintegrated wreckage of his jet, and after two years he had been officially declared killed in action. There were times when she would cry out his name in the middle of the night. Until she got over him completely, she'd told Avram once, she could never feel completely free to commit herself to another man. In the beginning he'd wanted to marry her, but finally he had backed off, accepting the relationship for what it was; always against the hope that one day she would come to him and say that she was ready.

Pocketing the key, he moved the rest of the way into the apartment and saw her standing on the balcony, looking out toward the sea, her back to him, her long black hair streaming down her straight back. For a long time he just looked at her, admiring the curve of her hips and her long tanned legs, bare in the brief shorts she was wearing.

Sensing suddenly that she was not alone, she turned. When she realized who it was she stiffened slightly, but made no move to come inside. "You're back," she said.

"Hello, Miriam."

"What are you doing here, Avram?"

"Coming back," he said shortly.

"You left, then?" she asked, her right eyebrow raising.

"I think so."

"Why?"

"I was hurt. I didn't want you to see me."

She came to the doorway, but then stopped. He could see the outline of her breasts rising and falling beneath the thin blouse. Her face was slightly flushed, as if she had just run up a flight of stairs.

"Are you all right now?" she asked.

"Not completely, but I'm healing."

Her nostrils flared. "You were involved in that Syrian thing. Is that it?"

It was big news, even though the censors had quashed the story in the Israeli press. She knew, of course, that he was Mossad, and she had put it together. He could see the understanding and then the hurt in her eyes.

He nodded.

"You were hurt, and you were ashamed to come to me. Is that what you're telling me now? Because if it is, Avram, God damn you to hell."

"If you want me to leave, I will," he said.

"Is that what you want? Is that what you've come here to tell me?"

"No," he said.

"What then, dammit?" she cried. She was beginning to shake. "What are you doing here like this? What do you want?"

"You."

For a moment she didn't seem to have heard him, but then she uttered a little strangled cry and came forward into his arms, her body molding against his. They kissed deeply for a long time, Avram barely aware of the pain in his arm, only that a deep longing ache was rising in his body.

He had been afraid to come back to her. But now everything was all right. Whatever decisions he had made were his, and he would stick by them. She was telling him as much by being in his arms.

When they parted she looked up into his face, and she could see the pain in his eyes. She tried to pull back, but he wouldn't let her.

"I'll never leave you again," he said.

"You're hurt. You're in pain."

"Nothing like it's been these past three weeks not knowing if you would take me back."

"Oh, God, Avram," she said and they were kissing again. This time he could feel her heart beating against his chest and the rising urgency of her passion in her lips. When they parted this time, her eyes were filling.

Careful not to pull the stitches in his arm, he

lifted her and carried her into the bedroom, laying her down on the big bed that faced the sea. The windows here were open, too, the light warm breeze rustling the curtains. He unbuttoned her blouse and gently kissed her breasts. She moaned, arching her back, then reached out for his face, pulling it to hers, and they kissed again, deeply, and for a long time.

Afterward they lay in each other's arms, her legs intertwined with his, and he watched her breasts rise and fall with her breathing. She was careful about the wound in his arm as she moved away and sat up.

"Was it bad?" she asked. "On the desert?"

"I can't tell you . . ."

She touched his lips to silence him. "It's all I want to know, Avram," she said. "Was it very bad?"

"Yes," he said after a while.

"How long can you stay here?" she asked, watching his eyes.

"Only for tonight."

"And then? Back to Tel Aviv? Jerusalem?"

"I've been stationed here, in Haifa," he said, and her face lit up. "But we won't be able to see each other for a while."

"Why?" she demanded, her anger suddenly flaring.

"I can't tell you."

"For how long?"

"I don't know. A few days, maybe weeks, I just don't know."

"But you'll be here in Haifa?"

"Part of the time. But I don't want you trying to contact me."

"There's so much that I want to tell you, Avram . . ." she started.

Avram hushed her. "I know, and there's so much I want to tell you, but it will have to wait. Just a little longer now. You're going to have to trust me. No matter what happens, no matter what you think you know, remember that I love you."

She studied his face. "There will be some danger for you?" she asked.

"Yes. And for you or anyone else who might be near me." It was more than he had wanted to tell her, more than she should know, but he wanted her to understand that he was not leaving her again. That he would be coming back.

"Then I'll wait," she said softly. She bent over him, her long hair trailing on his chest, and began to kiss him, softly, sensuously. "At least we have tonight."

Mossad Haifa Station, 9:16 a.m.

operation brother: the title was stamped on the front cover of the first spiral-bound book Avram extracted from the files. overview: goals and impact statement. The book was marked with the diagonal orange stripes signifying top secret material. Behind it were four other files, similarly marked, with the promulgation statement attached to the inside cover of each, marked for Class A Distribution. Somewhere there was a list of exactly who had received information regarding the operation.

"I don't want you digging through all our old dirty laundry," Geller had snapped this morning.

"I'm just going to bring myself up to date,"

Avram replied. "Give me an idea of what we've done and exactly where we're going. Is that all right with you?"

"Certainly," Geller said. "I just don't want you wasting your time with idle nonsense. As soon as you're ready I'm putting you on the night desk. Between the two of us we'll be able to cover this place twenty-four hours a day."

"I'll need a few days."

"It's all you'll have," Geller said sternly. "Regular staff meetings in Operations at ten sharp every morning. I expect to see you there. Every morning."

Avram glanced at his watch as he went to a corner table in Basement Archives and sat down. He had a little less than forty-five minutes before he had to be upstairs. At least he'd have a start.

The first volume began with a cover letter from Arik Ben-Or, outlining in broad strokes the reason for the mission; the first intelligence the Mossad had received indicating that the PLO were holding three deep-cover agents and had held them for more than thirty days without any public announcement. "Which leads us to the conclusion," Ben-Or had written, "that the PLO leadership has or is receiving instructions and/or planning advice of a more sophisticated nature than we've seen before."

The prime minister, his adviser, and the chairman of the Knesset's Intelligence Oversight Committee, had all agreed that Israel's top priority—morally as well as politically—would be to repatriate the three penetration agents with the absolute minimum of fuss and especially public outcry. "Time is of the essence," Ben-Or had instructed his missions and operations planners, "but the ultimate outcome certainly must outweigh all other considerations.''

A summary of recon photo analysis followed in which the PLO encampment south of the Syrian town of Hamāh was targeted as the likely holding spot for the three men.

An air force strike assessment was included in which the post-rescue surgical strike was outlined. An Israeli Navy equipment summary specified equipment that would be used, with the notation that timetable data could be found in an appendix to the final operational planning guide.

It was at this point, Avram recalled, that he had been designated as mission commander, over Ben-Or's personal signature. After the hasty meeting in Tel Aviv with Ben-Or, he had come up here to Haifa where the initial operational planning headquarters had been set up in a naval warehouse at the deep-water estuary of Kishon.

They'd compartmentalized the early stages. Only a handful of people understood exactly what it was they would be doing. The navy's operations man, for instance, had been told only that a mission involving two of his frigates and a pair of his helicopters would be carried out within an area yet to be specified, on a date and time to be announced through sealed orders once under way. The air force operations commander had been advised that he was to work out the details of a surgical strike somewhere in Lebanon or Syria—the actual target, date, and time to be supplied later. Photo Recon Analysis were given only the scantiest of information. And through it all there was no intermingling of details; cross-collateralization, it was called. The air force knew absolutely nothing of the navy's orders, and vice versa. In abso-

lute terms, then, the need-to-know list had been
kept to an absolute minimum.

Beginning with the prime minister himself and
working down to Yoram Geller and the Mossad
station chief at Be'er Sheva, plus the other four
who had actually gone on the mission with Avram,
everyone's loyalty seemed beyond question. Absolutely. They were all patriots to the highest order who had proven themselves over and over
again, their records absolutely clean.

Yet there had been a leak. Perhaps, he thought,
not a leak from within, rather an intelligence
gathering operation from the outside. Perhaps
they'd been looking in the wrong direction after
all. He hoped so.

Five men were seated around the large table in
the Operations Room across from Geller's office
when Avram came up from Archives in the basement. Besides Geller, he knew Sammuel Amit, who
was Haifa Station's operations chief; Joseph Geva,
a tiny man with a club foot who ran Mossad Communications with genius; and the husky Benjamin
Strauss, who until his emigration to Israel had
been a New York City cop and was now Haifa Station's chief of surveillance and the best leg man
in all of the Mossad. Avram didn't know the fifth
man, who sat quietly at the end of the table, a
hooded look to his eyes, like a cobra's. Geller introduced him.

"Michel Louk, Shin Beth out of Jerusalem."

The Shin Beth, a sister service to the Mossad,
was charged with the responsibility for Israel's
internal security. Just lately they'd been coming
under a lot of heat for what were called "exces-
ses" in carrying out their duties. A number of
prisoners had died recently in Shin Beth interro-

gation cells. "A necessary evil, the Shin Beth," Ben-Or had once said, his distaste for their methods obvious.

"What brings you to Haifa?" Avram asked, taking his seat.

"We've been asked to participate in a joint mission," Geller quickly answered for him.

"We don't normally conduct operations internal to Israel," Avram said.

"This time we will."

Louk nodded and sat forward slowly. He gave the appearance of being an exceedingly dangerous man. He was seated alone. Even Geller seemed wary of him.

"We are perfectly capable of handling this ourselves, Mr. Zemil, rest assured. But since the operation will take place here in Haifa, we thought this station should be included." His voice was gentle, perfectly reasonable, as if he were a schoolteacher talking to a class of young children.

"Naturally," Geller said.

"Have we got approval out of Tel Aviv?" Avram asked.

"Yes," Geller said smugly. "Yes, we do. Now let's get on with it."

"Sometime within the next ninety-six hours—I am sorry I cannot be more specific about the time—we will receive an emissary from the government of Lebanon," Louk began.

"Which government?" Avram asked. "Catholic, Druse, or Shi'ite?"

"The legally constituted government of Lebanon. The only government the United Nations recognizes at the moment."

And Israel's enemy, Avram thought, but he held his peace for the moment.

"While he and his party are here, it will be our

job to make certain they come to no harm," Louk continued. "They will be brought in through the naval base, but without escort because we don't want to create a stir, and from there they will be taken by windowless van to Nazareth where they will meet with members of our military and government."

Avram started to protest, the Mossad had no business in this sort of an operation, but Louk held him off.

"The meeting will occur, Mr. Zemil. That has nothing to do with us. We are merely charged with ensuring the delegates' safety while on Israeli soil."

"Who is this delegate?" Avram asked.

"Youssef Fawzi," Geller said.

"I see," Avram said, a sick feeling in the pit of his stomach. Fawzi was a long-time friend of Yasser Arafat and the PLO. He knew Abu Nidal personally, and had once sworn in public that if he had his way the streets of Jerusalem and Tel Aviv would one day run red with rivers of Jewish blood. And now he was coming to Israel under the protection of the very people he had sworn to massacre.

The others had the same reaction. Even Geller had had difficulty saying the name.

"Have we gotten confirmation from Tel Aviv?" Avram asked Geller.

"Yes. We've been ordered to help, and we will."

"Do we know the nature of this meeting?" Avram asked.

"It's not for me to say . . . ," Louk began, but Geller interrupted.

"He is bringing with him reliable intelligence that Syria is getting ready to attack Lebanon."

"That doesn't make sense," Avram said. "The Syrians have been the peacekeepers there."

"Evidently that policy has changed."

"He's coming to ask for our help?" Avram asked, not believing he was hearing any of this.

"Apparently," Louk said. "And we'll give it to him."

4

■

THE ROOM WAS EMPTY. THE SINGLE LIGHT bulb dangled from the ceiling. Now the lights were coming on all over the camp.

Avram thought back to that night in the desert as he stepped into the doorway of a closed shop and pretended to look in the window. You will be completely on your own, the prime minister had told him. Trust no one. Not even Ben-Or.

He had left the station a half-hour ago, and halfway across town he thought he might have picked up a tail, but he hadn't been certain. He'd stashed his car in a parking ramp on G'Ula Street and had made his way this far on foot. No one was behind him. Or if they were, they were very good and were probably working teams; a pair behind, one out front, and possibly one or more teams paralleling his track.

Either that, he thought, or he was getting paranoid, and no one was back there.

He waited until a bus rumbled past, then stepped away from the doorway and hurried down the street, around the corner at the end of the block and down a narrow, dirty alleyway. This section of the city was spread out over a slight hill that looked down over the Port of Haifa's oil-tank field and depot, the quarantine station for incoming agricultural products, the power station, and in the distance the Kishon Harbor Naval Base., The alley led to a dead end where Avram stopped in the shadows and waited; watching, his every sense straining to pick out the one stray noise, from a city of noises, that would mean someone had come after him. The scrape of shoe leather against the pavement; the distinctive rustling snap of a weapon being drawn from its holster; or the metallic click when a safety catch was flipped off or a hammer drawn back.

But there was nothing. No one had followed him here. After a full five minutes, he stepped out of the shadows and hurried halfway back up the alley to a glass door marked GROMIT IMPORT/EXPORT in Hebrew and Arabic. He knocked once, then twice, then once again. Immediately a light came on in the rooms above, and someone opened a window.

Avram stepped back into the light and looked up as Yakof Gromit stuck out his ponderous head and shouted down at the top of his lungs like the buffoon he pretended to be.

"Who is it has the gall to disturb an honest man's dinner!"

"Open up, you old thief," Avram shouted up, in no way trying to hide his presence.

"If you've brought me money or luck, you're welcome, otherwise get lost!" Gromit shouted. He slammed down the window, and moments later Avram could hear him coming down the stairs.

It was all an act, of course. If you wish to hide a grain of sand, Gromit was fond of saying, hide it in the desert. Openly he was an outrageously outspoken thief and cheat who imported and sometimes exported anything of value, including fake archaeological antiques supposedly from the Sea of Galilee. He'd never been above making a profit wherever he could, including the sale of arms to anyone with cash. Somehow, it seemed that any crucial shipment of weapons to unfriendly Arabs was discovered in transit by the Mossad. Gromit howled the loudest about betrayal and had managed against all odds to keep his skin intact.

They'd known each other for a very long time. Avram's father had mentioned Gromit's name in the late fifties in connection with an arms smuggling operation out of Jaffa, Tel Aviv's seaport. His name came up again when Avram was still in the service, working for Aman, the military intelligence unit. A shipment of Israeli-made Uzi submachine guns was going across the border into Lebanon for a militant Shi'ite cell in Beirut. Avram's investigation eventually led him to Gromit, who by then was operating out of Haifa. Instead of arresting the man, Avram had made a deal with him; Gromit's freedom in trade for a source of information, with the proviso that no arms shipments would ever reach any group hostile to Israel. This arrangement had been in place for more than ten years.

Gromit opened the door to Avram, shouted an obscenity, and dragged him inside. When the door was safely closed, the angry expression on his bloated face turned instantly to one of concern.

"You look as if you are still in one piece, my friend," he said, his voice cultured, his English highborn British. He'd been to Oxford in the early fifties.

"You heard?" Avram asked.

"The desert has no secrets in the end; you know this," Gromit said. "Come."

Avram followed him up the stairs. Gromit was a huge man—over six feet tall and more than four hundred pounds—but he moved with the grace of a ballet dancer.

In the main room, a young boy of fifteen or sixteen with long blond hair lounged naked on cushions in front of a big-screened television set.

"Go to your room, Jacob," Gromit told him. "And no eavesdropping this time, or I shall have to spank you again."

The young boy jumped up with a squeal and rushed out of the room, the odor of sweet perfume lingering on the air after he was gone.

Gromit turned to Avram and motioned him to one of the cushions with a sheepish look on his face. "What can one do, my friend? Fight the inevitable?"

"You're a dirty old bastard," Avram said.

Gromit laughed out loud as he poured them each a cognac in expensive crystal snifters, and then ponderously settled his bulk in the midst of a pile of cushions across a low table from Avram.

"So, you have survived again. I think perhaps you are a cat with your lives."

Avram shrugged. "We were set up, Yakof."

"I heard you walked into an ambush. Too bad about your people in Damascus. They are such pigs, the Syrians." He shook his head. "But then, they've had thousands of years to practice."

"What else have you heard?"

"Not much more. Sometimes it happens this way, Avram, you know this."

"I think we were betrayed."

"Not so uncommon," Gromit said, raising his

cognac in salute. "Cheers. So it's revenge you're after, is that it?"

"Not exactly, though I wouldn't mind a bit of it. I'm looking for something specific."

"*Someone*, I'd say. Insha'Allah . . . in God's hands. And what would you do with this someone once you found out who it was?"

"Arrest him, or her. If possible."

"If not?"

Avram simply raised his glass.

Gromit smiled. "It is a difficult game we play, you and I, my friend. If I tell you everything I know, then I am out of business. In the first place, there would be no reason for you to come back. In the second place, there are a lot of enemies out there who would gladly do me harm. If, on the other hand, you tell me everything you know, you would never again be able to trust me. In which case you would have to do something about me. Perhaps an accident. I hear the Shin Beth have become even more adept than in the old days."

"One name, it's all I want from you, Yakof," Avram pressed. "You need to steer me in the right direction. It's a big world out there."

Gromit chuckled, the sound rumbling deep in his barrel chest. "That, my friend, is an understatement." He rubbed the side of his nose with a forefinger. "But then, why come to me?"

"You hear things."

Gromit took it as a compliment and nodded his head in acknowledgment.

"For instance, how did you know I was involved in our rescue mission in Syria?"

"Trade secrets of the bazaar."

"It's important," Avram said steadily. With Gromit you could not lose your temper, or press too hard. He took out a thick envelope from his breast pocket and nonchalantly laid it on the table. Gromit made no move to reach for it; in fact, he pretended not even to notice it, but Avram had caught the flicker of his eye. The envelope contained five thousand U.S. dollars, more than half of what he had been able to draw from his bank in Tel Aviv yesterday.

"This is business, Yakof. Possibly very large business."

"You have always been generous in the past," the big man said. "In this matter I think a name is not so important, but the brother of a certain *bazaari* here in Haifa who does carpentry work in the city of Be'er Sheva. You know this place? A lovely old city. In the old days it marked the southern boundary of Palestine."

Some contract labor had been used in the construction of the mock PLO encampment outside of Be'er Sheva. But it wasn't enough. The connection was still too tenuous.

"They are building a Bedouin camp here in Israel, my friend tells me. A movie set, I tell him. Clint Eastwood is coming. But in my mind I am thinking perhaps it is something more. Then comes the announcement in the newspaper of the unsuccessful mission to a PLO base on the Syrian desert."

"I'm not after a carpenter with a big mouth," Avram said.

"I'm just a humble man with an admittedly large appetite but small ears," Gromit said. "There are others. You have your sources."

"One name, Yakof. Perhaps the Syrian Secret Service."

"It's possible," Gromit shrugged. He finished his cognac. "There are spies all around us. You know this."

"Perhaps PLO."

"I think not. Ever since they were scattered from Lebanon their real will has ebbed. No, if such a thing as you suggest is so, it would have to be someone with a great deal of sophistication."

"And dedication," Avram said.

"Yes, and dedication. But to what ends, have you asked yourself this, Avram?"

"I think it's obvious."

"Perhaps not," Gromit mused. "But there has been talk. Mostly idle gossip. A hint dropped here, a loose word dropped in the wrong place. Perhaps he is the one you seek."

"Who is he?"

"A Russian possibly," Gromit said. "But just as possibly not."

"A Jew?"

"I don't know, Avram. In this I am telling you the truth. He might be here in Israel."

"Do you have a name?"

"I have nothing yet," Gromit said. He poured them each another cognac, and when he was settled back in his cushions he sighed deeply. "If it is the same one, he would be called Palmyra."

"The city in Syria?" Avram asked, startled.

Gromit chuckled. "Coincidentally, yes. But this one would have no real connection with the Syrians, unless it was to advise them."

"Sophisticated advice."

"If Palmyra is here in Israel, he will not be your spy, but he will be directing your traitor."

"He could have been involved in the compromise of our mission?"

"That and much more."

"Which means he's turned one of our people."

"Or he has constructed a network of informants. A very large network."

"Or both," Avram said, half to himself.

"Yes, and perhaps even more that we cannot guess. For if he is the same man, he is very clever, and very wicked, my friend."

Avram looked up out of his thoughts. "You seem to be talking about the *same man*, Yakof. What do you mean?"

For the first time this evening Gromit seemed uncomfortable, as if he had said too much already and didn't want to go any further. But he was trapped by his own admissions. He turned his head so that he could look toward the window. "Were you followed here, do you suppose?"

"No," Avram said. He told the older man the precautions he had taken, but said nothing about his gut-level feeling that someone was out there. Someone very good.

"But you are looking for a traitor."

Avram nodded.

"With whom, Avram?"

"No one," Avram said evenly.

Gromit's eyebrows rose. "You are foolish, my friend. But it is good, because if my words got out I would be as good as dead." He chuckled and patted his own ample belly. "And I know I have much living yet to do."

"Palmyra," Avram prompted after a moment, even as he wondered if he had gone too far.

"Five years ago I had a partner, in Marseilles," Gromit began. "A good man—if you had no need to trust him too much. You understand?"

"He is no longer your partner?"

"He is dead."

"His name?"

"Jossele Saab," Gromit said. "Which is of no consequence now."

"I never knew this," Avram said, although he

had known that Gromit worked with people overseas, especially in France where many of his export deals of questionable legality were expedited. In fact, back in the early sixties the Israeli Navy had bought missile boats from the French at Cherbourg.

"We told each other things," Gromit said. "We traded information as well as goods, when the trade was of mutual benefit."

Avram waited for him to continue.

"Jossele was having some difficulty in securing an export permit for a shipment of . . . machine screws to a certain Latin American country."

"Which country?" Avram asked.

Gromit smiled. "Nicaragua."

"Go on."

"But Jossele was a sharp man. He discovered that a certain deputy in the Ministry of Defense—who could help him secure his permits—had a penchant for young, good-looking, virile men. Jossele sent the son of an old friend up to Paris to see what could be done."

"The deputy minister's name?"

"Roland Giot," Gromit said.

The name was familiar to Avram. He'd heard it before. He searched his memory.

"Yes, you will have read about him in the newspapers. He was found in his apartment, his brains scattered over his desk. He shot himself in the head."

"Because of his liaison?" Avram asked, vaguely recalling the story. It had been a minor scandal in the French government.

Gromit nodded. "Jossele received his permits and our deal went through, though to expedite it he sent his little *puffta* here to Haifa to see me."

"To pick up money."

Again Gromit nodded. "Two months later the little boy returned, this time very frightened. Jossele was dead. Killed by a Russian whose code name was Palmyra. Naturally I sent the boy away. I want no dealings with the Russians."

"But Jossele had."

"All along."

"Where is the boyfriend now?"

"Also dead," Gromit said. "He was found in Tel Aviv with his face blown off." He shook his head. "Poor little René."

"René Mercier?" Avram asked, suddenly remembering reading something about it.

"Yes," Gromit said. "I tell you I lived in fear that somehow my name would come out. That the silly little boy may have been followed here."

"Are you telling me he was also killed by this Palmyra?" Avram asked.

"Not directly. But he was set up. Just as Jossele had been set up. Just as Deputy Giot had been put into the position where he had to kill himself."

"All arranged by Palmyra?"

"Yes. He is a dangerous man."

Avram tried to think it out, tried to see where the connections between then and now might lie. "You'd heard this name before?"

"Once, a year before that. There were rumors in Paris that a certain cipher clerk at the British embassy in Paris was selling secrets to the Russians. He hanged himself just before they came to arrest him. He'd been dealing with Palmyra."

Avram sat back in his cushions. "If this Russian is here in Israel now, if he is doing something to us, running some operation, surely he wouldn't still be using his old code name Palmyra."

"From what I understand, Avram, this is a man of very great ego." He smiled.

"I want to know if he is here," Avram said.

"It would be very dangerous to pursue him."

"I have no other choice, Yakof. Whether he is involved in our present troubles or not, I must know. You tell me that there are rumors he is here in Israel?"

"Only rumors," Gromit said.

"Can you help me?" Avram asked.

Gromit sighed, and after a moment nodded his ponderous head. "You and I have had a very long and profitable relationship, my young friend. I wish for nothing to come between us. I will do what I can. But it will be slow and delicate, you understand this?"

"Yes," Avram said. "And expensive."

Gromit didn't respond. "The danger from a man as ruthless as Palmyra is great—for both of us. Human life means absolutely nothing to him."

"How soon will you have something for me?"

"Twenty-four hours," Gromit said. "Return here tomorrow evening. And we shall see."

HAIFA WATERFRONT DISTRICT, 11:35 P.M.

The Mossad safe house was a small white-plastered structure in a row of similar houses just off the Kishon Harbor Navy Base. Avram parked his car in the back courtyard and let himself in. There was no moon. The night was very dark, and he was tired. It seemed like years since he'd gotten any proper rest. The wound in his arm ached, and driving down from Gromit's apartment he'd begun to lose feeling in his left hand. There was some nerve and muscle damage, the doctors had told him. But in time, they promised, he would regain nearly full use of his arm and hand.

The safe house was sterile. There was food in the cupboards, linens on the beds and stacked neatly on shelves in the closet, pictures on the walls, and a few books in the bookcase in the living room. But the place had an unlived feel to it. Secret meetings were held here at times. At other times it was used as an isolation cell. And at still other times, like now, it served simply as a hotel. No one had made their personal mark on any of the rooms, though the place was kept neat and clean by housekeeping. More likely someone's wife. Avram thought, switching on the light in the kitchen and putting on water for tea.

Miriam was just across town, barely a couple of miles away. He wondered what she was doing at this moment. He wanted to be with her, but it was simply too dangerous. When this business was finished. She would understand.

Kicking off his shoes and pulling off his coat, he walked into the bedroom where this afternoon he had dropped off his two bags, one on the bed, the other on the floor. He unstrapped his holstered gun from the small of his back and laid it on the bed, and in the bathroom started the water for his shower.

Undressing, he laid his wallet on the dresser. He had a little more than four thousand U.S. dollars remaining. *Pikeesh*, the Arabs called it. Gromit and others of his ilk preferred hard Western currencies—American dollars, German marks, or French francs—over Israeli pounds. When this business was over he would submit a voucher for reimbursement, at the same time protecting Gromit's identity by listing it as a blind account.

He stepped into the shower and adjusted the spray to as hot as he could stand it, his aches and pains immediately easing. The Russians had been spying in Israel from the very beginning, just after the war when the British got out. Their goal, of course, was to do everything within their considerable power to ensure that the region remained unstable. And they'd been successful, to a point. A paranoia had been sown in the average Israeli's mind about Soviet spies in every dark corner.

It would be very easy, he thought, to blame all of Israel's troubles on the Russians. But hardly practical. Israelis, he thought wryly, were supremely capable of getting themselves into trouble without any outside help or influence. Perhaps Gromit was grasping at straws. Perhaps he had told Avram what he wanted to hear, not hard information.

Another thought suddenly struck him and he yanked back the shower curtain to look out into the bedroom, staring at the two nylon bags he had brought with him. One was large and square and held most of his clothing, including jackets and trousers. The other, slightly smaller but of the same make and color, contained shoes, boots, toiletry articles and some other clothing. The big bag was on the floor now, the smaller bag on the bed.

He turned off the water and stepped out of the shower. Not bothering with a towel, he stepped into the bedroom and listened. The teakettle was whistling in the kitchen, but there were no other sounds.

At the bed he pulled his SigSauer out of its holster, levered a round into the firing chamber, and switched off the safety catch. When he'd dropped his bags off he'd laid the big bag on the bed and the smaller one on the floor. They'd been switched. Someone had been here. Someone had gone through his things.

He doused the lights in the living room and in the kitchen. He took the teakettle off the fire and looked out the window into the rear courtyard. Nothing moved. In the distance, toward the harbor, he thought he could hear the diesel engines of a boat, probably a tug pulling out a big ship for a night departure.

Back in the bedroom he pulled on his trousers and shoes. He didn't bother going trough his bags. They contained nothing that would connect him with this investigation, or the Mossad. Whoever had gone through his things would have learned nothing, except the brands of toothpaste and after-shave lotion he used.

Once again in the kitchen, Avram eased open the window and slipped outside into the courtyard. He dropped down and moved quickly left into the deeper shadows in the lee of the concrete block wall that separated the courtyards of this house and the next in line. From where he crouched he could see down the driveway to the street, where a few cars were parked. But nothing moved, though now he could hear the traffic sounds from the busy Nazareth Road a quarter of a mile away, and he could see the glow of the downtown area of the city to the northwest, and the strong lights illuminating the naval docks to the north.

It was possible, he thought, that Geller had sent someone over from the station to check on him. He wouldn't put it past the man. It was more likely, however, that he had been followed here. Which meant that if there was indeed a leak within the Mossad, they were already becoming suspicious of him.

He moved around the side of his car, and keeping close to the house he moved up the driveway. There was no real reason to suspect that whoever had followed him earlier and gone through his bags would still be here except that all evening his feeling of being watched had grown. A couple of Fiats, an old Ford Cortina sedan, and a battered Mercedes truck were parked along the narrow street. There was no traffic back here at this hour. He moved away from the house and started to cross the street when the Mercedes's engine roared to life and the truck lurched away from the curb, accelerating down the street.

"Stop!" Avram shouted, raising his gun.

Someone popped up from behind the Ford Cortina and ran toward the harbor.

Avram started after him. A line of old houses ended at the edge of a steeply cut drainage ditch on the other side of which was an open field that led to a tall wire-mesh fence surrounding an oil-tank storage field. The tanks were lit, as was the naval base a half-mile away, but the deep ditch was pitch black.

The figure leaped down into the ditch and was gone as Avram rounded the corner of the last house and pulled up short. He waited a full five seconds for the man to reappear on the other side; when he didn't, Avram raced on a diagonal to the left, hoping to intercept the man before he reached the culvert that ran beneath the oil-tank farm access road.

The man was running up the middle of the deep ditch.

Avram scrambled over the side, slipping and half falling fifteen feet to the muddy bottom that smelled strongly of crude oil. He got to his feet and raised his pistol in the direction the man had gone. "Stop, or I'll fire!" he shouted.

Suddenly, someone was behind him. He ducked low and to the left as he started to swivel on his heel, when something very hard slammed into his back, driving the air out of his lungs and sending him to his knees. He'd made the most elementary of mistakes and had been led stupidly into a trap. As he struggled to raise his head he was in time to see a booted foot coming directly at his face. He managed in the last instant to fall back, so that the blow only grazed the side of his head, but a million stars burst in his eyes and he went down hard.

When he came around he was alone, the night dark, a boat's whistle hooting in the distance. Why hadn't they killed him? he wondered.

They could have. They should have.

5

■

THE SAFE HOUSE WAS SILENT AND DARK.
Avram crouched in the shadows across the street
watching for a movement, any kind of movement.
He hadn't really expected anyone to be here now,
not after what had just happened. But he had been
led into one trap; he wasn't going to go blindly
down that path again.

There had been at least three of them. The
driver of the Mercedes truck, the one he had
chased, and finally the one who had been waiting
in ambush in the ditch.

But they hadn't killed him. It didn't make any
sense. Nor did their coming after him in the first
place make much sense, unless they'd somehow
learned why he was in Haifa.

He thrust that thought roughly aside and hurried across the street around to the back of the
safe house, and climbed in through the kitchen
window, closing it behind him. He made a quick,
thorough search of the house making sure that no
one was waiting for him, and then in the bathroom splashed some water on his face, washing

the oil smudge from the side of his head where he'd been kicked.

His head ached from the blow, and there was a long, wicked-looking bruise already beginning to form on his back where he had been struck, probably with a piece of wood or pipe. They'd had him at their mercy. He was down on all fours, barely conscious, certainly unable to defend himself. They could have done anything to him. But they had just run off into the night.

When he was finished he quickly got dressed. Outside, he tossed his bags in the back seat of his car and got in behind the wheel. There was an outside possibility, he thought, that the safe house had been spotted for what it was, and whoever showed up was simply a target for an Arab group. It wasn't uncommon for suspected Mossad agents or informers to be found in the middle of the night with their throats slit. Somehow, though, he didn't think what happened tonight was going to have so easy an explanation.

He started the car and without headlights rolled to the end of the driveway, pulling up short just before the street. The houses were dark. No one had seen or heard a thing. No alarm had been raised. In certain places in Israel night was a time to be behind locked doors. It was a time not to see what moved in the darkness.

The insanity was beginning, he thought. And at this point he had no idea where it would lead him.

Traffic was very light by the time he got downtown. He'd taken pains to come in the long way, climbing up through the residential districts of central and western Carmel overlooking the city, and then doubling back through Kiryat Eliezer past the Haifa sports stadium. This time he was absolutely certain he was not being followed. Nor did he have the feeling any longer that he was being watched.

He turned onto Khouri Street, the Mossad station just a couple of blocks away. A blue-and-white police car pulled up beside him at the traffic light and the two cops looked over at him. When the light changed they went straight ahead, but he turned to the right down Prophets Street behind City Hall and the government complex, pulling into one of the parking lots of the Technion, Haifa's technical college. Dousing his lights and switching off the engine, he waited a full five minutes to see if the police cruiser would swing around the block. He didn't want any trouble with the police tonight. Once the report got back to Geller there would be questions asked that he didn't have the answers for: What were you doing downtown at that hour? for instance.

When they didn't come, he got out of the car and hurried into the campus, where he located a public phone across from a fountain, the sound of splashing water echoing off the building fronts.

Miriam Loeb answered on the first ring. "Yes?"

Avram felt the relief wash over him. Her voice sounded normal. "Did I wake you?"

"No. Where are you, Avram?"

"Here in town. I couldn't sleep. I just wanted to hear your voice."

"I'm glad you called," she said. "Are you okay? Is anything wrong?"

A guarded note had crept into her voice. Avram could hear it. He knew all of her moods. She sounded worried. "Everything is fine, shouldn't it be?"

"Uncle Arik called this afternoon," she said.

"Yes?"

"He asked if I had seen you."

"What did you tell him?"

"I told him that you had come here. And I told him that I was worried about you. That you didn't seem yourself. And you don't. I was angry at you and at him for not telling me anything. If you'd been killed, I wonder how long it would have taken for someone to tell me."

"What'd he say to you?"

"That whatever you had done, and were doing now in Haifa was simply none of my business, whether or not I was family."

"And it isn't," Avram said as gently as possible. "Nor is it Haifa Television's business."

"Then why did you bother calling?" she snapped.

"Because I was missing you," he said, the statement only a half lie.

"Then come talk to me."

"In a little while, Miriam. In a few days."

"What if I don't accept that?"

"I'm sorry . . ." he started to say.

"Something happened tonight, didn't it?" she cried.

"I have to go now."

"Avram . . ." she shouted, but he'd hung up the telephone and stepped away from the booth.

He'd told her too much already, far too much. He wondered just what she had told Ben-Or, and from that what the old man was guessing now. He should never have gone to see her, he thought, because by doing so he had put her in jeopardy. That and another, darker reason—a reason he didn't even want to think about. It was madness.

He checked into the Zion Hotel just behind City Hall on Bialik Street, leaving his car in the back of the hotel's parking lot. From his room he could look down the street at the Vulcan Foundary Computer Center less than a hundred yards away and see who came or went. For a long time he sat, lights out, by the open window watching the front entrance of the Mossad station, wondering exactly why he was doing what he was doing, until finally his fatigue overcame him and he lay down on the bed to get some sleep.

MOSSAD HAIFA STATION, 11:10 A.M.

The morning staff briefing had been a particularly busy one. Their Shin Beth liaison for Operation Sleeper (as their mission to provide protection for Youssef Fawzi was called), Michel Louk, had laid out the preliminary timetable in some detail. No one could find fault with the plan, though it was clear that even Geller felt uncomfortable with the role the Mossad would have to play in babysitting an avowed enemy of the state.

After Louk had finished and was dismissed, they covered the operational reports from six of their outstations, including Mossad's European headquarters, which was run from a well-known, highly visible travel agency in Paris. The unit had originally been formed in 1960 to provide secret travel arrangements for the team that had kidnapped Adolf Eichmann from Argentina. Since then it had grown into the most effective outstation they had, and coincidentally turned a substantial annual profit from its legitimate travel business.

The French government was again balking at providing Israel with technical equipment and aid, this time for the Ein Gedi nuclear power generating station.

"We've gone as far as we can with this," Geller told them. It was time to turn the project over to Tel Aviv, who would in turn, no doubt, drop it in the PM's lap. "As if he doesn't have enough troubles already."

"What does Frank want to do about it?" Avram asked. Frank Eshkol was head of the Paris Station and therefore chief of Mossad European operations. A tough man. Absolutely first-rate.

"He wants to pull another Frauenknecht caper," Geller said with a smirk. "Not while I'm in charge. Those days are past."

In the late sixties Alfred Frauenknecht was the chief engineer of the jet fighter division of the Swiss company of Sulzer Brothers that built the French Mirage jets on license from Dassault. The Israelis desperately needed spare parts for their Mirage jets (which they had purchased from the French) but DeGaulle had placed an arms embargo on Israel. Frauenknecht was convinced by Mossad agents to steal the Swiss copies of the jet fighter's blueprints—all two tons of them—which he did. Later he was jailed for his efforts.

"Has he got someone in mind?" Avram asked.

"We'll drop it," Geller said, glaring across the table. "In any event that's a decision for Jerusalem, not us."

He was right, of course, on both counts. It *was* a decision for the PM and his advisers, and the Mossad did not need the entanglements of another difficult operation that would have serious international political repercussions if it failed.

During the meeting, Avram had watched for a sign that anyone around the table knew about last night. But no one said a thing.

After the meeting, Avram went back to his office. Geller was going to Tel Aviv to talk with Ben-Or about the Paris situation, and Avram was about ready to go back downstairs to Archives to continue his research, when Benjamin Strauss, chief of surveillance, drifted across the corridor with two cups of tea.

"What do you think about that idiot, Michel Louk," Strauss said, closing the door with his heel.

"Fawzi is the enemy, not him," Avram said, looking up.

"Sometimes I wonder," Strauss laughed. "I brought you some tea." He was a very large man, but his voice was surprisingly soft and even gentle.

He set down Avram's tea on the desk and took a seat without being invited. He smiled. "You're getting your feet wet right out of the chute. I like that, but I don't know if it's too smart."

"What have you got on your mind, Benjamin?" Avram asked. Strauss had the reputation of being nobody's fool, always direct and to the point.

"Two things, both of them concerning our great white leader," Strauss said. He spoke Hebrew, but he preferred English, which he spoke with a Brooklyn accent. "The first is, if you want to stay around here for long, you don't cross him. He may not always be right, but he's damned sure of himself, he's a dedicated man, and he has Ben-Or's complete confidence."

"If he wants a yes-man, I'll have myself transferred out of here," Avram said evenly.

"Don't get your hackles up," Strauss said. "He doesn't mind disagreement, but when a decision has been made he expects his staff to be loyal."

"I've already gotten that lecture from him."

"He didn't send me in here, I came to give you

a bit of friendly advice on my own." Strauss sat forward in his chair. "I don't want to get off on the wrong foot with you. From what I've heard, you're just about the best we have. But no one expected you here like this. We thought you'd be running a station of your own, or at the very least be sent out on another operation. You're a field man, and a damned good one. Frankly, Yoram is a little intimidated by you. All of us are."

"Don't be," Avram said tersely. His natural inclination was to warm to the man, but he could not.

You will be completely on your own. You are to trust no one. Not a living soul must know what you are doing or why.

The prime minister's words. But he had already violated that confidence. Once partially with Miriam, and again with Gromit. At least one of those had been a mistake. He didn't want to make another.

"You said you had two things," Avram said.

Strauss looked at him for a long time, but finally nodded. He'd gotten less than he expected by coming in here, it was plain on his face. "Yoram isn't aware yet that you're no longer bunking at the safe house."

Avram held himself in check. "But you are."

"I dropped by early this morning to talk to you."

Avram tried to read something from the big man's expression. But if Strauss knew anything about last night, he wasn't obvious about it.

"Safe houses should be maintained as safe houses," he said. "I moved into a hotel until I can find a place of my own."

Again Strauss hesitated for a moment or two before he nodded and got to his feet. He wanted to say something else, but it was clear he was having trouble deciding if he should. As much as Avram wanted to help him out, he could not. Trust no one, the Prime Minister had told him. He hadn't realized just how difficult to carry out that order would be.

IN ARCHIVES, 6:15 P.M.

It was not the usual custom for Mossad outstations to maintain their own records once the files became old enough, or outdated enough to be considered of "historical value." In that case the actual paper files were destroyed and microfilm copies sent down to Central Records Keeping in Tel Aviv. Haifa Station was the exception to this rule, since by tradition many of the service's most important operations had been planned and actually run from there. Decentralization was the watchword; the paper Diaspora, the service wags were fond of calling it. Archives was Haifa Station's actual term for the rat's maze of poorly lit rooms cut into the rock beneath the building. Lara Kiesow, who had emigrated from Poland to Israel twenty years ago, ran Haifa Archives in a scholarly, bemused manner. But she had a mind as sharp as a tack, and a nearly perfect photographic memory. She'd come back twice to check on Avram during the afternoon.

"You'll go blind in this light if you keep it up," she said, peering at him through her bottle-thick glasses. "I can bring them up to your office a basket at a time. Wouldn't mind at all. Actually, I'd like to get out of here once in a while."

Avram looked up from his reading and smiled. "Not necessary, Lara. I'm just browsing." He'd

pulled a number of recent operational files out of
the stacks to conceal his particular interest in the
Operation Brother documents.

"Will you be long then?"

"Probably. I've got a lot of catching up to do. If
you've got something else to do, don't mind me. I
can manage."

Her smile was a little strained. Like all good
archivists she felt uncomfortable when an out-
sider was "mucking about" in her precious files.
"I suppose I could stay."

"Not necessary, believe me," Avram said. "And
I promise to put everything back where I found
it."

"Leave it on my desk," she said. "I'll take care
of it in the morning." She eyed him for a long time,
then turned on her heel and left.

Alone with the files for the first time, Avram
opened the fourth in a series of spiral-bound
books, marked TOP SECRET with the title OPERA-
TIONAL ANALYSIS AND PRE-IMPLEMENTATION SUMMARY:
OPERATION BROTHER. The inside cover had been
stamped "For Your Eyes Only" and had been directed to Ben-Or over Yoram Geller's scrawly signature, with the note that this document should
be considered the final operational planning guide.
A stamp at the bottom of that page, again over
Geller's signature, rescinded the For-Your-Eyes-
Only designation on a date three days after the
actual operation had taken place, thus bouncing
the document back into the bulk of the operational files.

The first section dealt in summary with Naval
Operations, directing the reader to supporting
files including those from Photographic Reconnaissance Division: See First Air Force, PRD, Lod
AFB. The second section dealt with the Air Force

strike, with supporting documents to follow. The third with timetable summaries, over Sammuel Amit's signature, maps in Appendix 1A. The fourth with results of training schedules at Be'er Sheva; the fifth with budget lines (see Accountability Annex 1101P 3/25); and the final section with mission personnel, Avram Zemil, commander, personnel dossiers, and psychologic indexing files available on request. Each section was prefaced with the list of personnel who knew the actual extent of that particular segment.

Avram began with the promulgation statement inside the front cover. He'd checked out a subminiature camera from Equipment Stores this morning. Propping the book open directly beneath the overhead light above his table, he photographed the first page, on which Ben-Or's and Geller's were the only two names. In quick succession he photographed the preface to each succeeding section in which the segment's personnel were listed.

No matter what he knew, or what he would discover, he had decided early on that he would need documentary evidence to show the prime minister. His proof. It was also a safeguard in case something happened to him.

Next he opened the first volume in the operational series: OVERVIEW: GOALS AND IMPACT STATEMENT, and again photographed the personnel lists, which included a lot of correspondence and "minutes of meetings" between Ben-Or, Harel, and the PM's adviser, David Sokoloff. The most sensitive of these minutes were in Ben-Or's handwriting, with an attached notation that no secretarial help had been used in their preparation. In each case the documents were originals, stamped COPY 1 OF 1 COPIES.

Delving into the individual operational detail files, he again photographed anything on which a name appeared.

In the reading he was again brought back to their training, and finally to the night out on the Syrian desert when he realized they had been betrayed. The same sick feeling he'd had then rose in him now.

Finished, he put away his camera and went back to the Operational Analysis and Pre-implementation Summary. It was a thick book filled with the minutiae so necessary to any mission: everything from weapons and ammunition selection to maintenance of the Phantom jets used on the surgical strike; from methods of operational funds disbursement to confirmation that mission personnel had received the necessary shots and had filed their 573/A statements, which were their wills in case they were killed in action.

He had the photographic evidence; now on a pad of paper he began jotting the names from the personnel lists. He was looking for the common thread, of course. The names that appeared on every section's list. The men, and in one case the woman, who knew the actual goals and timetable for Operation Brother. It took him only a few minutes, and when he was done he sat back with a deep sigh.

Thirteen names, including his own. Twelve men and one woman who knew everything. If there was a traitor to Israel, his or her name was on this list.

At the top was Prime Minister Harel. It was possible, Avram thought, that he had ordered the investigation knowing that it would fail, thus vindicating himself. If that were so, Avram thought, then making any sense of this would be not only totally impossible, but meaningless. He scratched off Harel's name.

Defense Minister Yitzhak Rabin had been included from the very beginning, naturally. If he were the traitor, all of Israel would be lost, her defenses would be useless. Avram crossed his name off.

Next came Arik Ben-Or. The prime minister had specifically forbidden Avram to discuss his investigation with the Mossad chief. Trust no one, he'd said. Why Ben-Or, other than to keep the investigation absolutely contained? He'd known the old man from the very beginning. Ben-Or had been like an uncle to him. Was it possible? he asked himself. Was it even conceivable? He thought not, and crossed Ben-Or's name off the list.

He crossed his own name off the list, and hesitated for a moment over the names of the other four who'd gone out with him. All good people, he thought. But so were the others on the list. All beyond reproach, none with any axe to grind, and all had stood to lose their lives by attacking the PLO camp. If one of them had been the traitor, he (or she) would have known it was likely he'd be killed when the operation went bad. Would one of them have risked it? More likely, if one of them had been the traitor, he would have managed to drop out the day before the operation began. Even breaking a leg in a contrived accident would have been better than the risk of being killed. He scratched their names off the list.

Which left five men.

David Sokoloff, the prime minister's adviser; Yoram Geller; Sammuel Amit, who'd been in on planning stages from the very first day; Peter Salinger, who was the chief of operations at the Be'er Sheva training camp; and Felix Louk, chairman of the Knesset Intelligence Oversight Committee and, coincidentally, Avram had learned from his reading, the brother of Michel Louk, the Shin Beth liaison here at this moment for Operation Sleeper.

Felix Louk. Avram turned that name over in his mind. He knew very little about the man, except that over the past few years he had become a highly visible and vocal leader in the Knesset. Of all the people on the short list, Louk would have the most to gain by the downfall of Harel's government. It was possible, Avram thought, that the man wanted to become prime minister himself. He'd been a very strong advocate of the rescue mission, arguing that to fail would be a severe slap in the face to the Israeli government. If it was he who had engineered the failure, it would be he who would now be agitating for another vote of confidence, which Harel might not survive.

Another intriguing aspect was Felix Louk's brother. As a high-ranking Shin Beth officer, Michel Louk would naturally have been privy to much of what happened during the operation's training phases. He wouldn't have known everything, of course, but his brother could have supplied him with the missing details. Michel Louk would have been the more logical Arab contact. It certainly would have been easier for a Shin Beth officer to make contact with a PLO or Syrian Secret Service informer than it would have been for a highly visible member of the Knesset.

Was he clutching at straws? he wondered as he closed the book and pocketed his notepad. Palmyra, the code name for Yakof Gromit's Russian, crossed his mind. If he was involved, it could be possible that he had turned the Louk brothers. He was a charmer, Gromit had intimated. A man of rare ego. But apparently he was also brilliant, and presumably very well connected. Was it possible that he had simply put it together from a mass of information gathered through the huge network of spies and informers? Gromit's friend whose brother was a carpenter in Be'er Sheva was one example. Gromit had put it together, though after the fact. Could Palmyra have put it together *before*?

Avram put away the Operation Brother files from where he had taken them out of the stacks, then laid everything else he'd taken out as cover on Lara Kiesow's desk so that when she came back in the morning she would have something to keep her occupied and would not snoop around trying to find out just which files he'd been meddling with.

When he was finished he put on his coat and trudged back upstairs. His list had been expanded to six names with the addition of Michel Louk, and seven if the Russian was involved. Trust no one, the prime minister had told him. There was an eighth name too. His own fault. But God, he didn't want to think about that. Not yet.

In the corridor he was in time to see Sammuel Amit, Haifa Station's operations chief, emerging from his office. He was of medium height and build, with slightly graying hair and a nondescript face that could just as easily be forgotten as remembered. He looked up.

"Burning the midnight oil?"

"I have a lot of catching up to do," Avram said.

Amit looked hard at him, managed a tight little smile, then nodded. "You'll be starting on the night desk in a few days?"

"Yoram wants us to split the duty roster between us."

"Good idea," Amit said. "See you in the morning, then."

He went down the hall and out the security door.

The corridor was silent. Avram waited a full ten seconds, watching the steel door close, listening for a sound, any sound. Except for Operations and Communications, almost everyone had gone home by now. He stepped across the hall to Amit's office door and tried the knob. It was locked. How much risk, he wondered, would he be taking by breaking into the operations chief's office? If he was caught, his assignment would be over before it began. Yet Amit was on his list.

There was a safe in Amit's office. What secrets did it contain? None, if he was any good. But everyone in this business got careless sooner or later. The door lock was the ordinary tumbler type, easy to get through, but he would need the combination to the safe. Tomorrow night, he thought.

Benjamin Strauss came around the corner from Operations just as Avram was crossing the hall to his own office, and the big man nodded perfunctorily without breaking stride, his eyes flicking from Avram to Amit's office door.

JERUSALEM, 7:30 P.M.

The Soviet Union had broken off diplomatic relations with Israel in 1967 just after the Six-Day War. Only recently had Poland, Hungary, and Yugoslavia begun to make overtures to restore relations. At the moment, they each maintained Interest Section officers at the Swiss embassy in

Jerusalem. The Soviet Union had offered to do the same, but Israel had flatly refused them: Full diplomatic relations or nothing, the Israeli government said. "There'll be no fence sitting in the peace process."

Ivan Roskov sat drinking a spiced vodka in the office of Jan Międyrzecz, the Polish Interests officer on the second floor of the Swiss embassy. Outwardly, they were warm old friends. In reality, Międyrzecz was frightened of the Russian, who he knew was KGB and therefore in Israel illegally; and Roskov despised the Pole, as he did all Poles, who he thought were even more subhuman than Jews. The two of them had been thrown together quite frequently over the past few months—in Mięedyrzecz's case on explicit instructions from Warsaw. Cooperate, he had been told, and cooperate he would, to the point of making his office Roskov's as well as his home.

The telephone rang and Międyrzecz picked it up. "Yes," he said softly. He nodded, handed the telephone to Roskov, then got up from behind his desk and left the room, closing the door behind him. It was a twice-daily routine.

Roskov picked up the phone. "Yes," he said in Polish, an added safeguard even though it was highly unlikely the Shin Beth monitored the telephone lines in and out of the Swiss embassy.

"We found nothing," Petor Bogachev, Roskov's aide, said. "But there was . . . an incident."

Roskov could hear the tension in the other man's voice. It was unlike the captain. "Tell me."

"There was an accident."

"Injuries?" Roskov asked circumspectly. Bogachev and his people had followed Avram Zemil to the safe house in Haifa. They had met with some trouble.

"Only minor and to the other driver."

"Were names exchanged?" Roskov asked, meaning had Avram recognized them?

"No, sir, it wasn't necessary."

"I see," Roskov said, relieved for at least that. Who was Avram Zemil? And why had he been sent to Haifa now of all times? "About the other matter. Inquiries have been made? It was confirmed?"

"Yes, sir. But that will be taken care of completely. This evening."

"Very good. We will talk again."

"Yes, sir," Bogachev said and broke the connection.

Roskov slowly hung up the telephone. Why had that oversized slug begun asking questions? Why now? Coincidence? He doubted it. He'd never believed in coincidences, and he wasn't about to start now.

HAIFA, 8:00 P.M.

Avram returned to his hotel. He had a meal sent up to his room and ate in the dark by the open window as he watched the front entrance of the Vulcan Foundary Computer Center. He took a long time with his dinner, but afterward he had no conscious recollection of what he had eaten or how it had tasted. Haifa was a seaport and he listened to the sounds of the harbor mingling with the traffic noises from below. Getting ready to keep his appointment with Yakof Gromit a deep loneliness came over him, bringing with it a sadness he thought would never leave him, no matter what the outcome of his investigation.

6

TEL AMAL DISTRICT OF HAIFA, 10:05 P.M.

TRAFFIC WAS STILL HEAVY AT THIS HOUR.
There was a stridency to the city that until this
moment Avram had never noticed. It was his
mood, of course, but it suddenly seemed as though
everyone was in a frantic hurry to get somewhere.
He kept watch in his rearview mirror, swinging
down side streets, holding back until the moment
a traffic light changed, then shooting through the
intersection so that anyone following him would
be cut off. It had become second nature to him in
his business. And the tradecraft seemed even more
important now because of the mission he was on.
"Be careful that the holy zeal doesn't come over
you," Ben-Or had told him once. "Israel needs patriots and dedicated men. We have had more than
our share of zealots."

Not zealotry, Avram thought, but anger. His anger had been building ever since that night on the
Syrian desert. This afternoon and early evening,
going through the Operation Brother files had
brought everything back to him as a bright, very

hot flame in his gut. It had all been a monstrous game. The traitor was a person totally without morals or commitment. The country he had betrayed meant nothing, and the country he was working for meant even less because when it was over there would be nothing there for him. No home, no birthright. Nothing.

Until last night all his evidence had been circumstantial. They could have been spotted coming up from the coast. Or they could have been spotted in Cyprus from where they had left on the second leg of their mission. Someone could have put it together and alerted the camp and a trap could have been set. Except for last night. He did not think the attack on him at the safe house had been a coincidence. Haifa was where the mission had been planned. He had been the mission commander. And now he was back in Haifa. Anyone on his short list could have found out that he had been reassigned here. Had one of them gotten nervous?

He parked his car on a narrow side street and worked his way back on foot, as he always did. Here there were a lot of people out and about, most of them Arabs in traditional dress. Peaceful coexistence: he wondered if it would ever be possible. Coming around the corner into the alley off which Gromit's office and home were located, Avram pulled up short and instinctively stepped back into the shadows. Something was wrong. The alley was empty of people. Gromit's house was dark. Even the upper-story windows were dark. But Gromit had been expecting him. Even if he hadn't, there were always people coming and going at all hours of the day and night. "There is safety in numbers," he'd once confided to Avram. "The man who surrounds himself with people will never be lonely, and most likely not the target for an assassin's knife." Nothing was foolproof, but it had worked for him all these years.

There was a back way to the house through the bazaar in the next block. He turned away from the alley and hurried down the street threading his way through the crowds, plunging into the bazaar in the next block with its plethora of sights and sounds and smells. Women in *chadors* and veils shopped at the dozens of stalls, while old men sat sipping coffee and talking. Vendors were hawking their wares mostly in Arabic but with a mingling of Hebrew and even some English and French. Someone was smoking hashish; he could smell the sweet burning odor as he passed one of the stalls. There were enough people in Western dress on the street so that Avram did not stand out, yet he was getting the distinct feeling that he was being watched. Many of the shopkeepers shrank back into the darker recesses of their establishments as he hurried by, and there were no hands grabbing for him, trying to get his attention, trying to sell him something.

Halfway into the bazaar he stepped into the tiny open stall of a silversmith. An old man sitting at a low table didn't bother looking up as Avram passed to the back of the shop through a curtained door into a very narrow, filthy open passageway between the buildings. Gromit's house was at the end of the passage.

Avram waited in the darkness for a little while, watching, listening, but there was nothing. The noise from the bazaar he'd just passed through seemed distant. He was alone here.

He took out his gun, checked to make sure there was a round in the firing chamber, then moved down to the door at the end of the passageway, keeping his eye on the one dark window on the second floor and the roofline above. If anyone were up there they would be silhouetted against the sky if they showed themselves.

Gromit was simply taking precautions, he kept telling himself. He'd found out something and now he was holed up in his house waiting for Avram to come to him. To give him protection. Let it be as simple as that, Avram thought.

The door was old and heavy, a desert oasis scene poorly carved in bas-relief on one of the panels. Avram tried the knob and it turned easily in his hand, the door swinging open an inch. The corridor was in darkness. A sweet incense odor wafted out to him.

He looked over his shoulder, back toward the rear of the silversmith's shop, and softly reclosed the door. Turning, he retraced his steps back into the shop. The same old man as before was still seated at the low table. He was drinking coffee and smoking from a *hookah*. Avram had holstered his gun.

"Has some one come this way in the past few hours, old man?" Avram asked, his Arabic only fair, but understandable.

The old man looked up at him and squinted his eyes, but said nothing.

Pikeesh. Avram tossed an American twenty-dollar bill onto the table. "I am a friend of Yakof's. Has anyone come through your shop this night?"

The old man made no move to touch the money, but he shook his head, the movement so slight as to be barely discernible.

"No one has come tonight?"

Again the old man shook his head.

"Many thanks to you," Avram said in the more

formal tone, and he turned and went back into the narrow passageway.

The back door should not have been left unlocked. It was unlike Gromit to be so careless. Something was definitely wrong, but if the old man were to be believed no one had come this way. Yet.

He pulled out his gun again, switched off the safety, and slipped inside, closing the door behind him, plunging the narrow corridor into almost complete darkness. Only a dim light filtered back from the windows in the front of the building. He felt for the door bolt and eased it home. A safety valve, or was it paranoia again? He wanted his back protected.

For a long time he stood stock still in the darkness, straining with every sense to detect the presence of someone, anyone in the building. He cocked his ear. Somewhere in the distance he thought he could hear a faint mewing, like a small kitten calling for its mother, or a little girl crying. The sound was nearly constant, but so faint he had to hold his breath to hear it.

With great care Avram moved down the corridor to the stairs. Straight ahead was the front door. To the right, another door led into Gromit's "business office," which was merely a front. Most of his real business was conducted upstairs in his living room over drinks.

Moving to the front door, he tested the lock. It too was open. He turned the lock, securing the door, and moved to the office door, but it was locked. He turned and looked up the stairs. The house was in darkness. Here, though he could hear the mewing sound a little clearer, he still could not quite make it out. Trouble. Danger. The entire house reeked of it. Whatever or whoever was making the noise was somewhere upstairs.

Avram started up, his stomach in knots but his muscles loose. Training, endless weeks and months and years of training had brought him safely to this point. But someday that would end. It had to. When the odds became overwhelming, or when the element of surprise was there, his time would come.

At the head of the stairs a broad hall led right through a curtained archway into Gromit's living room and straight back to a kitchen, the bathroom behind it, and stairs to the roof. To the left down a narrow corridor were two bedrooms.

He listened but the mewing sounds had stopped. Perhaps he had imagined them, or perhaps they had come from outside after all, though he didn't think so.

Moving on the balls of his feet he went to the curtained archway and with the barrel of his gun parted the heavy drapes so that he could look inside. In the dim yellow street light the two big windows were silhouetted. Gromit, naked, lay on his side in the middle of a pile of cushions, his massive legs parted obscenely, his obese belly sagging. There was a lot of blood from where they had cut strips of skin from his flanks, the long stripes running from his left armpit all the way down to his hip. His face was mutilated as well, and Avram could see between his parted lips that most of his teeth had been knocked out, blood oozing down his chin. A lot of blood had come from his anus. Avram spotted the long metal rod they must have used. The room was in a shambles. They had searched the place, and then they had tortured the big man to death.

He wondered about the noise. Gromit was a big

man. He had many friends in the bazaar. He would
have cried out. Someone would have heard him.
Unless he'd been gagged.

All this ran through Avram's mind quickly. They
had come here looking for information. He
stepped the rest of the way into the main room,
the stench of fear and death and blood suddenly
assailing his nostrils, making him nearly gag.
Stepping over the debris of the search he bent
down over Gromit's body and reached out, gently
touching the big man's cheek with his fingertips.

Gromit's body heaved a massive sigh and his
eyes flickered open! Avram's heart skipped a beat!
Gromit was still alive!

"Avram . . ." Gromit gurgled, fresh blood welling out of his mouth, a big rose bubble forming
on his lips and then bursting.

"Don't talk, I'll get an ambulance," Avram said,
and he started to rise, but Gromit reached up with
a bloody hand and brushed his sleeve.

"Avram," Gromit gurgled again, his voice all but
lost because of the blood in his throat. They had
broken him up inside. He was bleeding internally.

Avram leaned down to him, his ear close to the
man's lips, anger rising so sharply in him now that
it was hard to keep from shaking with rage. The
bastards! "I'm here, Yakof," he said gently. "What
is it you want to tell me, old friend?"

"Your own . . ." Gromit struggled to form the
words.

A chill rose up Avram's spine. "What about my
own?"

"Your own . . . look to your . . . own," Gromit
whispered hoarsely. His eyes flickered, and Avram
noticed for the first time that his left eye was
sightless. It looked as if they had placed a lighted
cigarette directly against the eyeball.

"What about it, Yakof? What are you trying to say to me?"

"Your own . . ." Gromit croaked. "Limassol . . . Limassol . . ."

"Limassol. What is that, Yakof? Who—"

A huge gush of blood welled up from Gromit's throat. His massive body shuddered, and he sagged, his frame seeming to shrink, his body almost caving in on itself. And he lay still, his eyes open. He was dead.

Avram sat back on his haunches, the blind rage threatening to consume him. Limassol. He thought for a second. Limassol was the coastal city on the southeastern corner of the island of Cyprus. They'd left for Syria by boat from the British naval base at Cape Gata barely ten miles to the south. Limassol. Their traitor was there? The ones who had done this to Gromit had come from there? The answers were there? What?

Someone screamed with a high-pitched wail from behind him, and Avram barely managed to spin around as Gromit's boy, Jacob, nude, his long blond hair streaming down his back, came through the archway, a big curved sword upraised in both his hands. He brought the sword down as he charged. Avram rolled left, the blade hitting Gromit's body with a dull smack, opening a long, bloodless gash. The boy screamed again, seeing what he had done, and he spun on his heel and slashed wildly at Avram, the blade cutting the air inches from Avram's shoulder. Avram managed to scramble in beneath the boy's next swing and he grabbed the kid's arm, twisting it sharply backward until with a shriek he dropped the sword and stumbled backward.

"Who did this?" Avram demanded, getting to his

feet. His insides were churning. He had almost shot the boy.

Jacob was shivering with fear or rage and he kept shaking his head and wringing his hands, his eyes flicking from Avram to Gromit's body and back. The same mewing sounds Avram had heard from downstairs came from the back of the boy's throat.

"Who did this?" Avram asked more urgently. "When did it happen, Jacob?"

The boy looked up and took a step backward. "You . . ." he cried, the sound strangled.

"No, it wasn't me. I just got here. Did you see anything, did you hear anything?"

"Oh, Papa," the boy cried. "Oh, Papa!"

"Jacob!" Avram snapped.

The boy jerked as if he had been physically slapped. "They tortured him. I could hear them. I could hear . . . Papa crying even though they gagged him."

"You saw them? You watched?"

"I was frightened. I ran away and hid in my room. In the closet like I was always told to do if there was trouble."

"Why didn't you call the police? Why didn't you go for help?"

The boy's eyes were wide with fright and confusion. "Police? No police. Papa said no police, ever. But now he is dead. What will Jacob do? Oh, what will poor little Jacob do?"

"Did you see them? Did you see who they were?"

"They came from the back and the front. Three of them. Big men. Bad men. Oh, what will little Jacob do now? Poor, poor Jacob."

The old silversmith had lied. "When, Jacob? How long ago?"

"Just now, *effendi*. Just now. I couldn't stand it any longer. I heard my master crying. I heard you talking . . ."

"Stay here," Avram told the terrified boy. He cocked the hammer of his pistol and moved to the curtained archway. Both the front and rear doors had been left open. Had they already left, or had someone been out on the street watching for him to show up? They could have been warned. They might still be here.

Avram eased the curtains aside and slipped out into the corridor. Again his senses went outward. Was there someone else in the house? He moved down the back hall to the kitchen, pulling up short at the doorway and just easing around the corner so that he could see inside while presenting the smallest target. A small fire burned on the grate, providing enough illumination for him to see that no one was here. He stepped softly past the doorway and moved farther down the corridor to the bathroom. He eased the door open, hesitated a moment, then leaped inside, his gun sweeping left to right. A modern toilet and bidet stood side by side facing a sink, beyond which was a large sunken tub. No one here.

Avram started to move back out of the room when a motion from above caught his eye. He looked up in time to see a face disappear from the skylight. The roof!

He turned and raced the rest of the way down the corridor to the door leading up to the roof. Sometimes, in the spring and fall, Gromit had held parties in his rooftop garden. "A bit of peace in a world upside down," he'd once said.

Flattening himself against the wall, Avram eased the door open and looked up the stairs. The door above was open; he could see the black sky and the glow of the city. If they'd known he was here, why hadn't they ambushed him? Unless they didn't want a confrontation with a Mossad agent. Unless they'd only come here to get information from Gromit. About Palmyra? If that were the case, Avram knew that he would be dealing with Soviet KGB agents. Trained, and probably very good. Contrary to popular belief, the Russians fielded no fools.

Avram started up the stairs, keeping low, his knees bent so that he could spring left or right the instant someone appeared in the doorway.

Someone moved just beyond the doorway; Avram could hear the brush of fabric against a plant. Gripping his automatic tightly in his right hand, he leaped up the last two steps and burst out onto the roof, rolling right and diving for the cover of a line of potted trees. He fired at a dark figure halfway across the roof, the sound shockingly loud in the still night air. The man cried out and fell forward. Two dull, muffled pops came from the left, the bullets shattering the pottery plant holders inches from Avram's head. He scrambled to the right, then rose up on one knee as the second man leaped up on the parapet at the rear of the building overlooking the narrow alleyway two stories below. Avram fired once; the man screamed as he was driven forward over the edge and disappeared.

Avram got to his feet and rushed over to the body of the first man. His bullet had caught the man in the back of the neck just at the base of his skull. His eyes were open and lifeless, his features thick and dark and Slavic. Avram hurriedly searched the body. He carried Polish diplomatic identification, but the silenced pistol he still held tightly in his right hand was a nine-millimeter Makarov. It, and the bigger Graz Buyra, were the KGB's weapons of choice. This one was no Pole, Avram thought. Gromit had gone looking for Palmyra, and the Russians had come after him.

He was going to have to get out of here before the police came. The two shots he had fired would have been reported. Jacob was going to have to come with him. If he was burned, Avram's mission would be over before it had barely started.

But there was a third man. Jacob had said three had come in the night from the front and back.

Avram jumped up and started back to the doorway when an ear-piercing screech came from below, and was suddenly cut off. A moment later there was a crash as if something or someone had fallen over a table laden with dishes. It was the boy.

At the head of the stairs Avram was in time to hear someone below, on the first floor. He fired twice, straight down the stairs toward the front door as he raced headlong down into the darkness.

The curtains into the main room had been torn off their rod. Jacob lay in a bloody heap on top of the low table, broken dishes and coffee service scattered around him. He was dead. He'd taken two shots to the chest at close range.

Avram turned and went to the stairs at the same moment the back door opened with a crash. He hurried down, careful to make as little noise as possible, mindful that he could even now be walking into another trap. The third man could be waiting within the dark corridor.

At the bottom, Avram leaped left, moving fast and keeping low, his gun swinging toward the end of the corridor, his finger tightening on the trigger.

In the distance now he could hear the first of the sirens. The shots had been reported already and the police were on their way. He had to leave! Now!

The open door at the end of the corridor was framed in the dim light coming from the passageway that led through the silversmith's shop. Nothing moved. From where he crouched in the darkness Avram could see the body of the Russian who'd fallen from the roof. His left leg was bent at an unnatural angle beneath his body. He lay in a big pool of blood.

Darting to the end of the corridor, Avram pulled up short just at the doorway. The sirens were much closer now. He could hear the rising shouts of a crowd outside in the bazaar. He started to move out into the alleyway, when two silenced shots were fired from the silversmith's shop, the bullets smacking into the doorframe, woodchips and plaster dust splattering his face.

He fired one shot high. He didn't want a stray bullet hurting an innocent bystander out in the bazaar. A moment later the crowd began screaming hysterically in fear.

Avram leaped out into the alleyway, raced the thirty or forty feet to the silversmith's shop, and burst inside. The old man he had spoken to earlier lay back against the wall, his arms akimbo, half his forehead blown away where he had been shot just above the bridge of his nose.

In the bazaar there was pandemonium. Men and women were screaming, scrambling in every direction, trying to get out of the path of the madman who had passed through with a gun. Across the street a woman lay in a pool of blood where she had been shot; a few yards up the street a young boy lay on his side, his right leg twitching, blood pumping from the big hole in his neck.

Create a diversion to cover your trail, to assure your escape. It was the oldest tactic in the book. But these were innocent people murdered in cold blood not because they had any real part to play in the operation, but only because they happened to be in the wrong place at the wrong time.

The gunman had gone right, deeper into the bazaar. The first of the police cars was just approaching the main street to the left as Avram emerged from the silversmith's shop and turned right.

"Stop!" a familiar voice roared from behind him.

Avram feinted left, spinning on his heel as he brought his gun around. Benjamin Strauss was just coming through the crowd, a pistol in his hand.

"This way," Avram shouted. There was no time to explain now. They had to get away before the police arrived.

Strauss hesitated for a precious second or two, the crowd still scattering hysterically, indecision on his face. But then he nodded grimly.

Avram raced deeper into the bazaar pushing panicked people out of his way as he ran, Strauss right behind him. They reached the end of the bazaar, the crowd spilling out onto Nazareth Road, in time to see a dark Mercedes with Polish diplomatic plates racing to the north, darting dangerously into traffic. Avram rushed out into the middle of the street, mindless of the cars and trucks streaming around him, and brought up his gun. There was a moment he could have fired, but he hesitated for fear of hitting a civilian and the Mercedes was gone.

He had failed! Whatever secrets Gromit had given up to his torturers were now safe in the Russians's hands. Where was this madness leading him? When would it end?

"Unless you want us involved with the police, we'd better get away from here," Strauss said from behind him.

There were sirens everywhere now. A lot of them, converging on the bazaar from all directions. Avram holstered his gun. "Come on," he said, starting across the street.

DOWNTOWN HAIFA, 11:30 P.M.

They sat in a booth in the Windsor Hotel bar on Carmel Boulevard a block up from the harbor. The dark room was crowded. Everyone was watching the singer on the raised platform. Benjamin Strauss held his glass of beer in his massive paws. He was mad.

"I won't screw around with you, Zemil. I want explanations now, or I'll inform Yoram and take this to the police myself. There were a lot of dead people in the bazaar."

"And one more in the silversmith's shop, one in the alley, and three in the house," Avram said.

"Yakof Gromit?"

Avram nodded. It was going to be impossible to keep Strauss out of this now, and equally impossible, he thought glumly, to tell him everything without completely blowing his investigation.

"You were following me," he said. "Why?"

"First things first. What the hell is going on? What are you involved with here?"

"I need your answers before I can say anything,

Benjamin," Avram said. "And if I'm satisfied I'll tell you what I can."

Strauss said nothing; he just stared across the table.

"You're going to have to trust me when I tell you that this is very important, and that what I'm doing is legal."

"Murder is hardly legal . . ." Strauss snapped in anger.

"I killed two men tonight, both of them in self-defense. Both of them . . . Russians."

Strauss's eyes widened. "KGB?"

Avram nodded. "You were following me. Why? Did Yoram tell you to watch me?"

"No," Strauss said after hesitation. "It was my own idea."

"Why?"

"You've been acting oddly ever since you got here. I wanted to know what was going on."

"By spying on one of your own people?"

Strauss didn't flinch. "I've been around a long time, Zemil. I learned the hard way that when something *seems* to be rotten, it usually is. Who were these Russians? What are they after?"

"Yakof Gromit is . . . was an informer of mine. He has been for a number of years."

Strauss said nothing.

"He was looking for something for me. And he was killed for his efforts."

"Looking for what?" Strauss demanded. "You and I both know the Mossad does not involve itself with internal matters. That's the Shin Beth's province."

"I can't tell you," Avram said. "And on this you are going to have to trust me."

"Bullshit!" Strauss exploded.

"Are you questioning my loyalty?" Avram asked harshly, his eyes locked into Strauss's.

The big man backed down immediately. "Of course not," he said. "But I'm going to need more than that. Let's talk to Yoram."

"No," Avram said. "We'll talk to no one. Not yet, not until I give the word. I want you to be perfectly clear on that."

"What if I don't go along with you?"

"You won't be happy with the consequences."

"I don't take kindly to threats!"

"It's not a threat, Benjamin, but you must keep out of it for your own good, for everyone's good. Just for a little while now. You're going to have to trust me." Strauss was one of the innocents. He had known nothing about Operation Brother until after the fact.

"You're asking too much," Strauss said. "Those were innocent people lying on the street back there."

"I may need your help. But I also need your silence."

"Help with what?"

"I'll tell you when the time comes. But you must stop following me, and you must say nothing to anyone. That includes Geller."

"I repeat: If I don't, then what?"

"You will have ruined everything, my friend," Avram said tiredly. "And you cannot possibly imagine the consequences of that, for you, for me . . . for Israel."

"Goddammit," Strauss said softly. "Goddammit to hell. What do you want me to do?"

7

■

To DAVID SOKOLOFF'S WAY OF THINKING the Israelis were too informal a lot with their open collars and rolled-up shirtsleeves. Kitchen table diplomacy, he'd heard it called. Even at the highest levels of government no one seemed to take appearances seriously. He sat across from Ezra Harel in the prime minister's office, watching an artery throbbing at the side of the old man's neck. The third man in the room was dressed the same; dark suit, white broad-collared shirt open at the neck. It was a uniform that seemed to typify the Israeli government. From these offices, with men such as these, they had won wars. So far.

"You cannot convince me that Avram Zemil was responsible for the massacre in the Tel Amal bazaar last night," Harel said for the third time in as many minutes. "The reports are very confusing, you've said so yourself, David. Fragmentary. Can anyone be absolutely certain it was him? I for one am not."

"Nor I," the third man said. "Such an act would

be inconceivable for him. They were innocent women and children for the most part."

It was the cult of personality, of course, Sokoloff thought. Friends did not do those sorts of things. "He was placed at the spot."

"In the company of another man," Harel insisted. "Has he been identified?"

"Not yet, but Michel Louk is working on it."

"I thought he was conducting Operation Sleeper," the third man said, sitting forward slightly.

"He is, but since he is already in place in Haifa with a team, he's gotten himself involved. He's taking it personally."

"His brother-in-law is Haifa chief of police," the third man said.

"And his brother is in the Knesset," Sokoloff said. Israel was too small for any kind of a real investigation of itself to be conducted by one of its own. He'd not argued that point at the time. Now he wasn't so sure his silence hadn't been a mistake, for more than one reason.

"Michel Louk is a dedicated man," Harel said.

"One whom everyone dislikes," Sokoloff added softly.

"Which is taking us far afield," the third man said. "The dead man in the alley and the one on the roof were carrying Polish diplomatic identification."

"The Poles have denied that they were their people," Sokoloff said.

"Let me finish. They were both armed with Soviet weapons. Makarov nine-millimeter automatics."

"Anyone who wants such a weapon can purchase it on the black market."

"You're denying they were probably KGB agents?" Harel demanded.

"I'm denying nothing, Mr. Prime Minister," Sokoloff said. "It's not my point."

"Then what is?"

"The first of the ballistics reports have come up from Haifa."

"Louk?" the third man asked.

Sokoloff nodded. "Not one of those people was shot with a Makarov. In every case they were shot with a German-made nine-millimeter automatic. Fifteen-round. A SigSauer."

"Easier obtained than a Makarov," the third man said tightly.

"Yes," Sokoloff conceded. "But it is the weapon Avram Zemil carries. And he is very good with it."

There was a stunned silence in the room as each of them considered the implications of what was being said and where it was apparently leading them. Harel was the first to recover.

"Are you saying that we . . . that I've made a mistake in selecting Zemil?"

"I honestly do not know, Mr. Prime Minister," Sokoloff said. "But we must consider the facts at hand. Perhaps he's gone over the edge. He has put himself under a lot of pressure because of the failed rescue mission. Seeing the photographs of our people hanging in the square in Damascus might have done it. Perhaps he is seeking a personal revenge."

"Not by shooting down innocent women and children," Harel said, his voice rising in anger.

"May I remind you, sir, that it was an Arab bazaar?"

"Monstrous," Harel said, looking toward the other man. He shook his head. "I would certainly need more compelling evidence."

The third man again sat forward. "But that wasn't your only point, was it, David?" he said.

"No."

Harel's eyes narrowed, but he said nothing, waiting instead with barely concealed anger for his aide to continue.

"I think it is a possibility that Avram Zemil is the traitor we have been seeking," Sokoloff said. "By hiring him you not only tipped our hand, but you've given him the perfect means to cover his tracks."

"Which he is doing by shooting up a bazaar, and being spotted with a second man?" Harel retorted.

"Not to mention the fact that he's apparently gunned down two Russians," the third man said. "If he were our traitor, and I'm not saying for a moment he is, why shoot KGB officers? I would think they'd be his allies."

"It's the only thing that doesn't fit," Sokoloff said reasonably. "Perhaps they had a falling out. Perhaps he isn't working with the Russians after all. Perhaps he is working for Syrian Intelligence, and the Russians simply saw what they thought was an opportunity of some sort and got in the way. There could be a dozen explanations."

"Including the probability—and you notice, David, that I use the word *probability*—that Avram Zemil is simply doing his job, and that someone else was on the scene with a SigSauer," the prime minister said impatiently.

Sokoloff nodded slightly. The old man was clutching at straws. Of course, they all were. They were frightened out of their minds. And frightened men often did foolish things.

"He has, from what I understand, been digging

into the records at Haifa Station. That's consistent with his assignment."

"Yes, sir," Sokoloff said. "Which means he has the list."

"The same list we have," Harel said. "A dozen names. The only people in the world who knew about Operation Brother, its exact timetable, and its real purpose. Our traitor is among them."

"Presumably," Sokoloff said. "Avram Zemil's name is also on that list."

Harel's eyes narrowed. "So is yours, David," he said.

"Yes, it is," Sokoloff said unblinking. The old man was definitely clutching at straws, which ultimately would do none of them any good. Yet Sokoloff felt compelled to continue. He could not leave this. Not this late in the game. He glanced at the third man. "The man found tortured to death in the house was an arms dealer, an Arab himself."

"And also a Mossad informer from what I understand," the older man said carefully. "What's your point?"

"Zemil went there, presumably to see him."

"And do you suspect he tortured this one to death?" the third man asked sarcastically. His right eyebrow rose. "Avram had a very busy evening."

"He had some dealings with the man, that much at least is obvious."

The prime minister leaned forward. "I must be missing something, David," he said. "First you tell me that Avram Zemil may have shot up a bazaar—an Arab bazaar, as you pointed out. So, he hates Arabs. In the next breath you tell me he had dealings with an Arab arms dealer."

"We've made use of our enemies before," Sokoloff said. "Youssef Fawzi is a case in point."

"You're well informed," the third man said.

"I read the reports," Sokoloff replied, holding back an angry retort.

"You said Avram had been spotted in the area of the bazaar with another man. A man unidentified so far."

Sokoloff nodded.

"By whom, David? Who spotted Avram there? And how did that information get to you?"

For the first time, Sokoloff realized that he might have gone too far. But again he reminded himself that it was too late for him to back out. "The Shin Beth," he said. It was only a partial truth, but at this moment he figured it was the lesser of two evils.

"Michel Louk?" the prime minister asked.

Sokoloff nodded.

"What was he doing in the bazaar? Was he following Avram? At your orders?"

"No, Mr. Prime Minister," Sokoloff said, holding up his hand as though defending himself against a physical blow. "It was just coincidence that he was there at the same time as Zemil. He'd gone up to Tel Amal to check on this arms dealer. You remember, sir, you asked me to look into the possibility that the Iran-Contra connection was still alive here in Israel. This Gromit had international connections. If anyone would know, it would have been him. Michel went up there to see if he could find out anything. He just happened on the scene when he spotted Zemil."

"And the second man," the prime minister said angrily.

"Yes, sir."

"Whom he did not recognize, though he knew Avram."

"He only caught a glimpse of them. It was dark. There was shooting, and it happened very fast."

The prime minister nodded and glanced again at the third man. "I'm going to ask you something point-blank, David. I have the utmost confidence in you and in your judgment; I always have, and I want to keep it that way."

"I appreciate that, sir."

"Are you having Avram watched?"

"No, sir," Sokoloff said.

Harel nodded after a pregnant moment. "For the time being, then, nothing has changed. I also have the utmost confidence in Avram Zemil. As far as I'm concerned he is doing his job and he will be left to do it. He's unaware, of course, that anyone else but me knows of his mission, and we'll keep that fiction alive at least for the moment." The prime minister hesitated for a second. "No matter what happens in the coming days he is not to be interfered with . . . nor is he to be helped, in any fashion. Do I make myself perfectly clear?"

"Yes, sir," Sokoloff said.

The third man nodded, though clearly he did not like it. What was running through his mind? Sokoloff wondered. What secrets was he carrying around in his head?

"Which brings us back to the incident at the bazaar," Sokoloff said.

"Avram's name will be kept out of it," Harel said. "Tell Louk that Avram was not involved. Tell him that Avram was there only by coincidence."

"There'll be hell to pay if we don't come up with the killer."

"PLO terrorists," Harel said grimly. "The same

ones responsible for the killings at the Wailing
Wall."

"The air force will want to retaliate."

"We've plenty of legitimate targets," Harel said.
"I'll sign the order." He swiveled around so that
he could look out the windows. The morning was
bright, warm, peaceful. "We must find our traitor.
That is our first obligation against which nearly
everything else pales. And he is not Avram Zemil."

"I'm not so sure, Mr. Prime Minister," Sokoloff
said softly.

"I am," Harel said.

JERUSALEM, 9:20 A.M.

It was still the same morning. The Jerusalem
Hilton, located in a western section of the city
known as Givat Ram, rose form a stark yellow hill
next to Binyanei Ha'ooma (the National Convention Center). Sokoloff lingered in the coffee shop
for ten minutes before taking an elevator up to a
room on the eighth floor. The hotel was filled just
now with convention guests from the States, so
his was just another anonymous face. Something
was being hidden from him. It had never happened before, at least not here in Israel, and he
didn't like it.

The shits, Sokoloff thought.

As a young man his grandfather had emigrated
to the United States from the Soviet Union just
after the Revolution, settling in a Manhattan
neighborhood of Russian Jews where he'd opened
a small, highly succesful restaurant. His son, David's father, took over the business after the Second World War, though he'd hated it and had

wanted something better for himself. He'd wanted to get into politics. "It's my country, I want to help run it," he was fond of saying.

Young David was a gifted student. When he graduated from high school in 1957, he was admitted to Harvard first as an undergraduate and was subsequently accepted into the Law School, graduating with top honors. He worked for a few years at a large, prestigious New York law firm, gravitating at his father's urging to Washington, D.C., where he formed a lobbying organization involved with what Sokoloff called the "reeducation of the American Congress in foreign affairs." A representative or even a senator coming from Iowa or Nebraska or New Hampshire often knew nothing about the Soviet Union or its satellite countries.

Sokoloff's firm was funded in part by U.S. businesses that wanted to expand their commercial interests in the Soviet Union, and later, in secret partly by the CIA, who wanted a conduit for their spies heading east. Reagan had picked him up as an adviser, and two years after the election Sokoloff had emigrated to Israel. He had never married; he had never met a woman "precise" enough for his liking, so his move, though sudden and stunning in some quarters, had not created much of a stir.

Gregory Ballinger opened the door for him and without a word went back to his telephone conversation. Sokoloff came in and made sure the door was locked. He felt the need just now to take extra care with his movements.

"He's here now," Ballinger said. "I'll call you later." He hung up the telephone. He was a large, raw-boned American with dark eyes and thick black hair. He was also CIA.

"You haven't used my name on an open line, for God's sake?" Sokoloff asked.

"Don't worry about it, David, the line's clean."

"How can you be sure?"

Ballinger smiled, his expression boyish, which was irritating to Sokoloff. "It's my job, remember?"

"Nevertheless . . ."

"Want some coffee?" Ballinger asked, pouring himself a cup.

"No, I can't stay that long. I'll have to get back in a few minutes before they miss me."

"Starting to put the squeeze on you, is that it?"

"I think they might suspect something," Sokoloff said. He hated what he was doing, had from the start, and yet becoming what had been termed a "soft-double"—a spy for a friendly government that you wished no harm—had seemed somehow exciting at the time. "Harel asked me point-blank not more than an hour ago what I was doing."

"He thinks you're the nigger in the woodpile?"

Sokoloff hated that expression. "I don't know for sure, but I think he's lost at least the edge of his confidence in me. I think they're holding something back."

Ballinger thought about it for a moment as he sipped his coffee and looked out his window down toward the city. "That's serious, David. We'd hoped to keep you in place for at least another year."

"I don't know if it will last that long," Sokoloff said. "I don't know if *I'll* last that long."

"It's the Syrian thing."

Sokoloff nodded. "They've convinced themselves that there is a traitor within the government. At high levels."

"You said that was a possibility, David. We both

knew it was coming. Will they find him, do you suppose? Are they close?"

"I don't know. It's strange over there, and getting stranger by the day. Felix Louk is agitating for another vote of confidence."

"Will Harel make it?"

Sokoloff shook his head. "I seriously doubt it. Not after this Damascus thing, plus everything else that's been happening."

Ballinger turned back, his eyes wide, almost innocent. It was another of his studied actions. "What else is happening, David? Exactly what else?"

"There was another incident last night. Another killing."

"Here in Jerusalem?"

"Haifa. In an Arab bazaar. Half-a-dozen women and children were gunned down."

"PLO?"

"The Russians were involved. Two of them were found dead in the house of an Arab arms dealer. Polish IDs. Of course the Poles are denying any knowledge. The two were armed with Makarovs."

Ballinger was definitely interested now. "Who was the trigger man?"

"We don't know yet. But Avram Zemil was spotted in the area."

"Operation Brother?"

"Right. But he was in the bazaar with another man, so far unidentified. The arms dealer and his little boyfriend were also found dead. Tortured."

"Zemil?"

"It's possible. I just don't know, Gregory. It's getting strange, as I've said. They've set Zemil to find their traitor."

Again Ballinger grinned. "Poetic justice, I'd say. Is he any good?"

"Yes," Sokoloff said.

"Then he'll succeed."

Sokoloff looked at the American. "Unless he's stopped," he said.

"What are you asking me, David?" Ballinger said, his grin so broad that Sokoloff could see his gums. It was disgusting. "Exactly what is it you want me to do for you? Order a hit on this Zemil?"

"Good God, no," Sokoloff said aghast.

"But?" Ballinger asked, reading something of his thoughts.

"IF he finds out about me . . . about us, it'll destroy everything."

"You're right, of course," Ballinger said, the grin finally fading from his face. "Something will have to be done, especially if you're right and the Russians are involved. There have been some rumors."

"What rumors?" Sokoloff snapped. Like the prime minister, he found that he, too, was suddenly clutching at straws. But he was frightened. For the first time in his life he was truly afraid for his own future.

"Ivan Ivanovich Roskov. KGB. He's said to be in the area."

"What's he doing here?"

"I don't know, David."

"Then find him. Get rid of him."

"It won't be quite so easy as that. In the first place, he's supposed to be very good. The best. And in the second place, we don't know what he looks like. Not really. No photographs, and what descriptions we have are all contradictory. Some say he's old, others young. He's supposed to be tall and heavyset by some accounts, while others say he's short and thin. Finding him will be like finding the proverbial needle in the haystack. And even if we do, taking him won't be so easy."

"Then how do you know he's here in Israel?"

"I don't, David. There have simply been rumors, as I've said. He goes by the code name Palmyra. One of my people overheard a conversation here in Jerusalem in which the name was mentioned."

"Could have been talking about the city in Syria."

"Yes, they could have. But my man got the impression they were talking about a person. Like I said, only a rumor, but I'll look into it. In the meantime, what do you want me to do about Zemil?

"Can you put someone on him?"

Ballinger thought about it for a moment or two, then nodded. "You say he's good?"

"Yes."

"Then we'll have to be careful. If Harel has set him to find your traitor, he'll be on the watch. But you said he wasn't alone in Haifa."

"I don't know who the second man is. Zemil was supposed to be working alone."

"And you don't think he had anything to do with the killings in the bazaar?"

"I don't know," Sokoloff said. "I don't think he did, but the incident had something to do with him and what he's looking for."

"Palmyra," Ballinger said. "It has all the earmarks."

"Could one of the dead Russians be him?"

"Not likely," Ballinger said, thinking. He shook his head. "No, that's not likely. But I'll see what I can do for you, David. We'll watch Zemil, and I'll put the word out for Palmyra." He smiled. "Who knows, maybe one will lead to the other."

"That's what I'm afraid of," Sokoloff said.

JERUSALEM, 9:45 A.M.

Ivan Roskov slapped his hand against his leg in irritation as he looked out at the passing scenery. "You've very nearly put an end to this entire operation by your ineptitude," he snapped angrily.

"We didn't see him coming until the last possible moment," Captain Peter Bogachev replied. They were seated together in the back of Roskov's Mercedes on their way to the Wailing Wall.

"Gromit was looking for Zemil. They have my code name. They know that I'm here."

"Not necessarily, sir. The Arab was only guessing."

"He could have been holding back!" Roskov nearly exploded with rage.

"No, sir, he did not, I can guarantee it. He answered our questions. All of our questions."

"Except for one," Roskov said, finally getting his anger under control. "Except for one, Petor. The fact that he was expecting Zemil to show up."

"We'll kill him," Bogachev said with feeling.

"Yes, we will, Petor," Roskov said, thinking ahead. "But not yet. First I want to know what he is looking for."

"When the time comes, I want him," Bogachev said.

Roskov looked at him. "From what I've seen and heard already, I don't think it will be quite so easy as you imagine." He sat back in his seat as he tried to work out his next moves. Just at the edge of his thoughts, far back, he could feel the first hint that somehow his long, carefully drawn out plans were beginning to unravel a little at the edges.

* * *

Roskov stood very close to the Wailing Wall a few yards south of the Gate of the Chain, his face barely inches from the roughly hewn, uneven ancient stones. A few Haredim, in the same traditional dress Roskov wore, also stood praying at the Wall. The military had mounted a guard since the shooting incident, but they stood at a respectful distance.

The morning was already quite warm, and Roskov was hot in the thick coat and hat, yet he felt a certain peace here that he could barely admit to himself. There was a power to this place. An overwhelming feeling of age and history and religion.

A man in a long coat and broad-brimmed black hat stepped up to the Wall next to him. From the corner of his eye Roskov glanced over.

"This is very dangerous, meeting like this in the day," his contact said softly.

"Have you something for me?" Roskov asked.

The man was holding a prayer scroll in front of his face. He turned to look at Roskov, nodded his head and handed him the scroll. He turned back to the Wall. "It's all there. Another opportunity."

"Yes, I see," Roskov said, focusing on the scroll.

"But very dangerous. Nothing must go wrong."

"Something may already be going wrong," Roskov said softly, and he could see out of the corner of his eye that his contact had stiffened.

"What is it?"

"There was a shooting incident in the Tel Amal bazaar last night."

"Yes, I know about it."

"The Arab killed had my code name. He was looking for me. He had put out the word that I was here in Israel. Someone is looking for me."

"Why?"

"I don't know yet. But you and I together will find out."

"Were they your people with the Polish identification?"

"Yes, but they're not important for the moment. It is another man, Avram Zemil, whom we must worry about. He was seen at the bazaar last night."

"Are you certain?" the contact asked, and Roskov could hear the sudden fear and respect in his voice.

"Yes. I must know what he is looking for. It's possible that he knows about you."

"Then I will kill him," the contact said.

"Not yet. First I must know what he knows. I must know what he is after."

"It will be very difficult."

"But necessary," Roskov said. "Necessary for your survival as well as mine. Do you understand?"

"I'll see what I can do," the contact said. "Perhaps we should cancel our plans, or at least delay them."

"No," Roskov said sharply, but careful to keep his voice low. "No, we must go ahead. We've come too far."

"Yes, I agree. But with Zemil there will be trouble."

"Everyone has a weak spot. Find his."

His contact smiled. "I see what you mean."

8

■

Climbing the stairs from archives a couple of minutes before the morning staff briefing, Avram decided that he was no further ahead with his investigation now than when he had started, and yet already a lot of people had been killed—all but two of them innocent victims. That the Russians were involved came as no real surprise to him, but the savagery of their response to Gromit's inquiries was disturbing. Palmyra, if he was involved, had to realize that the massacre at the Tel Amal bazaar would not go uninvestigated. He had taken a very large risk. Yet Gromit had said the man was very good. Large risks were only taken for very large goals. Just how important was their traitor? What else had he done to Israel? What else was planned?

He'd gotten one name from records; a British expatriate who did about the same thing in Limassol that Gromit had done here in Haifa. One name to go on, nothing more.

Look to your own. Limassol. The words of a dying man. Had it meant that Gromit had found out who the traitor was? Did it mean a Mossad officer, or simply an Israeli? Look to your own. But why Limassol?

Benjamin Strauss, his eyes red from lack of sleep, was just coming down the corridor when Avram reached the door to Operations. They hadn't seen each other since last night. It was obvious that the surveillance man was having a hard time accepting his role as an unwitting accomplice to an operation he viewed as not only illegal, but extremely distasteful as well.

"Good morning," Avram said. "Has Yoram come in yet?"

"I haven't seen him," Strauss said tersely, his eyes avoiding Avram's.

Avram held the door for him. Sammuel Amit, the operations chief and Joseph Geva, their communications man, were in deep discussion with Michel Louk over a large-scale map of Kishon Harbor. They looked up when Strauss and Avram came in.

"I was just about to send for you," Amit said. "You're going to have to take charge of the briefing this morning. Yoram is still in Tel Aviv."

"When will he be back?" Avram asked, coming around the long table. Louk had an expectant, almost harried expression on his face.

"We don't know. Maybe not until tomorrow. He told me to tell you that you'll go by the book on this one."

"What's that supposed to mean?" Avram shot back. He was feeling mean after last night. Like Strauss, he hadn't gotten much sleep. Every time he closed his eyes he could see Gromit's battered body, hear his dying words.

"Operation Sleeper is on for tonight," Louk said.

"And Yoram won't be back in time for it?"

"He didn't think so," Amit said. "Michel here is in charge of this operation in any event. We're simply to provide backup."

"Get me Ben-Or on the scrambler," Avram told Geva and glanced down at the big map.

Geva hesitated for a moment, as if he were waiting for Amit to approve the order. Avram looked up.

"Now, Joseph," Avram said.

"Yes, sir," Geva said and he started for the communications console.

Avram managed a smile. "I think we can dispense with titles here. We're all on the same side."

"I . . ." Geva stammered. "Sorry."

Something was wrong, Avram could feel it thick in the air. He glanced at Strauss who avoided his gaze. Had the big man said something to them about last night? He doubted it. There would have been more of a reaction than a simple cold shoulder. Geller had probably given them instructions before he left that Avram Zemil was not one to be giving orders here.

"Now," Avram said to Louk. "How can the Mossad be of assistance to the Shin Beth?"

Again there was that curious hesitation, but Louk was a lot smoother than Geva or Amit and he recovered nicely, pointing to the missile boat docks on the western side of the naval base.

"Fawzi will be coming in on a private motor yacht about midnight. We'll be monitoring them from the moment they clear Beirut breakwater. Ten miles out we'll exchange recognition signals."

"How is their approach being handled?" Avram asked, studying the map. Beirut was just sixty miles north of Haifa. If Fawzi's yacht was large enough, it could make the trip in around three hours. Providing the weather held, and providing they ran into no trouble. There were a lot of boats out there, including Soviet trawlers that closely watched anything departing or approaching the Israeli coast.

"Four of our gunboats will be on station, out of visual contact but well within radar range. From that point inward we'll give them vectors."

"The navy is in on this?"

Louk nodded. "And the air force, who will be flying surveillance, long range as well as short range."

"How about at the Beirut end?"

"That's their responsibility," Louk said. "Ours starts ten miles out of Haifa."

Avram looked up. "That's a big ten miles."

"Yes, it is," Louk said.

"They'll be isolated once they enter the harbor?" Avram asked.

"Yes," Louk said. "That section of the base will be cleared ninety minutes before Fawzi's boat arrives, which will give us enough time to get our people into place. Once Fawzi steps ashore, the yacht will turn around and return to Beirut."

"From there we take him to Nazareth?"

"Right, without a visible escort," Louk said. "I'll have my people stationed at various spots along the twenty-mile route, leapfrogging by chopper as the van passes each position."

"Fawzi and a driver in the van; who else?"

"It was to be Geller and me," Louk said. "Now I assume you'll be in on it."

Avram glanced at Strauss. "No," he said. "I'm sending Benjamin along."

Louk and Amit were both startled, but Strauss nodded.

"You will, however, be at the base tonight?" Louk asked.

"Yes."

"Avram, I have Ben-Or on the scrambler for you," Geva said from across the room. "Do you want to take it in your office?"

"Here will be fine." Avram said, stepping around the end of the table and taking the phone from Geva. He wanted everyone to hear what he was about to say.

Ben-Or's voice was strangely distorted over the encrypted line, barely recognizable because it was reconstituted from scrambled digital data, but the words were understandable.

"Sleeper is on for tonight, is that right?" Ben-Or asked.

"It's why I'm calling," Avram said. "Yoram should be down here for this. Can you send him along?"

"You'll have to handle it yourself, Avram. Yoram is up in Jerusalem. Won't be finished probably until late tonight, or perhaps even sometime tomorrow. Is there some trouble?"

"No, no trouble at all. But he hadn't said anything to me about being out of the station for so long. Anything I should know about?"

"He had some meetings, I don't know all the details."

"With Felix Louk by any chance?"

"Yes, as a matter of fact. Why do you ask?"

"Just curious, Arik. His brother is here now."

"I see," Ben-Or said. "It's a Shin Beth operation. Let Michel Louk run it his way."

"Of course," Avram said, catching the exact meaning of Ben-Or's warning.

"We'll talk in the morning."

"Yes, sir," Avram said, and the connection was broken, the green light on Avram's console turning red to indicate there now was an open line down which raw encrypted data was being funneled. Avram hung up and went back to the others around the table.

The tension in the room had obviously increased.

"I take it Yoram will not be back in time after all?" Louk said.

"That's right," Avram said, once again studying the map. "What else have we got to go over here between us?"

"Placement of our personnel in and around the base, as well as along the route."

Avram nodded toward the operations chief. "Sammuel can handle that. What else?"

Louk's left eyebrow rose, but he offered no objection. Most likely Geller had planned on involving himself personally with every phase of the operation.

"Communications. Your people have the offshore stuff."

"You don't want the navy to handle that?"

"No."

Avram turned to Geva. "You can handle it, Joseph?"

"Yes, of course."

"Coordinate with Sammuel."

Geva nodded.

"Next?" Avram asked.

"Premission surveillance."

Avram turned to Strauss. "Do you have the staff to do double duty on this one?"

"I can manage," Strauss growled.

"Good," Avram said. "I want all reports on my desk no later than two this afternoon. I'll need a helicopter with a communications link to the boat, the vectoring crew, Benjamin's surveillance people, who will hang around the area until we have a confirmation that Fawzi has arrived safely in Nazareth, and of course with the transportation van itself."

Louk looked at Avram with renewed interest. "That wasn't in Yoram's plan."

"No, I don't suspect it was," Avram said. "I'll be going out to meet the boat, where I'll pick up Fawzi outside the ten-mile limit."

"Now, just a minute here . . ." Amit started to object, but Louk held him off.

"Let's hear what Avram has to say. Sounds interesting."

"All communications will remain the same as if Fawzi were actually being met at the boat and taken by van to Nazareth. I'll be watching from the chopper, just another security precaution. Once the van reaches Nazareth safely we'll set him down. But if anything goes wrong I'll get him the hell out of there."

"To where?" Louk asked.

Avram looked at him. "We'll decide that in the air. You want security, you've got it."

"I think this should be cleared with Yoram before we go ahead with it," Amit said.

"The change of plan stays within this room. No one, and I mean no one else will be told, and that includes your personnel."

"I agree," Louk said reasonably, but then his eye narrowed. "Fawzi's safety will be completely in your hands."

"I'll take the responsibility."

"Yes, you will," Louk said.

"Everything else stays the same," Avram said. "We'll go ahead with our planning as if we were sticking to the original schedule."

"How are you going to explain the chopper's approach to Fawzi's yacht?"

"A routine coastal inspection. It's done all the time. Have we got a recognition signal for Fawzi so that he won't believe he's kidnapped?"

Louk smiled. "Yes. It's *Áyios*."

It was apparently someone's little joke. But Avram didn't find it funny. *Áyios* was the Arabic word for saint, and Fawzi was anything but. "I see," he said. He looked around the table at the others. "Then let's get on with it, gentlemen. Reports on my desk by two." He turned back to Louk. "If you've a minute, I'd like to speak to you in my office."

"As you wish."

Avram's office was small and very plain. There had been no time for him to send for any of his personal belongings, but the room was comfortable and the window looked across a mall toward the Technion.

"What do you know about a shooting that occurred last night up in Tel Amal?" Avram asked without preamble, and he was gratified to see a startled look cross Louk's features.

He recovered quickly. "It's under investigation. How did you come to find out about it?"

"I was there," Avram said.

This time the surprised look on Louk's face remained. "What were you doing up there?"

"I went to see a friend."

"His name?"

An assumption that his friend was a he and not a she, Avram wondered, or did Louk know more than he was pretending to know? Strauss might have talked to him, but he doubted it. "Yakof Gromit. He is an arms dealer and a Mossad informer. I've known him for years."

"Did you see him?"

"No," Avram said. "There was shooting. By the time I got into the bazaar, everything was over and the police were on their way. I didn't think, under the circumstances, that it would have been good business to involve the Mossad in an internal affair."

"I see," Louk said softly. "Your friend Gromit was found tortured to death last night in his apartment."

Avram made an obvious show of trying to keep his expression neutral. "Who did it?"

"We don't know, yet. His boyfriend was shot to death at close range, and of course a number of innocent bystanders in the bazaar were hit by a third man who escaped through the crowd."

"A third man?"

Louk hesitated a moment. "At this point we have no idea who he might be. We found a dead man on the roof of Gromit's apartment building, and another in a back alley. Both carried Polish identification, but we think they were Russian."

"KGB?"

"Probably, though we've got no proper identification yet. Most likely we'll never know who they were."

They were playing a little song-and-dance here. Avram was almost one hundred percent convinced that Louk had been in Tel Amal to check on him. But why, and on whose orders?

"Ballistics?" Avram asked.

Louk shrugged. "Not completed yet, but the dead men carried Makarovs."

"Anything we should get the Mossad involved with?" Avram asked.

Again Louk hesitated for a beat. Whatever he'd expected here this morning, he'd obviously not

gotten it. He was almost nonplussed. "That may
depend upon what you went to see Gromit about."

"I've just been assigned here to Haifa Station,"
Avram said, sighing deeply, "I was on my way to
renew the old ties. I'm not surprised it was the
Russians, though. He led a dangerous life. He
passed the Mossad a lot of information over
the years."

"Source *Masabb*." It had been Gromit's code
name.

"You've read my reports."

"Yes, some of it quite good."

Avram had to wonder if Louk or his people had
been following him. The Shin Beth's presence here
and now, especially in the person of Michel Louk,
the brother of one of the men on Avram's short
list of possible traitors, seemed to be more than
coincidence.

"I'd be interested in being told whatever you
come up with," Avram said.

"At a personal level, or is this an official Mossad
request?"

"At a personal level. For now."

Louk got to his feet. He stopped at the door.
"Geller is not going to be very happy with you."

Avram grinned. "I think I'll be able to make him
see it my way. In any event, he's not here at the
moment, is he."

"No," Louk said. "No, he's not."

KISHON HARBOR, 3:17 P.M.

Mission operations had been set up in an old
torpedo arming shed on the western edge of the
naval base. Avram had driven out to see how the

preparations were going. They'd all dressed in navy work dungarees so that they wouldn't seem out of place, and their outside activities were being kept to a minimum. A naval officer had been assigned to act as their liaison and to run interference if any of the base personnel got a little too curious.

"How is it coming?" he asked Strauss, taking the big man aside for a moment. Louk was somewhere across base.

"Just fine, but what about last night?" Strauss snapped. "Louk gave me the third degree. Wanted to know if you'd said anything to me. He knows you were up there."

"I told him. He's running the investigation. It would come out sooner or later in any event."

"Did you happen to mention my name?"

"No, and we're going to keep it that way."

Strauss glanced over at the others huddled around the charts and the communications gear. "You're going to have some serious trouble with Yoram when he returns, and probably with Sammuel before then. In the meantime my ass is out on a limb. If you go down, so will I. We're talking about murder now, possibly espionage."

"Yes, we are," Avram said. "You're going to have to go along with me for just a little while longer."

Strauss let out a big breath slowly and shook his head. "Damned if I know how I got myself into this one, but I've come this far, might as well go all the way."

"What about this operation? Where are the holes?"

"Shit, they're everywhere. If there's been a leak, or if Fawzi is spotted leaving the base, there's not a thing we cold do to stop a rocket attack."

"He'll be in the chopper with me."

"That's what I'm talking about. You'd be a sitting duck. I don't think I'd care to baby-sit that bastard."

"Neither do I, but orders are orders."

Strauss laughed, disdainfully. "Somehow I don't think a little technicality like orders ever stopped you."

"Maybe I'll push him out the door offshore."

"Want some help?"

MOSSAD HAIFA STATION, 8:00 P.M.

The station was quiet for the moment. Everything out at the base was going smoothly. Fawzi's yacht was still several hours out from first contact, and Strauss had secured the area as well as possible. Louk's people were already stationed along the route to Nazareth. Over all of that, the business of Haifa went along at its normal pace. Avram had checked back at his hotel. None of his telltales had been disturbed, which meant no one had been in his room, not even the hotel maid with whom he had left strict instructions that his room was not to be disturbed. He wasn't due back at the base to pick up his helicopter and crew until ten-thirty.

He crossed the corridor from his office and entered the Operations Room. The night duty officer, a young man with prematurely gray hair, was seated at the communications console, his feet up, reading a magazine. When Avram came in he looked over his shoulder, then jumped up.

"Easy," Avram said.

"I wasn't expecting anyone, sir."

"Is Sammuel here by any chance?"

"No, sir, he left this afternoon. Hasn't been back."

"Right," Avram said. "Where are the duty logs kept?"

"In the Action Pending bin."

"How far back?"

"They go to Mr. Geller on a daily basis. After a week they end up downstairs."

"I'm looking for the week of May tenth."

"In Archives, sir."

"How about popping down and pulling them out for me, unless your board is busy."

"No, sir. It's a quiet night. Be glad for the activity. Just be a couple of minutes." The duty officer left the Operations Room.

Avram hurried to the door and looked down the corridor until the young man disappeared around the corner, then went to an old upright safe that stood beside the duty supervisor's desk. By regulation the safe was to be locked whenever the duty officer stepped out. Even for a moment. Avram couldn't find fault with the young man, though. If you couldn't trust the assistant chief of station, who could you trust? Quickly he pulled open the heavy door and rummaged through the current operational plans, coming up with the station's Plant Maintenance Manual, in which was listed, among other things, the lock numbers and combinations for every door, file cabinet, and safe in the station. It took him a couple of minutes to find and memorize the combinations for the safes in Geller's and Amit's offices, and he just managed to replace the book, close the door, and move away from the safe when the young duty officer came back.

"Here you are, sir. Told you it'd just be a minute."

Avram took the file from him and riffled through the first few pages pretending to look for something. "I'll be in my office. Get this back to you soon as I'm done with it."

"No hurry, sir."

Avram left the Operations Room and went down the corridor to his office. He flipped on the lights, hung his jacket over the back of his chair, and laid the duty log file open on his desk.

Back out in the corridor he left his door ajar and quickly stepped across to Amit's office, pulling a long, slender, case-hardened steel pick out of his shirt pocket. He had the lock opened in five seconds and slipped inside, closing and locking the door behind him.

Amit was busy out at the base, and the young duty officer wouldn't bother him unlesss something important came up, which meant he had all the time in the world. But he felt very nervous about spying on his own—disloyal, even though he understood that what he was doing had the prime minister's sanction. Get it over with, he told himself.

The safe was actually a big, old-fashioned cabinet with tall steel doors, set in the corner behind the desk. Avram went immediately to it, spun the combination and twisted the handle. The door came open with a slight squeal that for some reason reminded him of fingernails on a chalkboard, and school and playing hooky for the first time.

The current operational case files were arranged on a pullout shelf at eye level. The two shelves immediately below it contained, in bound volumes, the ongoing assessment reports in support of each operational file. Amit was a neat, very precise man, for which Avram was at this moment grateful. Careful to replace everything he touched exactly where he'd found it, he quickly worked his way backward through the files to a date that preceded Operation Brother without finding a thing on the mission. Everything had apparently gone down to Archives afterward.

On the bottom shelves he found one-time code pads, two small deciphering sets disguised to look like ordinary AM/FM radios, three pages like the one Geller had given him, and a steel lock box about a foot and a half square. He drew this out, picked the lock, and opened the lid. The box contained a Smith and Wesson .38-caliber revolver, a silencer tube, two military .45 automatics, and a flat Walther PPK, with holsters and about fifty rounds of ammunition for each caliber. They'd be the odd-lot operational supplies.

The top shelf contained a series of bound volumes: Amit's personal logs and encounter sheets. As chief of operations he was not exempt from field work. The Mossad was simply too short-staffed to afford the luxury of purely desk-bound officers, even at the highest levels.

Avram found the volume for the months preceding Operation Brother and took it over to the window, where in the light from outside he could just make out the entries in Amit's tight hand. He flipped through the pages quickly, coming almost immediately to the first time Operation Brother had been mentioned. The entry concerned an operational briefing Amit and Geller had attended in Tel Aviv with Ben-Or, Defense Minister Rabin, and agent Avram Zemil. In a few terse paragraphs Amit outlined in his own words the entire operation as it had been presented to him. He'd made

no editorial comments, made no judgments, made
no estimations or evaluations. In this and other
operations he'd written about in his logs, Amit was
completely neutral. He did as he was told, when
he was told to do it, and how he was told to do it.
There was nothing of the man in the entries, and
Avram found that he was disappointed. He hadn't
known exactly what he expected to find here, but
he'd hoped for more than this. Either Amit was
one cold fish, with no ambition, even with no feelings, or he was a very crafty man who might have
suspected that his personal logs would someday
fall into the wrong hands and wanted nothing of
himself to show through.

The remainder of the Operation Brother entries were in the same vein: cold, hard facts,
names, dates, and places, material assessments,
goals, even risks, but no personalities, no feelings.

Avram looked up as a telephone across the hall
began to ring. His office? Hurriedly he replaced
the last of the logs, made one last check to be certain nothing was out of place, then closed and
locked the safe and went to the door.

It was the telephone in his office and he caught
it on the fourth ring. It was the young duty officer
in Operations.

"Sorry to bother you, sir, but Mr. Geller is on
the scrambler for you."

"I'll take it here," Avram said. Geller knew, of
course, that Operation Sleeper was on for tonight. He'd probably spoken with Ben-Or, so
Avram wasn't surprised that he was calling now.
"I'm switching over." He depressed the flat red
button that synchronized his encryption device
located in the communications center with the

equipment connected to the phone Geller was calling from.

"I want to know what the hell is going on up there, Zemil," Geller shouted angrily without preamble the moment the line cleared.

"Operation Sleeper," Avram replied calmly.

"I know that! I'm talking about your change of my plans! I demand an explanation."

Avram was not surprised at Geller's knowledge, either. He would have almost bet that Amit would call. He wasn't going to make it easy. Geller and Amit were both on his short list. It was time to begin pressing them.

"What plans, Yoram? What are you talking about?"

"You know perfectly well . . ."

"It was my understanding that this was a Shin Beth operation, and that we were only to provide assistance. Was I incorrect?"

"Don't play games with me. Haifa is my station."

"Of course, Yoram. But at the moment you're not here, so as assistant chief of station, Haifa is mine . . . not Sammuel Amit's."

"He has his loyalty, something apparently you have not developed—at least as far as concerns my station."

Avram could have challenged him on that point, but he let it go for the moment. "If you don't like the way I'm running things in your absence, then come back and run this operation yourself. Or fire me."

"I can't do either. Not yet."

"Then let me run this operation the right way. Louk has no objections."

Avram could hear the barely suppressed rage in Geller's voice, even over the poor reception.

"If you screw this one up, Zemil, I'll have your head on the block. I guarantee it."

"When will you be back?"

"Not until sometime tomorrow. Late. Listen to me, Zemil, there is no place in my organization for you."

"In that we agree," Avram said. "Completely."

9

KISHON NAVAL BASE, 10:53 P.M.

AVRAM'S AMERICAN-MADE BELL UH-1 IRO-
quois helicopter was waiting on the tarmac, the
ground crew fueling it when he arrived at the
base. The pilot, co-pilot, and gunner were waiting
in the ready room. None of them had been briefed
on the exact mission except that they would be
heading out over the Med, and that they'd take
orders from a Mossad officer.

"We're just about ready, sir," the pilot said, getting to his feet. His name tag read Taber.

"I'll be about twenty minutes," Avram said. "In
the meantime, dig me up a flight suit, would you?"

"Sure thing," Taber said. "One question, sir. Are
we going to see some action, or is this going to be
routine?"

"You'll receive orders when we're airborne,"
Avram stated firmly.

"Yes, sir." the pilot said.

"Get me that suit," Avram replied after a moment. He looked at the other two. They seemed
young, but they had the look of competence about

them. "There might be some action, though I doubt it. There will be some tricky flying."

The pilot grinned. "I think we can handle it."

"I'll hold you to that, Taber." Avram said. He left the hangar and drove back to their makeshift operations center in the torpedo shed. It was time again, he thought, to push. This time a little harder, and with pleasure.

A dozen or so men were gathered in the ops center, including Amit and his assistant operations officer, Leopold Neumann, who like Avram was relatively new to Haifa Station; Geva and his people running communications; the navy's liaison officer; and Louk and some of his people. Strauss and his men were down at the docks making certain the area would be cleared in time.

"I was wondering where you'd gotten yourself off to," Louk said.

"What's his status?" Avram asked.

"They're about forty miles out and closing the coast at twenty knots. I'd suggest you get out of here within the next thirty to forty minutes if you want a chance to look him over before picking him up."

The offshore distance of Fawzi's yacht struck an odd note at the back of Avram's head, but before he could ask about it Amit's voice raised in anger across the room distracted him.

"Just a moment, there's something I have to do," he told Louk and he strode across the room to where Amit, Neumann, and several of the others were gathered around the operations table.

Amit looked up. "I'm going to tell you one last time that this isn't the way Yoram planned this operation."

Everyone was looking at them.

"Your objection is noted, Sammuel. In the meantime you're relieved."

"What?" Amit sputtered.

Avram turned to Neumann. "Can you take over this operation as of now?"

Neumann was flustered, but he nodded uncertainly. "Yes, I believe I can if need be."

"Just what the hell do you think you're trying to pull here, Zcmil?" Amit demanded, red in the face. Everything in the shed had come to a sudden standstill.

"You can consider yourself under house arrest. I want you out of here now. Yoram will be back sometime tomorrow, and at that time we will decide whether to have you court-martialed."

"On what charges?" Amit bellowed.

"Gross disobedience of a direct order," Avram said loudly enough for everyone in the shed to hear him. "Or are you denying that contrary to my direct order to you this afternoon you called out of the station with my operational plans?"

"Yoram is the chief of station," Amit said, looking to the others for support. No one moved a muscle or said a word.

"While he is gone, I am in charge."

Amit backed up a step, his face turning ugly. "You won't get away with this, you bastard," he hissed.

"It's you who won't get away with it, Sammuel. With *none* of it," Avram said.

A slightly puzzled look crossed Amit's eyes.

"Now get out of here, we've work to do," Avram said, and he turned his back on the operations chief and walked over to where Louk had been watching. If Geller was their traitor Amit would have to be replaced, innocent or not, because he'd allowed a personal loyalty to blind him from his larger responsibilities as an officer of the Mossad. If, on the other hand, Amit was their traitor he'd be isolated now and would probably make some kind of a move. A mistake perhaps. And, finally, if both Geller and Amit were innocent he would owe them an apology and his resignation, at least from Haifa Station. He neither liked nor trusted either one of them, and certainly after tonight would not be able to work with them.

"Perhaps I underestimated you," Louk said, a faint smile on his lips.

"Perhaps you did," Avram said.

"If you need a job after tomorrow, look me up."

"You said Fawzi's yacht is forty miles out?"

Louk nodded and turned to the chart spread out on his operations table. He stabbed a blunt finger at a spot forty miles northwest. Too far west.

"What's he doing out there?" Avram asked. "I would have thought they'd run ten miles off Beirut and then come straight down."

"No," Louk said. "His exact route wasn't included in your briefing reports because it was for the most part outside our territory. Our responsibility begins ten miles out."

Avram studied the chart, a horrifying thought suddenly coming to mind. "What was his track out of Beirut?"

"They left early this morning, before first light. Beirut direct to Limassol on Cyprus. They refueled and then headed here. We thought it best to insulate the point-to-point connection between us and Beirut."

Limassol, Gromit had said with his dying breath. *Limassol. Look to your own.*

Avram was staring at the chart. Limassol. It was about to happen again. But why? And who had set it up? Where was the connection?

"What is it?" Louk was saying.

Avram looked up at the Shin Beth officer. "Nothing," he said. "Soon as I'm airborne you can give my pilot the vectors."

"All right," Louk said thoughtfully. "Good luck, then."

"Yeah," Avram said. "You, too."

Over the Mediterranean, 11:38 p.m.

The sea was very calm and black, the stars reflecting from the oily swell that gently rocked the 165-foot motor yacht *Deniżi*, lying dead in the water twenty-seven miles off the coast of Israel. She was dark and had not answered any of the signals sent from the Mossad–Shin Beth operations center on Kishon, or from Avram's helicopter now hovering five hundred yards out just above the surface of the water.

They'd kept their radio traffic to an absolute minimum so they wouldn't attract any attention. A Soviet trawler with sophisticated electronic listening equipment was lying barely ten miles to the south-southeast, putting Fawzi's yacht and Avram's chopper well within their radar and listening range.

"What do you want to do, sir?" the pilot's voice came over Avram's headset.

Avram had been studying the yacht through binoculars from his position at the open door. Nothing moved on deck, nor were there any lights showing. The ship could have been deserted, or everybody aboard dead.

"Can you set down on the afterdeck?" Avram said into his mouthpiece.

"Can do. She's equipped with a chopper pad. A little small, but no problem."

"Soon as I'm clear, come back out here and stand by," Avram said.

"You got it," the pilot said.

Avram braced himself with one shoulder against the doorway as the chopper rolled left and sped, nose low, toward the dead ship. He took out the SigSauer holstered on his chest to make sure a round was in the chamber and the safety on, then reholstered it.

Limassol. He couldn't get it out of his mind that something bad had happened. He hadn't been terribly surprised when they'd come out to the ship and found her apparently lifeless. The answers were on Cyprus. The island was drawing him like a magnet—or rather, more like the bottom of a powerful whirlpool.

They came around the stern of the ship, port to starboard, made a wide, extremely tight turn inside their track, Taber expertly flaring the chopper so that their speed had been cut to zero at the last possible instant, and they touched down in the exact center of the helipad.

Avram leaped down onto the deck of the ship, yanking out his gun and keeping low as he raced for the stairs that led down to the stern deck proper. He'd gone barely five feet when the chopper lifted up and to the left, away from him, and then it was gone, leaving him alone aboard the ship.

Crouching in the darkness he could hear and feel the vibration of some distant machinery below decks. It didn't sound to him like the ship's main engines, but it was definitely a diesel, possibly one of the generators, which if that were the case meant the ship still had electricity. It also meant that the vessel's light had been turned off deliberately.

Above decks the big ship was laid out on four levels. On the lowest level, where Avram waited and listened for a full thirty seconds, wide passageways ran stern to bow along either side of the yacht. The second level contained the helipad and the entrance to what appeared to be the main saloon. The third level contained an open deck for sun bathing, a small swimming pool, and forward what probably was the owner's stateroom. At the top level was the bridge. Below decks were additional cabins, the galley, the crew's quarters, and the machinery spaces.

Avram crossed over to the port side of the ship and started up the passageway to where the boarding ladder was still in the raised position. If anyone had been aboard to sabotage the yacht and her crew, they had not left this way.

Forward, he took a companionway back up to the second level, hesitating just at the top. But nothing moved. No alarms were sounded, no shots fired, and he quickly moved to the broad glass doors leading into the saloon. A dim blue light illuminated a big, built-in tropical fish tank. He eased open the glass door and stepped just inside. He could hear the tank's aerator bubbling softly.

Back out on the deck he climbed the companionway stairs to the third level, again hesitating just at the top before he stepped out into the open.

The water in the swimming pool sloshed gently back and forth as the big yacht moved gently on the sea swell. The only sign that something was amiss was a deck chair overturned just beneath the overhang of the deck above. The sliding glass door to the owner's stateroom was open, the curtain half torn down. They'd not been able to see that from the air.

Slipping his weapon's safety catch to the off position, Avram approached the open door and looked inside. The sitting room was a shambles. It appeared as if there had been an intense struggle here. Furniture was overturned, a big plateglass mirror was broken, shards of glass scattered over the carpet, and near the door into the bedroom was a large pool of blood.

Avram quickly crossed the room, flattened himself against the bulkhead beside the bedroom door, and looked inside. A large man lay on his side on the floor beside a large circular bed, the back of his head blown away, a gun clutched in his outstretched hand. A bodyguard, Avram figured. Youssef Fawzi, two bullet holes in his chest and one just above his left ear, lay spreadeagled on the bed, the bedspread covered with blood. Avram went to the bed and touched Fawzi's neck. The man's skin was still warm. This had happened less than an hour ago. Possibly only minutes earlier.

Turning, Avram raced back out onto the pool deck, took the ladder to the upper level, and crossed the narrow deck into the bridge. The captain and two officers lay where they had been shot down; shell casings littered the floor. Avram bent down and picked one up. It had come from an Uzi light submachine gun. An Israeli-made weapon.

Stepping over one of the bodies, Avram went to the broad console and looked out over the bow of the ship. Still nothing moved. To the north he could just barely make out the helicopter, her lights out, hovering a few feet above the water. Some of the electronic equipment in the console had been shot up, but the radios seemed to be intact. He studied the switches for a couple of moments, then flipped on those controlling one of the communications radios. A moment later the sounds of static filled the speaker. He switched to their operational frequency, and picked up the handset.

"Base, sleeper down," he radioed. "Repeat. Sleeper down." It was the code that meant something had gone wrong.

"Understood," Geva's voice came over the speakers. "Say your location."

"Aboard. Our target has been terminated."

"Hold on," Geva said after a moment's pause.

Avram started to turn when a tremendous explosion shook the entire board, nearly lifting her out of the water, and sending him sprawling, his wounded shoulder slamming hard into the console, the sudden sharp pain driving him to his knees and pulling the air out of his lungs.

Before he cold recover, a second, even larger explosion shook the big yacht, sending her over nearly sixty degrees on her starboard side.

Avram tumbled down the sharply slanting deck against the bulkhead, the captain's bloody body falling on top of him.

The ship was listing even farther. It was about to turn over. Avram was seeing stars from the pain in his arm, and from where his head had slammed into the steel bulkhead. He fought to shove the lifeless body away, and he managed to get to his knees and pull himself to the high side of the bridge and outside. Somehow he had not lost his gun.

The rail was above him now, an impossible distance away. The portside wall and windows of the bridge itself had become the floor. It would only be a matter of seconds before the ship turned completely over, trapping him beneath her bulk and taking him down with her.

He had started to crawl up the bulkhead toward the big gas stack and mast when a burst of machine-gun fire raked the steel just in front of him, sparks and metal chips flying everywhere. He fell back, bringing up his gun with a smooth motion. A figure dressed in black was braced against the companionway ladder between the third and fourth decks just aft. He started to bring up his Uzi again, when Avram fired off four shots in rapid succession, at least one hitting his target. The figure fell backward into the companionway as a third explosion broke the ship's back and she started to roll over, picking up speed as she went.

Avram rolled over as a broad canvas loop attached to a cable brushed his side from above. It was Taber and the chopper hovering barely fifty feet overhead. As the ship started to go all the way over, Avram looped his arm around the strap, and the chopper pulled up and away from the rolling hull, nearly jerking Avram's arm out of its socket, but then he was clear, the ship's keel missing him by less than two feet.

Mossad Haifa Station, 5:43 a.m.

What remained of the shambles of Operation Sleeper had been hastily moved from the naval base back downtown. Louk was on the telephone with his people in Tel Aviv. The doctors had just left and Avram waited in Operations for Ben-Or to be reached. The Mossad chief had been among the government representatives who had gone to

Nazareth for the meeting with Fawzi. There'd been no reaction from anyone yet, but it was coming.

"There wasn't a damned thing we could have done about it," Louk shouted angrily into the telephone. "It was out of our hands from the start."

The young duty officer had told Avram that Amit had returned briefly to the station earlier, and had made one brief telephone call from his office before leaving.

"We're just lucky that there weren't any casualties among our people," Louk was saying.

They'd been betrayed again, of course. The man who had fired the shots at him had been willing to go down with the ship. His had been a suicide mission. Who was he? Had he started out with the yacht in Beirut, or had he somehow gotten aboard in Limassol?

"Yes, I know there will be repercussions," Louk said, lowering his voice finally. "But there was nothing, absolutely nothing we could have done to change what happened short of being on that boat when it left Beirut, so if you people want to place the blame somewhere, you can spread it around for all of us to share."

In a way Avram felt detached. He had tried on the Syrian desert, and failed. He had tried with Yakof Gromit, and failed. And he had failed again with Fawzi. His mood, he supposed, was probably due at least in part to the shot the doctor had given him to counter the pain in his arm. But the facts were there nonetheless.

Palmyra. The name was like a bright, very hot flame in his gut.

"No, there was nothing left," Louk said, glancing over at Avram. He turned back. "It went down in nearly six thousand feet of water, for God's sake. We'll have someone out there later this morning to search for debris, but there were no survivors."

Strauss had come back from the base after dismissing his people. He was working on his report, getting his notes straight. There would be an in-depth debriefing later today or possibly tomorrow, of course, and he wanted to make certain that he had his facts straight. They all did.

Louk finally hung up the telephone and came over to where Avram was leaning against the chart table. "Well, I think there is going to be a very big stink about this. I can smell it coming all the way from Jerusalem."

"Your hands are clean," Avram said directly.

Louk didn't flinch. "I talked to Taber and the crew. They saw what happened. There wasn't a thing you or any of us could have done to prevent that ship going down. I've told them that in Tel Aviv and Jerusalem."

"Have we got a crew and passenger manifest yet?"

Louk nodded. "I've seen it. The only passengers were Fawzi and one personal bodyguard. The ship carried a crew of eight men including stewards, and four officers plus the captain. It could have been any of them. We just don't have enough to go on."

Or it could have been someone else, Avram thought. Someone picked up in Limassol.

"But they'll be investigated?"

"So far as we can," Louk said. "But I don't expect there'll be much cooperation from the Lebanese."

"It wasn't our fault, you said so yourself," Avram said, yet he knew that it was. There is a traitor in Israel.

"Doesn't matter," Louk said. "They won't be blaming themselves."

How galling it was, Avram found himself thinking in the middle of Louk's sentence, to think that someone was rutting among Israel's secrets. It was even more difficult to accept knowing that whoever it was, was an Israeli.

"Are you all right?" Louk was saying. He reached out for Avram's arm.

"I think so," Avram said, rubbing his eyes. The room was a little warm. It seemed like years since he had last slept. His head was thumping, and the pain in his arm wasn't very far away. A mild concussion, the doctor had told him, and advised to stay off his feet for the next couple of days. Not possible, doctor. Israel is sicker than I am just now.

"Zemil?"

"I'm fine," Avram said.

"Go back to your hotel and get some sleep. This post-mortem can wait a few hours . . ." Louk was interrupted by the young duty officer."

"Mr. Zemil, there's an incoming for you on an outside line. In the clear. I can't make it out."

Avram pushed away from the table, crossed the room, and took the phone from the young man. "Yes?" he said.

"Oh . . . Avram," Miriam wailed, her voice high-pitched, a keening cry as if she were in great pain.

Her voice was like a dash of cold water on Avram's face. His head cleared instantly. "Miriam? What's happened?"

"Avram . . . oh, God, I need you. . . ."

"Where are you? What's happened?"

"Home," she cried. "Can you come to me? Now?"

"I'm on my way," Avram said. "Just hang on, I'll be there in a few minutes."

"Please . . . hurry," she said, her voice suddenly sliding down the scale so that he could barely hear her. Then the connection was broken.

Avram crashed down the telephone, spun on his heel, and headed across the Operations Room. Louk intercepted him at the door.

"What's going on?" the Shin Beth officer asked.

"It's a friend," Avram said, the effort to remain calm taking everything within his power.

"Miriam Loeb?" Louk asked.

"What the hell do you know about her?" Avram said, stepping a little closer to the man, his jaw tight.

"It's my job, so don't go off half-cocked. Is there anything I can do?"

Avram hesitated a moment, then shook his head. "No," he said. "I'll be back as soon as possible. In the meantime Neumann is in charge of this station."

"Ben-Or is going to want to talk to you," Louk said.

"That's my problem," Avram said. He lowered his voice. "I wouldn't want to be followed."

Louk's eyes narrowed. "I'll stay out of your way, Zemil. It's not me you have to worry about."

"No," Avram said, and he turned and left the station.

Miriam's Apartment, 6:03 a.m.

The sun was just coming up, bathing Haifa in a golden glow, when Avram reached Bat Gallim and let himself into Miriam's apartment. He'd drawn his gun, slipped off the safety and cocked the hammer. It was hard just at that moment to think straight because of his injuries and the drug, but his reactions were automatic, his body poised like a hair trigger.

Miriam, hearing him in the entry hall, came around the corner from the bedroom. Avram raised the pistol and nearly squeezed off a shot before realizing that it was Miriam standing in front of him, her figure silhouetted in the light from the balcony windows. He staggered backward, diverting his arm, and finally lowered the pistol.

For several long seconds she just stood there looking at him. His knees were weak and his hand shook badly as he uncocked his gun and reholstered it.

"Are you all right?" he asked.

"Avram," she cried, and she came to him in a rush.

He took her in his arms and held her close. Her entire body was shaking. He could feel her heart thumping through the thin robe she was wearing.

"What happened here, Miriam?" he asked. "Why did you call?"

"They were *here*," she sobbed.

"Who?"

"I don't know. God, there were two of them. Wearing masks. It was terrible. But they were here."

Avram held her so that he could look into her face. Her eyes were red from crying, and her complexion blotchy, but she didn't seem to have been injured, though he could see that she had been deeply frightened. His chest was tight and there was a deep, terrible ache in his gut.

"What happened? How did they get in?"

"I don't know. I was in bed asleep, and suddenly they were in my room. One of them held a flashlight in my face while the other went through my things. They searched my apartment!" She shuddered.

"Then what happened?"

She opened her mouth to speak but no sound came out. Her eyes were suddenly wild. It seemed as if she wanted to bolt and run.

"What happened, Miriam? Did they touch you?"

"I didn't know what to do. They said they would kill me if I screamed.'

"They talked to you, in what language?"

"Hebrew. They were Jews, Avram. They were our people. They were Israelis."

"What did they want?"

"They asked me about you. They wanted to know if we were sleeping together. If you told me things in bed. If you talked in your sleep. They said . . . they said you were a traitor." A little sob escaped from the back of her throat. "They said Syria was your fault. They said there would be more trouble because of you. Oh God, Avram, what does it mean? What were they talking about?"

"What else did they say? What else did they do to you?" He could see in her eyes now that something else had happened here. Something terrible. "What happened, Miriam?"

"They pulled the covers away and . . . they tore off my nightgown." Her voice was cracking. She was at the edge of hysteria again. "Their hands were all over me."

A red haze seemed to fill Avram's sight. He drew her close. He didn't want to hear any more. He didn't know if he could handle it. Yet he knew that he must, for her sake as well as his own. He had to know everything, he had to know the truth.

"They called me a traitor's whore," Miriam choked.

"Did they rape you?"

"No," she said, her voice barely audible. "The one with the flashlight stopped him. But they said they would be watching me, no matter what I did, where I went, who I spoke to. The next time, they said, would be different unless I helped them."

"With what?"

"They wanted to know about you."

"What did you tell them?"

"Nothing. They said they would be back. They'd give me time to think about it and they would be back, and the next time I would help them or something would happen to me." She sighed deeply. "I'm so frightened, Avram."

They lay fully clothed in each other's arms in Miriam's bed. It was midmorning. Avram had listened to the sounds of the city and of the harbor outside her window. Somewhere a radio was playing music.

"I want you to leave Haifa," Avram said. "You can stay with your uncle in Tel Aviv. You'll be safe there."

"I don't want to leave you," she protested.

"You must, Miriam. You have to promise me."

She looked up into his eyes. "What's happening, Avram? Why are they after you?"

"There's a traitor in the government," Avram said softly.

"My God," Miriam breathed.

"I'm trying to stop him."

"Who is it?"

"I don't know," Avram said. He stroked her hair. "But there have been killings."

"The bazaar?" she asked, her eyes growing wide.

He nodded. "And last night there was another incident. It won't stop until I'm successful."

"Then I'll help you," she said bravely.

"No, I want you to go to your uncle."

She started to protest, but Avram touched a finger to her lips.

"You have to promise me that, and one other thing," he said.

She wanted to fight him, he could see it in her eyes. But she was deeply frightened by what had happened to her. She finally nodded.

"I want you to tell no one what happened tonight, or what I've just said to you. It's very important."

"But Uncle Arik . . ."

"No one," Avram insisted. "Our lives will depend on it."

She nodded again after a long hesitation, then lay back and closed her eyes.

10

The day was hot and bright beneath a cloudless sky as the ancient taxi rattled along the main highway from Larnaca in the east to Limassol on the south coast, a distance of a little more than forty miles. The interior of Cyprus was a broad treeless plain called Messaoria by the Greeks—literally "between the mountains." Far to the west Avram could see Mt. Troödos rising more than six thousand feet above the plain, and as they came down out of the rugged Olympus mountain range Limassol was spread out along the coast that formed Akrotiri Bay, with several oceangoing ships anchored just offshore and traffic on the highway picking up.

In Limassol, Gromit had told him before he died. Limassol, where they'd set out for the Syrian coast in Operation Brother, and where Fawzi's yacht had called in an effort to insulate his journey from Beirut to Haifa. But what was here?

Cyprus was still a divided island, with the north being held by the Turks and the south by the Greek-Cypriots. But the official language through-

out most of the island was still English. Limassol,
like any other port city in the world, was a conglomeration of import/export companies, ware-
houses and docks, and waterfront dives catering
to the seaman.

A deep-throated ship's whistle boomed across
the bay as the cabby dropped Avram off downtown on the city square a couple of blocks up from
the water's edge. He walked immediately to the
opposite side of the square and sat down at a sidewalk cafe, placing his overnight bag at his feet.
When the waiter came he ordered a light coffee,
and without appearing to do so studied the comings and goings of the traffic.

Whoever was here, he reasoned, would have an
organization of watchers. He'd not spotted anyone
obvious at the airport, and so far as he could tell
he had not been followed down here. But there
weren't many roads on the island, and even fewer
destinations. He had arrived in Larnaca and had
immediately left. It would have been a logical assumption on anyone's part where he had been
headed.

He was worried about Miriam. Last night had
shaken her badly. If she could hold herself together long enough to get up to her uncle's in Tel
Aviv, she would be all right. But she was a bright,
extremely curious woman who had all her life
been used to getting the answers she was seeking.
It's why he had told her as much as he had. If she
poked her nose into things this time, they would
kill her. Avram had little doubt of that. Just go to
Tel Aviv, he thought. Run, and stay with your uncle until it's over. Short of bringing her there himself there was little more he could do than hope.
It wasn't very comforting.

Ben-Or would be looking for him this morning,

and so would Geller. When he got back there would be trouble. But he had work to do.

He took his time with his coffee, watching for the odd face or the odd car that seemed out of place or regular movements. If the setup was sophisticated enough they would have one or two vehicles—perhaps a car and a truck, and possibly two or three legmen. But, if they were doing their job covering the square, or even providing coverage for an individual, their pattern would have to emerge.

But there was nothing that Avram could detect: no pattern, no watchers. He paid his bill and took his leather bag inside to the rest room where in a toilet stall he took out his gun and holster and strapped them to the small of his back beneath his coat. He'd had to show his police ID in Haifa and again in Larnaca so that his bag would not be searched or even scanned; otherwise he would not have been able to come across armed. His name and face would be noted at passport control in Haifa, his number flagged, and soon Ben-Or would know where he'd gotten himself to. But that would take time; in the meantime he was on his own, and armed.

Back outside, his bag slung over his shoulder, Avram recrossed the square and walked the two blocks down to the waterfront. In his records search he had come up with the name of a man here in Limassol who could possibly help him, for the right price. He was Thomas Jenkins, an expatriate Brit, former mercenary, sometime gun-runner and Mossad informant; and at other times an outrageous drunk who would sell his mother—if he ever had one—for the price of a bottle of cheap booze. Avram vaguely remembered dealing with him on some operation once years ago, so the name had jogged his memory.

Jenkins. If anyone would know something and would be willing to talk to him, it could very well be he.

Within a block of the waterfront the character of the city changed from that of an ancient seaport struggling to bring itself into modern age, to one of industrial and commercial squalor. Dirt and filth were everywhere; garbage was piled along the curbs and in dark alleys, and overall was the smell of the sea at low tide, of stack gases and bilge waste from the big ships, and greasy odors from the many hole-in-the-wall cafes and bars.

Jenkins owned a bar called the Bombay Palace across the street from the motor launch quay that brought crews from the big ships anchored out in the bay. He was a wiry little man in his mid-forties with hooded eyes and a weather-beaten face crisscrossed with broken veins of a man who has drunk too much for too long. He was seated alone at a small table near the back of the bar, drinking something out of a coffee mug. There were only a few sailors at the bar, and a couple of whores at one of the other tables. Avram went straight back to Jenkins, who looked up at him through bloodshot eyes and grinned cynically.

"Slumming this morning, what, mate?" Jenkins said, his accent definitely Cockney.

Avram sat down across from him. "Do you remember me, Tom?" he asked, keeping his voice low. No one was paying them the slightest attention.

Jenkins shrugged. "Never forget a face. What're you doing here?"

"Looking for a little information."

Jenkins held up a hand. "Nope. I'm out'a that

business now, God's honest truth I am. I got all I can handle right here."

"I'll pay well," Avram said, reaching in his coat for his wallet.

"No you won't, Zemil, 'cause I won't accept your Jew money. Like I said, I'm out of the business. For you, for anyone else who comes sniffing around here like some dog in heat."

Avram forced himself to relax. He withdrew his hand from his pocket and sat back easily in the chair. He smiled. "Someone else been here, Tom, is that what you're trying to tell me?"

"I'm not telling you nothing. Now if you don't mind, get your ass out of here. I'm busy."

"But I do mind. I've gone through a lot of trouble to get here. And I'm feeling a little mean." Avram smiled again, patting his side to indicate his gun. "You know how it is, Tom. There's nothing worse than a mean Jew on your ass."

Jenkins was unimpressed, though for the first time Avram could see that the man was hiding something. "For a fiver I could have two dozen men in here who'd be happy to take you apart, armed or not armed. Now why don't you just leave like a good little boy and tend to your own troubles."

"Who says I've got troubles?" Avram asked softly.

"Get out," Jenkins said, starting to move away from the table.

Avram sat forward and took out his gun, showing it briefly to Jenkins, who blanched, before he let it rest casually on his lap beneath the table, the barrel pointed at the Brit's midsection.

"I don't think too many tears would be shed at your funeral."

Jenkins glanced toward the bartender but made

no move to signal him. "In my own club," he said. "I am threatened in my own club."

"What was that about troubles?" Avram asked again.

Jenkins shrugged. "A man hears things."

"Such as?"

"A certain yacht was blown up and sunk last night just off your coast. A certain Lebanese gentleman of some importance was said to have been aboard. The Israeli government was to have provided protection. Most likely . . . so I have heard . . . it was Mossad who arranged his . . . accident. He was not a popular fellow."

Avram knew that he should not be surprised by the extent of the Brit's knowledge, yet he found that he was. The operation had been tight from their end. Where was the leak? If Jenkins knew about it already, who else knew?

"The yacht called here before crossing," Avram said.

Jenkins nodded casually. "I'd heard something about it."

"Was there an exchange of crew?"

Jenkins's eyes narrowed. "What?"

"Did anyone get on or off that yacht?"

"I don't know, mate."

Avram leaned forward a little.

"No, I swear it, Zemil. I don't know. I only know she came here for a couple of hours, refueled, and then departed. Whether or not she took on passengers I couldn't say."

"There was a bomb aboard. Any way for it to have been placed aboard here?"

Jenkins laughed. "Don't be a bloody fool. Of course there was a way. A dozen ways. Ten thousand ways. This is Cyprus."

"Tell me," Avram said.

"Tell you what?"

"A place, a name. Just one of the ways that bomb could have been taken aboard past their security."

"I don't want your money . . ."

"But you do want your life, don't you, Tom?"

"Christ," Jenkins swore. "It didn't have to go aboard, now did it?"

"The ship blew up in the water. I was there. I saw it. There were at least three explosions. Lifted the entire ship half out of the water. Broke her back. These weren't missiles."

"You're not very smart, Zemil. Magnetic mines. A frogman could have swum them over. Attached them to the outside of the hull. One by the stern, one amidship, perhaps one in the bow. They wouldn't have had a chance."

"Is that what you think?" Avram asked. It was logical. It explained why the explosions were so effective. They'd probably ripped the entire bottom out of the big ship, broke her back. And just now such Soviet-made devices were easy to come by; probably through Syria, or possibly Iran for the right price.

"It's possible," Jenkins said.

"The frogman?"

Jenkins hesitated a beat. "There are many . . ."

"I'm interested in only one name."

"I can't give it to you, because I simply don't know it. Could have been any one of five or six ex–Royal Navy. They all hang out at the British Club."

"The golf club?" Avram asked. He knew the place. Years ago it had been exclusive.

"The Annex over at Episkopi. They took the overflow. Shall we say, the less than acceptable crowd?"

"Who do I ask for?"

"Charlie Nobel," Jenkins said, and Avram got the impression that the Brit was either lying or had just made up the name off the top of his head. It wouldn't take very long to find out. And if Jenkins was lying about this one thing, there had to be a reason.

"One last thing, Tom," Avram said. "I was aboard that boat. They were all dead. Shot to death. All but one of them, that is."

Jenkins said nothing.

"Any thoughts on that score?"

"What happened to the live one?"

"Went down with the ship, unfortunately."

"He was a fanatic, then. Probably a Shi'ite, maybe Druse. They're all crazy over there."

"Just like us Jews?" Avram asked.

"I didn't say that."

Avram got to his feet, holstering his gun as he rose. "I'm going down to Episkopi. I hope you weren't lying to me about anything, Tom. I do hate being lied to, old chap."

"Don't come back," Jenkins said, his eyes narrowed.

"No," Avram said softly. "You wouldn't want to see me back here. Believe me."

Haifa, 11:40 a.m.

Miriam Loeb parked her bright red Fiat convertible in the loading section in front of Haifa's small airport terminal, her Television One press pass on the dash, and went inside. After Avram had left her she had cleaned up and a half hour later telephoned the Mossad station and asked for him. She'd gotten someone named Neumann on the phone who hadn't wanted to tell her a thing. Finally, however, using Ben-Or's name she had gotten the information that Avram had not shown up, and that in fact at that moment no one knew where he was. A couple of telephone calls later and she'd found out that his car was parked at the airport. She'd not been able to get anything else out of her police contact so she'd come here in person. She'd spotted his car as soon as she drove in.

She crossed through the arrivals and departures lounge to the airport authority administration offices and walked past a flustered secretary into the office of Maurice Shapiro, the airport manager. Shapiro had been an air force buddy of her husband's. They went way back together. He was on the telephone when she barged in.

"Looks like I have company," he said into the phone. "I'll call you back later." He hung up.

"Hullo, Maurice," she said, slumping into a chair across the desk from him.

His secretary appeared at the doorway but he waved her back. "It's all right, Ruth, she's a friend." He was a well-built, dark-complected man about Avram's age. He was married and had four children. He'd made a play for Miriam years ago. "Somehow I don't think this is a social call, Miriam."

She couldn't get last night out of her mind: waking up and seeing the two men standing over her, going through her things, their voices boring into her skull, their hands all over her body. She shuddered.

Shapiro sat forward, sudden concern on his face. "What is it?" he asked. "What's wrong?"

"I need some help, Maurice," she said, trying to control the sudden constriction in her throat.

"Are you in trouble? Has something happened?"

"Do you know Avram Zemil?"

Shapiro's eyes narrowed a little. He nodded. "I've heard of him."

"He flew out of here this morning. I have to know where he went."

"I can't do that, Miriam. You know that."

"I have to know!" she said firmly, sitting up. "This is important or I wouldn't ask. You can't believe how important."

Shapiro studied her for a long moment. He was obviously moved by her outburst, and yet he was a man of regulations. "Is this for Television One, or is it a personal request?"

"For me, not the station."

"Why? What's this all about? Are you or he in some trouble?"

Miriam shook her head. "I can't tell you, Maurice. I just have to know where he went. No one will know who I got it from. I swear to God."

Still Shapiro was torn, but after a moment he picked up his phone, dialed a number and then turned his back on Miriam. He said something into the phone that she couldn't quite make out, and after a half a minute he said something else, then swiveled back and hung up the phone, an odd expression on his face.

"Larnaca," he said.

"Cyprus?" she asked in amazement.

"Yes. He left on the ten-fifteen. But there's something you're not telling me. He went through passport control on a police ID. It's my guess he was armed. His passport was flagged, Miriam," Shapiro continued. "Which means I'm going to have to report your query. Now, do you want to tell me what you've gotten yourself involved with before the shit hits the fan?"

"I can't, Maurice," she said, getting up. "Thanks for your help."

EPISKOPI, CYPRUS, 12:12 P.M.

The British Club Annex was housed in a big old barn of a house overlooking the sea. Fifty years ago it had probably been beautiful, but there was a ramshackle, unkempt air about it now. Sooner or later it would have to give way to a fine tourist hotel; the property was just too valuable to continue as it was.

There were only a few cars parked in the lot when Avram's cab pulled up under the canopy at the main entrance. "Wait here for me, I'll only be a few minutes."

"Of course, sir," the cabby said, pushing his hat down over his eyes and lying back.

Just inside, a large stairhall led straight back to the kitchen. To the left was a clubroom and to the right, the bar. No one was on duty at the reception desk. Plaster was cracked, paint chipped and peeling, and someone had tracked sand up the shabby carpet on the stairs. A couple of men were seated at the bar nursing drinks when Avram walked in and sat down.

The bartender, a barrel-chested monster of a man with huge arms, came over. "You a member?" he growled. "Ain't seen your face in here before."

"No, I'm not," Avram said. "I just dropped by to see a man recommended to me. I've got a little job of work for him."

The bartender looked at him appraisingly. "What's this man's name?"

"Charlie Nobel."

One of the men at the end of the bar snickered, but said nothing. The bartender was impassive.

"What do you want him for?" the big man asked.

"Is he here today?"

"That depends now, don't it?" the barman said. There was something wrong, Avram could feel it now. Jenkins had either sent him on a wild goose chase, or had set him up. Either way it meant the man did know something after all. If he had to take Jenkins apart to find out whatever it was he was hiding, he decided he was going to do it with pleasure.

"Maybe I've been sent to the wrong place." Avram said, getting off the barstool and stepping away from the bar.

"Maybe you have," the barman said, and he started to reach beneath the bar to his left.

Avram pulled out his gun. "Hands on the bar or I'll blow your head off," he said in a reasonable tone.

The bartender stiffened.

"Now," Avram said.

The big man complied, his jaw tight, the muscles in his arms rippling.

"Did Jenkins call you?"

The barman said nothing.

Avram raised the SigSauer a little higher and cocked the hammer, the noise loud in the quiet barroom. "I asked if Tom Jenkins called you."

The bartender nodded. "Get out of here while you still can."

"Who is Charlie Nobel?" Avram asked. "Where can I find him?"

The other two at the end of the bar were looking at him. "Charlie Nobel's not a he, it's an it," one of them said. "It's a bleedin' chimney on a small boat."

"Now get the hell out of here," the bartender said.

The question was, whom did Jenkins work for? Someone had paid him off. Someone who'd known that Avram would be coming to Limassol. Palmyra?

He backed away, keeping his eye on the bartender until he cleared the doorway back into the stairhall, then he turned, and stuffed the gun in his holster hurried outside. The cabby was still laying back, the hat over his eyes, when Avram climbed in the back seat.

"Back to Limassol," Avram said.

The cabby sat up and turned around, a big pistol in his right hand. He wasn't the same one who'd driven out here. The other one had been old, his face lined, half his teeth missing. This one was much younger, his complexion olive, his eyes dark.

"So what happens next?" Avram asked, gauging the distance, and his chances.

"Time for you to die," someone said in Hebrew at the open window to his left. He turned to look into the barrel of another pistol. This man was a little older than the driver, but he had the same olive complexion and dark eyes. They both wore dark watch caps and the rough clothes of a Cypriot peasant. There was something about him, something about the driver, too, that seemed somehow vaguely familiar to Avram. He'd seen these people before.

The second man climbed in the front seat next to the driver and held the gun in a steady hand directly at Avram's chest. "Get us out of here before someone comes, Jacob," he said to the driver. "I want to get this over with."

"Who sent you, the Russians?" Avram asked.

"Shut up," the gunman hissed. "Traitor!"

They pulled out of the driveway and sped down toward the highway that led back to Limassol to the right, and to the left back up into the cliffs along the southwestern coast.

"What are you talking about?" Avram said.

"Keep still, or I will kill you here and now."

"If you know who I am, then you obviously know that I'm no traitor to Israel."

"Enough of your lies," the gunman roared. "God in heaven, I won't hear more of it!"

"You say in God's name. Then in God's name if I'm to die, tell me why."

The gunman was becoming so agitated that spittle was beginning to form on his lips as his mouth worked to form words adequate enough to express his apparent hatred. The driver was getting worked up as well. It didn't make any sense to Avram. They were fanatics, and yet at first they had come on like professionals. The two were usually mutually exclusive. Professionals were almost always calm about their work. It was an opening, though.

"I deserve that much."

"Shut him up!" the driver shouted.

"At least that much," Avram pleaded. "I'm begging you in God's name for mercy."

"Nooo . . . !" the driver screamed. At that moment the gunman glanced over at the driver. It was the opening Avram needed.

He lunged forward, grabbing the gun with his left hand and a handful of the gunman's coat with his right, hauling the man bodily over the seat.

The car shot left out onto the highway, skidding nearly out of control toward the edge of the cliff that plunged more than five hundred feet down to the sea and rocks before the driver managed to regain temporary control.

"Traitor!" the gunman bellowed shoving Avram hard against the door; a tremendous bolt of pain shooting through his wounded arm, making him see spots before his eyes for a moment.

He managed to shove the gunman off him against the opposite door which popped open, throwing the man half in and half out of the car.

Avram grabbed the front of his jacket and tried to haul him back inside, but he was like a crazy man, kicking and screaming and struggling to get free.

"Stop!" Avram shouted, blocking most of the blows with his body. "Stop the car!"

The cab suddenly surged forward and swung sharply to the left. Avram looked up over the edge of the seat in time to see that they were heading directly for the edge of the cliff. He shoved the gunman out of the car, rolling out the open door right after the man, his shoulder bag catching momentarily on the window crank and nearly pulling him under the wheels.

But then he was tumbling end over end, his head and wounded shoulder banging against the pavement. Somewhere in the distance he heard a tremendous crash as the cab struck the barrier at the edge of the highway and arched out into space, the engine suddenly racing.

Seconds later another crash came from far below, then a second and a third as the cab careened off the rocks at the bottom.

Avram had ended up in a heap at the side of the road. He knew he could not stay here like this.

Someone was bound to be coming very soon. He had to get away fast.

He picked himself up gingerly. The pain in his arm was deep and throbbing, making his left hand all but useless, but he'd suffered no broken bones, only a few cuts and bruises.

At the edge of the cliff he looked down. What remained of the cab was scattered over the rocks and in the sea. No one could have lived through it.

About thirty yards back he found his shoulder bag, the strap broken, and twenty yards farther, curled up in a ditch against a rock, the side of his skull crushed, the gunman. Working as quickly as he could, Avram found the dead man's wallet and opened it. He carried a little money and an Israeli driver's license. In another pocket Avram found his passport. His name had been David Solomon, with an address in Jerusalem. In a left pocket he found a room key for the Pavemar Hotel in Limassol. These two had been waiting for him. They'd been sent here knowing that sooner or later Avram would be showing up. And when he did they had orders to kill him.

They were Jews, and yet they had called him a traitor. Why?

Avram brushed off his clothes as best he could and stepped back up on the road. The body was all but invisible to anyone in a passing car. Nor was there any debris on the road, or where the cab had crashed through the barrier. It might take some time before the accident was spotted and reported to the police.

Time, he only needed a little time, he thought as he limped down the highway toward Episkopi where he figured he would be able to find a cab back to Limassol.

Thomas Jenkins had some explaining to do. This time he wouldn't be able to lie.

LIMASSOL, 3:48 P.M.

Thomas Jenkins lay slumped over his desk in a back room of the Bombay Palace, his face in a big pool of blood. He'd been shot in the side of the head at close range with a large-caliber handgun.

Avram stood just within the doorway, hesitating with indecision for just a moment. The front door of the club was unlocked, yet when he'd let himself in there had been no one on either side of the bar. The place was deserted.

This was a setup. He wanted to stay to look through Jenkins's office, but he knew he had just run out of time. Completely. In any event, he figured, turning and starting back to the front of the club, whoever had killed the Brit had probably known what to look for and had already taken it. If there had been anything in the first place.

Limassol had been a complete setup from beginning to end. Three men dead now, and for what? What had he gained? Nothing more than the name of an Israeli gunman who thought he'd been sent to eliminate a traitor.

Trust no one, the prime minister had told him. But Benjamin Strauss had been pulled into it, at least partially. And so had Miriam. Who to trust? Who not to trust?

He was halfway across the barroom when the front door crashed open and half-a-dozen Cypriot policemen, all armed with MAC 10 submachine guns, burst in shouting at him.

11

THE INTERROGATION ROOM WAS SMALL and, except for a small square of glass in the door, windowless. A naked light bulb dangled from the stone ceiling over a steel table and two chairs. Avram, his back to the door, sat across from a tiny, intense-looking Greek-Cypriot who had identified himself as Lieutenant of Detectives Ándros Filiátes. They'd been together now for the better part of ten hours, the Greek drinking tea all the time without ever once getting up to relieve himself.

"Shall we begin again, Mr. Zemil?" the detective said pleasantly. They spoke in English. Throughout it all the detective had maintained a friendly, if firm, attitude. But Avram could feel that this was about to change. It was something in the man's eyes, in the set of his shoulders.

"I'm thirsty and hungry and very tired . . ."

"Yes, I know all that. In addition, it would seem you need some medical attention."

"I slipped and fell. A slight accident."

"But first there is the troubling matter of your

identification." Filiátes glanced down at the blank
pad of paper in front of him. "You tell me that
you are not a Mossad agent—though heaven
knows what a spy would be doing here on my
island—yet your name is unknown to me. It is not
on the rosters of my brother police officers in Israel. Shin Beth perhaps? But then you wouldn't
be here. Puzzling."

"I've recently been discharged from the army.
My assignment to Haifa has come within the last
month."

"I commend you on your promotion, sir, but
alas, I don't believe your story." The Greek shook
his head as if he were actually sorry. "Tell me
again, then, why you brought a weapon here to
Cyprus."

"We suspected that Jenkins was smuggling
arms from Israel into Lebanon."

"Through Limassol?"

"Yes."

"Then why wasn't my office informed of this,
please, sir?" Filiátes asked. "That would be the
normal procedure. Cooperation. Hands across the
sea."

"Because I wasn't certain of my source. I
wanted to look him over first."

"Very dangerous."

Avram shrugged.

"So you walked into his office only to find him
dead?"

"That's right."

The Greek nodded sadly. "Then tell me, what
did you two discuss earlier in the day? You were
seen speaking with him."

This was something new. The Greek hadn't mentioned that bit of information before. "I asked him

a couple of questions, but he refused to cooperate."

"So you left?"

Avram nodded.

Again the Greek nodded sadly. "You carry an exotic weapon. German-made. A SigSauer. Poor Mr. Jenkins was killed with such a weapon."

"Mine has not been fired."

"Determining such a thing is, as you well know, a very inexact science. Your weapon has been fired within the last twenty-four hours." Filiátes looked up. "And now I think I would like to begin hearing the truth from you. Why did you kill Thomas Jenkins?"

"I didn't," Avram said tiredly. "I found him that way." Evidently the wreck outside of Episkopi had not yet been found; either that or it hadn't been connected to him. Or at least he hoped it hadn't and the Greek was merely holding back that information for the moment. He wasn't particularly worried about being linked with Jenkins's murder; ballistics was in some respects an inexact science, but even an amateur with a cheap microscope would be able to see the differences in rifling marks between a bullet fired from his gun and one fired from another SigSauer.

"But I believe you did. And I believe it has something very definite to do with the unfortunate death of Youssef Fawzi at sea. Poor Mr. Jenkins, as you undoubtedly know, was a guest aboard that yacht hours before she was blown out of the water."

Avram fought to keep any sort of reaction off his face.

"You Israelis," the Greek said. "So many troubles. First Syria, then Fawzi, and just hours ago, from what I'm told, two of your people were ar-

rested in New York City, at the United Nations of
all places, for spying. I trust your prime minister
will soon find himself in retirement. Too bad, he
was a good and just man." The detective held his
hands apart. "But then, this is a terrible world we
live in."

"I would like to see a representative of my government," Avram said, forcing more calmness into
his voice than he felt. At least one key to the puzzle had finally fallen into place for hm. Their traitor definitely worked with someone else, someone
very well organized—which of course pointed to
the KGB agent Palmyra—and together they were
working for nothing less than the downfall of Ezra
Harel and possibly the entire government. At this
point it looked as if they were doing a good job of
it. Everything he had done, every move he had
made had been thwarted.

Filiátes glanced past Avram and nodded. "As it
happens, someone from your government is here,
with protests. Perhaps too loud, too special."

"Then I demand to see him. Immediately."

"Her," the Greek corrected absently. "But need
I remind you, sir, that you are in no position to
make any demands? You are a foreigner on Cypriot soil. Armed, in contravention of our laws. At
the very least you are a Zionist spy, and most
likely a murderer. I may keep you indefinitely. Or,
you might be shot trying to escape. Believe me,
Mr. Zemil, when I tell you that without cooperation your life is forfeit."

"My government would take a dim view of anything happening to me at your hands . . ."

The detective slapped his open palm on the
tabletop, the noise like a pistol shot in the close
confines of the little room. "My government takes
an exceedingly dim view of aggressive acts against

it. Who knows, you may even be working for the northern Turks. Stranger things have happened here."

As long as someone, probably from the embassy, knew he was here, nothing would happen to him. "My people will identify me as a police officer."

"Lies!" Filiátes shouted. He was becoming extremely agitated.

"I've killed no one on this island."

"Lies," the Greek shouted again. He pushed himself abruptly away from the table, knocking his chair over, and with shaking hands, his face red with rage, he fumbled his pistol out of its holster at his side, cocked the hammer, and leaning across the table placed the barrel of the gun in the middle of Avram's forehead. "The truth," he screeched. "I will have the truth from you, or so help me God I will scatter your Zionist brains all over this cell."

"I did not kill Thomas Jenkins, though I would have had I gotten to him first," Avram said, very careful to keep his voice at an even level. There was no telling what the Greek was capable of doing in his present state.

"Why? Why did you want to kill him?"

"Because we believe he was responsible at least in part for the sabotage of Youssef Fawzi's yacht," Avram admitted, tempering the larger lie with a small truth.

"Then who killed him, if not you?" the detective asked, his rage subsiding.

"I don't know. But a man in his position has many enemies."

Filiátes laughed once, the sound harsh and sharp like a dog barking. He stepped back suddenly, uncocked his pistol and holstered it. "When will you Israelis ever learn that Cyprus is not your play toy? We are not all fools here." He took a pen from his breast pocket and a printed form from the file folder on the table and handed them to Avram. "This says that you will never again set foot on Cyprus soil," he said. "Sign it."

Avram did so. The Greek didn't care about Jenkins, he'd only wanted to catch a Mossad spy redhanded.

The Greek whisked the paper away and shoved another form across. He was smiling again. "This says that you were not harmed or subjected to harsh treatment here. Sign it."

Avram signed it as well.

Filiátes snatched the paper, the file folder, and his blank tablet from the table and strode across the room, where he flung open the door and stepped aside. "You are free to go, Mr. Zemil. Your Tel Aviv flight leaves from Larnaca at six sharp. If you are still on Cyprus when it leaves, you will be arrested and executed for the spy you are."

Avram got up from the chair and passed swiftly out into the corridor and down the way he had come this afternoon. The placed reeked of sweat and urine and feces, and fear. He had no doubt that if he remained on Cyprus or came back any time soon, Filiátes would make good his threat.

Miriam Loeb was waiting in the outer hall. When she spotted him coming around the corner she jumped up from the bench where she had been sitting. She had his jacket and overnight bag. She looked all in. Obviously she'd been waiting a long time.

"Mr. Zemil," she said formally, crossing to him and extending her hand. "I'm Miriam Loeb. When we heard that you'd been arrested, the embassy

sent me." He could see the hurt and the fear in
her eyes, along with the warning that they could
not speak openly.

"Thanks, you don't know how surprised I am to
see you."

"Are you all right? Have you been harmed in
any way? We were told you might need some medical attention."

"I'm fine," Avram said. "I was told there was a
flight out of Larnaca?"

"Yes, back to Tel Aviv. I will be returning with
you. Transportation to the airport has been provided for us."

"Have you got my things?"

She nodded. "In the bag."

"All my things?" he asked pointedly.

"Everything is here, Mr. Zemil," she said. "Now
if you will just come with me?"

ABOARD THE EL AL JETLINER, 6:07 A.M.

"What the hell were you doing in Cyprus?"
Avram asked, careful to keep his voice low. The
DC-8 was barely half full. He and Miriam were
seated alone near the back.

"I found out that you'd flown out," she said. The
was the first they'd felt able to talk since she'd
picked him up at the police barracks.

"How?" he shot back.

"I have my contacts," she said defensively.

For the last twenty-four hours Avram had been
operating mostly on adrenaline. It was beginning
to run out; he was crashing and he knew it.

"This is very important, Miriam," he said. "I

have to know how you traced me to the police at Cyprus."

"You're hurt . . ." she started to say, but he cut her off savagely.

"Damn you, I asked a question!"

She reared back as if she had been slapped. Her eyes moistened. "I called your office and got them to tell me that you weren't in, and in fact no one knew where you were."

"Of all the stupid things . . . What next?"

"I have a friend on the police force. Traffic Control. I asked them to look for your car. That took a bit of doing, but I found out that it was parked at the airport."

"So you drove out to the airport and checked with another of your contacts who told you, just like that, that I'd taken a flight to Larnaca."

She nodded.

"Who was it?"

"I can't tell you that, Avram," she said.

"You're going to have to, Miriam. Sooner or later you're going to have to. My life, your life depends on it."

She told him, including the fact that Shapiro had intended to report her query. "So I called Uncle Arik."

Avram realized he had been holding his breath. He let it out with a deep sigh as he lay his head back, "And told him what?"

"That I was worried about you. That no one knew where you had gone, except for me. That two men came to my apartment in the night. That I thought . . . that I was frightened."

"Then?"

"Uncle Arik found out that you had been arrested so he sent me to get you."

"Just like that he sends his niece, a television

journalist, to a foreign country to bail out a man accused of being a spy and a murderer." He opened his eyes and looked at her. "Miriam, that just doesn't make sense. What is it you're not telling me? What else did you tell him?"

She had turned away and she was looking out the window at the clouds below. "There is something you don't know about me, Avram. Something I never told you. Uncle Arik never told you either. We both thought it for the best."

Avram held his silence; he was beyond surprise.

She turned back to him. "I've worked for my uncle for ten years now."

"What is that supposed to mean?"

"That I'm a Mossad operative. That I know who and what my uncle really is. That I know who and what you are and have know it from the beginning."

"Do you carry a gun? Have you been trained? Have you . . ." Avram could hear the harshness in his voice, and he didn't really know why he was reacting this way. Yet he felt hurt, in a small measure betrayed.

Miriam's nostrils flared. "I don't do that kind of work."

"But you have a gun, you've been to school?"

"Yes" she said. "I have a gun. I know how to use it. Does that make me less of a woman in your eyes, Avram? Is that it?"

He lay back again without answering her. He didn't know what he felt now. Fatigue. Pain. Fear, he supposed. Uncertainty about the future. A mixed bag of feelings. Ben-Or was going to have to be brought into this investigation. He would make the prime minister see the necessity of it.

"Why did you go to Cyprus, Avram? What was there, your traitor?"

"No one," he said. "I was mistaken."

"Who was murdered? They never told me."

"No one of importance."

"Did you kill him?"

"No."

Miriam was silent for a minute or so, leaving Avram to his own thoughts. His head was spinning. He wanted nothing more than to lie down somewhere and sleep for a very long time. Sleep. Rest. Peace.

"I'm not going to be able to help unless you trust me, darling," Miriam said from a distance.

He looked at her. "I don't want your help."

"The other night—"

"Forget it," he snapped. "Forget everything I told you." He softened. "Listen to me, Miriam. I told you then, and I'm telling you now, your life, my life depends on you keeping out of it. You may have already caused irreparable damage by going to your uncle, and by coming to Cyprus."

"What were we supposed to do, let you rot in that prison?" she flared.

"Leave it alone. Get out of Haifa. Stay with friends or with your uncle, but leave it be."

"Don't you think I deserve an explanation after . . . after what happened the other night? They said they would be back."

"Go to your uncle," Avram said. "I won't be long. I promise you."

TEL AVIV, 8:15 A.M.

They took a cab into the city without saying too much to each other. She dropped him on Yafo, just around the corner from the Mossad's headquarters in the Land Registration Annex and left with nothing settled between them and no plans to see each other later in the day.

Avram stood on the street corner, the morning traffic thick, and watched until the cab had disappeared around the corner. He loved her. There was no question about that in his mind. But just now he was deeply frightened because of her, and because of the thoughts he had harbored very deep in the back of his brain. Thoughts that refused to be buried any longer. Miriam knew too much; some of it he had told her, some of it she had guessed, but she knew even more. How? God in heaven, was it thinkable? With her access to him as well as her uncle, practically all of Israel's secrets were hers for the asking.

He shuddered at the thought, then turned and walked around the corner and into the courtyard where he entered the annex, leaving his bag and gun at security before taking the elevator up to the third floor.

A stern-faced Yoram Geller was waiting for him when the elevator doors opened. "He and Alex are waiting for us in the briefing room."

"Right," Avram said tiredly. He'd wanted to get up to Jerusalem to see the prime minister first, but the urgent message to come here had been waiting at the airport.

"Before we go in, have you anything to say to me?" Geller asked pointedly. "Anything I should know?"

"Fawzi's yacht called at Limassol before crossing. I got a tip that Thomas Jenkins might have been involved somehow, so I went to see him."

Geller's right eyebrow rose. "He's the one you've been accused of murdering?"

"Yes, but it wasn't me. By the time I got to him he was dead."

"Who killed him?"

"I don't know, Yoram. Whoever set the bombs aboard Fawzi's yacht, I suppose."

"Shi'ites?"

"It's possible."

Geller looked at him. "Why didn't you call me first? Tell me what you were up to."

"I didn't know where you were. And in any event I thought time was more important."

Geller nodded. "Well, you were wrong again. But I don't care, because you're no longer my problem."

"What's that supposed to mean?"

"I'll let Ben-Or tell you since you're such close family friends."

Geller turned and hurried down the corridor to the briefing room, where he knocked once. Avram followed him inside, the door automatically locking behind them. Ben-Or, his mane of white hair in disarray, was seated at the conference table next to his chief of staff, Alex Paderewski.

"Are you all right?" Ben-Or asked without preamble.

Avram nodded. "Yes, sir."

Geller took his place at the table, but Avram was not invited to sit.

"The Cypriot ambassador has already telephoned this morning. The prime minister telephoned me wanting to know what was going on." Ben-Or shook his head. "What *is* going on, Avram?"

Avram told him the same thing he'd told Geller in the corridor, leaving out the business at Episkopi and the two dead Jews who had been sent to kill him.

"So you found out nothing?" Ben-Or asked harshly.

"No, sir."

"Nor did you inform anyone where you were going?"

"No, sir."

"I see," Ben-Or said with a sigh. He sat back.

"Who was your interrogator at the police barracks?" Paderewski asked.

Avram told him.

Paderewski glanced at Ben-Or. "He's a tough one," he said and turned back to Avram. "Is that where you got those?" he asked, indicating the large bruises that had formed on Avram's forehead and the side of his face, and his generally disheveled appearance.

Avram nodded. He was a little disappointed in Ben-Or. He knew something like this would happen, but he'd thought the old man would have given him the benefit of the doubt and talked to him first in private.

"Do you want to lodge a formal complaint against the Cypriot police?" Geller asked.

"Under the circumstances, no," Avram said.

"What circumstances?" Paderewski queried.

"They've got a dead body on their hands, and no killer. I think we should let well enough alone. For the moment."

"I agree," Ben-Or said. "Was Filiátes aware the you are a Mossad operative?"

"He accused me of it."

"Then he knows," Paderewski said.

"Probably," Ben-Or agreed. "What about our people in place over there?"

"They'll have to be warned, or course," Paderewski said. "I don't think we'll have too many worries about Nicosia; there still isn't much cooperation between the Turks and the Greeks. But Larnaca will be difficult for a while, especially if Filiátes goes on the warpath." Paderewski was a transplant from a little town in South Dakota. It had been a lot of years since he'd left there, but he still occasionally spoke in quaint little western-isms that somehow managed to creep even into his Hebrew.

"You have caused a lot of trouble, Avram," Ben-Or said without malice. "I'm pulling you out of Haifa and bringing you here for the time being. You'll go back on the Syrian desk, I think."

"Yes, sir," Avram said glumly. It was worse than he expected, but he wasn't really surprised.

"Take a day or two sick leave to get yourself back in shape, and then when you get back I'll want a complete written report, as well as two letters of apology."

"Sir?"

"One to the government of Cyprus, and the other to Yoram and his Haifa staff."

Geller was clearly gloating, even though he was trying to hide the triumphant look on his face. Even that didn't seem to matter to Avram.

"Yes, sir," he said. "I'll have it all on your desk in the morning."

JERUSALEM, 1:20 P.M.

Avram had taken the slow train up from Tel Aviv and had gone directly to his apartment just out-side the Walled City's Jewish Quarter, where he cleaned up and changed clothes. His body was a mass of scrapes and bruises and it hurt when he breathed deeply. At the very least he figured he had cracked a couple of ribs in the fall from the car. He wrapped the tape around his chest, which made the pain bearable, then telephoned the prime minister's office, getting his adviser, David Sokoloff.

"I'd like to see the prime minister sometime this afternoon if that's possible," Avram said.

"He was just about to telephone you, Mr. Zemil. Can you come now? Are you here in Jerusalem?"

"Yes. I can be there in ten minutes."

The day was a little hazy and not overly warm, but Avram found that he was sweating in the cab on the way to the prime minister's office. He had no idea what he was going to tell Harel, except that a lot of people had already died; and the only thing he had learned was that in truth there was a traitor in either the Mossad or the government, and that their traitor was working for a certain KGB agent code-named Palmyra.

"You never listen," his father once told him. He couldn't recall the occasion just now, except that he was young, and that he was being punished for something. "You're headstrong. You don't believe that anyone is smarter than you. Well, you're wrong, and you're going to find it out the hard way one day."

But if he was wrong, his father had been wrong too. Because he'd always looked up to the old man with respect, a certain amount of fear, and even a little awe. Everyone had looked at his father that way. "Large boots to fill," Ben-Or had told him at his father's funeral. Perhaps impossible, he thought.

He was shown straight in to Harel and they were left alone. As in the Mossad briefing room, he was not invited to sit down. Unlike Tel Aviv he was not asked for any explanation.

"I have made a mistake, Avram," the prime minister began.

"Sir?"

"I am relieving you of your obligation. The search, for you, is over."

This Avram had not expected. He was stunned.

"I can only give you my thanks for what you have tried to do for me, for your country, and ask that you never tell what happened here to anyone, under any circumstances. Do you understand?"

"Yes, sir," Avram mumbled.

"I'm sorry, Avram," the prime minister said heavily. "Truly sorry."

"I could work with whomever else you have picked for the job."

The prime minister looked at Avram for a long time. "No," he said finally. "There is no one else. It has all been a tragic mistake." Harel glanced down at the papers spread out on his desk. "Now if you will excuse me, Avram, I have much work to do."

The prime minister stared at the closed door after Avram Zemil left, and sighed deeply for everything that had happened since he'd taken office, for everything he'd had to do in the name of Israel, and for what certainly was yet to come.

Another door opened and he looked up into the face of the one man in all of Israel he trusted implicitly, and he saw the sadness and weight there, too.

"You had no choice, Ezra," the man said. "It must be done this way."

"No choice," Harel said. But God help them all if he was wrong.

12

TEL AMAL DISTRICT OF HAIFA, 10:00 P.M.

BENJAMIN STRAUSS WAS AN HONEST MAN
who believed with all his soul in the idea of Israel.
He personally had no relatives who had died in
the Nazi concentration camps, but he knew many
people who had. The State of Israel guaranteed
that such a thing would never happen again. Come
to Israel and be safe. The Diaspora is over. Israel
was home.

But Benjamin Strauss was also a pragmatist. He
had worked the streets of New York City as a cop
until emigrating eight years ago. He knew that
even the most noble of ideals could go seriously
awry if they involved human beings.

Sitting in his dark car smoking a cigarette,
Strauss had been watching both the entrance to
the bazaar half a block away and the entrance to
the alley leading to Yakof Gromit's home and
business, sealed now by the yellow crime-site rib-
bons placed by the Haifa Civil Police. So far as he
had been able to determine, however, the police
had done nothing here except remove the bodies.

No one had come to look through Gromit's papers, nor had anyone even come to dust the place for fingerprints. The investigation, he had learned, was at the moment proceeding at the diplomatic level.

"Best to keep your nose out of it, Benjamin," his friend Moshe Cantor told him over supper three hours ago. Moshe was a desk sergeant with the Haifa police. He'd been Strauss's first friend here in Israel. They shared the common bond of police work.

"I was just curious," Strauss said. "I worry about things like that, you know me. Innocent people killed. Murderers allowed to run free. They were Russians, two of those bodies, you have confirmed that?"

Cantor shrugged. He was a big, raw-boned man, even larger than Strauss. Nearly a *sabra*. His father and mother had come from Europe after the war with him still in diapers. They'd been on the *Motorvessel Exodus*. "No one's saying. The Poles are denying them, of course, but with the weapons they had . . . I'd say it would be a safe guess that they were Russians. Spies, Benjamin, that's your line. Is that why you're so interested? Have you gone over to the bad boys of the Shin Beth?"

"Nothing so dramatic as that, Moshe," Strauss had said, without really answering his friend's question. But that's how they talked to each other. In their oblique way they had aided each other's work from time to time. Theirs was a comfortable, no-strings-attached relationship.

"The house itself is sealed, of course, until whatever has to be worked out, is worked out—up in Jerusalem. You have any contacts up there?"

"A few. If I hear anything I'll pass it along."

"Ah, Benjamin," Cantor had said, sitting back

with his after-dinner drink and sighing. "This certainly is no land of milk and honey, but it's worth fighting for, wouldn't you say?"

"To the death," Strauss said. "No question of it."

Land of milk and honey or not, something was now manufacturing a terrific stench of death and decay. From all accounts the rescue mission to the Syrian desert had been tight, and yet it had gone awry. Someone had blown it. Just as someone had blown the Fawzi operation. In both cases Avram Zemil had been involved, as he had been involved here with Gromit the night of the killings. Someone was trying to set Zemil up, and Strauss thought he had a fair idea of who it was. He needed proof, though, before he could act. Whatever Zemil had been looking for here that night could still be in place.

Finishing his cigarette, Strauss flipped it out the window, then got out of the car and crossed the street. Just now there wasn't much traffic here or within the bazaar. After the shooting the Arab community had been quiet. So far there had been no reprisals or demonstrations, in part, he supposed, because no one knew whom to blame, and partly because of the savagery of the attack. Innocent women and children. It made no sense to them, and it made even less sense to Strauss, even though he understood why it had been done: to cover one man's escape. The third man. A Russian, most likely, who was working with a turncoat, a traitor to Israel. A traitor whom Avram Zemil was trying to uncover.

Strauss turned his face away as a truck rumbled by. When it was gone he hurried up the street, slipping into the dark alley to Gromit's house. At the door he quickly picked the lock, checked one last time that no one was watching, then ducked beneath the ribbon and into the stairhall, closing and locking the door behind him.

The house was dark and silent as a tomb, which in a way it was. From what he knew of Gromit, his import/export business had merely been a front for his other activities, which meant in all likelihood there would be nothing of interest in his office. Whatever was here, he reasoned—if indeed anything was here—would be upstairs in the man's living quarters.

He waited in the dark hall for a full three minutes to allow his eyes to adjust, listening for a sound, any sound. But there was nothing.

Pulling on a pair of thin leather gloves, he went up the stairs, moving on the balls of his feet to make as little noise as possible. At the top he stopped again to listen. A dim light filtered from the outside through the heavy curtains over the windows in the main room. Strauss stepped inside, and at the window adjusted the drapes so that no light would come in or go out. He took a small penlight from his pocket and switched it on.

The room was a shambles. The police had done nothing more than pick up the bodies, the weapons, and the shell casings, leaving everything else as they had found it. The large pools of blood on the carpeting and splashed on the furniture had dried black and crusty.

Careful not to disturb a thing—he figured at the very least the police had taken photographs of the crime scene—he stepped across to a large, ornately carved wooden cabinet standing along one wall.

Holding the penlight in his mouth, he had the lock picked in a few seconds, and pulled the door open. Whatever had been in the cabinet had been taken away. Bending a little closer and holding the light beam on one of the shelves, he could see by the dust around it where a book, or perhaps a file folder, had rested and where the dust had been disturbed as it had been removed. But by whom? If the police had cleaned out this cabinet they wouldn't have closed and relocked the door. There would have been no need of it. Besides, the police did not work that way. Possibly Avram had come back, but Strauss doubted it. Because of Operation Sleeper he hadn't had much time between the shooting and now. So who had come here, and why?

A sudden slight noise came from behind him. He spun around on his heel as he reached for his gun, but he heard the noise of a silenced shot at the same moment the impact of the bullet in his side shoved him back against the cabinet, driving the air from his lungs.

"Oh shit," he whispered, all the strength going out of his legs as he sank to the floor.

He had dropped his penlight, the narrow beam shining up toward the ceiling. He managed to raise his head as a face swam into view in the red mist above him.

"You," he said, his voice soft, coming as from a great distance.

"Why did you come here, Benjamin? What are you doing here?"

"How . . . ?" Strauss croaked. "How did you know I . . . was here . . . how . . . ?"

"That was easy. I followed you. But I'm sorry. You can't know how sorry I am that this had to happen."

"Why . . . ?" Strauss whispered.

"It's a matter of . . . loyalty."

Strauss could do nothing more than watch help-

lessly as the barrel of the silenced pistol was
pointed just inches from his forehead. *First loyalty*, he thought as a tremendous thunderclap
burst in his head. . . .

Tel Aviv, 9:00 a.m.

Avram Zemil was a pariah at Mossad headquarters; Yoram Geller had made certain of it. The
staff even here was small and close-knit. Everyone
knew, if not exactly what had happened, at least
that Avram had done something to disgrace the
service and to make everyone's work even more
difficult in an exceedingly difficult time. The word
was that if and when Ezra Harel fell, so would
Ben-Or. Avram had been a Ben-Or man, which
made him doubly an untouchable.

He'd come in early, having hired a driver to
bring his car down form Haifa. He moved a few
of his things from his apartment in Jerusalem to
a small hotel in Givat Herzel where he usually
stayed when he had to spend time in Tel Aviv. On
the way down he stopped at the post office and
mailed a small package to his post office box in
Jerusalem, where it would remain until he called
for it, safe for the moment. Included were the film
canisters from his reading in Haifa Archives, and
a complete written report of everything he had
found out so far. If anything happened to him now,
which he felt was a very strong possibility, the
information he had gathered would be safe.
Sooner or later it would find its way into Ben-Or's
hands. He'd checked in with the service doctor,
who retaped his ribs, which were badly bruised

but not broken, and had then moved into his small
new office.

"I'll look at the Syrian day reports for the past
ten days," he told Leopold Gezira, the operations
chief, a tiny man with a large head and protruding
eyes. Gezira brought the files and laid them on
Avram's desk. "If there's anything else you need,
just give me a call. I'm right down the hall." He
left, closing the door softly behind him. They
would be watching him, of course, Avram thought,
to see what mistakes he would make, as if what
had already happened wasn't enough.

There was nothing much new in the day reports.
Some intelligence was still coming from the Mossad's few remaining Syrian networks, but after the
debacle on the desert, operations, especially in
Damascus, had been sharply curtailed. At some
point he realized that he was going to disobey the
prime minister. He knew there was a traitor and
he was going to find him . . . or her. No matter the
cost. Too many innocent people had been killed,
too much had gone wrong for him to stop now,
though this time he understood that if something
else went wrong he would no longer have the protection of his government. He was on his own.

Another thought struck him. He had been pulled
off his search most likely because the traitor had
gotten to Harel. Somehow the traitor had convinced Harel that their troubles were not due to
one person, but were due to a string of circumstances beyond their control. Avram Zemil's running around Syria and Haifa and Cyprus wasn't
helping matters. In fact, his actions so far had
caused Israel a lot of embarrassment. It was all a
terrible mistake, the prime minister had told him.

Yes, Avram thought, but not the mistake the
prime minister evidently thought it was. It also

meant that their traitor knew what Avram had been up to. Had he known all along? Or was he simply guessing? Whatever the case, there wasn't much time. The traitor would be digging in, burying himself in Harel's confidence. If he was going to be exposed, it would have to be done soon.

Gathering up the day reports, Avram left his office and went down the hall to Gezira's, knocking once, then letting himself in. The operations chief was on the phone. He looked up and waved Avram to a chair.

"He just walked in," Gezira said. "Do you want to talk to him?" He avoided looking directly at Avram. "Yes, I agree it's terrible, I had no idea. What does Yoram have to say about it?"

"What's up?" Avram mouthed the words, but Gezira waved him off.

"We'll be right up," Gezira said and hung up the phone. Now he looked at Avram, a very odd, questioning expression on his face. "Alex wants to see us upstairs."

"What's going on?"

"There's been another killing in Haifa," Gezira said.

Avram steeled himself or the worst. "Who was it this time?" he asked.

"One of our people. Benjamin Strauss."

Avram sat forward so fast he almost dumped the files he'd been holding. "What the hell happened, Leo?"

"I don't have the details, except that his body was found in a house in Tel Amal."

"Yakof Gromit's house?"

Gezira's eyes narrowed. He nodded. "Yes. What do you know about it?"

"Nothing, except that Gromit was an informer

of mine, and he was killed the other night in that big shootout in the bazaar."

Gezira sighed. "I don't know what the hell is going on with you, Zemil, but I think it's time now for an explanation. Was Benjamin working on something for you?"

"No," Avram said. "I have no idea what he was doing there. That is a police matter so far as I know, unless Yoram is involved. But if he was, if Haifa Station was doing something, no one told me. Benjamin Strauss was a friend, that's all. And Gromit was an informer."

"Right. We'll let Alex decide what he wants to do about this." Gezira got to his feet. "He's waiting for us."

Avram glanced at the computer terminal on Gezira's desk, then got up. "I'll meet you upstairs. I'll just put these away in my office," he said holding up the Syrian files.

Gezira gave him a hard look. "Be quick about it," he said.

They stepped out into the corridor; Avram turned right toward his office and Gezira headed left to the elevator. Avram took his time down the hall until he heard the elevator door open, then close. He looked back as the car started up, then turned and hurried back down the hall, letting himself into Gezira's office. He figured he only had a couple of minutes before they'd wonder upstairs what was keeping him. But what the hell had Benjamin been doing at Gromit's house? The place had been sealed by the police. Was he looking for clues? Avram had warned him, but he felt sick about his death. And angry. There wasn't one chance in hell now that he was going to give this up. Even if he had to quit the Mossad, he was not going to give it up.

Stepping around Gezira's desk, he hit the Archives access code, which he remembered from his days on this desk before Operation Brother, hoping against hope it hadn't been changed in the interim. It hadn't. The Archives menu came up and he punched in the codes for the General Information Index: Personnel Search, typing in the name of the man who had tried to kill him outside Episkopi, his description, and the fact that his partner's name had possibly been Jacob.

Someone passed in the corridor. He could hear the low murmur of voices, and then they were gone.

A file reference number came up on the screen, followed by "Solomon, David M.," with the same address and date of birth that had been on his driver's license and passport. According to Mossad files, he was a member of the ultra-conservative religious sect called the Haredim, which over the past couple of years had grown strong across the country. Their message was as simple as it was deadly: If they had their way they would take Israel back to the days before the war when it had been a simple protectorate of the British government. Jews and Arabs must live in peace and harmony, they preached. All weapons must be abolished. The military must be disbanded. The police must be restricted in their powers, allowing them only a charter to mediate in Jewish problems. Back to basics was their theme. Jews did not belong in the military-industrial world conglomeration that was on an accelerating downward spiral. Trust in God. It was the same message many Arabs were preaching: *Insha'Allah*—in God's hands.

The Haredim did not practice what they preached, however. At least not completely. Over the past year or so, certain of their members had become quite militant, among them Solomon, whose police file listed numerous acts of suspected terrorism. Nothing had been proven, but Solomon, along with half-a-dozen other Haredim, had been placed on a Shin Beth list of people to be watched. The controlling officer on the project was none other than Michel Louk, whose brother had the most to gain if Harel's government were to fall.

Circles within circles. Plots within plots. All leading toward the embarrassment and eventual destruction of the present government, with the Louk brothers's names popping up in all the wrong places.

Avram didn't think the Haredim themselves were at fault. Basically they were a deeply religious, peace-loving people who wanted to dismantle all government so that their people could return to a simpler age. But he suspected that they had either been terribly misled by someone, or were perhaps being used as a front by people like Michel Louk and David Solomon.

Quickly Avram punched the expand key to pull up more information on the Haredim's leadership who were also suspected of anti-government terrorist activities. Solomon's name remained on the list, along with two others: Jacob Ahrens and Hiram Mizel, a former army major who had resigned his commission eighteen months ago.

According to the records, Solomon and Ahrens had left the army about the same time as Mizel. The connection was loose, but it was there. Two of them were dead, leaving only Mizel on the expanded list. Three other names had also come up on the screen for which there was little or no further information in Mossad files except that one of them, Moshe Cantor, was a Haifa Civil Police officer.

For the moment Mizel was his mark. Where was his connection with the Russian, if any?

Avram quickly blanked out the screen and waited a moment at the door before he opened it and looked out into the corridor; at the moment it was empty. He stepped out, hurried back to his office where he dropped off the Syrian day reports, then took the elevator up to Paderewski's third-floor office. If the Haredim were involved, he figured it was a safe bet that its general membership knew nothing about a traitor or that the traitor was in all likelihood working for or with the Russians. But just now they were a very powerful force within Israel. If they were pushed from the wrong direction, by the wrong person, there was no telling what they might do. Israel could end up in a bloody revolt. This time when the Syrian tanks rolled across the desert there'd be no one to stop them.

Gezira and Paderewski were waiting for him upstairs. When he came in they stopped talking.

"Leo told me about Benjamin Strauss," Avram said. "What happened up there? Was Yoram running an operation?"

"He says not," Paderewski said, his voice soft, his eyes hooded. Something was wrong. The atmosphere in the chief of staff's office was thick with hostility.

"Then there's nothing I can add to what I've already told Leo."

"Arik is out of the office at the moment, so what I'm doing is on my own authority—subject to immediate review, of course," Paderewski said.

Gezira looked up defiantly at Avram.

"Do you think I had something to do with Benjamin's death?" Avram asked point-blank.

Paderewski shook his head. "You didn't pull the trigger, but he was working for you. He went to Gromit's house at your orders, for what reason we don't know."

"That's not true."

"The Shin Beth believes it to be true."

Michel Louk again.

"I have no other choice but to relieve you of all duties until a board of inquiry can be convened. Of course Arik can rescind my order, but under the circumstances I don't think he will, Avram."

"I see," Avram said. The jaws of the vise were closing tighter. "Am I under arrest?"

"No," Paderewski said heavily. "But I suggest that you keep yourself very visible. Go back to your apartment in Jerusalem and stay there." Paderewski sat forward. "Is there anything you want to tell me?"

"Only that you're wrong, Alex. I had nothing to do with Benjamin's death."

"Then who did? What was he doing at that house?"

"I don't know."

Paderewski nodded. "You will be watched, Avram. I would suggest that you do nothing further to aggravate the situation."

"I've done nothing wrong," Avram said. "Nothing against Israel, or the Mossad."

"I hope not," Paderewski said. "I sincerely hope not."

LOD AIRPORT, 2:18 P.M.

Ivan Roskov watched from the back seat of his Mercedes taxi as Petor Bogachev emerged from the passenger terminal, his single black leather overnight bag slung casually over his shoulder. He hesitated in the crowd on the broad sidewalk until he spotted the car, then came directly across and got in beside Roskov.

The driver flipped on the occupied sign and pulled away from the curb. It would take them an hour to get up to Jerusalem, plenty of time for Bogachev's report, and his new orders. They were going into the next phase of operations, and Roskov was anxious to get on with it. Soon, he told himself. Very soon they'd be going home in triumph. He could almost taste the victory.

"The Fawzi thing went without a hitch, and Jenkins has been eliminated as ordered," Bogachev said. "In that, there was no problem. Absolutely none."

"Very good," Roskov said, but something in his aide's manner wasn't quite right. "But?"

"There has been no word from Solomon or Ahrens. In fact, no one has seen them. But Zemil was spotted departing from the Larnaca Airport."

"Damn," Roskov swore. "When?"

"This morning. Early."

"Was he alone?"

"He was with a woman. From her description I'd guess it was Miriam Loeb."

"What was she doing there?" Roskov demanded. Again he was getting the feeling that somehow all his carefully laid plans were starting to come unraveled. It couldn't be allowed to happen. If drastic measures were called for, then drastic measures would be taken. But first he had to move with care.

"I don't know. From what I understood, she'd been taken care of, scared off."

"Evidently she doesn't scare easily."

"Neither does Zemil," Bogachev said. "The question is, what is he after?"

"I don't know, Petor," Roskov mused, half to himself. "But it makes you wonder."

"Then let's kill him and get it over with," Bogachev said. "I can find him and do it tonight."

"Not yet," Roskov said. "There's no telling what repercussions might develop if he were suddenly to be hit. First we have to learn what he's up to. If it's us he's after, the network, we'll have to find out how much he knows and who he's told it to. He's not working alone."

"We don't have a lot of time, sir," Bogachev continued his argument. "A little more than forty-eight hours."

"A lot of things can happen in that time, my friend," Roskov said. Zemil fit somehow. But where? He looked up. "In the meantime there is another little job for you in Haifa."

"Miriam Loeb?"

"No. This one is a policeman."

"Cantor?" Bogachev asked.

Roskov nodded.

"All hell will break loose when he is found dead."

Roskov smiled. "Yes, it will, Petor."

"Do you want me to use the SigSauer again?"

"Of course," Roskov said, but he was thinking ahead again, to a moment a little more than forty-eight hours from now when he would finally be vindicated. When at long last he would be given his rightful place in Moscow. An accident of birth, nothing more, had made his struggle so terribly difficult that he had to be doubly tough, doubly merciless . . . if such a thing were possible.

"When I am finished, what then?" Bogachev was asking.

"Call. There will be other work for you."

"Yes, sir."

Roskov looked at him. "Where did you say Zemil has gone?"

"I don't know. He and the woman took a flight direct here to Lod. After that I don't know. Perhaps back to Haifa."

"I doubt it," Roskov said. "Somehow I doubt it." He looked out at the passing scenery. "He's here, Petor."

JERUSALEM, 5:00 P.M.

David Sokoloff sat in a dark booth at the back of the Intercontinental Hotel's Peacock Bar nursing an ice-cold martini with shaking hands. It was the first real drink he had allowed himself in a very long time. Keep a clear head, he'd told himself at the beginning. You'll need it. But at this moment he figured he needed the strong drink more than he needed a clear head.

"I don't believe it," he said.

Gregory Ballinger, his CIA contact, was seated across from him. He'd insisted on meeting like this out in the open. "Keeps us all honest," he said. "No hidden microphones, no tricks."

"It looks that way," Ballinger said. "If there is a traitor in the Mossad, it's most likely Zemil."

"Impossible."

"Look, David," Ballinger said, leaning forward

and dropping his voice, a boyish expression of
earnestness in his eyes, "first he goes out on the
Syrian rescue mission and blows it."

"He was wounded."

"Convenient. From what I understand of the
setup out there, he and his team should have been
killed. But they weren't." Ballinger shook his
head. "Then this Fawzi mission of yours goes all
to hell, and who's the only man on the boat before
she goes down? Zemil."

"Why, for God's sake? What would he have to
gain?"

"I don't know, I just read the facts as they come
in. But your pal Zemil was spotted in Limassol,
Cyprus, talking with a known Soviet sympathizer.
A British arms runner. And from what I'm told he
wasted a couple of Jews outside some little coastal
town."

"What?" Sokoloff asked. He was having a hard
time keeping up with Ballinger.

"We don't have that for sure yet, but the timing
is right. The Cypriot authorities just picked up
their bones a few hours ago from what I'm told.
About the same time your prime minister cans his
ass. Now, to my way of thinking, that's damned
interesting."

"But Zemil is family friends with Ben-Or and
Harel."

"Then why was he fired?" Ballinger asked. "And
I'll let you in on another little secret. Remember
that Russkie we were talking about?"

"Roskov?"

"Right. Goes by the code name Palmyra. Well,
he's definitely here in Israel. And the word is, he's
working with someone within the Mossad. You got
any other candidates?"

Sokoloff was stunned. "What are you going to do?"

"Look into it, pal. And if he's your man, I'll hand his head to you on a silver platter. Ought to put you in very good grace with his nibs Harel."

"If his government survives."

Ballinger grinned broadly as he sat back. "Might be time now for you to begin actively cultivating Felix Louk, if you catch my drift. But I don't think you'll have to sweat Zemil much longer."

13

JERUSALEM, 5:05 P.M.

WALKING INTO THE MENORA HOTEL ON
King David Street downtown, Avram had the feeling that a gigantic clock was ticking over his head,
the hands rapidly approaching the zero hour when
a trip lever would finally fall and a gigantic explosion rip his world apart. The prime minister had
fired him, he'd been relieved from his Mossad duties, and Benjamin Strauss was dead. He was truly
on his own now, and in a curious way he felt free,
that he was no longer encumbered by any re-
straining hand.

Earlier he had tried to reach Miriam, to apolo-
gize and to make sure that at least for the next
couple of days she kept her head down, but there
was no answer at her apartment, nor had Ben-Or's
housekeeper seen her.

He'd picked up his car at the Central Railway
Station in Tel Aviv where the driver had dropped
it off, checked out of his hotel in Givat Herzel, and
driven directly to his apartment just outside the
Jewish Quarter. On the way up he had taken his
time, watching the same dark blue Fiat sedan that

had tailed him from the station hanging a few cars behind him.

The Fiat had been parked outside his apartment when he'd emerged a half hour later with two suitcases in hand, dumped them in the backseat of his car, and driven directly over to the Menora. And now, just inside the busy lobby, he looked over his shoulder in time to see the Fiat pull up in the driveway, two men in the car.

"I'll need some peace and quiet for a couple of days," he told the desk clerk.

"Of course, Mr. . . ."

"I'll pay in advance," Avram said. He laid two hundred American dollars more than the room rate, down on the counter. The clerk smiled knowingly and discreetly picked up the money.

"Will there by any . . . special request?"

"Only that I do not wish to be disturbed under any circumstances. Do I make myself clear?"

"Perfectly."

Avram registered under a false name, and the clerk didn't bother looking at the card.

"Do you wish a bellman to help you with your bags, sir?"

"That won't be necessary," Avram said, picking up his suitcases. "When it is time for me to leave, I promise you that I will reward good service."

"I understand perfectly, sir. I noticed that you came by automobile."

"Have it parked for me, I won't be needing it."

"Of course, it will be taken care of."

As Avram crossed to the elevator he saw that one of the men from the Fiat had come in. He went to the front desk as Avram stepped aboard the elevator and the doors closed. The clerk would tell him whatever he wanted to know, once he was shown a Mossad ID. But his instructions would be simple: Do exactly as your guest asks of you, except that we will want to know everything he does. The Mossad in effect was going to provide him with around-the-clock protection so long as he *apparently* remained in this hotel, his car parked in plain view in the hotel's parking lot.

His room was on the third floor, halfway down the narrow carpeted corridor between the elevator and the emergency stairway. Just around the corner was the floor maid's station and linen closet, unlocked, the door standing slightly ajar.

Avram let himself in, dumped his suitcases on the bed, switched on the television, and in the bathroom started the bathwater running. He hadn't been in his room more than thirty seconds before he let himself out again. The elevator had returned to the ground floor and was already starting back up as he hurried around the corner and flattened himself against the wall next to the linen closet. From here he could see the elevator to his right, past his room, and the stairwell door at the end of the corridor to his left.

The elevator door opened seconds later and the man from the Fiat who had checked at the registration desk came down the hall. Avram stepped back out of sight. He could hear the soft footfalls on the carpeting coming closer, until they stopped. He peeked around the corner. The man had stopped outside Avram's door, his ear pressed to the wood. He would be hearing the television and the sounds of the bathwater. Normal sounds. Sounds of a man preparing for a rest. Not the sounds of a dangerous man, of a man on the run.

Avram moved back out of sight again as the man straightened up and walked back to the elevator. Moments later he was gone, the elevator heading back down to the lobby. Avram stepped back around the corner, hurried to his room, and let himself in.

He was still tired and sore; he hadn't gotten much rest last night and the wound in his left arm was still giving him some trouble. He hadn't yet regained complete use of that hand. He shut off the water in the bathroom and then quickly changed from his gray slacks and sportcoat to dark slacks, a dark jacket, and soft slip-on boots. On the bed he disassembled his SigSauer, wiped down the parts with an oily rag, and reassembled and reloaded it before stuffing it in the holster at the small of his back.

From his suitcase he pocketed a small penlight, his lock-picking tools, a subminiature camera loaded with ultrafast film, and his tiny voice-activated tape recorder.

Two of the men who had come after him in Cyprus had been Haredim. They'd wanted to kill him. He was going after a third Haredim tonight. This time he wanted more proof to send to his post office box in case something happened to him. Proof that Ben-Or could use to good advantage.

He arranged the pillows beneath the bedcovers so that from the door someone might be fooled for a few moments into believing that he was in bed asleep. Then he turned off all the lights but left the television on, the sound turned way down.

At the door he waited until someone passed in the corridor, and he reflected that what he was about to set in motion was strictly illegal. He no longer had a charter to operate, or even to carry a weapon. If he was arrested now there would be no way out for him. In fact, he would be like a duck in a shooting gallery, easy prey for an "accident" that would undoubtedly be arranged by the traitor. The Mossad and Ben-Or were no longer his safe havens. In Tel Aviv, in Haifa, or here in Jerusalem he was no longer among friends. In fact, in some respects he had become the enemy.

When the corridor was clear he let himself out, making sure the door was locked, then hurried down the corridor to the emergency stairwell. It was possible that the two from the Fiat had either split up or had help and were now watching both the front and rear of the building, but he doubted it. Avram was under a loose house arrest. They had confirmed that he was settled down in his room, and his car was in the parking lot. As long as nothing changed, they probably wouldn't move. Though it was likely that from time to time through the night they would come up to check on him, he didn't think they'd try to make contact with him.

On the ground floor Avram cautiously let himself out into a broad corridor that led around the corner from the lobby, past the bar, which was full with the after-work crowd, to the rear door that led out to the parking lot.

Avram turned left, passing the bar, and then instead of going out the back door turned immediately right down a service corridor that led to the kitchen and storage areas. A fire exit was partially blocked by boxes stacked in a white-tiled corridor. There was no alarm on the latch bar, nor could he be seen from the kitchen as he let himself out into the early evening and walked directly away toward King George Street and Jaffa Road, West Jerusalem's main thoroughfares.

Yemin Moshe District of Jerusalem, 10:18 p.m.

Hiram Mizel lived extremely well for a Haredim in an area of Jerusalem that catered to accomplished artists, who occupied red-roofed houses with huge skylights for their studios. Avram had found his home with no problem, and had parked diagonally across the corner up the street from his two-story house partially hidden behind a tall white block wall. He'd rented a Volkswagen van from Hertz on King David Street that was perfect for his needs. He'd drawn the curtain that separated the driver's compartment from the rest of the van, and from a side window he was able to watch Mizel's house without himself being spotted.

He'd been watching now for several hours, not knowing whether Mizel was even in residence but waiting for the household to settle down so that he could go in for a look. No one had come in or out in that time, though with the darkness the house had been lit up.

The brief information he had been able to glean from the Mossad files he'd called up on Gezira's computer terminal included this as a home address and another in Mea She'arim where Mizel operated a religious rare book and art shop, a description, and a summary of the police files which listed the man as a "suspected antigovernment activist." Mizel was also a fully accredited rabbi, though the files had not been specific about his students or which synagogue he attended. Most curious was the fact that Mizel was a Haredim, yet he lived here and not in Mea She'arim with the bulk of Jerusalem's religious zealots in his sect.

There were differences even among the Haredim, of course. Listen in on two Jews discussing something and you'll hear three opinions. Some of them were strict traditionalists, ultra-orthodox with their views against autopsies, driving cars, the Sabbath religious laws. Others, though they had moved into the twentieth century, still preached a return to an earlier age. It was this one notion that they all had in common.

Israel had always had her religious zealots. Only now, if the Haredim as a group were truly involved with the traitor, and with the Russians, they had become willing to kill for their beliefs. Avram shuddered to think what that could do to the country.

An outdoor light went on just inside the walls of Mizel's courtyard, and Avram sat up. A minute or so later the main gate swung open and a gunmetal-gray Mercedes sedan shot out onto the road and roared past Avram, giving him just an instant to see that the driver was alone and was definitely Hiram Mizel before it was around the corner.

Avram scrambled into the driver's seat of the van, got the engine started, and raced after the Mercedes, which had a big head start. Wherever Mizel was going, he was in a big hurry.

Traffic was much thicker outside of the residential district, and passing the intersection with Mamillah Road, Avram nearly missed the big Mercedes, spotting it out of the corner of his eye turning up toward Jaffa Road. Stepping on it, he wove through traffic, squealing around the corner in the next block and cutting diagonally to the northwest. The Mercedes was just pulling into the parking lot of the central bus station when Avram slowed down and cruised past. He found a parking spot on the street half a block up, and with his lights out but engine running he watched in his rearview mirror as Mizel got out of the big car.

Was he leaving the city by bus? That didn't make much sense. He was dressed in dark slacks and a plain white open-collar shirt, no jacket, no hat. Hardly traveling clothes. Nor was he carrying a suitcase or overnight bag.

Avram watched as Mizel left the parking lot and hurried on foot down the block, ducking into the Ram Hotel a few doors away.

Shutting off the engine and pocketing the keys, Avram crossed the street and hurried down to the hotel. Traffic was quite thick here and he had to slow down so as not to be conspicuous. He wanted no trouble with the police. With all of Israel's troubles just now, a running man in a crowd was bound to attract unwanted attention.

Reaching the hotel, Avram stepped inside and went immediately to one of the house phones in the lobby and picked it up, pretending to talk to someone while scanning the faces. There were fifteen or twenty people in the lobby, a knot of them at the registration desk, but none was Mizel, who was short and thick-waisted and wore a thick, dark beard.

Avram put down the telephone and walked directly across the lobby, past the registration desk and beyond the bank of elevators to a broad hall that led into the hotel bar.

He stepped inside and hesitated a moment while his eyes adjusted to the relative darkness, a moment later spotting Mizel seated at a back booth with another man. Avram moved smoothly to a stool at the end of the bar from which he could see the booth.

Avram ordered a beer from the barman. Even if Mizel knew him, Avram didn't think he had been spotted. The Haredim rabbi was in deep discussion with the other, much younger, much rougher-looking man. It seemed to Avram that they were bargaining, as if they were haggling over something.

His beer came and he paid for it. Mizel said something, sat back in his seat, looked at the other man for several seconds, then pulled a sheet of paper from his shirt pocket and passed it across. The second man carefully unfolded the paper, spread it out on the table in front of him, and bent a little closer to read what was written on it. He used his finger, running it slowly down the page as if he were reading something off a list. But a list of what, or whom? Avram wondered.

At length the second man looked up and said something to Mizel, who shook his head, replied, and stabbed a finger at the paper. Finally, as though coming to a difficult decision, the second man nodded as he folded the paper and stuffed it in his pocket. He said something and stuck out his hand. Mizel hesitated only a beat before reaching out and shaking hands. He smiled and the other one laughed.

Whatever business they had discussed seemed settled between them, because for the next twenty minutes or so they both seemed much more relaxed, even animated at times with their gestures and laughs, though Avram could see that Mizel held himself with a certain amount of caution. He was a careful man. Avram could see that even at a distance.

They got up, finally, Mizel leaving money for

their bill, and they left the bar together; Avram turned away as they passed him, then got up and followed them out.

He held back behind a large steel column as Mizel and his friend crossed the lobby. Once they were through the doors he hurried after them, reaching the sidewalk in time to see them, still together, head down to the bus station parking lot where Mizel had left his Mercedes.

Avram waited for a break in traffic, then crossed the street and hurried as fast as he dared to where he had parked his VW van. By the time he reached it Mizel and the other man had climbed into the Mercedes and were pulling out of the parking lot. This time Mizel didn't have as great a head start. Avram was easily able to catch up with them and keep behind them without being noticed, sometimes falling well back, switching lanes, always keeping cars or trucks between him and the Mercedes.

MEA SHE'ARIM, 11:20 P.M.

Mea She'arim was a world within a world, much like the Eastern European Jewish ghettos of the eighteenth and nineteenth centuries. Men in black, wide-brimmed hats and long black coats hurried through the narrow streets deep in conversation; what few women were out at this hour were dressed puritanically in high-collared long dresses, black shawls around their shoulders, and scarves tightly wrapped around their heads. This was one section of the city that Avram rarely frequented, though sometimes as a young boy his

mother had sent him down here to one of the bak-
eries for fresh bread and rolls.

The Mercedes pulled up and parked along Mea
She'arim Street just outside the district. When
Mizel and the other man got out they were both
dressed in the long black coats and hats of the
Haredim. They headed immediately into the dis-
trict.

Avram found a parking spot half a block away
and hurried after them. His modern dress would
be tolerated if not accepted on any day but the
Sabbath, still three days off. But he would attract
attention if he lingered too long in the open. He
passed beneath a big banner strung across the
road which proclaimed in Hebrew and English:
JEWISH DAUGHTER—THE TORAH OBLIGATES YOU TO
DRESS WITH MODESTY. WE DO NOT TOLERATE PEOPLE
PASSING THROUGH OUR STREETS IMMODESTLY DRESSED—
COMMITTEE FOR GUARDING MODESTY. The Haredim
took their laws seriously.

Away from the main street the district was a
warren of narrow alleys and dark cobbled roads,
the two- and three-story buildings jammed so
closely together that a person could easily step
from one second-story window to another across
the lane.

It was late, so not many people were out and
about. The few that Avram passed only glanced at
him, their looks disapproving, but nothing was
said to him.

Within a couple of blocks it became obvious to
Avram that Mizel and the other man were headed
toward Mizel's rare book shop deep within the
district. Whatever business they had discussed
back at the hotel had evidently not been finished.
But what was here? The second man hardly looked

the type who would be interested in old religious books.

The narrow lane the two had taken opened finally into a small square off which five streets radiated outward. The bookstore occupied the first floor of a three-story building directly across from where Avram waited in the shadows. Attached to the bookstore was what appeared to be a garage or warehouse. The service door, Avram figured, was large enough to accommodate a fair-sized truck.

He watched as Mizel opened the front door of his shop, switched on a light, and stepped inside with the other man, closing the door behind them.

The instant the door was closed Avram moved out of the shadows, crossed the square, and hurried up one of the lanes that led diagonally to the northeast. As he had hoped, an alley that led back behind Mizel's building intersected with the lane and he turned down it, plunging again into a darkness that was relieved only by the dim light coming from a couple of second-story windows.

He reached the rear of Mizel's shop as a light came on in the garage, and he eased a little closer. Brown paper or cardboard had been taped over the window, so that although he could see light he could make out nothing inside. Taking out his lock picks he moved to the shop door, feeling around the edges of the frame first for any signs that the door was alarmed. It wasn't. The lock was of an old Yale design and was stiff with age and apparent disuse. It took him nearly a minute to get it open, and he eased the door open just a crack.

From inside he could smell the distinctive musty odor of old books and manuscripts, a museum smell, and see that the door led to a small workroom, beyond which a narrow corridor led to the front of the shop. A light showed from the front, and another from a door that led left into the garage.

Avram silently let himself into the workroom, carefully closing the door behind him, and he crept out into the hall to the garage door.

Mizel and the other man stood in a pool of light at a large worktable loaded with packages of some sort, on the far side of the garage. Avram could just make them out over the hood of a Mercedes truck that took up half the garage space, but he couldn't quite hear what they were saying.

Keeping low, he slipped into the garage and worked his way around the rear of the truck. Mizel and the other man were hunched over one of the packages, their backs to Avram, as he moved away from the truck and ducked behind a pile of large crates.

". . . first-rate stuff," Mizel was saying, his voice soft but the words coming clearly to Avram, crouched less than ten feet from them.

He took out his tape recorder, switched it on, and laid it carefully on one of the boxes.

"I'll be the judge of that now, won't I," the other man said in English with a Cockney accent. "What's your source?"

"I can't see what difference that could possibly make."

"You're new at this game, mate, so don't get cold feet on us, or you'll fuck it up for yourself and your people."

"Iran," Mizel said, the admission obviously a bitter one.

The Brit laughed. "What about the factory?"

"Egypt," Mizel said. "But beyond that I can't tell you anything else, simply because I don't know it."

Again the Brit laughed, the sound low and completely without humor. "You've got yourself into a dangerous little game here, my friend."

"We need the money."

"And we've got the money. How much stuff can you get us?"

"Two hundred kilos, for now."

The Brit was impressed; he whistled long and low.

"And there's more. As much of it as you can handle."

"Pardon the pun, mate, but this shit doesn't grow on trees. My people are going to want to know more about your source."

"We'll supply you with as much as you can handle, no questions asked," Mizel said, his voice hardening. "It'll be shipped to London in the frames of paintings, and as a paste underlay in the artwork itself. Now, is it yes or no? You have the list of paintings."

"I don't know if they'll go for it," the Brit said.

"Then get out. We'll find someone else . . ."

"Keep your britches on, mate. I'll take a little sample with me and get back to you say within twenty-four hours. Forty-eight at the most."

"Forty-eight hours will be too late. I can give you twenty-four, no more. And when you come back I'll expect to see the money. Dollars or pounds Sterling, I don't care."

"You Jews are all alike," the Brit said, laughing again. "Twenty-four hours it is. Just have this shit ready for transport, and I'll bring the money."

"See that you do," Mizel said, and he started to move away from the table.

"Don't bother," the Brit said. "I'll find me own way back. With all the shit that's been going down

around here lately, the streets ain't safe any-
more."

"It's just the beginning," Mizel said. "Just the
beginning."

Avram had to duck a little farther into the shadows as the Brit walked past him and went back
into the bookstore. A moment later he heard the
front door open and close. Mizel had waited by
the table, his back bowed, his head bent.

"Trust in God," he muttered.

Avram picked up the miniature tape recorder
and stood up, moving softly away from behind the
crates. "Why will forty-eight hours be too late,
Hiram?" he said.

Mizel spun around so fast he nearly lost his balance, and he had to hold onto the table to steady
himself. "God in heaven," he cried.

Avram held up the tape recorder. "It's all here."

Mizel's eyes were wild, his nostrils flared, his
jaw slack. In his severely cut clothes he almost
looked like a Rasputin, unpredictable, maniacal.

"Heroin, is that what you're getting from Iran?"
Avram asked, glancing beyond Mizel at the tubu-
lar plastic packages stacked on the table. "The
Russians would be involved in that sort of a trans-
action. The KGB. You do know that, don't you,
Rabbi Mizel?"

"Who are you?" Mizel stammered.

"Avram Zemil. Mossad. Why does the Haredim
need so much money? And what's going to happen
in forty-eight hours?"

"If you're from him, you already know that!"
Mizel spat.

Avram held himself in check. *Him.* Their traitor
was someone in the Mossad. And whoever it was
worked for or with the Haredim. "Maybe he wants

to make certain that everything runs according to schedule. That there'll be no problems this time."

"None of that has been my fault!" Mizel shouted. "I warned them, God in heaven, I warned them all."

"About what, Hiram?"

"You know."

"Yes, I do. But we have to make certain that you understand everything, perfectly."

"No," Mizel said, shaking his head. "This is all wrong. You shouldn't be here like this. Who sent you?"

"Palmyra," Avram said.

The color drained from Mizel's face. He seemed on the verge of collapse. His knuckles had turned white from gripping the table so tightly for support. "I don't know what you're talking about," he said.

"You don't want to know, but you do," Avram said. "Does your trust in God extend to the Russians?"

"You're not from him," Mizel choked.

"Who?" Avram snapped. "A traitor to Israel?"

"No," Mizel hissed. "You're the traitor! You, and your kind!"

"We're not trying to tear the government apart, your people are."

"What government?"

"We don't kill innocent people. Nor do we deal in drugs."

"Only weapons," Mizel shouted, extremely agitated. "Fighter airplanes and bombers and even atomic weapons. Or are you denying Israel has nuclear devices they are ready to use?"

"Only to save our lives."

"God will save us!" Mizel screamed. "Trust in God!"

Avram looked at him. The man was more than
a religious fanatic, he was probably insane. He
firmly believed that the only way to Israel's salvation, and therefore his own, was to destroy the
present government. To dismantle the military.
What made it all the worse was that the man, and
others of his kind, had probably lost relatives at
Auschwitz and Dachau and the other Nazi concentration camps. But they had forgotten. Or they na-
ively believed it could not happen again.

"I think you will talk to me, Hiram," Avram said
softly, reasonably. "I think I'll be able to persuade
you."

"Trust in God!" Mizel shrieked, the sound almost inhuman. He reached behind him, snatched
up a plastic packet of the raw, uncut heroin, and
before Avram could make a move to stop him,
ripped it apart and began eating the white powder, taking huge mouthfuls and forcing them
down his throat by swallowing over and over
again.

Avram lunged forward, ripped the package out
of Mizel's hands, and tried to jam his fingers down
the man's throat in an effort to make him vomit,
but Mizel had the sudden strength of a madman,
and he shoved Avram aside against the hood of
the truck.

"No," Avram shouted.

Mizel took three steps forward, then a high-
pitched, keening sound came from his throat, his
back arched, and he fell backward, his legs jerking spasmodically, his eyes rolling up in his head,
and his chest heaving.

Avram shoved away from the truck, but by the
time he reached Mizel the Haredim rabbi's body
had shuddered deeply and he slumped back dead,

blood filling his mouth from his bitten-through tongue.

"Trust in God," Avram said to himself, sitting back on his haunches.

After a while Avram got to his feet. He picked up his tape recorder where he had dropped it, switched it off, and pocketed it. In the back of the garage he found a five-gallon jerry can half-full of diesel fuel that he brought back to the work-table. With his stiletto he cut open all the plastic packets of heroin, each one containing at least two kilos of the uncut drug. Finally he opened the can of diesel fuel and poured it carefully over the table, making sure that every gram of the white powder was soaked with fuel and completely ruined. Whatever the Haredim would be doing within the next forty-eight hours, it would not be financed with drug money from this lot.

14

AVRAM HAD WATCHED THE DAWN RISE over the city. From his room he could see the Mount of Olives lit in a golden glow at this hour. He'd managed to catch a few hours' sleep last night, but when he awoke in the dark his heart had been racing and his clothes were soaked with sweat. The Haredim, or at least some of its leadership, had been maneuvered by the Russians into heading the country toward civil war. Step by step they had managed over the past weeks to embarrass Israel all over the world. Harel's government would probably fall soon, and there was no telling who would take over. It was a possibility, Avram thought, that Felix Louk would be a prime candidate.

Mizel had inadvertently given him three pieces of information. The first was that the traitor worked for the Mossad, which seemed to rule out Michel Louk, although it certainly was possible that the Shin Beth was also involved. The second was that the Russian code-named Palmyra was definitely playing a large part. Mizel had denied knowing the name, but when Avram had brought it up the Haredim rabbi's reaction had been obvious. The third, and to Avram's thinking most important bit of information, though, was the forty-eight-hour deadline Mizel had given the drug dealer. Something important was scheduled to take place tomorrow night. But what would happen? And where? Here in Israel, or elsewhere? It wasn't much to go on, but it was something. At least something.

Avram ordered breakfast sent up to his room, and while waiting for it to arrive he wrote out a complete report of everything that had happened to him yesterday and last night, including how he came by the information on Mizel and what had transpired at the garage next to the bookstore. He wrote it on hotel stationery, enclosed the tape recording he had made, and once again addressed the envelope to his own post office box.

After breakfast he took a shower, not bothering to shave, and changed clothes, leaving his suitcases unpacked in his room. He went downstairs. Crossing the lobby he picked up his tail, the same pair as yesterday. He wondered if they'd gotten any sleep or if they'd had a relief team spell them last night. Outside, he hailed a taxi, ordering the driver to take him to the prime minister's office near the Knesset building across town.

Everything was changed now. Harel would have to see it. The one piece of good news Avram was bringing him was that their traitor was not a member of Harel's cabinet, but rather someone within the Mossad. But that included, Avram thought morosely, Ben-Or and Miriam. No matter what, though, it was going to be over with by tomorrow night at the latest. Another thirty-six hours or so was all he needed. Just a day and a half.

Traffic was thick by the time he was let off in front of the government complex across from the Shrine of the Book. Crossing the entrance plaza he saw the dark Fiat with his tail pull up and park. Just inside, he stepped to one side and watched from one of the plate-glass doors to see what they would do. But neither one of them got out of the car. He had caused them no trouble so far, so they were content merely to wait for him to emerge and take another cab to wherever he was going.

Avram turned and hurried down the broad, busy corridor to Security, where he showed his Mossad identification and dropped off his gun before being allowed to go upstairs to the office of the prime minister's appointments secretary. It was already filled this morning with people wishing to see Harel.

"I'm sorry, Mr. Zemil, but the prime minister will be busy the entire day. Perhaps you could try tomorrow."

"Just tell him that I'm here, would you?" Avram asked the young man. "It's important."

The secretary sighed deeply; he was used to this sort of thing, but picked up the phone and said something softly into it that Avram couldn't make out. He hung up almost immediately. "I am terribly sorry, Mr. Zemil, but it will be impossible to see him any time today, or tomorrow for that matter. He asks that you be patient. Perhaps after the weekend."

"You told him that I was here, and wasn't merely telephoning?"

"Yes."

"I see," Avram said. "Thank you." He turned

and left the office, taking the stairs back down to Security, where he retrieved his gun.

Outside he hesitated only a moment before he cut across the plaza to the Knesset building, passing the eternal flame that guarded the entrance. Once again, just inside he looked back the way he had come. The Fiat had not moved, nor had either man gotten out. They had seen him crossing the plaza, of course, they couldn't help but see him. They would be content to wait out front for a while yet. Time enough for him to do what he had to do, he hoped. With or without the prime minister's help he was going to stop the Haredim and their Mossad traitor and Russian spy.

At a telephone kiosk in the main entry hall, Avram called Ben-Or's private number at Mossad Headquarters in Tel Aviv, but his secretary said that he was not to be disturbed by anyone for any reason. *Especially not Avram Zemil*, Avram thought. Next he tried Ben-Or's home, but his housekeeper said he wasn't in.

"Is his niece Miriam there, by chance?" Avram asked.

"No."

"But she has been there?"

"No, sir, she's not been here at all."

"Thanks," Avram said, disappointed. Yet in his heart of hearts he hadn't really expected her to be there, nor had he really expected the prime minister or Ben-Or to be in for him.

"Shall I tell her you called?" the housekeeper was asking. "Is something the matter?"

"No," Avram said. "It's nothing at all. I'll talk to her later."

He checked again at the front doors; the Fiat was still parked in front. He turned and headed across the entry hall toward the rear corridor. Fe-

lix Louk was just stepping off the elevator with a
number of other people as Avram passed, and
their eyes met. Avram had never been introduced
to the man, but he knew him by sight. And he
would have bet that Louk wouldn't know him. Yet
the man pulled up short for just an instant, his
face darkening in recognition. The moment
passed, Louk turned to say something to the people he was with, and they headed across the entry
hall.

Avram watched until they were gone, then
turned and left the building by one of the rear
exists, crossing the big parking lot and working
his way on foot all the way over to Hanasi Boulevard before catching a taxi back to the Menora
Hotel.

One from the Mossad, one from the Shin Beth,
and one from the Knesset, all working with or for
the KGB and using the Haredim as their instrument of political upheaval. Was it possible, he
wondered? Felix Louk had definitely recognized
him, and had definitely been upset. Why? The
Haredim's idealism, even their naivete he could
understand, but Felix Louk was a man of the
world; very bright, very knowledgeable. He knew
the score. He knew that if the Israeli government
were to fall the entire country might find itself
embroiled in a war it could not win because of
lack of leadership. What game was he playing at,
if indeed he was one of the players?

As he rode back across town Avram realized that
Jerusalem was a dead end for him, at least for the
moment. He was getting no help from the prime
minister; and Felix Louk knew that he was here.
Before long his Mossad watchdogs would realize
that they had been sidestepped and would be coming after him.

The answers, if there were any answers, would be in Haifa, where most of the killings had taken place, where Gromit had evidently struck a nerve with his inquiries about Palmyra, where Miriam had been roughed up, where Benjamin Strauss had been killed, where Operation Brother and Operation Sleeper had been planned, and where Michel Louk, at last count, was still holding court.

He could not get Miriam out of his mind. What part had she played, was she playing in this business? He wondered if he really wanted to know.

Moving fast, he checked to make sure that nothing had been touched in his room, then took the back way out of the hotel and around to the parking lot, where he retrieved his Peugeot with his spare keys. He drove directly to the train station, where he bought a one-way ticket to Tel Aviv, then back outside he hurried to the taxi stand on the corner and took a cab to within a block of where he had parked the rental Volkswagen. When the cab was gone he approached the van with extreme caution, making as sure as he possibly could under the circumstances that no one was watching.

On the way back across town he stopped at a postal station where he mailed his report update and the audiotape, and by noon he was on the highway to Haifa, conscious of the fact that this was gong to be his last chance, and that a lot of people would be gunning for him soon.

HAIFA, 2:15 P.M.

The day had turned out very warm, though a good breeze blew from the sea. Avram lingered near the big casino two blocks from where he had parked his car on a side street and watched the people playing in the big municipal swimming pool next door. The normalcy of the scene seemed somehow out of place to him in his present state. Israel was in a battle much more dangerous than the Six-Day War, and yet there weren't a handful of people in the country who knew about it. There was no call to arms this time. No mobilization that would save them. It wasn't going to be that easy.

On his way up from Jerusalem he had taken care with his tradecraft, stopping at roadside inns, sometimes driving ten kilometers an hour over the speed limit, sometimes ten less, once pulling onto the shoulder of the road and opening the hood of his car as if he were experiencing car trouble. But no one was behind him, or if they were they were damned good. Yet he had the feeling all the way up that he was being watched, that someone was back there, that someone knew where he was going, what he was about to do.

Coming into Haifa itself, however, he had spotted one of Strauss's people, heading in the opposite direction. He wasn't sure if he had been spotted or not, but he thought there ws at least a fifty-fifty chance of it. His excuse, if he was approached, would be Miriam. He was worried about her and had come down to see her. It wouldn't hold for long. The first question would be, why had he ducked his tail in Jerusalem? Why hadn't he told someone? But he figured he'd cross that bridge if and when he came to it.

In the meantime he *was* worried about Miriam. She hadn't been at Ben-Or's, nor had there been any answer at her apartment when he'd tried to telephone halfway up.

He waited for a break in the traffic along busy Ha'aliya Street, then crossed and hurried up the block to her apartment building. Her car was not in the parking lot, nor did she answer when he rang the doorbell. He let himself in with his key, pulling up short in the entry hall and reaching for his gun. The apartment was a shambles. Someone had been there and taken the place apart. The couch and chairs had been cut apart, stuffing lay everywhere; the carpeting had been pulled up, and even the wallpaper and light fixtures had been ripped from the walls and ceilings.

He shut the door with his heel and, flattening himself against the wall, eased to the corner and then stepped out into the living room, dropping automatically into a crouch, sweeping the room with his gun, the safety off, the hammer cocked.

Nothing moved except for the balcony drapes blowing in the breeze.

"Miriam," he called softly. His heart was hammering. This could not be another Yakof Gromit. Please, God, not Miriam. He could not handle finding her body in a pool of blood. Not that. Almost anything but that.

The apartment remained silent. Moving swiftly, he went to the kitchen, also a shambles, then on to the bathroom and her bedroom, also completely taken apart. But there was no blood. Nothing but an incredible mess, and he breathed a silent sigh of relief.

Whoever had been here had been very thorough. If they had been looking for something, there was little doubt that they had found it. It was possible,

however, that this was just another warning, like
the near rape of the other night.

Or, he thought glumly, holstering his gun, Miriam—if she were the traitor—had ordered this
herself, knowing that he would be showing up
here sooner or later, and wanting to throw him
off.

But which was it? And how could he find out?

Back in the living room, Avram was about to
pick up the telephone to try to reach Ben-Or again
when he heard a soft metallic noise from the front
door. Someone was using a key to open the door.
The lock snapped softly open.

He yanked out his gun and quickly stepped
around the corner from the entry hall, where
again he flattened himself against the wall. He
heard the door open, and a moment later someone
stepped inside and closed the door. Whoever it
was hesitated in the entry hall for a full ten seconds and then came forward. Avram tensed.

Yoram Geller stepped out from the entry hall,
and even before recognizing him Avram reached
out and placed the barrel of his automatic against
the man's skull, just behind his left ear.

"God in heaven," Geller said, pulling up short.

Geller was on the list. Avram did not remove his
gun. "What are you doing here, Yoram?"

"Looking for you," Geller said, keeping his
hands away from his sides in plain sight, his body
held rigid.

"Was it your people who took this place apart?"

"It was like this an hour ago when I came looking for you," Geller said. "Unless you mean to
shoot me, how about taking that gun away from
my head?"

Avram stepped back after a beat, lowering his
gun and uncocking it but not reholstering it.

Geller turned to face him, a tight little expression of satisfaction on his face. "You've done it now," he said softly.

"Where is Miriam?"

"I don't know," Geller replied, shaking his head. "I'm placing you under arrest."

"I think not," Avram said evenly. "How did you know I would be coming here?"

Geller grinned and started to say something, but Avram held him off.

"I'd be careful what I said and how I said it."

Geller's eyes narrowed. "When you turned up missing from the Menora Hotel, Alex called and said you might be headed this way."

"So you waited for me."

Geller nodded.

"Did you notify the police that her apartment was ransacked and that she's missing?"

"Under the circumstances, no."

"What circumstances?"

"Put the gun away, Zemil, and come back to the office with me. We'll talk it out."

"What circumstances?" Avram demanded. "Talk to me now, Yoram."

"This is your doing. Somehow you got up here faster than we counted on, and you pulled the place apart. We know that you've been looking for her ever since you were brought back from Cyprus, so you came here to find what you could."

"What the hell are you talking about?"

"She went to her uncle for help. She's worried about you. Frankly all of us are. Ben-Or called me and asked me to see what I could do. Now, either give me your weapon or put it away, and let's go back to the office."

"Do you know where she is?"

"I've already told you . . ."

"Does Arik know where she is?"

"Come with me and I'll personally put through the call to him. You have my word on it. Just give it up."

"No."

"Who the hell are you working for? Have you gone to the other side, then? Talk to me, Zemil. We can work it out."

"Not until I find Miriam."

"She's not here."

"Then she's in Tel Aviv. I'll go there. I've got to find her . . . before tomorrow night." Avram watched Geller's eyes, but if the mention of a specific time had any significance for him he didn't show it.

"Then go," Geller snapped. "Get the hell out of Haifa. I don't want you here any longer. Whenever you're around there's trouble. Go to Ben-Or, he'll hold your hand, you're old family friends."

"If you try to stop me there will be trouble, Yoram, I guarantee you won't like it."

"I already don't like it. Just get out of Haifa."

"Who is downstairs? Who came with you?"

"No one," Geller said.

Avram stepped into the entry hall and holstered his gun. "Just stay here for a little while, Yoram. Don't try to follow me."

"Not me," Geller said. "You're no longer my problem."

Avram turned and left he apartment, half expecting Geller to come after him, or at the very least to see someone on the street waiting for him. But there ws no one, and the feeling that he was being followed diminished by the time he got to his car and headed out of the city, ostensibly south toward Tel Aviv, but with a far different destination and purpose in mind.

NAZARETH, 4:20 P.M.

Avram was reasonably certain that he had not been followed out of Haifa, though passing through the suburb of Kefar Shamir in the south he thought he saw another of Strauss's people parked at the side of the road. But the car didn't pull out and Avram didn't turn back to make sure.

A few miles farther south he left the main highway for a secondary road that cut east across the desert, skirting the airbase at Zippori before turning back to the northeast, and then into the pilgrimage town of Nazareth. This was where the meeting with Fawzi was to have taken place, and the irony of coming here like this to throw off anyone who might be following him, and to acquire the means of continuing his investigation, was not lost on him. Israel was a very small country, and what secrets she had were kept jealously guarded. Still, wherever he went, he always ran the risk of being spotted and recognized.

He parked the van in a tourist parking lot just off the city center and went the rest of the way into town on foot. On the drive through he had noticed a number of clothing shops. With a minimum of fuss he purchased a long dark coat at one of them, and carrying it wrapped in paper walked to another shop a block away where he purchased a broad-brimmed black hat, which he also had wrapped.

In the public rest rooms attached to the central post office downtown he donned the long black coat, after first stuffing his gun in his belt so that he would be able to get to it more easily, then the hat, and wrapped his own jacket in the paper

sacking. He looked at himself in the mirror, pulled
the hat a little lower, set a stern expression on his
unshaven face, and left the men's room, Avram
Zemil the devout; a Haredim, one of the faithful.
"Trust in God," he mumbled.

He walked over to the bus depot conscious of
the fact that the looks he now got from passersby
were tinged with a little respect, some envy, and
even a little fear. Nazareth was a Christian town,
or at least it had always wanted to be, though it
did have a fair population of Haredim if his memory served him correctly. He also became conscious of the fact that there were very few
similarly dressed people out and about at this
hour, which he found slightly odd. But then again,
the Haredim were certainly not a majority here,
as they were in Jerusalem's Mea She'arim district, or in Haifa's Hadar HaKarmel section. Still,
it was odd to see so few of them. In the small concourse there were three ticket counters, lines at
two of them. At the free one he bought a round-
trip ticket for Haifa with the return date left open.
The bus, he was told, would be leaving within the
half hour. As he turned to leave he heard his ticket
clerk say to one of the others, "If this keeps up
they'll all be gone by tomorrow," and then he was
out of earshot.

The Haredim were evidently moving out of Nazareth. But to where, and for what purpose? What
was going to happen tomorrow night, and where?

Haifa's Hadar HaKarmel Section, 7:38 p.m.

Haredim men never strolled, they always strode
purposefully, their eyes and thoughts focused on
some Talmudic problem, perhaps, but their outward manner and movements brisk and certain.
On the other hand, once they were settled in a
sidewalk cafe they could spend hours discussing
the Talmud with each other, or simply sitting back
alone to contemplate the wisdom of God and His
chosen people

Coming into Haifa as a Haredim, and climbing
briskly up the steep Mount Carmel avenues into
Hadar HaKarmel, Avram felt like a fish swimming
upstream. It seemed to him that the Haredim were
moving out of the section, in ones and twos and
threes, many with overnight bags or valises;
women and children, too, entire families in some
cases. It wasn't a mass exodus, or any sort of an
evacuation, but he was noticing more people leaving than arriving. There were less Haredim than
usual in the cafes and along the side streets. More
of the houses were unlit, their occupants gone.

Avram sat down at an outdoor cafe across from
a traffic circle. Behind him were apartment
buildings and storefronts, across the way the avenue was lined with palm trees. It was already
starting to get dark, and the traffic was running
with headlights. Here the city seemed more tour-
isty and relaxed than did the Haredim district of
Jerusalem. There were more people in ordinary
clothes, the attitudes seemed less strict, and yet
there was the undercurrent that God's work was
closer here than it was downtown in Haifa
proper. And Avram did not stick out because of
his dress.

"You will be leaving soon, brother?" the young waiter asked.

Avram looked up and smiled peacefully. "There is time yet," he said in classical Hebrew. "And thou wilt be leaving as well?"

"No," the young man said. He was dressed in a white shirt and dark slacks. He was no Haredim.

"Trust in God."

"Yes, but where are you going? No one will say."

"To do God's work," Avram said. "I will have tea, if thou please."

"Yes, sir," the young man said, and he turned and went back into the cafe, leaving Avram once more alone to watch the traffic passing.

If not here at this place, he thought, then somewhere else in Hadar HaKarmel there would be an answer. Short of that he would pick one of the departing Haredim and follow him. That would be dangerous, because there was no way of knowing what he would be walking into, so it would be his last resort. But if need be he wouldn't hesitate.

A blue-and-white police car cruised slowly by, the two officers staring at him, and then they were past. It had almost seemed to Avram that they had recognized him. Which meant they would have to have been looking for him. It was unlikely, unless Geller had turned his name and photograph over to the police.

A half-minute later the same police car came around the traffic circle from the opposite direction and stopped. Neither cop made a move to get out of the car, but one of them was talking on the radio. Avram was starting to get a very bad feeling about this.

The young waiter came back and laid out his tea things. "I don't know what the big mission is all about, brother," he said conversationally. "After all, there is nothing of importance in Hadera."

Avram had almost missed it. He looked up at the young man. "Hast thou said Hadera?"

The boy nodded uncertainly. "I didn't mean to offend. It's just . . . I overheard some talk . . . I'm sorry . . ."

Avram forced a smile. "No offense," he said. "As thou sayest, there is nothing in Hadera. Nothing at all."

The police car pulled around the traffic circle, screeching to a half directly in front of the cafe. Avram started to move as both cops leaped out of the car, but instead of coming for him they took off running in the opposite direction.

"Down," Avram shouted, pushing the waiter down and pulling the table on top of them both.

A moment later a tremendous explosion shattered the night air with a rush of flames, car body metal, glass, burning palm fronds, blood, and body parts.

The tabletop had protected Avram from most of the blast effects, but the young waiter was dead, his head nearly severed from his body and a large piece of metal jutting from his chest.

At first he couldn't hear a thing except a loud ringing in his ears as he pulled himself out from beneath the debris. There were flames everywhere. As he crawled away he began to hear screaming as from a very long distance. An old woman lay in his path entangled in a piece of twisted metal that had probably been the chair she'd been sitting in, bright arterial blood spurting from a gash in her side, most of the flesh on her face and chest flayed away by flying glass. She screamed once again, then slumped back, her eyes open.

In the distance Avram could hear sirens too, and more screaming, and men shouting, and car horns honking. The bomb had been meant for him, of course. Which also meant that he had either been spotted in Nazareth and followed here, or somehow he had been spotted downtown at the central bus depot when he'd come in. They knew now that he was dressed as a Haredim. And they might even guess that he'd learned that the Haredim were all gathering in Hadera.

Would they believe he was dead? Would they call off their search?

Reaching the blown-away remnants of the cafe's front wall, Avram took off his hat and his long black coat, then plunged through the flames into the interior of the building. The serving counter had been shoved over, and two waiters lay in pools of their own blood. Avram had to crawl around them and over the counter and shove his way through a half destroyed door into the kitchen. The cook and his helper were sitting on the floor looking at each other. The flames were already reaching this part of the building, and outside the sirens were much closer.

"Is there a back way out?" Avram shouted.

The cook looked up and mumbled something.

Avram helped him and the other man to their feet and pulled them around the big preparation table. Beyond a storage area a door was propped half open. He led the two outside into the alley, and when they were far enough away from the burning building he left them.

The street was in pandemonium. People were coming from everywhere. A fire truck screamed around the traffic circle as Avram stepped around the corner from the alley and hurried the opposite way down the hill toward town.

Hadera. Whatever was happening tomorrow night was taking place in Hadera, he thought, and involved the Haredim. A lot of Haredim. Those from Nazareth and those from Haifa. What was going to happen in Hadera that was so important that Hiram Mizel was willing to die rather than reveal it?

15
───

Kᴳᴮ MAJOR IVAN ROSKOV LOWERED HIS binoculars and stepped away from his fourth-story hotel room window as an unmarked olive-drab army van pulled up in front of the Uri Dan Hotel. Four men dressed in civilian clothes went into the hotel, and the van immediately took off, circling the square once before heading east.

It was starting, he thought, Within twenty-two hours his task here in Israel would be completed, and he would be hailed as a hero of the state. But at what price? he stopped to wonder.

He'd been groomed for just this kind of an assignment. Mistrust. *Lies, deceit, uncertainty.* "You are the expert, Ivan, because you have no conscience, you understand the goal. The only goal. We trained you that way."

He did not remember his parents, but he did remember his early schooling with a clarity that at times was almost preternatural. He remembered training exercises when he was barely two. They had taught him young. Even before the State of Israel had become an established fact, Roskov and a few others like him had been trained so that someday they could come here and wreak their special havoc.

Only one Jew can understand another Jew. That was the concept. And that's why he had been trained for this assignment—because he had been born a Jew. Still, he had his own secret, even from them, and sometimes even from himself.

He shuddered once as he turned away from the window and checked his watch. Bogachev was late. He should have been back from Haifa by now unless something had gone wrong. They were so close, and yet, incredible as it had been for him to believe, the entire operation could very well fail because of one man who knew or had already guessed too much. Mizel's body and the ruined heroin was proof enough of that, without even considering everything else that had gone on. How he knew what he knew, was the big question.

The money had gotten into the correct hands just this afternoon, but it had been close. Too close for Roskov's liking.

Again back at the window he studied the square and the approaches to the Uri Dan. By tomorrow the square would be filled with a mob chanting "Trust in God." And tomorrow night the government of Israel would fall.

Already there were at least two thousand Haredim in the city. By morning that number would be doubled, and by evening there would be ten thousand of them. Pliable fanatics, who under the correct circumstances could be more powerful than nuclear weapons. Look what students had done to America's resolve in the Vietnam war.

The Israeli army would be here in force, as would the Shin Beth and the Mossad, but it would do them no good. No good at all.

Someone knocked at the door. Roskov laid down his binoculars, took out his Makarov 9-mm automatic pistol, and quickly stepped across the room. "Yes?" he said softly, in English.

"It is I," Bogachev whispered from the corridor.

Roskov reached out, undid the lock, and stepped back. "Come," he said. With care, he told himself. It was too late in the game to make foolish mistakes. Any mistake.

The door opened and Bogachev stepped into the room, his eyes wild, his hair and clothing disheveled. He'd done nothing more to disguise his appearance than throw a jacket over his civil police uniform. He was out of breath.

"Lock the door," Roskov ordered. As Bogachev did so he crossed the room, closed the curtains over the windows, and switched on the lights.

"The man is a devil," Bogachev said hoarsely.

At the bureau Roskov poured his aide a stiff vodka and brought it to him. Bogachev knocked it back and then let out a deep sigh.

"Is he dead, Petor? Did you personally identify his body?"

"He should be dead. I swear everything was perfect. But he just got up and walked out the back door. Before we could do a thing about it he had disappeared into the night."

"Where is he?" Roskov demanded, his insides churning.

"I don't know. But he must know something. At least about the Haredim. Somehow. He was dressed in a black coat and hat. At first I didn't recognize him."

"You're certain it was Zemil?"

"Yes, Ivan, I am certain. I will never forget those eyes, nor will I ever forget seeing him rise from the ashes like . . ."

"He's just a man, Petor," Roskov said sharply. "Nothing more. Just a man. Why didn't you continue following him like before?"

"There is no signal from him now," Bogachev said. "The tracer we placed on him must have been damaged in the blast."

"Do you think he suspects about it?"

"I don't know any longer, I just don't know," Bogachev said, finally catching his breath. "But devil or not, he's a hard man to kill. We've missed too many times."

Roskov turned away for a few moments. He had to think. He lit a cigarette and poured himself a drink. Zemil had run to Haifa. Why there? Because of Miriam Loeb, most likely. He'd gone to her apartment; they'd seen that barely hours after they'd searched it.

"Was he wounded in the blast? Was he hurt, Petor?" Roskov asked, turning back.

"I don't know. He got out of there under his own power. But he must have been shaken up. The car went off less than thirty feet away from him."

Roskov was nodding. "He's been relieved of duty from the Mossad, which means no one believes that all this time he has been looking for us."

Bogachev's eyes widened. "He knows . . . ?"

"It would seem that way. But even if he knows everything, or most of it about tomorrow night, nothing will happen until then. Which means he has time to hide and lick his wounds. He's been on the go now for a long time. He'll need rest."

Sudden understanding dawned on Bogachev's face. "The woman's apartment," he said.

"That's right, Petor. He'll probably go back there to rest for tonight. He'll believe that no one would think to look for him there. He'll believe he's safe for the moment."

"What about the girl?"

"After tomorrow she won't matter," Roskov said. "I want you to get back to Haifa. Wait until it's late, then go in and kill him."

"Yes, Ivan . . ."

Roskov held up his hand. "This time, Petor, don't fail me."

MOSSAD HAIFA STATION, 10:05 P.M.

When the security door buzzed, Michel Louk pushed his way through into the corridor and headed directly down to Operations.

Yoram Geller had agreed to meet him here, though from what he had been led to understand, the chief of station had been here most of the evening.

Sammuel Amit, who had been reinstated as operations chief, met Louk at the door and ushered him inside. "We're just about ready for tomorrow evening. Yoram and I were going over the last-minute details."

"Good," Louk said. "But there may be a change." He personally did not like Amit or Geller, and he had been on Zemil's side the night of Operation Sleeper. But then one could not choose one's friends—or allies—in this business. Something he had learned a long time ago. His brother Felix was preaching the same message up in the Knesset.

Geller came out of his office with a sheaf of papers. "Ah, Michel, you're just in time. We can go over where you want our people placed."

"We have to talk first," Louk said. He hadn't wanted to come here like this. Louk expected that Geller was going to get a great deal of satisfaction from what he was going to tell him, but there was simply no help for it. He'd found it hard to believe himself. Yet the facts spoke for themselves, no matter how disagreeable and surprising they were.

"Is there something wrong?" Geller asked.

"Yes, there is, Yoram," Louk said. "Let's use your office."

"Of course," Geller said. He handed the papers to Amit. "Work up the three alternate timetables. We'll be with you in a minute."

"Right," Amit said, and he went back to the situation table, while Geller and Louk went into Geller's office.

"Has this got something to do with tomorrow night?" Geller asked when they were alone.

Louk thought the station chief was a worried man. It was the look in his eyes. The job did it to everyone sooner or later. "I'm afraid so. Or at least, I'm saying I sincerely hope not, for all of our sakes, but I suspect it's so."

Geller's eyebrows knitted. "What the hell are you talking about?"

"Avram Zemil," Louk said softly.

"What about him?" Geller asked harshly.

"Do you know where he is right now?"

"No. But he was here in Haifa this afternoon. I sent him back to Tel Aviv."

"Has he shown up there yet?"

Geller shook his head. "No."

"I'd like to see a copy of his service record. Tonight. Right now, if possible."

"Before I can do that I'll have to have a pretty

convincing reason, and depending upon what that reason might be, authorization from Tel Aviv."

Louk just looked at him. Geller had always had the reputation of playing everything exactly by the book. He was doing it now. Louk couldn't blame the man, but still he didn't have to like him. "I have reason to believe that Zemil has, at the very least, participated in as many as nine or ten murders and has had a continuing contact with a Soviet KGB agent."

The color drained from Geller's face. It was the first real reaction Louk had ever seen the man exhibit. Geller sat down behind his desk. "God in heaven," he said softly.

"He was spotted in the bazaar the night of all the trouble, and there have been several other incidents since then, not to mention Operations Brother and Sleeper."

"He's no traitor," Geller said softly, and to Louk's mind unconvincingly. "He goes way back. His father was an important general, and he's close personal friends with Arik Ben-Or."

"I know," Louk said. "And I find it hard to believe myself. Last night there was another murder here in Haifa."

"The cop."

"Right. Moshe Cantor, a friend of mine. And, perhaps not so coincidentally, a friend of Benjamin Strauss."

"Found shot to death in Yakof Gromit's home," Geller said. "Are you saying Zemil killed them both?"

"We don't know about Strauss, but Moshe was shot to death with a German-made 9-mm automatic. A SigSauer."

"Zemil carries a SigSauer."

"So I understand."

"Why?"

"I don't know," Louk admitted. "I've seen him in action, he doesn't come across as the type to turn on his own country. He's sharp."

"He's a maverick."

"Yes, he's that," Louk said. "From what I've been told he's been relieved of duty. Can you tell me why?"

"There have been a number of incidents since he was assigned to me."

"Such as?"

"I don't think I can go into it right now. And before I give you his dossier I'll have to get authorization from Tel Aviv."

"Your loyalty is touching, Geller, but I will be issuing an all points bulletin on him, in conjunction with the army and the civil police. I want him off the streets before tomorrow."

"It won't be so easy, I don't think . . ."

"He will be considered armed and extremely dangerous. My people will be instructed to defend themselves, of course, but that at all costs he is to be brought in."

Geller sat forward. "If Zemil is . . . a traitor, a killer, that is, do you think he'll try something tomorrow night in Hadera?"

"I don't know," Louk said, sighing deeply. "I simply haven't any of the answers. Until the last twenty-four hours I would have been willing to bet that Avram Zemil was anything *but* a traitor to his country. Now . . ." He let it trail off.

Geller got up from his chair. "I'll see what I can do from my end," he said. "I'll call Tel Aviv now for authorization to release his dossier to you, but I don't think they'll give it tonight. Perhaps in the morning."

"In the meantime, where did he go?"

"I don't know," Geller said. "I honestly don't know. But the word will go out to all of my people, and to everyone in Tel Aviv and Jerusalem to be on the lookout for him."

"And Hadera," Louk said.

"Yes, and Hadera," Geller replied.

TEL AVIV, 10:10 P.M.

Miriam Loeb had a terrible secret that had been eating at her for seven years. There wasn't a night or a day that went by she didn't think about it. Think about what it had done to her. Sometimes, though, she found herself giving thanks that it had not done more. It had always had the potential of destroying her. In the beginning years she'd told herself she could handle it. But she had been young and oh so very idealistic. But just lately, with everything that had been going on, she realized that she had been a complete and utter fool. She'd been used; passively perhaps, but used nevertheless.

Now it was over. Now she was finally being called to account.

She'd been sitting in the garden room of Ben-Or's Ramat Aviv home on the grounds of Tel Aviv University ever since eight o'clock when the messenger had delivered the package to her. Uncle Arik had gone out. She had immediately recognized the handwriting on the envelope as Avram's, but when she'd opened it her entire world had collapsed around her.

The garden room was dark except for what light filtered in through the large bow windows, but it was enough for her to look at the photograph on the table before her and read the attached note. The words at once so simple, and yet so terribly complex and hurtful. "Miriam," he had written. "I know." Nothing more except for his signature and the photograph.

He knew. But for how long? And why had he sent this to her now, except to destroy her, except to totally ruin her credibility, except to get her off the track and keep him off?

"Oh, Avram," she cried, tears welling up in her eyes for everything that had been, for everything that could have been, and especially for a youth that had been so uncomplicated. All that was changed, irrevocably changed, and there was absolutely no way of getting any of it back.

"Miriam?" Ben-Or's voice came from the front hall. The lights went on in the living room on the opposite side of the garden.

Miriam straightened up and dried her eyes with her handkerchief, but she didn't answer immediately.

"Miriam?" Ben-Or called again, and he came out into the garden, stopped a moment, then looked straight across at her.

"In here," she said, the words thick in her throat.

Ben-Or crossed the garden and came in. He reached for the light switch.

"No," she said. "No lights, not yet."

"What is it?" the old man asked. He sat down across from her and reached for her hands. "What's happened?"

"This came tonight," she said, pushing the note and the photograph across to him. She got up. "You'll need some light after all," she said and walked over and switched on the light.

Ben-Or was looking at her. He turned after a

moment, glanced at the note, and then looked at the photograph. He took out his glasses, put them on, and looked closer at the big ten-by-thirteen black-and-white print. It was taken from a long distance overhead and showed a group of men dressed in coveralls, in a large plowed field. To the left were a series of low barrackslike structures, and to the right was a shoreline of what could have been an ocean—a wave was breaking on the rocks. Several of the men were looking up toward the sky. One of them was circled in red.

"He knows what?" Ben-Or asked. "Who is this in the picture?"

"Dennis," she said.

Ben-Or didn't understand.

"Dennis Loeb," she said, her throat constricting. "My husband."

"He's dead. More than seven years ago."

"It's him," Miriam said. "And the picture was taken recently."

Ben-Or looked at the photograph again. "You can't be sure, Miriam. It's impossible to say . . . "

"I'm sure," Miriam said.

"How?" Ben-Or asked, looking up.

"Because I've known all along."

The old man sagged visibly. He sat back in his chair. "This wasn't taken in Lebanon or Syria," he said softly as if he were afraid of his own voice.

"The Soviet Union," she said.

Again Ben-Or seemed to shrink a little further into himself. "What does this mean?"

"Shortly after Dennis was shot down, a photograph and tape recording were sent to me. It was him. They said if I wanted to keep him alive I would say nothing to anyone, but that for the moment nothing else would be required of me."

"Why didn't you come to me immediately?"

"There was nothing you could have done. He was in Moscow. I saw the photographs. They would certainly have killed him."

"You couldn't have been sure . . ."

"They sent me his severed finger, our wedding ring still on it."

"So you said nothing all these years?"

She nodded.

"Nothing was ever asked of you?"

"Nothing."

"No contact was ever made?"

"Never. Until now."

Ben-or looked at the note, and again at the photograph. "You believe the time has come?"

She nodded, her voice finally failing her.

"And you believe that Avram is working for the Soviet government? That he is their contact?"

Again she could only nod. She was so terribly confused and frightened, she did not even know her own emotions. She loved Avram and yet she felt something for her husband. She had lived with that for seven long years.

"Then what does he want, Miriam? What do the Russians want you to do for them? Why now after all these years?"

"Avram told me that he believed there was a traitor in the government."

"Yes, and why would he tell you this if he were the traitor?"

"At first I thought he knew about me, or perhaps had guessed and was giving me a chance to admit it to him."

"But that wasn't the case?"

"I didn't think so, until I told him that I was Mossad, that I had done some work for you."

"Yes?"

"He disappeared, and then this came by messenger today. Avram was the only one who knew I was here."

"That's not quite true," Ben-Or said strangely. "But it's close enough."

"Uncle?" she asked softly. "Is he a traitor? Is he working for the Russians?"

"What do you think?"

"I don't know," she cried. "I don't know what to think any longer."

GOVERNMENT CENTER, JERUSALEM, 10:15 P.M.

All of his life David Sokoloff had wanted to do some good in the world. Not just for the Jewish people, but for the world in general. In part his desire had been nurtured by an altruistic father, but in part his desire had been driven by a need to succeed in a very large way, to be looked up to with respect and even a certain admiration. An old friend had once called it his "Henry Kissinger complex." Shuttle diplomacy that through the sheer force of intelligence and personality of one man *could* make a difference: ending the war in Vietnam, or establishing relations with China. Big, sweeping accomplishments. Even those who didn't like the Kissinger type respected it. Sokoloff wanted to be counted as one of those world-class diplomats.

But sneaking into the prime minister's office on a grubby little spying mission seemed very far away from his goal, despite the fact that he was doing it for his government, and his purpose was, in Ballinger's estimation, "honorable."

He had spent the entire day arranging for and then sitting in on meetings between Harel and

members of his cabinet, leaders of the Knesset
and spokesmen, it seemed, for nearly every splin-
ter group within Israel; from the East African and
Oriental Jewish community to the National May-
ors Association, whose chairman was the Mayor of
Gaza; from the leaders of a moderate Palestinian
group, to the rabidly fanatical Haredim. Harel had
displayed his gentleness and understanding, and
his genius for compromise, while still maintain-
ing his leadership. Sokoloff had always admired
the man, but today he had seen Harel at his very
best, which made what he was doing tonight even
worse.

A sweeping change might be on the verge of
happening in Israel, and perhaps such a thing
should be welcomed, Harel had told them. But let
us never forget that we are surrounded with a
people who have publicly avowed our complete
annihilation. "A people, might I add, who are sup-
ported by the Soviet government."

"Throw down your weapons," a Haredim rabbi
had argued vehemently. "The world will never allow another Holocaust."

Sokoloff's office adjoined Harel's. He knocked
once and let himself in. Harel had left for his home
two hours ago and would not be back until morning. Sokoloff stepped around his desk, flipped on
the light, and laid out his analysis report of the
day's meetings. He could have brought it to Harel
in the morning, but the report was his excuse for
being here, should someone see the light, or passing in the corridor decide to see if Harel was
working late. Here it was a lot different than in
the States. Here the prime minister was far more
accessible than the president.

He started with Harel's appointments calendar.
Ballinger had told him what to look for, if not ex-

actly where to find it. Avram Zemil had been in to
see Harel twice in the last weeks. Ballinger
wanted to know what they had talked about. It
could provide them with a clue to exactly what
Zemil was up to. "Zemil is your traitor, but it
would be interesting to find out what he has told
Harel, to see just how he has been covering himself." The calendar made absolutely no reference
to either meeting, however, which was very unlike
Harel who, among other things, was noted for his
precision and attention to detail

Next he moved to Harel's in/out trays, which
contained nothing more than a few routine reports, one of which dealt with plans for deepening
Kishon Harbor in Haifa and was classified confi-
dential. Nowhere was there any reference to
Zemil.

The desk drawers contained governmental di-
rectories; some routine circulars, including one
from Physical Security claiming that members of
the international news media were being given too
free access to all levels of government, including
the prime minister's office itself; and the current
weekly précis of world events gleaned from the
foreign press.

Closing the desk drawers, he moved to Harel's
security file cabinet in which classified documents
were kept under lock and key at all times when
the prime minister was out of his office. He opened
it with his key, and starting with the top drawer
flipped through the files one at a time looking for
any sort of reference to Zemil, even an oblique
one, such as the jacket title for Operation Brother.
Again he found nothing. Not a single reference to
Zemil.

Closing and relocking the safe, he stood looking
toward the window for a long moment, wondering

what he had expected to find, and wondering also why he wasn't particularly disappointed that he had found nothing.

He turned finally, ready to switch off the light and leave, when his eyes fell on Harel's briefcase on the floor next to the couch. He hadn't noticed it when he'd come in because he'd been concentrating on the desk. Harel always had his briefcase with him. Seldom, if ever, did he leave his office without it. Tonight was an exception, but he'd had a lot on his mind. He'd been distracted by the day's events.

Sokoloff brought the briefcase to the desk, and with a paper clip had it unlocked in a few seconds. It was one of the little skills he'd been trained to do by the CIA before he emigrated.

There were a few reports in buff folders, with the orange diagonal stripes signifying classified material, mostly having to do with the state of Israel's military readiness, one from Ben-Or dealing with Mossad operations, and another from Ariel Eshkol dealing with the Shin Beth. Again Sokoloff could find not a single reference to Avram Zemil, which he found astounding considering everything that had been going on recently.

A few other file folders contained routine correspondence that Harel was working on, and in the center compartment was an unabridged staff directory—classified secret—which listed the names, addresses, telephone numbers, and positions of the entire Israeli government including the security services. Next to that fat volume was a slim leather-bound notebook. He pulled it out and opened it on the desk. A handwritten list of names was stuck in the middle of the book. Sokoloff's heart skipped a beat looking at it. His own name was on the list, along with Avram Zemil,

Geller, Felix Louk, Sammuel Amit, Peter Salinger, the operations officer at the Operation Brother training camp outside Be'er Sheva, Ben-Or, and Defense Minister Yitzhak Rabin. Ben-Or's and Rabin's names had been crossed out.

Each of the people on the list had known the complete details of Operation Brother. Each could have sabotaged the effort. He'd sat right in this office discussing the fact that there was a traitor within the government or the Mossad. They had discussed who would be the best one to investigate. Avram Zemil had been selected. But now his name was on a list that could only be a list of possible traitors.

Ben-Or's name had been scratched out, of course, and so had Rabin's. But his own name was still on the list. Harel suspected him, as well as Zemil. Why? What had happened in the past weeks to make Harel change his mind? What had he learned to make him fire Zemil?

Sokoloff crossed the entry plaza past the eternal flame, nodded to the security guard on duty, and got into the passenger seat of the waiting Chevrolet sedan. Gregory Ballinger put the car in gear and pulled away.

"He thinks Zemil might be his traitor," Sokoloff said.

Ballinger glanced at him. "What'd you find?"

"A list," Sokoloff mumbled. "Nothing more than a list." He looked up. "And my name is on it, too."

16

AVRAM SAT ON THE FLOOR IN THE SHAM-
bles of Miriam's apartment by the sliding glass
doors, smoking a cigarette. His body was a mass
of aches and sharp pains. He'd probably suffered
a mild concussion in the explosion because at
times he saw double, and twice when he'd gotten
suddenly to his feet he had become so dizzy he
almost blacked out. His chest hurt and his left arm
was all but useless, the intense pain in his shoulder numbing his muscles all the way down to his
fingertips.

The shower he'd taken had helped a little. So
had a change into some fresh clothes he'd left
here, and the dinner he'd made. But he had not
been able to get much sleep. Every time he closed
his eyes he saw the explosion, and afterward he
heard the screams and smelled the blood mingled
with raw cordite and plaster dust, and could feel
the heat of the flames consuming the restaurant.

Somehow he'd been traced to that restaurant.
But how, or by whom? He'd seen one of Strauss's

people on the way into the city yesterday, and he'd had his confrontation with Geller. But he would have sworn that he had not been followed to Nazareth, or back here in his Haredim costume. It was possible that whoever the traitor was had staked out all the train and bus depots as well as the highways leading into Haifa. If that were the case, it would mean they'd expected him back here, and they were willing to run the risk of mounting what for the understaffed Mossad—or Shin Beth—would be a major operation.

There was something else. Something he was missing, and just at the back of his brain he knew that he should be able to figure it out given what he already knew. But he could not. He was tired and battered and worried. Time was running out. In another twelve or fifteen hours whatever it was the Haredim were planning would happen. Whatever it was would take place in Hadera. But what? And why Hadera, which was nothing more than a small town about twenty-five miles down the coast? A tourist town, but the tourists there were mostly Israelis. Not many foreigners found Hadera enchanting.

Again, like with Limassol, he had only a part of a clue with no real idea what it meant, though he knew that somehow it fit with everything else that had happened. Only this time he was afraid that Hadera was going to be very big. Too many Haredim were evidently gathering in Hadera. Mizel had needed a lot of money, presumably to finance whatever was going to happen in Hadera tonight. But money for weapons? And if that were the case after all, just who were they planning on shooting?

He stubbed out the cigarette in an ashtray on the floor next to him and got painfully to his feet.

A truck rumbled by on the highway below. The casino had been lit up until late, but it was dark now. Out to sea he could see the lights of a big boat moving toward the south. Life went on at its own pace, but somehow none of it seemed real to him any longer. His thoughts and actions were focused now on one thing: Hadera and exposing Israel's traitor there. Nothing else mattered.

It was late. If Ben-Or was going to be at home, he would be there now. Across the room Avram picked up the telephone, but it was dead. He saw that the wire had been yanked from the wall, the wall plate taken apart and the contacts disassembled. The searchers had been thorough.

He left the apartment, taking the elevator down to the ground floor and hesitating at the front doors for a moment before going outside. Nothing moved on the streets. There were no police, no watchers. No one waiting. Outside, he turned right and hurried to the public telephone on the corner, just down the long drive that led across to the casino, and dialed Ben-Or's Tel Aviv number.

It had come too far, and he was getting too close now to keep this to himself any longer. Harel had told him to trust no one, but that had been before. Everything was changed now. The traitor knew that Avram was coming after him. Palmyra knew it. And if they kept trying to kill him like they had on Fawzi's yacht, and in Limassol, and again in the restaurant last night, they would succeed. Sooner or later, no matter how good or how lucky you were, the odds would finally catch up with you.

The connection was made and Ben-Or's telephone began to ring. The household would be settled down for the night, he figured, so he was surprised when the phone was answered on the second ring and even more surprised that Miriam answered it.

"Yes?" she said cautiously. Her voice was husky. It sounded to Avram as if she had been crying.

"I have to talk to your uncle," he said.

"My God, Avram, it's you," Miriam blurted. "How could you call here? What do you want? Haven't you done enough?"

"Miriam, what is it? What's wrong?"

"You bastard!" she shrieked. "You used me all along. All these years you've lied to me. And now you think I'll just curl up and die. Well, you're wrong. I told Uncle Arik everything. He knows what you are!"

"What are you talking about?"

"Your little package arrived last night. There's no use for you to pretend any longer."

"What package?" Avram shouted, "What are you talking about? What's happening down there?"

"Why are you doing this to me, Avram?" she cried. "Why are you doing this to Israel? Don't you have any loyalty? Or didn't you ever have any?"

Avram forced himself to calm down. "Miriam, believe me, I don't know what you're talking about. What package? Who sent it to you?"

"You did," she moaned. "And I admit it. All these years I've known that Dennis was alive. But besides me only the Russians knew it. Until now."

Avram could hardly believe what he was hearing. One name flashed through his mind, and it was Palmyra. "I had no idea, I swear it," he said.

"I don't know what you're trying to do now, but the photograph came with a note. In your handwriting, Avram. Your handwriting!"

"But it didn't come from me."

"You're the traitor, Avram! It's been you all along, and now you're trying to use me, but it won't work. Traitor!"

"Miriam, it's not true! Listen to me. Tell your uncle it's going to happen at Hadera tonight. Tell him Hadera . . ."

Avram realized in mid-sentence that he was talking to a dead line; the connection had been broken. He wasn't sure she had heard what he'd said, and he didn't think it would be of any use to try to reach her again. She would either hang up or have a trace put on the line. Traitor. She had called him a traitor. But what had she meant about Dennis and the Russians? Was her husband still alive and being held by the Russians? Was that what she meant? Had she been blackmailed all these years?

The room was empty. The single light bulb dangled from the ceiling. Now the lights were coming on all over the camp. There was a traitor. They had been betrayed.

He shook his head in an effort to clear the haze that was threatening to envelop him. The Russians had gotten to her years ago, she said. Whether or not her husband was still alive didn't matter, so long as she believed he was. And they had bided their time until now. Until she had become a threat to them by association with their only real threat. They had convinced her that he was the traitor. But what about her uncle? She'd said she told him everything. Considering everything that had happened over the past days, what else could Ben-Or believe except that Avram Zemil was a traitor to Israel?

Hadera. At this point it was his only salvation, and perhaps even the salvation of Israel.

He turned and walked back down the street to Miriam's building and let himself in. On the way up in the elevator he tried to think out his next moves. It was going to be difficult at best. He would be going into a city searching for an unknown.

He needed more information, he thought, as he went down the corridor. He needed to have some idea of what he was looking for. A start, of course, would be with the Haredim. He'd found out that they were going to Hadera. Now it was time to find out why.

First he would write out what had happened since his last report, and mail it. Then he'd make his way to Hadera—again, he expected, as a Haredim. This time he would take a little more care with his tradecraft to make absolutely certain he wasn't being followed.

He let himself into the apartment, closing and locking the door behind him. The instant he stepped out of the entry hall he instinctively knew something was wrong. A split second later he understood what it was. When he had gone downstairs to make his telephone call he had left the balcony curtains open. They were shut now, the apartment was in almost complete darkness, and he was at the disadvantage because his eyes had not had a chance to adjust after the lighted corridor.

Someone moved to the left. He spun right and dove toward the overturned couch as two shots were fired in rapid succession from a silenced pistol, one of them plucking at his coat sleeve, the other smacking into the wall inches above his head.

He went down with a crash, a sudden wave of dizziness coming over him. He cried out in genu-

ine pain as he clawed for the gun at the small of
his back.

The ruse worked, but too well. Before he could
get his gun out a dark figure loomed overhead,
barely silhouetted in the scant light filtering
through the closed curtains. He kicked out with
his right foot, just catching the gunman's hand,
diverting the next shot, and then he scrambled up,
his shoulder crashing into the man's chest, driving him backward, both of them tumbling over the
couch into the pile of debris on the floor.

The gun smashed into the side of Avram's head,
deflecting downward to his wounded shoulder in
a bone-jarring blow. Instantly his left arm and
hand became useless. Using his legs to suddenly
push himself forward, he managed to grab a handful of the gunman's thick hair in his right hand
and he smashed the man's head against the floor.
The gun came up and fired, the bullet creasing
Avram's neck with an extremely hot stitch. Again
he smashed the gunman's head against the floor,
bringing his knee powerfully up into the man's
groin. A grunt exploded in his face, the gunman's
breath foul with fear and death.

Again and again, Avram smashed the man's head
into the bare concrete of the floor where the carpet had been pulled up in the search. The gunman's struggles became weaker and weaker, until
finally he was limp beneath Avram's weight, and
his gun clattered to the floor.

Avram rolled off the man, and for several long
moments he could do nothing more than sit
hunched over while he tried to catch his breath.
The room seemed to be slowly spinning round and
round and his stomach was churning, threatening
at any moment to make him violently ill. He could
feel the warm blood streaming down the side of

his face from a cut on his scalp, and down his
shirt collar from the wound in his neck. There was
a lot of blood. Too much blood, he thought.

Somehow he managed to get to his feet and
across the living room into the bathroom. By feel
alone he grabbed a towel from the rack and
wrapped it around his neck to staunch the flow of
blood.

They had followed him to the restaurant and
now they had traced him here. How? How had
they known?

*The room was empty. The single light bulb dan-
gled from the ceiling . . .*

But Miriam had known he was calling from
Haifa. That much at least would have been easy
to check. Not such a big guess to think he might
come here to hide, to lick his wounds. Calling him
a traitor could have been meant to do nothing
more than throw him off.

Something crashed in the living room. Avram
pulled out his gun and stepped around the corner
as the dark figure rose up on one knee and fired,
the shot barely missing. Avram fired once; the shot
caught the man high in the chest and drove him
backward, the noise from the unsilenced weapon
shockingly loud in the close confines of the apartment.

He lurched to the left and, keeping low, his gun
trained out ahead of him, rushed the rest of the
way back into the living room. But the gunman
was dead. His eyes were open, and already the
blood that had pumped out of his chest in bright
arterial spurts had slowed and stopped.

Avram slumped down beside him. Someone
would have heard his single gunshot. The police
would be summoned. Someone would be coming
very soon. Letting the gun rest in his lap, he pulled

open the dead man's coat with his right hand and awkwardly fished for his wallet, flipping it open when he had it. He couldn't seem to make his eyes work. Something was wrong. Until it dawned on him that the apartment was too dark. Shoving his gun in his belt he staggered to his feet and went to the window, where he parted the curtains only enough so that he could read the dead man's identification card. He was a Pole. From the Polish Interest Section in the Swiss embassy in Jerusalem.

Avram turned and looked back at the man on the floor. Not Polish, he thought, but Russian.

Whatever the case, this apartment was no longer safe for him. He was going to have to get out, and now. There would be others coming for him. Soon.

Pocketing the dead man's ID he started across the living room when a scratchy sound came from the body. He spun around reaching for his gun, automatically stepping left into a crouch. The dead man hadn't moved. The scratching sound came again, followed by a low-pitched hiss.

"Petor?" a voice said, as from a great distance.

A walkie-talkie, it suddenly came to him. The gunman, whose first name was Petor—which didn't match the name on his Polish ID—was being summoned. He had not come alone.

Avram found the walkie-talkie attached to the man's belt. He pulled it off the loop and keyed it once, but said nothing.

"*Da,*" the voice came from the speaker.

Someone was outside waiting. Down on the street. In a car. Avram shoved the body over and scooped up the silenced pistol, which he immediately recognized as a SigSauer, exactly the same model as his, except this one was silenced. Jenkins had been killed in Limassol with a SigSauer, and Avram had just found his assassin.

He went immediately to the door, which he unlocked and opened just a crack. The corridor was
empty as before. No one had come to investigate
the single unsilenced pistol shot. Perhaps no one
had heard it, or if they had, had not recognized it
for what it was. He stepped out, closing and relocking the door behind him, and hurried down
the corridor to the stairwell.

It was going to be very dangerous for him to be
out on the streets like this, with a bloody towel
wrapped around his neck, more blood down the
side of his face, with a silenced gun in his hand
and another weapon in his belt. There'd be no explaining it to anyone. The instant he was seen the
alarm would go out.

At the bottom he slumped against the wall, spots
before his eyes, another wave of dizziness and
sickness coursing through his body. He wasn't going to be able to keep this up much longer. He
needed to stop somewhere to tend his wounds and
get some rest.

The lower corridor was empty when he stepped
out and made his way to the back door, which he
opened barely a crack and looked outside. A Mercedes taxi was parked up the street. He could just
make out the front half of the car, the driver behind the wheel. Holding the walkie-talkie well
away from his body, he keyed the transmit button.

"You won't get out of this apartment alive, you
bastard!" he whispered urgently and released the
transmit button.

For a moment nothing happened. But then the
driver jumped out of the cab and came up the side
street in a run. Avram stepped back farther into
the corridor and raised the silenced pistol.

Seconds later the door was yanked open and the
driver, a large, swarthy man wearing a cabby's

cap and coat, burst into the hall, a big Makarov automatic in his left hand. He pulled up short when he saw Avram.

"If I have to kill you, I will," Avram spat in English, hoping it was a common language between them.

The driver's gun was pointed downward, Avram's was pointed directly at the man's chest, the hammer cocked, his finger tight on the trigger. The other man realized his disadvantage for the moment. He held his body rigid, his eyes on Avram's.

"You won't leave this city alive," the big man said.

"You won't leave this building alive unless you answer my questions," Avram said. "What is going on in Hadera tonight?"

The driver laughed, the sound low and guttural. "Fuck your mother, Jew," he said. It was a Russian national expression of disgust. That much Avram knew, which solidly identified this one.

"Petor is dead. Soon the police will be coming."

"Good," the Russian said, unperturbed. "Then we shall wait for them."

"The moment I hear a siren I'll pull this trigger. Hadera. The Haredim are gathering there. Why?"

"You're a traitor to your country, Zemil. There is no place for you to hide. No place to run."

"Hadera," Avram repeated. "Five . . . four . . ."

The Russian smiled, a little uncertainly this time. "I know your kind. As long as I don't move a muscle you won't shoot me. Not in cold blood."

"Three . . . two . . ."

"It won't happen," the Russian said, clearly nervous now.

"One," Avram said with finality. "Hadera?"

"Fuck your mother," The Russian said and started to raise his gun.

Avram pulled the trigger twice, the muffled sound of the silenced weapon echoing dully in the narrow corridor. The first shot hit the Russian high in the chest, driving him backward against the steel fire door, and the second destroyed his throat, taking out most of his spinal cord at the base of his skull, blood with bits of flesh and bone flying everywhere.

NETANYA ON THE COAST, DAWN

The sun was just coming up at Avram's back as he used salt water from the sea along a deserted stretch of beach to clean his wounds, the pain at times so sharp, so immense that it threatened to drive him to his knees. He had regained only a slight use of his left arm and hand. Not enough, not enough, he kept telling himself. Yet it was all he had. He had truly run out of time.

Driving down here in the taxi the Russians had used, he had passed the turnoff to Hadera. Two army Jeeps had been parked beside the road, a civilian truck stopped for the roadblock. Not only were the Haredim interested in Hadera, but so, it seemed, were the military authorities. He had heard nothing about any operation for this region, unless the army was simply expecting trouble from such a large gathering of religious fanatics and had brought troops up here to prevent any problems from getting out of hand. Then why the roadblocks? They had to be protecting something in Hadera.

Twice on the way down here he had nearly

blacked out with pain and loss of blood, but looking at his wounds in the taxi's door mirror he was
relieved to see that for the most part they were
relatively minor. One of the bullets had cut a long
crease in the side of his neck. The four-inch-long
wound had puckered and the blood flow had
slowed to an ooze. There was a fairly large cut in
his hairline just above his left ear, but it, too, had
stopped actively bleeding. But his clothes were a
mess. He had pulled on the Russian driver's coat
and cap, which in addition to his shirt were badly
blood-stained. He might have gotten away with
such an appearance last night, but in the light of
day the first person to see him would sound the
alarm.

At the back of the car he unlocked the trunk,
hoping he might find something, but not for a moment dreaming he would find what he did. A lot
of mysteries suddenly became clear to him. The
trunk was filled with suitcases and leather satch-
els containing several changes of civilian clothes,
two complete Israeli Civil Police uniforms, and the
long black coat and broad-brimmed hat typically
worn by the Orthodox sects such as the Haredim.
The satchel contained two Uzi submachine guns
and ammunition. In a small leather case he found
what appeared to be a duplicate of the pager that
Geller had given him. He'd left his at Miriam's
apartment because it had been shattered in the
restaurant explosion, though why he had carried
it as long as he had he didn't know. Habit. He took
the pager out of its case and looked at it, turning
it over in his hands, his mind running to a dozen
different possibilities. It was possible, just possible, that the pager he had carried was something
more. A homing device, perhaps, which meant either that Geller was the traitor and had planted

the device on him, or that somehow, somewhere, the Russians had managed to switch devices on him. He tried to think back; there could have been the opportunity, he supposed, in Larnaca when he'd been held by the police. Filiátes had allowed him to leave too easily. Was the Greek in on it? He'd also seen a couple of the devices in Sammuel Amit's safe. If Amit were the traitor, he could have given Geller the doctored pager to give to Avram without the chief of station realizing what was happening.

Circles within circles. Plots within plots. All of it, though, led directly toward a three-cornered triangle, two sides of which he already knew about: The Russians and the Haredim. The third was Israel's traitor: the last leg that, when exposed, would cause the entire triangle to collapse. He hoped.

First he needed one more bit of information, and then he would go to Hadera. Tonight, he kept telling himself. One way or another, tonight would see the end of it. In some ways he didn't know if he wanted to see it through for fear of what he might find.

Quickly he changed into one of the civilian outfits in the trunk, the trousers a little short and the jacket slightly too large, not so badly cut that he would attract undue attention, though he would be marked as a foreigner. All the labels were Polish.

He repacked one of the suitcases with a police uniform, a Haredim hat and coat, and the walkie-talkie he'd taken off the dead man in Miriam's apartment, tossed the bag in the backseat of the taxi, and drove up from the beach to the main highway leading back into town.

* * *

The day was already bright and warm when Avram parked the taxi on the out-of-the-way street just off the downtown section, and with the suitcase in hand walked six blocks over to the railroad station, entering by a side door and crossing directly to the men's room. He washed his hands and splashed some cold water on his face, looking at himself in the mirror as he smoothed his hair straight back with a lot of water. His eyes were bloodshot, and with his jacket collar up the wound at his neck was barely visible. He no longer looked like an Israeli, he decided. With the poorly cut suit, his hair slicked back, and the sour, determined expression on his face, he looked more like what he was presenting himself as: a Polish diplomat.

Outside, he strode across the small concourse to the rank of public telephones, where he set down his bag and dialed a long-distance number that he dredged up from memory.

"Operations," the duty officer at Zippori Air Force Base answered.

"This is Sammuel Amit, I'm calling from Haifa Station. Has Joseph left yet?" Avram said, using a fictitious name.

"Joseph who?" the OD asked. "Who is this again?"

"Amit. I need to know if Joseph Schummach has left for Hadera. This is Mossad business. Priority blue. Haven't you been told?"

"I don't know any Schummach, but the others left last night."

"They're in place then in Hadera?"

"I don't know, but I imagine they are. But if you're calling from Haifa you should know that."

"Look, I've got a job to do, you know. I'm just trying to do as I'm told. To make sure everything is set for tonight. Make certain everyone understands their orders."

"Sorry, Amit, but this is an open line."

"That doesn't matter. Do you understand your orders?"

"What the hell are you talking about?" the OD demanded.

"Hadera," Avram snapped. "Tonight. Good God, man, where have you been?"

"Hold on, I'll check with my captain."

"Better yet, why don't you check with Tel Aviv? I'm done screwing around here."

The OD hesitated on the line for a pregnant second. The morning train was getting set to depart and Avram looked up as a number of school children dressed in uniforms hurried, giggling and shouting, across the concourse.

"Tel Aviv?" the OD asked uncertainly. "I would have thought the orders would come out of Jerusalem, under the circumstances."

"Yes, and what circumstances are those?" Avram asked. He was moving onto shaky ground now.

Again the OD hesitated.

"Look, as I said, I'm just following orders." Avram said. "I'm supposed to find out if everyone knows and understands their orders."

"Well, that's not for me to say," the OD said. "Just let me get my captain, you can talk to him."

"Right," Avram said, disappointed he hadn't been able to get more, and yet satisfied that he had at least picked up one more piece of the puzzle. Whatever was drawing the Haredim to Hadera tonight had the interest not only of the army and the Mossad, but also the attention of the government in Jerusalem.

He hung up the telephone, picked up his bag,

and had started across the concourse when he spotted a civil policeman watching him from across the hall. He took care not to falter in his stride, or to outwardly appear hesitant or nervous, but the cop was definitely interested in him.

Outside, several taxis had drawn up, discharging passengers for the morning train to Tel Aviv. Avram crossed to one of them, tossed his bag in the back, and crawled in after it.

"Can you take me to Hadera," Avram asked, injecting a Slavic accent into his English.

The cabby glanced at him in the rearview mirror and nodded. "Sure," he said. "Of course. Everybody is going to Hadera, why not Ivan?" It was the Israeli common name for a Russian or anyone else from a Warsaw Pact country. Avram smiled inwardly.

As the cab pulled away from the curb he looked back toward the station entrance. The cop who had taken an interest in him had come out and was looking this way. But he made no other move, nor did he pull out a notebook to jot down the license number. But he definitely had something on his mind. What? Why now?

Hadera was about ten miles north of Netanya and a couple of miles inland from the coast. The army roadblock was at the coastal highway turnoff. His first trouble, if he was going to have trouble getting into the city, would happen there.

Avram sat back in his seat and, careful to keep his hands low enough so that the cabby could not see in the rearview mirror what he was doing, checked his gun to make certain it was fully loaded and ready to fire, the safety on. He wasn't going to shoot one of his own people, of course, but there was no telling what he would be running into in Hadera.

Next he took out the wallet he had lifted from the dead man and again checked his Polish diplomatic identification. The photograph was vague enough so that he might pass. The name was Stanislaw Sikorski, the red passport proof of his diplomatic status.

Outside the town the cabby sped up, the morning developing into a beautiful day. Already there was a lot of traffic on the road, and by the time they reached the army roadblock on the highway to Hadera the line was backed up, a lot of the drivers impatiently honking their horns, some of them standing out on the side of the road arguing with the soldiers.

Avram watched for a few minutes. As each car reached the barricade, the driver and passengers were required to get out and were searched after they showed their identification. In the meantime, other soldiers went through the car looking through luggage and packages. It was a search, Avram realized, that he would never pass.

He tried to think as a Polish diplomat might think under the circumstances. Such a delay would be intolerable to him. A search of his person and suitcase totally out of the question.

Avram sat forward in his seat. "Drive around to the front of the line," he said.

The cabby looked at him. "We can't do that."

"Oh, yes, my friend, we most certainly can and will," Avram said arrogantly. He took out his diplomatic passport. "I have important business in Hadera. Now drive to the head of the line and there will be a bonus in it for you."

The cabby mumbled something under his breath that Avram couldn't quite catch, but he put the cab in gear, carefully eased out of the line, and bumped up the side of the road to the army barricade. One of the officers stepped away from the car they were searching and held up his hand for them to stop. He seemed angry.

"What the hell do you think you're doing here," he shouted.

The cabby shrugged, but Avram leaned out the window, waving his passport. "I have business in Hadera that cannot wait," he shouted in broken English.

Avram had expected an argument from the officer, or at the very least that his passport would be checked. But the officer just stepped back and saluted.

"Of course, sir," he said, and he waved them through.

17

Driving into the city of 30,000 people, two things were immediately obvious to Avram. The first was that whatever was going to happen here tonight was going to be very big. Traffic, both vehicular and pedestrian, was thick, every second person, it seemed, dressed in the Haredim costume, soldiers stationed on every street corner. And the second was that activities seemed to be centered at the Uri Dan Hotel downtown. Some sort of a joint military-civilian checkpoint had been established at the hotel's main doors. Everyone coming and going was stopped.

Avram's driver had become impatient. "Where is it you wish to go, exactly?" he snapped on their second pass through the downtown section.

Avram had ordered the driver to circle around the square without explanation. "I'm looking for a friend," he said finally.

"You have no friends here," the cabby muttered in Hebrew, certain that his Polish diplomat fare would not understand.

"What is that?" Avram snapped.

"It's your money," the driver said in English. "I'll drive all day if you want."

"It's not necessary," Avram said. He had already seen what he wanted to see. "I'll be staying at the International. You can take me there." He sat back in his seat.

The International Hotel was just across the street from the Uri Dan. If he was able to get a front room he would be able to watch what was going on across the street. As much as he wanted to get started immediately, he realized that it was going to be very dangerous for him to be out on the street during the daylight hours, so he was going to have to wait until darkness. It would be cutting everything very thin . . . too thin, perhaps, but if the Mossad were here in Hadera in force, it was very possible he would run into someone who would recognize him no matter how he tried to change his appearance.

They came back through the square and the cabby pulled into the International's driveway. Avram paid him well, adding the promised bonus, and with bag in hand hurried into the hotel and across the crowded lobby.

As incredible as it seemed, Hadera was filling with people and yet no one was saying exactly why everyone was here. If he had still had the prime minister's confidence, he thought bitterly, he would know what was going on here, what to expect. Or if Ben-Or would answer his telephone calls he could find out something, anything. But as it was he was totally on his own. This time the advantage belonged to the traitor.

"Your reservations please, sir?" the clerk said at the desk.

Avram laid out his diplomatic passport. "I have

none. But I wish to have a room overlooking the square if that is possible."

"Totally impossible," the clerk said, apparently unimpressed by the credentials. "We have been fully booked since last night."

"It is extremely essential that I have a room."

"I am sorry, sir," the clerk said insincerely. "Perhaps the other gentleman in your party can help you?"

Avram just stared at him. Other gentleman? Pole, or was he Russian? The clerk was waiting for him to respond. He was going to have to make a decision now. "We're not in the same party," he said. He reached in his pocket and took out his Mossad identification. He was taking a terrible risk. Partially covering his name with his thumb he held the plastic card out only long enough for the clerk to realize what it was, then withdrew it. "I am a Polish diplomat," he said softly, urgently, in Hebrew. "Do you understand?"

The clerk's eyes had gotten round. "Yes, sir," he stammered. "I think so. Do you wish to speak to the manager?"

"Definitely not," Avram said. "No one must know who I am. No one on your staff, and especially not this other Polish diplomat you spoke of. This is a matter of national importance. I want to make that very clear to you. And I want you to understand that your help will not go unrewarded, if you take my meaning."

"Perfectly, sir," the clerk said, pleased. "A front room you wished?"

"If possible," Avram said, glancing over his shoulder. So far as he could tell no one had noticed the brief exchange. He turned back and filled out the guest registration card as Stanislaw Sikorski, paid for his room in advance, and the clerk handed him his key.

"You will be in room five-oh-four."

"And the other Polish diplomat? What room does he have?"

The clerk glanced at his registration list. "He is two floors up and one room over in seven-oh-six."

"His name?"

"Jan Międyrzecz, if I have the pronunciation correct."

The clerk had. Avram recognized the name. Międyrzecz was the Polish Affairs officer out of the Swiss embassy in Jerusalem. He had a gut instinct that whoever was in 706, it wasn't he. Palmyra? It was possible.

"Thank you," Avram said. "Not a word to anyone."

"Yes, sir."

Ivan Roskov entered the lobby of the International Hotel in time to spot a figure he took to be Petor Bogachev entering the elevator. But something didn't seem quite right to him. Some instinct made him keep from rushing forward. The figure turned and Roskov found himself looking into the face of Avram Zemil. He stepped back behind a large potted plant, certain that Zemil had not spotted him, his heart thumping nearly out of his chest. The elevator doors closed and the car started up. Roskov hung back until the elevator stopped on the fifth floor and moments later started back down.

Zemil here! But dressed in one of Petor's suits. It explained why he hadn't heard from his aide. Zemil was truly the devil that Petor had feared. But what had happened in Haifa? How had Zemil overcome them both? And how had he managed to make it through the roadblocks?

Roskov opened the newspaper he'd been carrying under his arm. Zemil's photograph appeared beneath the headline ARMY CAPTAIN WANTED FOR MURDER. The story had appeared in this morning's editions. They were calling Zemil an army officer so that the Mossad's name wouldn't be dragged into it. It was a standard ploy. The Shin Beth had issued an all points bulletin on him, and the army was looking for him as well. The fools, Roskov thought bitterly. The utter fools. All of them put together could not stop Zemil. Well, that wouldn't last much longer.

It was time, Roskov thought, to earn his KGB pay. But quickly this time, and with finesse. Zemil was going to die this day, but before that happened he was going to tell them everything he knew. That information was vital if all their plans were to succeed.

Roskov turned and left the hotel and headed back to the apartment he had just left on Hamara Street.

THE INTERNATIONAL HOTEL,
9:53 A.M.

The voice on the long-distance line spoke English, with a German accent. "Good morning, you have reached the embassy of Switzerland."

"Yes, please connect me with Mr. Międzyrzecz, the Polish Interests officer."

"One moment please," the woman said. Seconds later the number rang and was answered, again

by an English-speaking voice, this one with a
heavy Polish accent.

"Three-seven-eight."

Avram deepened his voice and held his hand
partially over the telephone's mouthpiece. "This
is the international operator, I have an extremely
urgent call for Mr. Jan Międyrzecz. Is he there
please?"

"I don't believe so, operator. But hang on a moment, I'll check."

"We are holding with Mr. Międyrzecz's Warsaw party."

A moment later a man's voice came on the line.
"Hello, this is Jan Międyrzecz."

Avram smiled and hung up the telephone. The
Polish Interests officer was safely tucked away in
Jerusalem, unavailable, it seemed, to anyone ex-
cept a priority call from the Polish capital.

He picked up the telephone again and dialed
room 706 two floors above him. He let it ring five
times before he hung up again. Odd, wasn't it, he
thought, that Jan Międyrzecz was registered here
at this hotel and yet answered his telephone in
Jerusalem.

He checked his gun once again, then let himself
out of his room and took the stairs up to the seventh floor. He had to wait in the stairwell for a
party to get off the elevator and make their way
to their room. A half-minute later the bellman
emerged and took the elevator back down. The
moment the elevator door closed, Avram stepped
out into the corridor and hurried down to 706. He
knocked at the door and then put his ear to the
wood. No sounds came from within.

Making sure no one was coming up the corridor, he hurriedly picked the lock and let himself
in, slipping the security chain into its slot. The

room was a twin of the one he'd been given; twin beds separated by a nightstand to the left, a bureau with television to the right, a large bathroom, and a table and two chairs placed in front of the large windows. The curtains were slightly parted. A few clothes hung in the closet, but there was nothing else in the room.

Avram stood with his back to the door for a long moment. Was this Palmyra's room or was it really Jan Międyrzecz's, rented for the Polish diplomat who would be showing up later today? But no, the clerk downstairs had intimated that the Polish gentleman was already in residence.

Starting in the bathroom, Avram quickly looked through all the drawers and shelves, as well as all the obvious hiding spots; in the toilet tank, under the bed, inside the television, behind the light fixtures. But there was nothing other than the few articles of clothing in the closet and a few toiletry articles in the bathroom, the razor Swedish-made, the cologne, French.

He was left with two choices: He could remain here to see who would show up. If this room belonged to the Russian Palmyra after all, the man could get spooked and avoid the room, or he might be out on the streets right now putting into effect whatever was going to be happening here tonight, not planning on returning until it was over. His second choice was to leave an obvious sign that someone had been here, which might spook the Russian into tipping his hand, and then get on with his own investigation.

He opted for the latter, pulling the bedcovers back, shoving the mattress aside, pulling the man's clothes out of the closet and rearranging his toiletry articles in the bathroom before letting himself out and making his way back downstairs to his own room.

At his window he checked the street below and the entrance to the Uri Dan Hotel. A man in civilian clothes stood just at the army checkpoint, his back this way. He didn't seem to be trying to get into the hotel; rather it appeared to Avram that he was conferring with the officer. After a moment he turned to look out at the street and Avram got a good view of him. It was Yoram Geller. Not terribly surprising, Avram thought. The Mossad was definitely on alert. Geller would be here.

Seconds later Michel Louk came out of the hotel and said something to Geller, then the two of them turned and walked to the driveway as a black Ford sedan drew up. Louk opened the door and David Sokoloff got out of the back. The three of them spoke for a few seconds, then turned and walked past the checkpoint into the hotel.

All three of them were on Avram's short list as possible traitors. All three of them were together now. What the hell did it mean? What was going on here? In addition to the Haredim gathering, and security precautions, those three were together: a Mossad station chief, a Shin Beth officer, and the prime minister's chief adviser. Whatever it was, it was damned important.

In the bathroom Avram peeled off his clothes and took a long, hot shower, the spray in some small measure easing his aches and pains. Drying himself off, the towel came away bloody from where his neck wound had begun to ooze, but by the time he was finished it had closed up again.

He dressed in the civil police uniform, then pulled on the long black Haredim coat and hat, pulling it low over his eyes. He had no identification as a Haredim, but he didn't think he would be singled out among the several thousand already on the streets, unless he was already recognized. In that case a fake ID wouldn't do him any good anyway.

With the police sidearm in its holster, he reloaded the silenced SigSauer he'd taken from the dead Russian and stuffed it in his coat pocket. His stiletto was strapped to his chest.

Before he left his room he checked himself in the mirror. The Polish diplomat Sikorski was gone, replaced now with an ordinary, God-fearing Haredim here on a pilgrimage. But a pilgrimage for what, or to do what? he wondered. Time now to find out.

First checking to make certain the corridor was empty, he let himself out of his room, took the stairs down to the third floor and then the elevator the rest of the way down to the busy lobby.

He had a feeling that the rank and file of the Haredim had no real idea what was about to happen here tonight. Their leaders had simply called for a rally here, and nothing more. If he was going to find out what was going on, he would have to isolate one of the leaders; or his other, much more distasteful choice would be to find and isolate someone from the Mossad or the Shin Beth and persuade him to tell what he knew. This last was very dangerous. He could not, would not, hurt one of his own. But if he was given no other choice he didn't know what he would do.

The answers, however, were not to be found sitting alone in his room waiting for something to happen. The answers were out on the street, or short of that, across the way in the Uri Dan Hotel.

The elevator stopped at the ground floor and the doors opened. Two thick-necked men dressed in dark suits were waiting. They stepped aside as

Avram got off, sudden recognition dawning in their eyes. One of them stuffed his hand in his right pocket. The other moved smoothly to the left so that they were momentarily blocked from view by anyone else in the lobby. They were Russians, it was clear from their appearance.

"If you reach for your gun we'll kill you here and now," the nearer one said softly. He was a professional, Avram could see it in his eyes. If there was a shootout here, innocent people would probably get hurt.

Avram inclined his head slightly. The entire exchange had taken less than two seconds. A bellman leading a couple was coming across from the registration desk.

"We have a car waiting just outside. Walk straight across the lobby. Now," the Russian ordered, and he stepped aside.

Avram smiled and nodded as he passed the couple, and headed for the main doors, the Russians falling in on either side and slightly behind him.

Outside, a gray Mercedes sedan had drawn up to the curb. One of the Russians went ahead, yanked open the rear door, and got in. When Avram bent down to climb in after him he saw that the Russian had drawn a big automatic and was holding it in his lap. He got in, the second Russian piled in next to him and shut the door, and the driver pulled smoothly away from the curb and headed away from the square.

"So now what?" Avram said.

"Shut up," the Russian on his left said harshly.

"We're off to see Palmyra, is that it? You know that your friend Petor and his driver are both dead. Up in Haifa."

The Russian jammed the barrel of his gun into Avram's ribs hard enough to cause a sharp bolt of pain driving up into his lungs. "Shut your filthy Jew mouth, or I'll kill you here and now."

"I doubt it," Avram gasped through clenched teeth. "I doubt it seriously, Ivan. Your master might yank on your leash so hard it would break your fucking neck."

The other Russian had pulled out his gun, and he smashed its butt into Avram's skull, the blow totally unexpected. A burst of stars exploded in Avram's head as he was driven sideways. He wasn't unconscious, but he allowed his body to go completely limp, slumping over the first Russian's legs as he reached inside his coat for the stiletto strapped to his chest.

The Uri Dan Hotel, 10:00 a.m.

Gregory Ballinger lowered his binoculars as the gray Mercedes sedan turned the corner and disappeared from view. It had been Avram Zemil in the back seat of the car with two KGB operatives. He'd recognized their faces from his files. It meant that Palmyra was near, and it meant that their worst fears about Zemil were probably correct: He *was* working for the Russians. For just a moment, though, he had almost doubted his own assessment. It had seemed that just as the car turned the corner some sort of a struggle was going on in the back seat. But the angle was wrong, and the car was too far away for him to be certain. He was sure, however, that Zemil had emerged from the hotel willingly with his Russian pals. There'd been no struggle there, no coercion, no hardware showing.

Maybe the Shin Beth was correct after all.

Maybe Zemil was a killer and their spy. But he wasn't after Sokoloff, or at least it didn't seem that way to Ballinger. Who then? What was he up to? Having a man like Zemil in this close right now, however, made him extremely nervous. Everything could blow up in their faces. Sokoloff's name was after all, on the prime minister's short list of suspects.

Ballinger worked in the consular section of the American embassy. His cover was as Deputy Vice Consul for Economic Affairs. He turned away from the window, put the binoculars aside, and in the bathroom straightened his tie. He pulled on his coat, picked up his attache case, and left his room, taking the elevator up to the top floor of the hotel, where a Shin Beth security post had been set up. He showed his credentials to the duty sergeant.

"Mr. Sokoloff is expecting me," he said.

"He just arrived, sir," the sergeant said. "I'll call him for you."

The corridor was alive with security people and mid-level government officials. Telephones were ringing, typewriters were clattering, and over all was the muted hum of a dozen conversations.

David Sokoloff emerged from a room and waved Ballinger down. The sergeant nodded for him to go ahead. Sokoloff seemed pale and very nervous.

"I'm glad you could see me on such short notice, Mr. Sokoloff," Ballinger said for the benefit of anyone who might be listening. "I'll just need a moment of your time, sir."

"Sure," Sokoloff said. "Come in."

Ballinger stepped past him into the room, and Sokoloff closed and locked the door, then turned on him.

"What the hell are you doing here like this?" he

blurted. "You could ruin everything. My God, I'm on his short list. You know that."

"And so is Avram Zemil," Ballinger said. "He's here."

"In Hadera?"

"I saw him two minutes ago coming out of the hotel across the street. He wasn't alone."

"Are you sure it was him?"

Ballinger nodded. "He was with two KGB legmen."

Whatever color had been left in Sokoloff's face drained away, and he sat down on the edge of the bed all of a sudden, as if his legs had collapsed under him. "Here," he whispered. "With Russians. Then it's true. He is our traitor."

"It would seem so."

Sokoloff looked up. "What is he doing here? Now of all times?"

"Think the worst, and it's probably true."

"Insanity," Sokoloff said shaking his head. "That's total insanity."

"I agree. But I thought you'd better be warned."

"Yes," Sokoloff said absently.

"When are the others due to arrive?"

"This afternoon and early evening. The first meeting is set up for eight o'clock sharp."

"Here?"

"There is a conference room at the south end of this wing."

"Security is tight?"

"Very. But Zemil is damned good." Sokoloff shook his head again. "I can't warn anybody. They'd want to know how I got my information."

"He was dressed as a Haredim."

"That's just great. Every other person in this town right now is Haredim."

"Listen," Ballinger said. "You have another

problem as well. I suspect that Ivan Roskov—Palmyra—is probably here as well. And that could mean very large trouble, so watch yourself."

"What about Zemil?"

"We're working on it. I'll see what I can do. Just watch yourself."

Sokoloff nodded.

"Are you armed, David?"

"No, I don't like weapons, you know that."

"Well, I suggest you get a gun, and keep it with you at all times. At least until tonight is over with."

"Do you think I'll need it? I mean, is it possible . . . ?"

"With Zemil and Palmyra working together anything is possible, David."

HAMARA STREET, 10:02 A.M.

The Russian shouted something unintelligible. In the momentary confusion Avram had managed to withdraw his stiletto and he held it in his right hand. The timing would be tight, split-second, the odds in the back seat two to one. He would concern himself with the driver later.

As he expected would happen, the Russian who had hit him grabbed a handful of his coat and started to haul him back at the same moment the other Russian was pushing him away.

Avram cried out in pain, and as he suddenly sprang backward, shoving the one Russian up against the opposite door, he thrust the stiletto in and up, the razor-sharp blade easily penetrating the man's heavy jacket and slipping between two ribs directly into his heart.

The Russian reared back, blubbered something, and slumped over dead.

Avram continued shoving backward, butting his shoulder into the second Russian's chest as he swiveled in his seat, yanking the stiletto out of the dead man's chest.

"Yuri!" the Russian screamed, trying to bring his gun around so that he could fire.

The driver hauled the big car around a corner, his foot jammed on the accelerator, slewing both Avram and the other man momentarily off balance.

It was all the opening the Russian needed. He brought his gun up and fired at the same moment Avram reared backward, his head banging off the roof, the bullet shattering the window. He fired a second time, and the bullet caught Avram in the side with a dull, sickening hammerblow. Avram batted at the gun with his nearly useless left hand, but it was enough to throw the Russian's third shot off. In the next instant he brought the stiletto around in a long, arching slice, opening the Russian's throat with a gush of arterial blood and air from the lungs. The man tried to scream but only a hoarse gurgle came out as he clawed at his throat, then slumped over dead.

Avram grabbed the gun and hauled himself upright. "You're next, Yuri, unless you slow down now!"

The driver knew that his life depended upon his compliance. He immediately slowed the big car to a normal speed.

They'd come only a few blocks from the downtown square and were now on a much quieter residential street of apartment buildings. Someone had to have seen the struggle and would be reporting it to the police by now. They were going

to have to get off the streets, and very soon. Avram
held the gun on the driver with his right hand,
while with his left he applied as much pressure as
he could to the wound in his side. He felt weak,
light-headed, and sick to his stomach. He could
not continue much longer.

"Where were you supposed to be taking me?"
he demanded.

"Somewhere," the driver growled, glancing at
Avram's reflection in the rearview mirror.

"Where?"

"An apartment, very close now."

"Is Palmyra there? Were you bringing me to
him?"

The driver didn't answer. Avram jammed the
barrel of the big pistol into the base of his neck.

"Talk to me or I'll kill you here and now. I don't
have anything to lose. I think you understand
that."

"Yes," the driver said. "We were to take you to
. . . Palmyra."

"What is his real name?"

Again the driver hesitated. Avram began to
squeeze the trigger.

"Major Ivan Roskov," the driver blurted.

"In two minutes I'm going to pull this trigger,"
Avram said, working with everything in his power
to keep his voice steady and to keep from drifting
off. "Unless you have brought me to Roskov."

"I can't."

"Then you'll die."

The Russian said something Avram couldn't understand, but at the corner he turned onto Hamara Street, and half a block farther he slowed
and turned into a driveway that led to a parking
area at the rear of a small apartment building. No
other cars were parked in the lot.

"He's here?" Avram asked.

"Yes," the driver said.

"Take me to him," Avram said. He fumbled with the door handle and when the door popped open he lost his balance and nearly fell out of the car.

The driver jumped up and came around to him. Avram looked up and raised his pistol, but it was beginning to get dark, and he was having trouble focusing his eyes. He'd miscalculated his own abilities. Gromit had said Palmyra was very good; the best. A man of enormous ego but with a talent to match.

Avram could no longer hold up the heavy weapon. The driver reached in and took it from him, then helped Avram out of the car as another, much shorter man with large, intensely dark eyes came from the apartment building.

"So, Mr. Zemil," he said. "We meet at last."

"Palmyra?" Avram heard his own voice as from a very great distance.

"Just so," Roskov said. "Very clever of you to have come this far."

18

HADERA POLICE STATION, NOON

"AVRAM ZEMIL IS A KILLER," MICHEL Louk told the others around the conference table. "And I have reason to believe he's here in Hadera at this very moment." Besides Louk, who represented the Shin Beth at this meeting, the others included Yoram Geller for the Mossad, Daniel Eisele, the husky middle-aged Hadera chief of police, and Captain Zvi Amer, who was in command of the special army security forces brought up for tonight. The tension that gripped the city was reflected in their faces.

"If that's true, then we all know why he's come here," Eisele said, his voice gentle like wind in a wheatfield. He was a good man, and quite bright.

"I don't know what other conclusion we can come to, gentlemen," Louk continued. "He has apparently gone through a great deal of trouble to remain at large, despite our best efforts to catch him, over the past day or so. And everything he's done seems to point in this direction."

"I'm sorry, Michel, but I just don't see it that way," Captain Amer said, leaning forward, his bony elbows on the tabletop. He'd served with Avram in the army, and a couple of times since on joint Army-Mossad operations.

"I'm afraid the information we have is overwhelming," Louk said.

Amer looked at the others around the table. "I read the headlines too, but under the circumstances I think it would be wise if you shared what you know. If Zemil is our man—and I'm telling you I'm having a hell of a hard time accepting that—but if he is, my people are going to need every scrap of information they can get if they're to do a good job."

Louk glanced over at Geller, who had been strangely silent from the start of this meeting. He supposed it was because Zemil had been one of their own. A Mossad agent whose first loyalty was supposed to belong to the State of Israel. "It's up to you, Yoram. Some of this information is sensitive."

Geller took a moment before he spoke, as if he were gathering up his thoughts. "We're here to protect the life of the prime minister of Israel, among others. Don't let's quibble about interservice rivalries."

No one said anything.

"It began several weeks ago with a Mossad mission called Operation Brother," Geller said.

"Actually it began a few months before that," Louk corrected, and Geller glanced sharply at him. "But let's start with Operation Brother. From what I've been told it was an airtight operation that only a handful of people in all of Israel knew about, yet it was blown, and because of its failure three Mossad penetration agents were hanged in public in Damascus."

Recognition dawned in Amer's and Eisele's eyes.

"Avram Zemil was mission commander. By rights he should have been killed on the desert. But he was not. Somehow he managed to escape."

"There were others who knew about the mission, you said," Eisele interjected.

"Yes. But Zemil was involved recently in another operation, this one a joint Shin Beth–Mossad mission in which a Lebanese diplomat whom we had guaranteed protection was killed. Avram was the only man on the scene. Again he escaped unharmed."

Amer had heard about that operation. "I would have killed the bastard myself, given half the chance," he said. "Did anyone actually see Zemil killing Fawzi?"

"No. But I've learned that afterward Zemil flew to Limassol, Cyprus, where he murdered, among others, a British expatriate who probably was involved in the sinking of Fawzi's yacht."

"Among others?" Geller asked.

"I'll get to it in just a moment, Yoram," Louk said. "It's my guess that Zemil took out the Brit to keep him quiet. At this moment the Greek-Cypriot police have a warrant for Zemil's arrest on the murder charge."

"Who is he working with?" Eisele asked.

"We thought the Russians," Louk said. "But now we believe he is working alone. To date we've found the bodies of four men whom we believe were KGB agents. They were all shot with a SigSauer nine-millimeter automatic. Deadly weapon. Fifteen-shot. It's the weapon Zemil carries."

"How do you know these men were KGB?" Eisele asked.

"Except in one instance they carried Polish diplomatic identification, but the Poles are not claiming them. It's a common dodge for the KGB."

Captain Amer sat forward. "You said in all but one case?"

"Early this morning two bodies were found in the apartment building of a friend of Zemil's. One carried a Polish ID, the other did not."

"Then he's here in Hadera," Amer said. "My people passed a Polish diplomat through the main seacoast highway checkpoint shortly after dawn this morning."

"Was he alone?"

Amer nodded.

"Did your people get his name?"

"No. We've been instructed hands off on all diplomatic passports."

"It's him," Louk said. "He is definitely here in the city."

"Then we'll find him," Eisele said quietly.

"It may not be so easy," Louk said. "He's very good. Possibly the best operative in all of Israel at the moment."

"He's only one man," Eisele said. "And we know what he's come here for."

"There may be something else going on with him as well. Something I don't quite understand myself. At least it hasn't made any sense to me yet."

"What is this?"

Louk turned to Geller. "In answer to your earlier question, I need to ask a question."

Geller nodded, but said nothing.

"Has Zemil ever had any connection with the Haredim?"

A startled look crossed Geller's features. "No," he said. "Not that I'm aware of."

"Nothing in his records, or from his past that you might know about, even a rumor, that would indicate he's got an axe to grind with the Haredim? Something that would have caused him to hate them so much he would be willing to murder them?"

Sudden understanding dawned in Geller's eyes. "You're talking about Jerusalem. Three months ago. The Wailing Wall massacre."

"Exactly," Louk said. "We've actually got nothing to tie him to that, except that on Cyprus, at the same time Zemil was gunning down the British expatriate, two Jews were found dead in a car crash. Both of them were members of the Haredim sect, and there were signs of a struggle in what remained of the car. Two nights ago, in Jerusalem, the body of Hiram Mizel, a prominent Haredim leader, was found in his bookshop; though the connection between his death and Zemil is a little thin, the timing is too coincidental for my liking. There were some other factors in the case that were highly unusual as well. Finally, last night in Haifa a bomb was set off in front of a cafe frequented by the Haredim. A number of people were killed and injured. One of the cooks firmly identified Avram Zemil, unharmed, at the scene." Louk sighed deeply. "Whatever else Avram Zemil is or isn't, gentlemen, it would seem that he has a fanatical hatred of the Haredim, who, as you all are painfully aware, have gathered in force here in Hadera at the moment. It makes for a very dangerous combination."

"We could have a full-scale riot on our hands," Eisele said, definitely worried now.

"One that could cause the Haredim themselves to run totally amok. They are at the edge of hysteria now as it is. One more incident could push them over the edge, and we would be hard pressed to guarantee anyone's safety, especially the prime minister's."

"Then the meeting should be canceled."

"I've already tried," Louk said. "But Ezra Harel, several of his advisers, and at least three prominent members of the Knesset, including my brother, will be here tonight with the Haredim leadership in an effort to hammer out their differences and save this country for all of us."

"God help us if Zemil starts something," Eisele said.

"Yes, God help us," Geller mumbled. "He'll have to be killed."

"Shot on sight, I'm afraid," Louk said heavily. "He's one man, I think, who will not give up."

"We'll start with the hotels," Eisele said.

"Yes," Louk said. "But you'd better begin with the Uri Dan itself and work outward."

"We don't have the manpower to do a house-to-house search."

"Start at the Uri Dan," Louk repeated. "Sooner or later he'll be drawn there."

HAIFA, 2:30 P.M.

Miriam Loeb was more confused and hurt than she'd ever been in her life; even more hurt than when she had been told her husband of just a few months was probably dead, and even more confused than when she'd received his severed finger in the mail.

She stood just within the doorway of the shambles of her apartment, surveying the wreckage and the big splotch of blood on the bare concrete floor. There was a lot of blood. The Haifa Civil Police lieutenant who had released her apartment back to her only long enough for her pick up a few items of clothing had made her promise to create the least possible amount of disturbance, which was a joke, she thought now. It couldn't be any worse. Nothing could. Her apartment was sealed as a crime site in what the lieutenant called an "ongoing investigation of some importance." Only the fact that she had identified herself as a Mossad officer had convinced the lieutenant to allow her up here like this on her own.

"Oh, Avram, what has happened?" she cried softly to herself. She wanted to believe in him. With all her heart and soul she loved him still, despite everything that had happened. Trust in me, he had asked her. But God, it was so difficult. Even Uncle Arik had abandoned him.

Tell your uncle it's going to happen at Hadera tonight. Those were his last words to her. But when she'd told Uncle Arik what he'd said, he had no idea what it meant. Forget him, Miriam, he'd told her. But she could see in his eyes that he didn't mean it. Not completely. He's not what you think, Miriam. Nothing is, Miriam. Nothing ever is.

But she could not forget him, because she loved him even more than she loved her uncle, more than she had loved her husband—they'd known each other barely two weeks before they'd married, and he was listed as missing in action three months later—and more, she supposed, than her country, because if he walked in the door this moment and told her point-blank that he was a traitor and that he wanted her to go with him, she would.

Whatever happened, she was going to have to hear it from his own lips. She would have to con-

front him with it face to face, and tell him about
Dennis. It would all depend, then, upon him.

Stepping carefully over the debris, she went the
rest of the way into her apartment. The struggle
had been violent. Both of them had been Russian,
probably; one of them had been carrying a Polish
diplomatic identification. The same two, she wondered, who had come to her in the night and
pawed her body, warning her to stay out of it? She
shuddered thinking about it.

She walked into her bedroom and looked
around. She'd come here looking for a sign, she
supposed. Something Avram might have left behind for her. But the police had gone over everything. If Avram had left a message, they would
have found it.

In the bathroom she switched on the light dangling by its wires from the ceiling fixture. Avram
had been here. She could smell him. A bath towel
was missing from the pile on the floor, and there
was a little blood on the counter.

She turned. What had happened here, exactly?

Back in the living room she watched how the
light deepened the almost black color of the dried
blood on the concrete floor. There was more blood
on the ruined remains of the couch. Violence. So
much death and violence.

And there was more to come, she feared. Much
more.

She left her apartment, and without looking
back jumped in her car and headed back downtown, parking ten minutes later in the side lot of
the Zion Hotel on Bailik. She no longer gave much
of a damn about her tradecraft. Now she was in a
hurry because she had made a decision in her
apartment, seeing the blood in the living room and

bathroom, knowing that some of it almost certainly had to be Avram's.

She entered the Vulcan Foundary Computer Center building, and after identifying herself to the young duty officer went back into Operations, where Sammuel Amit was holding down the fort in Geller's absence.

"Hello, Miriam," Amit said a little coolly when she walked in. Avram was on the outside, and in a small measure so was she, by association.

"Is Yoram here?" she asked.

"No," Amit said. No one else was in Operations at the moment.

"Where is he?"

"I can't discuss that with you. You know that."

"Has he gone to Hadera with the others?"

Amit just looked at her for a moment or two. "What is it you want here, Miriam?"

Miriam looked around the operations room. "I imagine most of the staff is down there helping the Shin Beth with security. No matter," she said, turning back to him. "You can help me. I need a weapon."

Amit shook his head. "I'm sorry, but I can't do that."

"If I have to telephone my uncle, believe me I won't hesitate. I want a handgun and I want it now!"

Amit seemed unimpressed by her threat. "May I ask why you need a weapon?"

"My apartment has been ransacked and two men were found dead there, as you no doubt know. I want protection."

"I'll assign a man . . ."

"You will not," she snapped, her voice rising. She stormed over to the operations desk and picked up the telephone. "I want to talk with Arik Ben-Or, immediately. This is his niece."

"Is this a priority code, ma'am?" the station operator asked.

"Yes," she said, looking directly at Amit. "Red-one."

"Yes ma'am," the operator started to say, but Amit came forward. "Hold it," he said.

"Hold that call," she told the operator and she placed her hand over the mouthpiece. "I need something with stopping power. Preferably an automatic."

Amit's eyebrows rose. "Nine-millimeter Beretta?"

"That'll do nicely," Miriam said. "And an extra clip of ammunition."

ON THE SEACOAST HIGHWAY, 3:15 P.M.

Miriam drove very fast, the convertible top of her Fiat down, the wind in her hair, her eyes filling behind her sunglasses. She'd made her decision in Haifa, but now that she was actually on her way she could feel her resolve weakening a little. It hurt so badly.

She glanced at her purse on the passenger seat. The Beretta was loaded and ready. Avram, according to the Shin Beth and the police, was a murderer. According to the evidence, he was a traitor. He'd known about her and Dennis, and he'd sent the photograph that he could only have gotten from the Russians.

But he had denied it. His handwriting, but he had denied sending her the photograph. A forgery, or was he lying to her? She was confused about

everything except one thing. She wanted to see
him, face to face. She wanted to hear what he had
to say from his own lips, at which time she would
know in her heart of hearts whether he was finally
telling the truth. If he was, she would stick with
him no matter what he asked of her.

She glanced over at her purse again. If he wasn't
. . . she would kill him.

THE HAMARA STREET APARTMENT, 6:30 P.M.

When Avram finally came around it was late. He
was in a small bedroom. Through the window curtains he could see that the sun was very low in the
sky. From the open bedroom door he could hear
the muted conversations of at least two men, perhaps three, speaking in guttural tones, urgent at
times he thought, but he wasn't quite able to make
out the words.

He was lying on a small bed, a single blanket
thrown over him. His shoes were off and he was
naked from the waist up, though he felt the band-
age around his side with his fingers. He'd been
shot in the side, and when he tried to move an
extremely sharp pain shot through his body and
he slumped back, an immediate sweat popping out
on his forehead and nausea rising to the back of
his throat. He felt beaten and bruised and very
weak.

Palmyra had won. But why hadn't they killed
him? There was more here that he didn't know.
He suddenly felt like a terrible fool. One seriously
wounded man against at least two presumably
healthy and well-armed Russians, however, wasn't
exactly his notion of good odds.

He shoved the blanket aside and pushed himself up, gritting his teeth against the pain and swallowing back the nausea as he swung his legs over the edge of the bed. That small effort had momentarily cost him what little reserve of strength he had left. He sat hunched over trying to catch his breath.

The voices from the living room seemed to fade in and out, but now he could hear that they were speaking in Russian, and there were three of them. One of the voices he recognized as the driver's, and one of the others . . . Palmyra.

He stood up slowly, holding the edge of the bed for support, then lurched drunkenly across the narrow room to the bureau, his legs nearly buckling under him. Again he had to stop to catch his breath, frightened at how weak he had become. But the dizziness didn't last as long, and moments later he was able to look out the window.

It was approaching early evening. His window looked down on the parking lot behind the apartment building. Two cars were parked there. The one he had been brought here in, and another Mercedes, this one red. Whatever was going to happen here in Hadera would be happening soon, he figured.

He looked around the room, searching for something, anything, that he could use as a weapon. But there was nothing. Even the bureau was empty, as was the tiny closet. The legs of the narrow bed were metal, but even if he could pull one of them loose there wouldn't be much he could do with it against armed men. Not yet, he told himself. For the moment he was going to have to bide his time. They had kept him alive this long, apparently because they wanted something from him. His opening, he thought grimly, would come. He would make it come, somehow.

He pulled himself together, turned, and as steadily as he could manage walked across the room to the doorway. The driver and another heavyset men, both of them dressed now as Haredim, were just leaving. The third man—Palmyra—had just picked up the telephone and was about to dial.

"Major," one of the men by the door said urgently and reached for his gun.

Roskov turned. "You are a man of great recuperative powers, I see."

The one by the door said something in Russian which Avram couldn't understand, but Roskov shook his head and waved him away. He hung up the telephone.

"I think Mr. Zemil and I will get along just fine, Yurianovich," Roskov said in English. "Time is getting short and you two have much to do yet. Get on with it."

The Russian objected, and Roskov turned on him, uttering a few sharp words. The one at the door blanched, and nodded. *"Da,"* he said. He and the other one left the apartment. Avram could hear them on the stairs and then they were gone.

The odds, Avram thought, had just improved.

"May I have something to eat and drink?" he asked, holding onto the doorframe with one hand, pretending an even greater weakness than he actually felt.

Roskov eyed him for a long moment. "I think you are a very dangerous man, Mr. Zemil, even with your injuries, and with a bullet still lodged in your body."

"Even a condemned man gets his last supper," Avram replied, allowing a little pleading to creep into his ragged voice. The tactic went against his grain, but this was life in the real world. Kill or be killed. The equation had gotten simple, at least here and now it had.

"I'm not going to keep you alive long enough for you to derive any benefit from a meal, but you can have a drink if you'd like. Vodka?"

Avram inclined his head and started away from the doorway.

"Stay there," Roskov barked sharply.

Avram halted.

Roskov was in shirt sleeves, his tie loose. He stepped over to where his coat was lying over a chair and took out his pistol, a big Makarov automatic. From a pocket he pulled out a silencer tube and screwed it onto the end of the barrel. He levered a round into the firing chamber, cocked the hammer, and flicked off the safety switch, all with his eyes never leaving Avram's. Back at the coffee table, which was laden with what appeared to be the remains of a light meal, he poured a healthy measure of vodka into a tall glass, placed the glass at the far end of the table in front of an easy chair, then stepped back.

"Now you may sit and have your drink," he said.

Avram lurched forward, nearly stumbling for real, and Roskov flinched, instinctively raising his gun. "For God's sake, don't shoot me."

"Not yet, but soon," Roskov said. "Just how soon will depend entirely upon you."

Avram made it the rest of the way to the chair and sat down gratefully. He picked up the vodka and downed it in one swallow. At his right elbow was a lamp table. He set the glass down and sat back, the liquor rebounding in his stomach threatening to make him sick. The room seemed terribly warm to him.

"What's going to happen here tonight?" he asked, his voice again coming from the end of a long tunnel. His legs seemed impossibly long.

"That's for you to tell me, Zemil," Roskov said, cautiously perching on the arm of the couch. "What are you doing here?"

Avram managed a slight, sardonic smile. "I killed your friend Petor . . . or should I say diplomat Sikorski. And I killed his driver. They weren't very good."

Roskov's jaw tightened a little. "Answer my question or I'll kill you this instant."

"I went to your room at the International. Overlooks the Uri Dan. Curious."

Roskov said nothing.

Avram closed his eyes. "I came here looking for you."

"Why?"

"You are a Soviet spy operating in my country, why else?"

"How did you trace me to Hadera?"

"Hiram Mizel told me before I killed him."

"He died of a heroin overdose . . ." Roskov started.

Avram opened his eyes. "I stuffed the drug down his throat. He told me you'd be here, along with the other one."

"Yes, who is this?"

"Our traitor. The one in the Mossad with whom you've been working for some time now. What are you after here? Is the Soviet Union so frightened of tiny little Israel?"

"You would be truly surprised if you knew the entire answer to that question. Why haven't you exposed your traitor, or killed him?"

Avram's heart skipped a beat. Roskov had said

him. Their traitor was within the Mossad after all, and it was a he. Not Miriam.

"Because I don't understand the connection with the Haredim," Avram admitted honestly.

Something crossed Roskov's eyes. A small triumph? It was troublesome.

"Who hired you to find me? Harel?"

"Yes."

Again there was that troublesome change in Roskov's expression. The man was obviously hearing what he had hoped to hear. What was missing here? Avram wondered. Something important.

"And you're still working for him?"

"Of course."

Roskov laughed. "Either you are an extraordinary liar, Zemil, or else your people have gone to great lengths to throw me off guard by discrediting you in public."

Avram had absolutely no idea what he was talking about. "We've used such tactics before."

"I can't remember when," Roskov started, but then something else occurred to him. "But then, you have been on the run for at least the last twenty-four hours, and you might not know." He got off the couch, moved cautiously over to the small dinette set and brought back a Tel Aviv newspaper. He tossed it, front page up, on the coffee table in front of Avram, knocking over the vodka bottle.

Avram's photograph was printed beneath the headline ARMY CAPTAIN WANTED FOR MURDER. That was the Shin Beth's doing. Was there more than one traitor? One within the Mossad *and* Michel Louk?

"Every cop and soldier in Israel is looking for

you," Roskov said. "Nice tactic, if a little dangerous."

Avram wondered what Ben-Or was thinking at
this moment. And the others, the people he had
worked with all these years, his army friends. It
was galling to think this bastard and the traitor
had brought him this far. He needed time to
think.

"What about Dennis Loeb," he asked.

The question was obviously unexpected to Roskov. "He's dead, I'll give you that much."

"In the plane crash?"

Roskov nodded. "Now your girlfriend thinks
you're a traitor, unless she's another of your
tactics. Nice body, by the way, my people tell
me."

Avram forced himself to remain calm, although
his gut was seething.

"You're no longer working for Harel, are you?"
Roskov said from a distance. "He'll be here tonight, along with his advisers and a few key Knesset leaders. Perhaps we can arrange for you to be
together again. The prime minister and his rene-
gade agent gone wrong."

Assassination. Avram finally put it together.
The Haredim would riot ... the heroin money
was for weapons ... and the crime would be
blamed on them, with Avram as their leader. It
fit. It all fit. Israel would fall, the borders would
be open, or they would fall, and this time when
the Syrian tanks rolled there would be no stopping them. This time when the war came, and it
surely would, Israel would lose, and every man,
woman, and child would be massacred. The Holocaust of Nazi Germany would be tame by com-
parison.

The telephone rang and Roskov picked it up.

"Yes?" he said, the gun never wavering from Avram's chest.

Now, Avram thought. He sat forward, clutching his chest and wheezing with a large gasp as though trying to catch his breath.

"He's here. I have him," Roskov was saying.

"Help me . . . for God's sake . . ." Avram cried weakly. He half rose out of the chair, then fell to the left against the lamp table, causing it and the lamp to crash to the floor, the spindly legs splintering as he fell in a head atop it all.

At any moment he expected a bullet in the back of his head. He willed his body to remain absolutely still despite the massive waves of pain. In his right hand he grasped one of the splintered legs.

"He just fell over," Roskov said after a long second or two. "I don't know. But is everything set at your end?"

Avram could feel blood rolling down his side from the bandaged wound that he had torn open in the fall.

"Then God bless you," Roskov said with feeling. "This is for Israel, you know where your loyalty lies."

Avram could hardly believe his ears.

"Yes," Roskov said. "Go with God." He hung up.

It had been the Mossad traitor on the telephone. But he was Haredim. Go with God. The Haredim used that as a regular greeting.

Roskov was just above him now. Avram waited, his muscles bunched up, his strength rapidly fading.

Roskov grabbed Avram's shoulder and had started to turn him over when Avram, with his last ounce of strength, thrust around and upward with the long, jagged-edged table leg, driving the splintered end into Roskov's stomach just above his groin; the pistol went off, the bullet smacking into the floor a half-inch from Avram's head, and an inhuman scream of pain, agony, and absolute rage escaped from the Russian's lips.

19

OUTSIDE THE URI DAN HOTEL, 6:40 P.M.

MIRIAM LOEB SAT AT A SIDEWALK CAFE ON Hadera's downtown square, sipping a Pernod to calm her nerves and watching the comings and goings of the crowd that had been gathering for the past half hour or so. The Uri Dan Hotel with its security post in front was across the square to her left, the International to her right. The cafe was mostly empty. Most of those who were taking part in the gathering demonstration—mostly Haredim by their dress—were out in the streets. And the townspeople, for the most part, had sense enough to stay indoors. There was going to be trouble here, she could feel it ripe in the air like the stench from an open sewer.

A half-hour ago her uncle had shown up, before most of the crowd had gathered. He'd spoken briefly with the officer at the security post and had then entered the Uri Dan. Since then the Haredim had seemed to materialize out of the woodwork, coming on foot from every direction, their black, amorphous mass coagulating on the square, choking all but the most persistent traffic.

There were police and army troops everywhere, but they were already outnumbered ten to one, and still the Haredim continued to stream into the square.

"Avram, my love, where are you?" she whispered to herself.

She'd not seen her waiter or anyone else from the cafe staff for the past ten minutes or so, but she didn't care. Every face that passed her was subject to her scrutiny. Avram was here in Hadera. Somehow everything would be resolved. All her fears, she knew at an instinctual level, would this night be either confirmed or put to rest. Her life, she decided, was on the line here just as surely as was Avram's.

"Come to me," she whispered. "It will be all right. I'll understand. Tell me so that I can know."

She spotted a head of white hair coming out of the Uri Dan but then she lost it in the crowd. She sat forward. Again she saw something white against the black background across the square, but again she lost it. It wouldn't be her uncle. He would not be out in the open alone; it would be rank foolishness. The chief of the Mossad did not go for early evening strolls, especially not through the midst of a crowd on the verge of turning hostile.

She'd known about Hadera now for a couple of days. Her uncle had counseled Harel against such a dramatic meeting, but the prime minister had been adamant. "Israel's future is more important than my safety," Harel had said. She'd read the top page of the notes on the meeting they'd had. The Haredim would have to be appeased. The meeting would take place on neutral grounds—so far as such a place could be found in Israel—and with the minimum of publicity.

For the past two days, however, the Haredim had been streaming into Hadera. Already the international press was showing up in droves as well, though for the most part they were being kept away from the square, at least for the moment, by the army on the grounds that the situation could become dangerous.

Hadera had suddenly become a magnet.

A movement directly to her right startled her and she turned and looked up into the concerned face of Ben-Or.

"Uncle," she said, surprised.

He sat down beside her. "What are you doing here, Miriam?" he asked. He looked and sounded very tired.

"You shouldn't be out here like this," she said. "It's too dangerous for you."

"What are you doing here, Miriam?" Ben-Or repeated. He reached out and covered her hand with his. "Waiting for Avram to show up?"

She dragged her eyes away from his, a lump rising in her throat again. "I have to know," she said softly.

"Not like this, not now."

"He's coming here, isn't he?" she said, turning back. "To assassinate Harel, is that it, Uncle?"

"I would like you to get your car and leave Hadera. For me, Miriam. Please."

She shook her head after a moment. "I still love him, Uncle. I have to know if he is a traitor, a killer. I have to hear it from his own lips, see it in his eyes. I won't leave until then."

A great struggle was going on inside Ben-Or, she could see it in his eyes and in the way he held himself perfectly erect, like the old soldier he was, at attention ready to receive orders he knows will be extremely disagreeable. In Israel, to survive, you were either that, or a religious zealot such as the Haredim. There didn't seem to be a middle ground here these days, if there ever had been.

"I could order you to leave," he said. "If necessary I could have one of my people take you back to Tel Aviv."

"I'd just come back," she said. "If he got me that far. I'm not leaving."

"You could be hurt."

"I'm already hurt."

"I meant physically," Ben-Or said. "This is a war."

"Yes," she said softly. "I know it. And I intend being on the front line no matter what you have to say."

Again Ben-Or hesitated. He shook his leonine head. "I'm afraid I can't accept that, Miriam. You're going to come with me now, back to the hotel." He looked at her with a sad but stern expression on his face. "If I have to take you back by force, I will."

She was shocked. He had never acted this way toward her before. It was out of love, she knew. But there was something else there too. Something he was hiding form her. She nodded and got to her feet, leaving money for her bill. "All right," she said.

Ben-Or got up and took her arm, and they started back the long way around the square, avoiding the bulk of the mob, which Miriam estimated was already in the thousands. The noise of their shouting, and in some cases chanting "Trust in God," was deafening.

Half a block from the restaurant she slipped out

of his grasp and without looking back hurried directly into the crowd. Once she thought she heard her uncle calling her name, but his voice, if it had been his, was lost in the din. She was free.

HAMARA STREET, 7:00 P.M.

Avram was operating in a dream state in which the world seemed to drift in and out of focus and his body seemed to float an inch off the floor. He had cleaned himself off in the bathroom—his body had been covered with Roskov's blood—and had painfully rebandaged the wound in his side. He was very aware of the passage of time, yet he couldn't seem to make his arms and legs move any faster; his fingers on the buttons of the shirt he'd found in the second bedroom seemed like thick sausages with no feelings. And pulling on the trousers he'd doubled over with pain, nearly blacking out.

The Russians and the Haredim. The connection was no longer conjecture. Hanging in the closet were several black coats and broad-brimmed hats, and on the bureau was a battered book of Torah studies next to his own pistol and stiletto.

He pulled on one of the coats and a hat, pocketed his weapons, and went back into the living room. Roskov lay in a bloody heap on the floor, the table leg jutting from his abdomen, his legs curled up beneath him.

The room was empty. The single light bulb dangled from the ceiling. Now the lights were coming on all over the camp. There was a traitor. They had been betrayed!

Palmyra was dead, and the Haredim's involvement was known. Two legs of the triangle were eliminated. All that was left was their traitor.

The apartment was on the second floor, and it seemed to take him forever to make it outside to the red Mercedes, which was the only car in the parking lot. Then he realized that he had forgotten the ignition key. He stood wavering at the side of the car trying to make a decision. Most Haredim did not own or drive an automobile, especially not a Mercedes. Mizel had been an exception.

He looked toward the north. It was already starting to get dark. He heard the noises of a very large crown. The Uri Dan Hotel was only a few blocks away. A Haredim heading toward the square on foot would be just another figure in the crowd. Approaching the city center alone in a red Mercedes, however, would attract some notice.

He glanced up at the apartment, then, girding himself for the final effort, turned and started down the driveway to the street, one careful step at a time, sweat immediately popping out on his face and blood beginning to trickle through the bandages over the bullet wound in his side.

OFF THE TOWN SQUARE, 7:18 P.M.

Chief of Hadera Police Daniel Eisele pulled to a screeching halt just at the edge of a large knot of police, army, and civilians blocking the Hamara Street approach to the square. Without bothering to switch off the flashing blue lights of his car he jumped out, and holding his ID up over his head pushed his way through the crowd.

An ambulance had already arrived and was backed up to the curb. One of his young uni-

formed police officers was sitting on the pavement
while the medics administered first aid to him. He
was pretty banged up, his uniform torn and
bloody and a large patch of his face scraped away
where he had skidded across the street. His partner's body was in the gutter covered by a blanket.

"What happened here, Eli?" Eisele asked his
sergeant, who had been the first to respond to the
call.

"There were two of them. Gray Mercedes.
Looked as if they were going to stop, but at the
last minute the bastards ran them down."

"Did we get a number off the plate?"

"No, sir. It happened too fast. Debre was killed;
broke his back and crushed his skull. Gertner was
lucky."

"Anyone else see it?" Eisele asked.

The sergeant just nodded toward the civilians,
many of the Haredim. "We questioned a few of
them, but all we can confirm is that it was a gray
Mercedes and there was a driver and another man
in the front. No one in the back seat."

Eisele sighed deeply. This was just the beginning, he thought. Before this night was over there
would be other casualties. He decided that he
should have remained in the army. At least there
you knew who your enemies were. He just thanked
God that a Haredim hadn't been killed. The mob
would have gone crazy.

He went over to the ambulance and hunched
down beside his injured officer, who looked up.

"We'll get you to the hospital in just a minute,
Paul," Eisele said.

"It's all right, sir, I can manage. I'll just need a
fresh uniform."

"The fight's over for you, for tonight anyway.
You didn't get a look at the registration tag?"

"No, sir," the young cop said, hanging his head in shame. "It was just a routine check like you asked. We weren't expecting anything like that."

"Did you get a good look at them?"

"I got a look at them, but I just don't know, sir. Rudi was closer. He was right in front of the car . . ." He closed his eyes with the pain of the memory.

"Easy now," Eisele said gently. "From what you saw, could you come up with a description?"

"Nothing that would hold up in court."

"We're not in court here, boy. Just think. Big men? Husky? Small men?"

"Husky, I think. Dark."

"Foreigners?"

"I don't know. Maybe. It was hard to tell because of their hats."

"Haredim?"

The young cop nodded.

"Careful now, son. You've seen this Zemil's photograph. You've got his description. Could one of the men in that car have been him?"

"I don't know . . ."

"Think, son, this is important. Is it possible?"

The boy nodded. "It's possible, sir, but I just can't be sure." He looked up, his eyes wide. "But he's one of us, sir. Why would he do something like that?"

"I don't know, son. But I sure as hell am going to find out," Eisele said. He straightened up and took his sergeant aside. "It's my guess that Zemil was one of them, and the other was one of his Russian playmates."

"Which means he's in the square."

"Right. Dressed as a Haredim in the midst of ten thousand of them. I'll alert the others, I want you in charge here." Eisele gazed toward the square. "From this point on, check everyone coming out of the square. He's in there now. When he finishes with his dirty business he'll want to get out. No matter what happens we'll nail the bastard."

THE URI DAN HOTEL, 7:22 P.M.

Michel Louk entered the conference room at the north end of the top floor corridor. Everything had been set up for the meeting: tables, chairs, microphones. And everything that could humanly be done, considering the crowds on the street, to provide security had been done. Yet Louk still had the feeling that he was missing something, that they were all missing something.

None of the principals had shown up yet, though some of them were already here in the hotel. Harel and his entourage had left Tel Aviv by helicopter minutes ago and were scheduled to set down on the roof at eight sharp when they would be escorted directly down here. When they were in place, the others would be summoned.

Yoram Geller was talking with some of his people. When he spotted Louk just at the doorway he broke off his conversation and come over.

"We're about ready here; how about downstairs?"

"It's a madhouse, but no one else is being allowed in the hotel. Absolutely no one," Louk said.

"Good. Starting at seven-forty-five I want no weapons whatsoever on this floor."

Louk was startled. "What are you talking about?"

"Downstairs is covered, and the roof is being manned. The only people on this floor will be Harel and his party along with your brother and the other Knesset members. Ben-Or will be here as well."

"What about the Haredim? There'll be six of them."

Geller nodded. "I'll personally screen them as they step off the elevator. I'll be armed of course, but no one else. The situation is explosive enough as it is without having a show of force up here."

"Any one of them could be armed."

"I know that, but it's extremely unlikely, Michel. If we have a lot of our people up here frisking them there'll be hell to pay."

Geller was correct, of course, but it made Louk uneasy to think that they'd be so vulnerable up here. "I'll stay here, then, in the conference room," Louk said.

"As you wish," Geller replied. "Any word on Zemil?"

Louk sighed deeply. "That's why I came up. He's probably here on the square somewhere, dressed as a Haredim. But he's with a Russian."

Geller was clearly shaken. "I don't understand."

Louk explained what had happened at the police checkpoint minutes earlier. "They weren't positive it was him, but Eisele seemed to think it was likely."

"What are you doing about it?"

"He's not in the hotel, we know that much for a fact. Everything is sealed up tight. And he won't be able to get in."

"But he'll try."

"Probably. But he won't make it."

A faint smile played across Geller's thin mouth. "No," he said. "I don't expect he will."

ON THE SQUARE, 7:35 P.M.

The mob was a living animal now. It had a life
of its own as it ebbed and flowed, like eddy cur-
rents in an enclosed bay just before a big storm.
All the streets leading in and out of the square
were blocked off. Avram looked back the way he
had come, through the Hamara Street checkpoint. He had expected trouble. He would have
been willing to bet almost anything on it. But he
had been allowed through, with barely a glance,
in a knot of other Haredim streaming into the
square.

Now as he watched he could see that the few
people leaving the square were being stopped and
searched. The opposite of what he thought should
be happening. What was going on? It didn't make
sense to him.

From where he stood, just within the crowd in
front of the Uri Dan Hotel, he had a clear view
of the security post at the front doors. No one
was being allowed inside. The army had actually
barricaded the doorway and stood shoulder to
shoulder with their weapons drawn. They were
dressed in riot gear with helmets, face shields, and
body pads. At least one of the civilians he recognized as Shin Beth. Louk's people.

There were soldiers at some of the first- and
second-floor windows, and he saw a helmeted head
pop up over the parapet on the roof and then disappear. They were taking no chances. The hotel
would be sealed front and back.

Absolutely no one who wasn't already inside
would be getting in now. That single fact was important. Avram knew that it should mean something to him. But what?

Palmyra's two soldiers had left the apartment dressed as Haredim. They would not be allowed inside. Which meant what? Probably they were somewhere here in the square ready at some signal to work the crowd into a frenzy. A riot outside, while inside the hotel was . . .

Then he had it. The obvious. No one else would be allowed inside the hotel, which meant that their traitor was already there. The Russians on the outside working the Haredim, the traitor on the inside ready to assassinate Harel.

The Uri Dan was flanked to the south by a five-story office building, its roof two stories below the Uri Dan's. To the north was a three-story parking ramp used in common by the Uri Dan, the International across the street, and the downtown office workers, merchants, and shoppers.

There was little or nothing he could do to stop a riot form occurring with this crowd. From what he was hearing they were ready for something to happen, their mood made all the uglier by the presence of so many armed troops in front of the hotel and hedging them in on all the approach roads.

He was going to have to get into the hotel somehow. And very soon.

He studied the Uri Dan and the adjacent office building for a minute longer. It would be possible, he thought, now that it was dark, for him to make his way to the roof of the office building, and from there hopefully through a window into the hotel's sixth floor. Whatever was happening would probably be on the top floor, he reasoned, but once inside he would be able to make certain of that by how the security people were placed.

It wasn't much of a plan, especially for the condition he was in, but it was better than nothing.

He happened to glance over toward the parking ramp before he turned toward the office building, in time to catch a brief but clear glimpse of a face beneath a broad-brimmed hat looking down at the crowd from the second floor of the ramp, and he froze in his tracks. It was one of the Russians from the apartment. The one Palmyra had called Yuri-anovich. The driver.

A short burst of gunfire from up there into the crowd would cause the entire square to erupt in violence. The army and the Shin Beth together would not be able to control them.

It would be a perfect cover for whatever was happening inside. The security people would of necessity be drawn down to the square. All eyes would be turned this way, while inside . . .

Avram turned toward the ramp and started working his way through the crowd, chanting "Trust in God," over and over again with them as he pushed his way across the square.

THE URI DAN HOTEL, 7:36 P.M.

Gregory Ballinger, like all the other guests in the hotel, was restricted to the sixth floor and below. No one was being allowed into the hotel now, but from what he had learned there was no restrictions on leaving. Once outside, however, no one would be able to return.

He had spent most of the afternoon and early evening at his sixth-floor window overlooking the square, watching through powerful binoculars. He had seen the exchange between Ben-Or and his niece, and had watched as she slipped away. He had spotted her a couple of times more in the crowd but finally lost her fifteen minutes ago.

Now he watched as Avram Zemil made his way through the crowd and then disappeared into the parking ramp next door. What the hell was the bastard up to? With Harel and everyone else getting set to show up within the next few minutes, Zemil's presence so close by was extremely dangerous. There were Russians out there too. He could practically smell them.

Ballinger pulled on his jacket, checked to make sure his Walther PPK was loaded and ready to fire, then left his room, taking the elevator down to the ground floor. Sokoloff had been warned already, and he at least had an idea of what was possible. Warning him again would accomplish nothing unless there was something concrete to report. Do not meddle in the affairs of the Israeli government, but keep your ear to the ground, had been his brief. Sokoloff was his main source. But he was damned if he would simply sit idle and watch an assassination take place that would embroil the entire country in a civil war. He just wasn't built that way. Brief or no brief.

The lobby was filled with people, but no one even noticed him as he crossed to the main doors and went outside, nor did the security people so much as acknowledge him as he stepped past the soldiers and hurried down the driveway next door.

The Parking Ramp, 7:42 p.m.

The noise of the chanting mob echoed and re-echoed off the low concrete ceilings as Avram hesitated on the sloping driveway onto the second floor. A hundred feet away he could see the tail of the parked gray Mercedes, nose toward the street.

"Trust in God," the Haredim were screaming, the words pounding inside Avram's head, at times making it nearly impossible for him to think.

He'd drawn his SigSauer and switched off the safety. The gun was silenced, the shots would not be heard down in the street over all the noise of the mob.

Traffic was impossible down on the square so that there was no chance that anyone would be entering the ramp by vehicle. The Russians knew that they wouldn't be disturbed. When all hell broke loose they would slip away in the confusion.

Avram ducked down below the trunkline of the first car in the row, pain shooting up from his side and taking his breath away for a few seconds. Then he crawled forward to the front of the car and rose just enough to look over its hood. He could see the Mercedes's hood, but the angle was wrong for him to see into the car. They were there, though. Probably waiting inside.

He worked his way carefully around the front of the car, between its bumper and the low concrete wall, to the second car in the line, his legs shaking with fatigue. Just a little longer, he told himself, and there would be peace. But he didn't know if he could hold on. A frightening weakness was coming over him. There wasn't much left.

Two cars up from the Mercedes he heard a low, guttural voice say something, and he suddenly smelled cigarette smoke. Crawling on his hands and knees he worked his way to the rear of the car, waited for just a moment, then scrambled to the rear of the Mercedes itself.

He cocked the hammer of his gun and rose up far enough to see the tops of two heads in the front seat, then ducked back down again.

Time, he thought. There was none left. It was either now or never.

Gathering his strength he suddenly leaped to his feet and in three steps was around to the open window on the passenger side of the Mercedes. The big Russian was turning around, his mouth open, his hands reaching for an Uzi submachine gun when Avram shot him in the face, the heavy nine-millimeter bullet destroying the man's eye and blowing the back of his head off.

The other Russian was faster. He'd brought his silenced Makarov around with one hand while shoving his partner's body against Avram's gun hand with the other.

For a breathless moment Avram was staring into the barrel of the big gun, knowing that he had lost, that there was no time for him to bring his gun into play, when a single shot was fired from behind him and to the left, crashing through the Mercedes's rear window and catching the Russian in the shoulder, throwing his aim off. The Russian fired reflexively, the bullet slammed through the roof of the car, and Avram had his gun around, firing once, catching the Russian in the side of the head just above his ear; his head bounced off the doorpost before he slumped down against the steering wheel.

Avram spun around, nearly falling backward off

balance in time to see a tall man dressed in a business suit step back and lower his pistol.

For a moment they both stood there like that, the sounds of the mob growing even louder in the parking ramp.

"Who are you?" Avram called out.

"It doesn't matter. I know who you are."

"I have to go."

"I won't interfere with you."

"They were Russians," Avram said.

The other man nodded. "I know. What about Palmyra?"

Avram's eyes narrowed. The man was an American. But what the hell was he doing here? What did he know? "I killed him."

"Good," Ballinger said.

Avram stepped away from the car. "If you come after me I'll have to kill you."

"I won't."

Avram turned, and pocketing his gun hurried as fast as his legs could carry him down the ramp, back toward the street.

Ballinger gave Avram a head start before following him. By the time he reached the street Avram was nowhere in sight. Just at the corner was a public telephone kiosk. Ballinger hurried down to it and placed a call to the Uri Dan next-door, catching David Sokoloff just as the man was about to leave his room.

"Avram Zemil is not your traitor," Ballinger shouted into the telephone over the noise of the crowd.

"What? What are you saying?" Sokoloff demanded.

"Zemil is not your traitor. But he probably knows who is. The crazy bastard has got some way figured into the hotel, I'm sure of it. You'd better warn your people ... someone, anyone, that he's on his way, and that he is *not* your traitor."

"How can you be sure, Gregory?" Sokoloff asked.

"You've got to trust me on this one."

"But who the hell do I tell? If Zemil is innocent, that means the traitor is someone here in the hotel."

"I don't know," Ballinger said. "And I can't help you with that. You're just going to have to go with your instincts. But hurry."

20

The Office Building Roof, 7:48 p.m.

It had taken Avram precious minutes to make his way through the crowd, past the Uri Dan and then into the adjacent office building through a locked side entrance. He didn't have the time to pick the lock so instead had broken the heavy plate glass, reached inside, and undone the bar release. Somewhere in police headquarters an alarm would be ringing on a board, but by the time the police got here it would be too late for them, perhaps for all of them.

No one in the crowd had noticed what he had done, and he didn't suppose they'd care if they had. The religious fervor was upon them. They had gathered here to make their voices heard. "Trust in God," they chanted over and over again. The government of Israel would hear them. It would have to hear them.

Though it was a normal workday, the building was deserted. No one had wanted to get caught in the middle of what was shaping up to become a major riot. Better to stay home, out of harm's way, on such a day as this.

The elevators had been switched off so he had to make his way up to the fifth floor on foot, and by the time he reached the top he was seriously winded and seeing spots before his eyes. The wound in his side had started to bleed again, and it felt as if someone were jabbing a white-hot poker in his side. The bullet was still inside his body. Every time he moved it shifted. There was no telling how much damage he was doing to himself. His left arm and hand were mostly numb as well, and wave after wave of nausea washed over him, each time leaving him a little weaker than the last.

So close, he thought, resting against the wall for support. He could not give up now. Not yet.

The room was empty. The single light bulb dangled from the ceiling. Now the lights were coming on all over the camp. There was a traitor. They had been betrayed.

That vision etched clearly in his head had become his call to arms, his rallying cry. It had brought him this far. Only a few more steps. So close.

With a nearly superhuman effort of will, Avram pushed himself away from the wall, pulled out his gun, and started up the stairs to the roof access door. Most of the security, he suspected, would be concentrated on the roof of the Uri Dan. But it was possible they'd stationed someone here. He wasn't going to shoot his own people. He could not, no matter the stakes.

At the top he tested the door. It was unlocked. He pushed it open just a crack and was about to look outside when the door was jerked all the way open and he sprawled flat on his face.

"Here, what the hell are you doing up here?" the uniformed cop demanded. He apparently hadn't seen Avram's pistol, but he had drawn his own.

Avram looked up at him. "I've hurt myself, could you help me up?"

The cop's eyes suddenly went wide. "Zemil," he said, and he started to bring up his gun.

"Stop right where you are," Miriam Loeb said from the bottom of the stairs.

The cop looked past Avram and started to stammer something.

"Give him your gun, or I'll shoot you now, so help me God," Miriam demanded. "Now!"

"No," Avram said. "Don't shoot him."

But the cop was watching Miriam, who had started up the stairs, the big Beretta automatic held expertly in her right hand. He handed his gun to Avram, who'd rolled over and gotten up. He swayed on his feet, bumping against the doorframe until he caught his balance.

"You're hurt," Miriam cried, hurrying the rest of the way up the stairs.

"What are you doing here?" Avram asked, shocked at how weak his own voice sounded in his ears.

"I've been waiting for you," she said, looking closely at him. But her gun never wavered from the cop.

"The traitor is already in the hotel," Avram said, pulling himself together. "He's here to assassinate Harel. They want the government to fall. There were Russians here too, but they're dead. You must believe me."

The cop started to edge away. Right here they were blocked from view by anyone on the Uri Dan's roof.

"If I have to shoot you I will," Miriam told the cop. The young man stopped.

"No," Avram said. "Call your uncle, tell him what I've said. I'll stay here with him."

Suddenly they heard the sound of a helicopter in the distance to the south.

"It's too late," Miriam said.

"You've got to believe me," Avram shouted weakly.

Miriam hesitated, torn between what she thought she'd known, and what she was being told now.

"Once Harel gets inside they'll kill him," Avram said.

She nodded finally. "I believe you. But what can you do?"

"Is there anyone else on this roof with you?" Avram asked the cop.

The cop shook his head.

"Take off your uniform, and be quick about it," Avram said, handing his gun to Miriam and pulling off his hat.

The cop hesitated.

"Now," Avram demanded, and the cop flinched. He started hurriedly to unbutton his shirt.

Avram undid his coat and painfully pulled it off his shoulders, dizziness washing over him again. Miriam gasped when she saw his bloody side.

"You can't go in there," she told him. "Not like that. You need a doctor."

The helicopter was coming much closer, the sound of its beating rotors loud now even over the roar of the crowd. It would be the prime minister and his party. No doubt they'd be touching down on the roof of the Uri Dan. The guards up there would be distracted for just a little while as it landed. Long enough, he hoped.

The cop had pulled off his shirt. Avram pulled it on awkwardly, his blood immediately staining the material. He had to fumble with the buttons, and it seemed to take him forever to tuck it into his trousers, then buckle on the thick belt and holster.

The helicopter was hovering just overhead now, then slowly settling on the roof above. Avram pulled on the cop's cap.

"Keep him here," Avram said.

Miriam brushed a kiss on his cheek, then he stepped past the cop and out onto the open roof. He glanced up toward the Uri Dan roofline. A soldier standing up there was looking down. Avram waved up at him, and a moment later the soldier waved back, then turned away. Avram glanced back at Miriam standing just within the open doorway. She was white-faced and frightened. So close, he thought. There was so much he wanted to tell her right now. It would have to wait.

Looking up at the Uri Dan roof again he saw the helicopter sinking out of sight behind the parapet, and he hurried straight across to the line of windows on the hotel's sixth floor.

THE URI DAN HOTEL, 7:55 P.M.

David Sokoloff was passed through security on the seventh floor and he hurried down the corridor to the conference room where Yoram Geller was giving his people their last-minute instructions. He looked up.

"Just in time, sir," Geller said. "The prime minister's chopper has just landed."

Who to trust? Sokoloff had been asking himself that question all the way up here. Was it possible Ballinger had been mistaken after all? Was it pos-

sible that the voice on the phone wasn't even his
American contact? It could have been an imposter.

"If you'll wait just inside, sir," Geller was saying.

Sokoloff started to ask Geller for a moment of
his time when he spotted Michel Louk in the conference room, and he made his decision.

"Right," he said.

"Oh, by the way, sir, are you carrying a weapon
by any chance?" Geller asked.

Sokoloff looked at him. He nodded.

"Give it to me, please," Geller said, holding out
his hand. "Security precaution. No one on this
floor is to be armed."

Sokoloff hesitated a moment, cursing his own
stupidity for admitting he was armed. But he was
a diplomat, not a soldier. He pulled out the pistol
and handed it over.

"Thank you, sir. You can go in now. The prime
minister will be down in a couple of minutes."

Sokoloff went into the conference room and
headed directly across to where Michel Louk had
been standing watching.

Avram stood in the middle of the room, wavering on his feet, listening for the sounds of alarm
to be raised. The hotel was very busy. He could
hear people passing in the corridor, and next door
a telephone was ringing over and over again, while
on the roof the sounds of the chopper began to die
away, and the noise of the mob below on the
square continued to rise.

The guest room he had entered was a mess. The
beds were unmade, dirty clothes were strewn on
the floor, and the television set had been left on.

Avram went to the telephone and dialed for the
hotel operator. He was wasting precious seconds

but he had to make sure, and if possible he wanted to even the odds a little.

"Uri Dan Hotel," the woman answered.

"This is Sergeant Herzog. Connect me with the security post, please," Avram said.

"Which one would that be, sir? In the lobby?"

"No, of course not. The prime minister is on his way down right now."

"Oh, the seventh floor. One moment, I'll connect you."

Avram had to hold onto the table for support while he waited for the call to go through. His wound was bleeding harder now. He pressed his arm against his side.

"Security," a man answered.

"You'd better get down to the third floor on the double. Someone is shooting up the place."

"Who is this?"

"Herzog, but if you don't get down here now, I'm not taking the blame. He's already shot one cop, maybe more." Avram broke the connection.

He waited a moment, then dialed the operator again. Spread confusion where you can. It was in the handbook.

"Uri Dan Hotel," the operator answered.

"This is Herzog again. Connect me with the downstairs security post."

"Yes, sir," she said, and moments later the connection was made.

"I don't know what the hell is going on, but there has been a shooting up here. We think they're on the third floor."

"Who is this?"

"Herzog, seventh floor. The prime minister is just coming down, and some nut is running around with a gun. It's probably Zemil. They're

on their way down to the third." Again Avram cut
the call short, hanging up the telephone.

At the door he listened for just a moment. There
were still people out there. He was going to create
havoc right now, but there was no help for it.

He took a deep breath, let it out slowly, then
yanked open the door and lurched out into the
corridor. "Into your rooms," he shouted, waving
his gun around. "Into your rooms now. He's there.
He's in that room!"

There were at least a dozen men and a few
women, perhaps more, in the corridor. Most of
them were in shirtsleeves. A few carried clip-
boards or file folders. Avram thought he might
recognize a couple of them from Jerusalem. This
floor had evidently been taken over by the mid-
level government employees here in support of
Harel's mission.

Instant pandemonium broke out in the corridor.
A woman screamed, "My God, he's wounded."

"Get out of here," Avram shouted, heading down
the corridor. "Now! Move! Move! Move!"

They scattered, shouting and screaming. At the
end of the corridor Avram glanced up at the elevator indicators. The down elevator was already
stopped at the third floor, the up elevator was
passing the first floor and rising. They had taken
his bait. He turned away from the elevators and
shambled to the far end of the corridor, shoving
his way through the fire escape door into the stairwell.

Someone was coming up from far below. He
could hear booted feet on the concrete treads, and
someone shouting something. But no one was
coming from above. He started up.

They would not have bled all their security people from the seventh floor, at least he didn't think

so. But they'd sent at least one man down in the
elevator to see what was happening on the third
floor.

At the seventh floor landing he had to stop again
to catch his breath. He felt so damned weak. The
lights in the stairwell seemed so terribly dim, yet
intellectually he understood the electricity had not
failed, it was his eyes. He was fading. He could
feel himself disconnecting.

At the small square window in the door he
looked out into the corridor in time to see Ezra
Harel, Felix Louk, and a couple of other Knesset
leaders emerge from a service stairwell halfway
down the hall and head immediately past the elevators toward the end of the corridor.

Yoram Geller appeared at the doorway in greeting and a moment later so did Michel Louk, David
Sokoloff, and several other security and government people. But no Haredim. There were no Haredim here. What did that mean?

There were other security people in the corridor, and all of them seemed agitated, very nervous. But something else was wrong. He knew he
was going to have to concentrate. Then he had it.
None of the security people were armed. There
were no weapons.

Geller came back out of the conference room
and hurried to his security people at the elevator.
He said something to them, and moments later the
elevator door opened and all but one of them
crowded aboard and the door closed.

The lone security man—probably Shin Beth,
Avram figured—turned and looked toward the
conference room. Avram eased open the door and
stepped out into the corridor. He got about ten
feet when the security man realized that someone
was behind him and spun around.

Avram raised the silenced SigSauer. "Make a noise and I'll have to kill you," he whispered urgently, his voice hoarse, as he hurried forward.

The security man stepped back, but Avram was on him, and he jammed the pistol's barrel into the man's throat.

"Why aren't you carrying a weapon?"

The security man stammered something.

"Be quick," Avram snapped.

"Mr. Geller's orders. No one of this floor is to be armed."

"Why?"

"Security precaution because of the ... prime minister and his party."

"Where did Geller go?"

"To get the others."

"What others?"

"The people for the meeting. The delegates ..."

"Haredim?"

"Yes," the guard stuttered.

Was it Geller after all? It fit; his knowledge, his abilities. Everything was there except for the Haredim connection. And why would Geller become a spy, helping the Russians? His wife had been killed in a PLO shootout. It didn't make sense to him.

He glanced at the elevator indicator. The car had reached the ground floor. There wasn't much time. If no one else was armed on this floor, and Geller returned with six armed Haredim, the fight would be over before it began. The prime minister had to be gotten out of here. Immediately.

Avram took the gun away from the security man's throat and stepped back. "Listen to me carefully," he said. "Yoram Geller is a traitor."

"Bullshit," the security man hissed, his muscles bunching for the attack.

"When he comes back he and the six Haredim will be armed. They mean to assassinate the prime minister and everyone else on this floor."

"You're crazy," the security man spat. "Why should I believe you . . ."

The elevator started up from the lobby.

Avram pulled the cop's pistol from the holster and handed it to the started security man. "If you value your prime minister's life, get him the hell back up on the roof to his helicopter. Now. I'll stay here and hold Geller off. But you'd better damned well hurry."

The guard was wracked by indecision. He looked at the rapidly rising elevator indicator, then back at Avram. "I don't . . ."

"Move!" Avram roared. "Do it now!"

The security man spun on his heel, raced down to the end of the corridor, and burst into the conference room. The elevator indicator had passed the sixth floor. Avram pulled the table the security people had used for a checkpost over on its side in front of the elevator door, then rushed a dozen feet down the corridor where he flattened himself against the wall and brought his pistol up.

Time, he thought. It had come down to a last few seconds. Hopefully there was a back exit from the conference room and a way for the prime minister and his people to get up to the helicopter on the roof. If he could hold them off here for a half a minute there was a chance, just a chance that Harel would make it.

The security man came out of the conference room at the same moment the elevator door started to open.

"They're gone," the security man shouted. "They've all left . . ."

Two Haredim armed with Uzi submachine guns

leaped over the table blocking the elevator door and opened fire, raking the corridor. The security man went down. Avram fired three times in rapid succession, the first shot knocking one of the Haredim off his feet, the second going wide, and the third hitting the other Haredim in the chest, driving him backward.

It was all happening with split-second timing. Avram rolled right and dropped to the floor as more Haredim, their long black coats flying, emerged from the elevator, firing as they came.

He hit one, and then another as he rolled wildly across the corridor. But there were too many of them. The odds had finally caught up with him.

A burst of machine-gun fire slammed into his legs just above his knees. He felt no real pain, only sickening dull slaps as the bullets entered his flesh, tore at his muscles, traveled on through.

He fired again and again, without really seeing his targets. There was suddenly a lot of automatic weapons fire, coming from the end of the corridor, from the stairwell he had used to make his way up here. More Haredim? They must have been waiting below. A reserve force in case the first six ran into trouble.

Avram tried to roll again, but he had lost his weapon, and someone was just beside him, pulling at his bloody shirt, pulling him to a sitting position. Using him as a human shield, he realized, He turned and looked into the enraged face of Yoram Geller, spittle running from the man's mouth, his eyes wide and maniacal.

"Come closer and he dies, right now," Geller screamed.

Avram tried to make his eyes focus on the end of the corridor. All the Haredim were down in front of the elevator. But it had not been Haredim

who had come up the stairs. They were army
troops, and just within the corridor itself Michel
Louk crouched on one knee, his pistol at arm's
length pointed directly at Avram's chest.

"Get back! Get Back! I swear I'll blow his head
off," Geller screamed. He pressed the barrel of the
Uzi against Avram's temple.

"Why?" Avram croaked. He held onto his chest.
Through the material of the shirt he could feel his
stiletto.

"No more killing! No more wars!" Geller
screamed. "It's over."

"Why?" Avram whispered hoarsely. "Your wife
was killed by the PLO. Why work for the Russians?"

Geller looked down at him. "My wife was Haredim. And she was killed by one of our soldiers.
If there hadn't been a shootout she would have
lived."

"If our government falls . . . everyone will be
killed," Avram croaked. He was having a hard
time speaking.

"Give it up, Yoram," Louk shouted.

"Get back or he dies! I swear to God!" Geller
screamed.

Avram reached inside his shirt and wrapped his
fingers around the stiletto's shaft. He could barely
feel a thing. It was very hard to make his muscles
work. His entire body felt loose.

*The room was empty. The single light bulb dan-
gled . . . The lights were coming on . . . There was
a traitor . . . they had been betrayed . . .*

So hard to think. To do anything. First loyalty.
It had to be to Israel, nothing else was possible.
Without Israel there would only be death for
them.

Someone shouted something from the conference room behind them. Geller looked over his shoulder. At that moment Avram yanked out the stiletto, and twisting away from the Uzi's barrel swung his arm around in a long, loping arc, burying the blade of the knife in Geller's left eye socket, the blade grating off the bone before penetrating all the way.

Geller reared back with an inhuman scream, the Uzi in his hands going off, the bullets slamming into the wall and the ceiling; and as Avram started to fall away, the blackness finally coming over him, he could hear the sustained firing of at least a dozen weapons from the end of the corridor, causing Geller to literally dance and jump in a final, gruesome, macabre ballet.

Epilogue

THE DAY WAS BRILLIANTLY WARM. MIRIAM looked stunning in her white bikini. She and Avram had come down here to one of the smaller resort hotels for his final week of recuperation. She looked up from the book she'd been reading and shaded her eyes against the glaring sun. She could just make out Avram's form nearly a half-mile out to sea, his strokes long and slow but powerful as he swam parallel to the shoreline. Only a few other people were on the beach at this hour.

"He'll want to push himself," the doctors had told her earlier. "But unless it looks as if he's going too far, let him. He's an extraordinary man."

"Yes, he is," she'd said. The wounds he had sustained had been enough to kill an ordinary man. As it was he would never regain one hundred percent use of his left arm, one of his kidneys had been removed, and there was the possibility that he would have recurrent blinding headaches because of his head injuries, perhaps for years to come.

His physical wounds were all but completely healed now, but it would take much longer for the psychological scars to disappear. Killing Geller had been the straw that very nearly broke him. Geller was a Jew, a Mossad, one of them, whose first loyalty was and always had been to Israel after all, even if his notion of what Israel's future should be was dangerously different from the norm.

"He'd been involved with the Haredim as a young, impressionable boy," Ben-Or had explained to them. "We just never made the connection until it was too late. After the army he met and fell in love with a Haredim woman, and he embraced their philosophy wholeheartedly. When she was killed he went berserk. It's too bad, he was a good man, in the beginning."

Avram had stopped swimming and was looking toward the beach. Miriam raised her arm and waved. He waved back as a shadow fell over her. She looked up into Ben-Or's kindly face.

"Ten years ago you would have been arrested for indecent exposure wearing a bathing costume like that," he said. He bent down and she kissed him on the cheek. Then he sat down beside her in Avram's chair.

"Daddy would have agreed with you," she said smiling. "I have a feeling Avram feels the same way, only he doesn't dare say anything about it."

"How's he doing?" Ben-Or asked, looking out to sea as Avram began swimming back to shore.

"Better," she said.

"Is he ready to go back to work?"

"Physically, yes."

Ben-Or looked at her. "Mentally?"

Miriam shrugged. "He still feels terrible about

354 GARY KRISS

Geller and about all the innocent people who were killed. It was a bloodbath.''

"It could have been much worse.''

Miriam nodded. "I know that, and he knows that, but still he feels that he could have prevented many of the killings if he'd done a better job.''

Ben-Or sighed heavily. "Has he mentioned the Russian, Roskov, to you?''

"Every day," Miriam said. "Still no word about him?''

"One of our people might have spotted him in Damascus, in the military hospital. Quite a man to get up and walk out of an apartment with a table leg sticking out of his gut.''

"Avram thinks he was a Jew.''

"We're trying to follow that up, but we're not having much success. It was only a hunch. It's over now in any event.''

"He'll be back," Miriam said.

"Possibly," Ben-Or said after a moment. "But for the moment at least he's been neutralized, as have the Haredim.''

"What's going to happen to them?" Miriam asked. Avram had been very concerned.

"There ware a few rotten apples willing to resort to force—Roskov duped them all, including Geller—but for the most part they're innocent. They simply believe that Israel should disband its military. They're willing to simply pray for that outcome, rather than murder for it. Which is logical, considering who and what they are.''

She thought about what he'd said as she watched Avram swimming in, his stroke sure and even.

"Does he resent us?" Ben-Or asked.

Miriam shook her head. "He understands that

it was the only way. You and Harel were working in the dark. You had no idea who your traitor was. Avram had to be isolated . . . even from me."

"Roskov got his handwriting from Geller, and they forged the note about Dennis."

"I know," Miriam said. She turned to her uncle. "I knew every bit of it the moment I looked into Avram's eyes on the roof of the office building next to the Uri Dan. I would have killed that cop for him, but he stopped him." She smiled again. "No," she said. "once I looked into his eyes I had absolutely no doubts about him."

Avram hurried up the beach laughing, his body hard and bronzed from the sun and from a twelve-hour-a-day regimen of work and exercise. "Good morning," he said, barely winded despite the long swim in the cold water.

"Miriam tells me you're feeling fit."

"I'm getting there."

"Are you ready to go back to work?"

Avram nodded.

"Haifa Station?"

A darkness came across Avram's face. He shrugged. "If that's were you want me. I don't know how good Sammuel Amit and I will be together . . ."

"That'll be totally up to you, Avram," Ben-Or said.

"I haven't forgotten how to take orders, if that's what you mean, sir."

Ben-Or grinned. "I'm sure you haven't; I just hope you remember how to give them."

"Sir?"

"I'm putting you in charge down there. I want you as my new Haifa chief of station. If you'll take the job."

"He'll take the job," Miriam said laughing. "When do you want *us* to start?"

"Wait just a moment ..." Avram started, but Ben-Or cut him off.

"Monday be okay?"

"Monday will be fine," Miriam said. "Just fine."

Watch for the exciting sequel to
First Loyalty
FINAL OPTION
coming soon from Lynx